By Glenda Young

Helen Dexter Cosy Crime Mysteries
Murder at the Seaview Hotel
Curtain Call at the Seaview Hotel
Foul Play at the Seaview Hotel

Saga Novels
Belle of the Back Streets
The Tuppenny Child
Pearl of Pit Lane
The Girl with the Scarlet Ribbon
The Paper Mill Girl
The Miner's Lass
A Mother's Christmas Wish
The Sixpenny Orphan

Foul Play
at the
Seaview
Hotel

GLENDA YOUNG

HEADLINE

First published in 2023 by
HEADLINE PUBLISHING GROUP

First published in paperback in 2023 by
HEADLINE PUBLISHING GROUP

1

Cataloguing in Publication Data is available from the British Library

ISBN 978 1 4722 8575 1

Typeset in 11.25/15pt Adobe Garamond Pro by Jouve (UK), Milton Keynes

Printed and bound in Great Britain by Clays Ltd, Elcograf S.p.A.

HEADLINE PUBLISHING GROUP
An Hachette UK Company
Carmelite House
50 Victoria Embankment
London EC4Y 0DZ

www.headline.co.uk
www.hachette.co.uk

To Scarborough, my happy place

Acknowledgements

The Seaview Hotel and the Vista del Mar in this story are fictional and are not based on any hotels in Scarborough. Likewise, Windsor Terrace and King's Parade are fictional streets. Norman's Nine crazy-golf course is also fictional.

My thanks go to the following: Angie Pearsall and her rescue greyhounds Monty and Carla for help bringing Suki the greyhound to life; Lynn Jackson at the Paragon Hotel, Scarborough, vice president of Scarborough Hospitality Association; Joe Parkinson; Gemma Alexander; Martyn Hyde and Stephen Dinardo at Eat Me Café, Scarborough. Special thanks go to Scarborough's Central Tramway funicular for their generosity in allowing me to research inside the cliff lift, even stopping it mid flight for me to make notes. It was a wonderful experience that I'll never forget. Their website is: https://www.centraltramway.co.uk.

For crazy-golf, adventure-golf and mini-golf research I'd like to thank Richard Gottfried of the Ham and Egger Files, at https://hamandeggerfiles.blogspot.com, and Andy Miller's book *Tilting at Windmills*. Thank you to the British Mini Golf Association for permission to quote from their rules; they have a great website at https://bmga.online.

To my husband, Barry. Together we make up the two crazy

golfers at http://twocrazygolfers.blogspot.com, where we often blog our games.

Thanks also to my wonderful agent Caroline Sheldon and to the wonderful team at Headline, including my editor Kate Byrne, Sophie Keefe, Caitlin Raynor and Isabelle Wilson.

And last but by no means least – thank you to Scarborough, my happy place, always.

Chapter 1

The Seaview Hotel was Helen Dexter's pride and joy. It was her home and her business, her life. The hotel had a lot going for it; it was an attractive building on the corner of King's Parade, overlooking Scarborough's North Bay on the beautiful Yorkshire coast. It had ten rooms, three storeys, and a rescue greyhound called Suki, who lived quietly and uncomplaining in the basement apartment with Helen.

Helen's next-door neighbour, Miriam, thought herself and her hotel, the Vista del Mar, a cut above the Seaview. However, Helen had invested her savings, time and effort into the place, and her hard work had paid off. After a recent visit from the hotel inspector, it had been upgraded to four stars. Her heart had burst with pride when she'd gained her award, while Miriam had reacted to the news with one of her cutting comments. 'They give four stars to anyone these days.'

However, the plaque that Helen had been sent displaying her four glittering stars wouldn't hang straight on the wall.

'This wall's wonky,' she moaned to Jean as she stood on the front step on a warm day in early June.

Jean was the Seaview's cook, a no-nonsense Yorkshirewoman in her mid-sixties, responsible for the hotel's award-winning breakfasts. She was short and stocky, with cropped blonde hair, and

1

wore large glasses that slid down her nose. She was constantly pushing them back, an affectation that was beginning to irritate Helen after a frustrating hour trying to hang the plaque.

Helen held an electric drill in one hand, a spirit level in the other. She laid them both down and picked up the plaque, but once again, it dipped to one side. Exasperated, she left it hanging at an angle and sat down on the step. Jean looked on with her hands on her hips, tutting and shaking her head.

'It's not the wall that's wonky. It's the way you've drilled those holes.'

Helen gritted her teeth. In all the decades they'd worked together, she'd never fallen out with Jean. When she had bought the Seaview with her husband, Tom, they'd taken Jean on with the fixtures and fittings. She'd come to rely on her more than ever since Tom had passed away. Jean had been her rock, the person she turned to when times got tough, the person who gave her advice whether she wanted to hear it or not. But right then, what Helen wanted was for Jean to stop complaining and give her some support. She didn't know what it was, she couldn't say for sure, but something about the woman had begun to annoy her lately.

'For heaven's sake, the holes are perfectly straight,' she said. Her words came out with more anger than she'd intended. She looked up at Jean. 'Sorry. I'm frustrated with the stupid thing. I've worked so hard to earn our four stars, but I can't even display them.'

Jean grabbed hold of the wall and eased herself down to sit beside Helen. When she was finally down, she pushed her glasses to the bridge of her nose. 'My knees aren't what they were. I hope I can stand up again.'

The two women sat in silence. Ahead, gentle waves rolled in to the wide, curved bay. To the right were the ruins of Scarborough Castle, while to the left, the coast turned to Scalby Ness. Clifftops of yellow and green stretched into the distance as far as Saltburn and Staithes. Helen turned her face to the sun, which was beginning to poke through the clouds. She felt herself begin to relax, her shoulders dropped, and with a pang of guilt, she glanced at Jean. 'I'm sorry for losing my temper.'

Jean grunted. 'If you don't mind me saying so, you've been losing it a lot lately. You haven't been yourself for some time. You seem to have lost your sparkle.'

'My sparkle?' Helen laughed. 'You really think I've got a sparkle?'

Jean shrugged. 'You used to. And there are still days when you throw your head back to laugh, or sing along to the radio, and I think to myself, "There's the old Helen, she's back." But you haven't done either of those things in a while.'

Helen let Jean's words sink in. 'Feels like it's going to be another nice day,' she said at last, staying safe on the topic of weather. 'I hope Sally's having a good time. I wonder what she's up to today?'

Jean gently nudged her in the ribs. 'The girl's on her honeymoon. What do you think she'll be up to?'

Sally was the cleaner at the Seaview. She was currently in a caravan in Norfolk with her new husband, local entrepreneur Gav, and her five-year-old daughter, Gracie.

'It was a lovely wedding, wasn't it?' Jean said. 'You did Sally and Gav proud holding the party here.'

Helen put her hand on her forehead. 'I've still got the hangover to prove it. You're right, though, it was gorgeous. It's the first time I've ever been a matron of honour. I was overjoyed when Sally asked me. And little Gracie looked gorgeous in her bridesmaid's dress. Mind you, Sally's mum wasn't what I expected.'

Jean shot her a look. 'In what way?'

Helen thought about Brenda, who'd never cracked a smile at the wedding. 'She didn't seem as happy as you'd expect the mother of the bride to be,' she said. 'I tried talking to her, but she didn't open up much, seemed a bit private, you know. Anyway, fancy you catching the bride's bouquet! Oh Jean, your face was a picture.'

Jean harrumphed with displeasure. 'I've already told you, I didn't mean to catch it, I only grabbed it before it hit me. I'll never get married again. I've got used to being on my own since Archie died.' She gave Helen a sidelong glance. 'Speaking of fellas . . .'

Helen shifted uncomfortably. 'Were we?'

'. . . any news from your Jimmy?'

Helen looked out at the sea. Jimmy was the first man she'd had feelings for since Tom died. So far, all they'd shared was a couple of chaste kisses. She couldn't bring herself to take it further, not with Tom on her mind every day. Besides, Jimmy kept leaving to work overseas in his job as an Elvis impersonator. She didn't know where she stood with him. One minute he was in Scarborough, the next he was jetting off to work in a bar in Benidorm, or Madeira, or on a cruise ship with his singing troupe of twelve Elvis imper-sonators, Twelvis. He was a good-looking man, tall and muscular, with dark hair greying around his ears. He was the same age as Helen, who currently felt that she was heading too fast to middle age. Her fiftieth birthday loomed. Jean had been pestering her to throw a party at the Seaview, but Helen had put her off. Reaching fifty didn't feel like celebrating a milestone, it felt like ushering in a mid-life crisis.

'Well, have you heard from him or not?' Jean asked.

'First of all, Jean, he's not *my* Jimmy. Second of all, as far as I know, he's still working in the Elvis bar on the Costa del Sol.' She stood, hoping to dismiss further questions, but she should have known better, because Jean rarely gave up. Jean reached for the wall and pulled herself to standing. She blew air from her mouth, then stood there with her arms crossed, glaring at Helen.

'When's he coming back?'

Helen waved her hand dismissively. 'The truth is, it's complicated, with Tom on my mind all the time. How can I even think about starting a new relationship with Jimmy when all I want is my beloved husband back?'

'You could have got to know Jimmy better and taken your mind off Tom a little. But you haven't even visited him in Spain, and he invited you out there all expenses paid,' Jean said.

There was a beat of silence while Helen chose the right words to say. The truth was, she'd deliberately held back on visiting Jimmy while he worked overseas. Before he'd left, her relationship with him had been developing at pace, and it scared her that some days he was on her mind more than Tom. It left her conflicted and guilty.

'I couldn't leave the Seaview and jet off to Spain, Jean,' she said.

Jean gave her a knowing look. 'Couldn't . . . or wouldn't?' she said.

Helen sighed. 'Just like when you married Archie, I swore to love Tom for the rest of my life. Now he's no longer here, there are still days when I feel lost without him.'

Jean laid her hand on Helen's arm. 'You're a young woman, with your whole life ahead of you.'

'Young? I turn fifty soon,' Helen sighed.

'And you should be celebrating it with a big party. The old Helen would have done so.'

'Oh Jean, there won't be a flaming party! Would you just drop it!' Helen cried, too loud and too sudden.

Jean dropped her hand and took a step back. Her glasses slipped down her nose again, but she was so stunned by the outburst that she just left them there. She stared at Helen open-mouthed. 'Well, someone got out of the wrong side of the bed this morning. If you'll excuse me, I've got work to do before our guests arrive.'

'I've upset you again, haven't I?' Helen sighed again. 'I'm sorry, Jean. I have lost my sparkle, you're right. I don't know what's wrong with me. I keep seeing problems instead of opportunities. It's not like me at all.'

'You're at a funny age, love,' Jean said gently. 'Turning fifty can do that to a woman. That's why you should celebrate it with a party and show the world you're not fearful of the big five-oh.'

Helen bit the inside of her cheek to stop herself from telling Jean to stop going on about a party she didn't want. She forced her thoughts instead to the guests arriving that day.

'One of the teams playing in the crazy-golf tournament is coming to stay with us. They're due before lunch.'

'Oh, don't talk to me about them,' Jean huffed. 'A woman called Olga has already emailed a list of sandwiches they want served on arrival. There's a lot of protein on their list – they say they need energy to play crazy golf. They've even asked for power breakfasts each day! What's a power breakfast when it's at home? I ask you! It's not as if crazy golf's a real sport, and yet they're behaving as if they're Olympians.'

As Jean was speaking, Helen's attention turned to the Vista del Mar. She was sure she'd seen a curtain twitch at the window. She took another look, concerned that Miriam was snooping and might have overheard her bickering with Jean.

'They're not even athletes,' Jean continued, unaware that Helen was no longer listening. 'I mean, crazy golf, adventure golf, mini golf or whatever you call it, it's just a game, isn't it? What do they need these so-called power breakfasts for? They'll have sausage and beans and be done with it. I can't be catering for whims at my age.'

Helen caught Miriam's eye through the window. Miriam nodded politely and made a show of arranging the curtains. However, Helen knew the other woman better than that, and knew she'd been prying.

'I've put their meal requests in the blue file in the kitchen, in the usual place,' Jean continued.

'Sorry, what was that?' Helen said as Miriam disappeared.

'You never listen to me these days, do you?' Jean tutted. 'Oh, before I head to the kitchen, is there any news from the staffing agency about getting a cleaner in this week while Sally's away?'

Helen pulled her phone from the back pocket of her jeans and glanced at the screen. 'Not yet.'

'You know I would have covered for her and done the cleaning, don't you? Getting an outsider in should have been a last resort.'

Helen tapped her fingers on the wall, remembering something Sally had told her. 'Sally said her mum would help out while she was away. She gave me her number, but I'm not sure about ringing her. I mean, she wasn't too friendly at the wedding. But I suppose we could do worse. Maybe I should give her the benefit of the doubt. At least we know we can trust her. Sally's a hard-working girl, salt of the earth; she must have got her work ethic from someone. I'll give Brenda a ring and ask her in for a chat over coffee and cake. Could you bake one of your lemon drizzles?'

'Course I can, love. It's been a while since we had one of those.'

Jean padded away inside the Seaview as Helen turned to look at the sea again. An ice-cream van, its engine spluttering, trundled along the road, leaving a whining, mournful rendition of 'Greensleeves' in its wake. Helen picked up the drill and spirit level, then walked into the hall and closed the Seaview's front door. As it slammed shut, the wonky plaque fell off the wall.

Chapter 2

Helen and Jean walked downstairs to Helen's apartment. It was small, with one bedroom, and an open-plan kitchen and living room that opened on to a patio. Helen's kitchen was where Jean prepared and cooked breakfast for the Seaview's guests, sending plates up to the dining room in the ancient dumbwaiter. When Helen entered the living room, Suki was pacing the floor. She recognised the signs and patted her hand against her jeans-clad thigh. 'Come on, girl, I'll take you for your walk.'

The greyhound walked obediently to her side.

'I'm taking the dog out, Jean. I'll be half an hour tops, and back before our guests arrive.'

Jean took a clean apron from a drawer, pulled it over her head and tied the straps around her ample frame. 'Right you are, love,' she replied. 'I'll try making this flaming power lunch they've asked for.' She scanned a sheet of paper on the bench, and as she read, her lip curled with distaste. 'Chia seeds, goji berries, manuka honey. It's like a foreign language. Alfalfa sprouts? Are they related to Brussels sprouts? I've never heard of half the stuff on this list. And if I've never heard of it, they're not getting it. You did tell them we've won awards for our full English breakfasts, didn't you? I mean, that's what I do, it's my thing. You've already pushed me out

9

of my comfort zone adding kippers and porridge to the menu. But this is too much.'

'Jean, we need to respect our guests' requests for different types of food. It's one of the requirements of keeping our four-star status.'

Jean pushed her glasses to the bridge of her nose, then tapped the list. 'Leafy greens I can cope with. Non-starchy vegetables I can cook. High-fibre, non-sugary cereals I can serve up at breakfast. But . . .' she peered at the list, 'matcha tea smoothies for breakfast? Oh dear me, no. I've never made anything with matcha tea, whatever it is, and I'm not about to start making it now.'

'Jean, please . . .' Helen began, but Suki was chattering her teeth, a greyhound trait that meant she was agitated. Jean sighed heavily, then pushed the piece of paper with the food requests away, dismissing it for now.

'I've got to take the dog out,' Helen said testily as she clipped Suki's lead to her collar, and led her out of the Seaview's back door.

Once outside, she took long, deep breaths of sea air. The June day was warm, there wasn't a breath of wind, and the sky was eggshell blue. She led Suki around the corner of King's Parade, then zigzagged her way down the hill to the beach. Walking the greyhound always helped calm her mind, and when she reached the sand, she let her off the lead. Suki trotted ahead. Helen was feeling troubled, angry at the world for reasons she couldn't explain. It wasn't the best frame of mind to be in at any time, never mind when new guests were due. And so, with each step she took, with each wave that frilled to the shore, she tried to process her thoughts, to get to the root of why she felt so upset.

Was it Jean, refusing to cook things she wasn't used to? Was it

Miriam, spying on her that morning when she'd lost her temper with Jean? Was it Jimmy, who, despite what she'd told Jean, had messaged her that morning to say he was on his way to Scarborough with surprise news, but annoyingly wouldn't tell her what it was? Was it her best friend, Marie, who still hadn't replied to her messages and calls and had been spending time with their old school friend Sandra DeVine instead?

Tears made their way to her eyes. She was feeling sorry for herself and she knew it. Oh, each one of those people – Jean, Miriam, Jimmy, Marie – was niggling at her in their own way. And turning fifty soon didn't help. It brought unwelcome thoughts of growing old, alone, trying to run the Seaview when she was past it, washed up. But deep down she knew the real reason she was feeling so low. It was the anniversary of her first date with Tom. It wasn't a wedding anniversary or a birthday, nothing she could mark with a card or a drink. It was a day only she knew, special just to her. She stopped walking, closed her eyes and raised her face to the sun.

'I miss you, Tom,' she whispered.

She felt a nudge against her leg and looked down, smiling when she saw Suki. She got down on her haunches and stroked the dog's long, thin head, running her hands over her smooth caramel coat. 'You miss him too, girl, I know,' she said. Suki gently nuzzled into Helen's hands. 'We both miss him and always will.'

She looked around for a dry spot on the sand and found one near the sea wall. She sat for a while with her back to the hotel, watching the sea, remembering Tom: how he looked, how he smelled. How easily the memories came. Suki stood at her side and Helen wrapped her arm around the dog's neck. She thought of their life together in Scarborough, the town they'd grown up in, the town they'd both loved, the town Helen would never leave. Scarborough would always be home. It was Tom and the Seaview, and it was Jean and . . .

Her heart dropped. She owed Jean an apology for being so terse, and decided to do it as soon as she returned. Once she'd done that, she planned to change out of her jeans and fleece, put on her favourite blouse, patterned with forget-me-not flowers, and get ready for her guests. Their rooms were prepared with fresh linen and towels, kettles and teacups, coffee sachets and milk pots. The lounge and dining room were spotless.

Helen smiled at the thought of crazy-golf teams coming to Scarborough. The tournament had been featured on the local news, and the organisers had invited a surprise celebrity to open it. The course they were using was Norman's Nine, a nine-hole course by the harbour on the South Bay. It featured models of Scarborough landmarks, including a scale model of the castle, where players hit balls through the gate tower, avoiding the moat.

She ran through in her mind what she'd do once her guests arrived and she'd checked them in. She'd ring Brenda to ask her if she'd like some cleaning work while Sally was on honeymoon. She'd enjoy coffee and cake and a proper catch-up with Jean. She'd google chia seeds and manuka honey and gently encourage Jean to take such things in her stride. Feeling more determined and less unsettled, she whispered again to the wind, 'Love you, Tom.' Then she stood, turned and walked back towards the Seaview with Suki.

On the way, she began to feel more relaxed and assured, ready to apologise. It wouldn't do to get on the wrong side of Jean. She depended on her for everything: cooking her award-winning breakfasts, cleaning the kitchen, being a shoulder to cry on, a rock to prop her up when she felt down, a source of news and gossip, a confidante. In short, without Jean, the Seaview wouldn't be the success that it was, and it certainly wouldn't have earned its four stars. She was a powerhouse of a woman, a sweetheart or a battle-axe depending on who she was dealing with and whether she needed to scare or seduce in order to get what she needed.

Helen hurried on, ready to throw her arms around her and tell her she was sorry for being so sharp. Then she changed her mind. Jean wouldn't appreciate being hugged; she baulked at too much physical contact. She was a woman who kept her emotions in check. Helen decided that instead she'd put the kettle on. She'd let Jean have a rest, ply her with coffee and biscuits – was it too late to pop to the shop to buy custard creams, to butter her up with her favourites?

She was about to walk past the end of King's Parade to head to the shop when she caught sight of two orange Gav's Cabs outside the Seaview. 'Oh no!' she cried. She looked at her watch, then back at the cabs unloading their passengers. There was no time for custard creams, she realised. There was no time to shower and change out of her dog-walking clothes. There was no time to warn Jean that their guests had arrived. For there could be no mistaking that these *were* their guests, the crazy golfers, clambering out of the cabs with golf clubs and sports bags and walking up the steps to the Seaview's front door.

Chapter 3

Helen picked up her pace and Suki trotted to keep up. When she reached the Seaview, she dug into her pocket for her key, then plastered on her professional smile.

'Good morning!' she called, waving at the group on the hotel steps. She noticed they were standing in line, one after another, politely queuing.

'I'm Mrs Dexter . . . Helen,' she said, slightly breathless. 'And this is my dog, Suki. She's not allowed in the front of the hotel, so I'll just leave her here for a few moments.'

She looked around, flustered, trying to find somewhere to tie Suki's lead while she dealt with her guests. They were over two hours early and had caught her on the hop.

'Sorry, everyone, I'm normally more organised than this,' she said as she attached the lead to the gate. Suki stood there without fuss. Helen brushed her hands on her fleece jacket, then pushed her bobbed hair behind her ears. 'And I'm normally better dressed when I greet my guests.'

She ran up the steps, and as she was about to slide her key in the lock, she noticed her new plaque lying on the ground. It was scuffed on one side from its fall. She scooped it up, then opened the door, tucking the plaque behind it, out of sight. Standing to one side, she allowed her guests to enter.

First in was a young woman with long red hair tied in plaits. Her eye make-up was dramatic, with green eyeshadow fading to pink. She wore blue jeans, and a denim shirt open to reveal a pink T-shirt. The end of each long plait was tied with pink ribbon. She bounded into the hall and thrust her hand at Helen.

'I'm Alice Pickle. We spoke on the phone when I made the booking.'

Helen looked at Alice, at the colours, the pinks and the reds and the immaculate eyeshadow. Alice was vibrant, alive, buzzing with energy, hopping from foot to foot, looking around her, taking everything in, taking Helen in. Helen felt herself being appraised and thought Alice must find her quite dull. Her green fleece jacket needed a wash, her old jeans had a tear at the knee, her dog-walking boots had seen better days. Her brown hair hung in the same style she'd worn it for years, and her face was blotchy and bare of make-up. She straightened her spine. There was nothing she could do about all that now. Her guests had arrived much earlier than arranged; they'd have to take her as they found her.

Alice looked around the hall once more, then back at Helen. 'We're early because we want to make the most of training time on the golf course. I should perhaps have called, but I was too busy reading my crazy-golf manual, going over the rules. Anyway, we're here now, and this . . .' she turned and waved a hand at the line of people outside, 'is our team. Come on in, everyone. Left, right, left, right.'

Helen's jaw dropped in shock when the line began to move in time to Alice's command. Left, right, left, right, they trooped into the hall. Left, right, left, right, arms swung and feet moved with precision.

'Company! Halt!' Alice cried once everyone was inside. 'Baggage! Drop!'

Bags thudded to the floor. Helen looked down and wondered why they needed so many clubs. Surely in crazy golf you just used one? Alice spun around to face her and gave a salute.

'Oh my word, that's very organised,' Helen said, trying to take it all in. In her years of running the Seaview, she'd never witnessed an entrance quite like it. She couldn't make head nor tail of this group. They'd taken the wind from her sails. She pulled herself back into professional mode and indicated the door to the lounge.

'Everyone, please come this way. I'll check you all in and give you the keys to your rooms.' She paused for a moment to steady herself before she continued. 'It's wonderful to have you in Scarborough playing in the crazy-golf tournament.'

'Oh, we're not here just to play, Mrs Dexter,' Alice said. 'Make no bones about it, we're here to win.' She narrowed her eyes before delivering a line that sent a shiver down Helen's spine. 'And we'll win by fair means or foul.'

Helen gulped. 'Oh, I see,' she replied, feeling unnerved by the woman's grave tone.

'It's not about luck, it's about skill,' Alice continued, more chipper now. 'But mainly it's about beating my arch-rival Ricky Delmont and his team.'

Lost for words, Helen collected the keys to the rooms. For the first time, she was able to take in the other members of the team. She hadn't paid them much attention so far; she'd been too preoccupied, too startled by their unusual arrival. When she'd passed them outside, she'd smiled and said hello, aware that there was an older man with white hair who was being helped up the steps by a young, pretty, blonde woman. There was a boy too, tall and skinny, with a short older woman who had cropped black hair. Beyond that, she hadn't noticed much.

As she walked into the lounge holding the keys, she glanced out of the window to see Suki lying by the gate, her skinny caramel limbs spilling on to the path. Then she turned to face her guests. The older man with white hair stuck out his hand.

'I'm Marty Highfield,' he said. Helen couldn't fail to notice he was looking good for his age. He was muscled, well-built. What was he, she wondered, in his seventies? Older? His face was weather-beaten, tanned, and his hair was wavy and thick. The young blonde woman at his side was stroking his arm protectively. Helen thought this was a nice touch and wondered if she was Marty's daughter, or his carer. But she was confused, as Alice had specifically requested a double room for the couple when she'd booked the team in.

'I'm Marilyn, Marty's wife,' said the young woman, in a breathy voice that sounded familiar, though Helen couldn't place where she'd heard it before. Her long, straight hair was dyed a shade that Jean would have called bottle blonde.

Helen wasn't sure she'd heard correctly. She looked from Marty to Marilyn and her smile froze on her lips. The age gap must have been two generations, but it wasn't her place to comment. Besides, she was all about live and let live. There seemed to be something genuine and warm in the way Marilyn regarded her husband. It appeared that true love had crossed this divide. 'Nice to meet you both,' she said politely.

'We do have a ground-floor room, right?' Marilyn asked. That voice again, that breath; where had Helen heard it before?

Marty gently patted his wife's hand. 'Now, Marilyn, there's no need to concern yourself. You know I can cope with stairs.'

Helen looked from Marty to Marilyn. 'I'm sorry, we don't have ground-floor rooms at the Seaview. I did explain to Alice on the phone when the booking was made. The lounge and dining room are on this level. There are twelve stairs to the first floor, with a landing after the first six. I hope that won't be a problem?'

Marty shook his head. 'No problem,' he said.

'But Marty . . .' Marilyn breathed.

And that was when Helen knew where she'd heard the voice before. The woman was talking just like Marilyn Monroe in her films, breathy and suggestive, as if she was about to run out of steam.

Marty smiled. 'I'm sure I can manage twelve stairs, darling. There's no need to worry.'

Marilyn held tight to his hand. 'But I do, sweetie, I do.'

Marty shot Helen an apologetic look. 'We'll be fine on the first floor.'

Helen handed him the key to room 1. 'Now then, let's see,' she said. 'Alice, I've put you on the second floor. As for the rest of your team . . .' She looked at the two remaining members: the short older lady with cropped hair and the tall, gangly boy, who was sprawled on the window seat tapping furiously at his phone.

'I need peace and quiet, whichever room you put me in,' the older woman said. Her tone was harsh and her words clipped. 'I spent most of my life in the military, and I know how important it is to have a space for pep talks and meditation sessions. Without a quiet room, the team will not win the tournament. And we need to win. It's important to win. We are here to win.' She raised her right arm and punched the air. 'We will beat Ricky Delmont and his team of losers this time!'

Alice leapt up from her seat. 'You betcha we will. It's about time he learned his lesson. I hate that son of a—'

The older woman put her finger to her lips and shook her head. 'Don't waste your breath on that man.'

Alice sat down, chastened. Helen looked at the remaining keys in her hand, averting her gaze from her guests. They really were turning out to be quite a strange bunch.

'Room 4 is a quiet room, it'd be perfect for meditation. It's on the first floor at the back, away from traffic and seafront noise.'

The woman nodded approvingly as Helen handed over the key.

'And your name is?' Helen asked.

The woman raised herself to standing. She was short, less than five feet tall, shorter even than Jean though around the same age. However, where Jean was stout, this woman was wiry, and her face was thin. Her skin was taut, her eyes beady and dark. She was dressed in a smart navy suit of jacket and trousers with a stiff-looking white blouse.

'Olga Stanovich. I am the team coach,' she barked, then sat down again.

Helen turned to the youngest member of the team.

'Freddy, don't be rude,' Alice Pickle called to him. 'Put your phone down and say hello to Mrs Dexter.'

Helen raised her hand. 'Please, everyone, call me Helen.'

'Sorry, Helen,' Alice said. 'This is Freddy Morgan, crazy-golf wunderkind. You might have heard of him.'

Helen smiled weakly. She had no idea who he was. 'Wunderkind?' she said.

Freddy lazily laid his phone on a table and looked up at her. His long, sprawling limbs reminded her of Suki. She glanced through the window again to make sure the dog was all right, then turned back to her guests. Freddy was slouched in his seat, his long legs extending into the room. He was a handsome boy, in his late teens. He wore a yellow short-sleeved polo shirt with a logo on it that Helen didn't recognise, black jeans, and expensive-looking spotless white trainers, branded with the same logo. He had neatly cut brown hair and clear skin, and when he smiled, which he did a lot, she noticed his perfect white teeth.

'A wunderkind is someone who achieves great success when they're young,' he said with a drawl. 'So I guess that kinda describes me. Sorta. I'm a crazy-golf genius, they say, as good as Ricky Delmont – whose ass, by the way, I'm gonna whop in this tournament.'

An American. There hadn't been an American guest at the Seaview in years. 'What a lovely accent,' she said. 'Where are you from?'

'Aldershot,' he replied. 'But I watch a lot of American TV.'

At first Helen thought he was joking, but his face was deadly serious. She was about to ask if he enjoyed Marilyn Monroe films, but thought better of it and bit the inside of her cheek. She turned to Alice. 'As requested, your team has the whole of the first and second floors while you're here. There are two empty rooms on the top floor in case I have any walk-in guests requiring accommodation at the last minute.'

'I need a separate room for yoga,' Olga said.

Helen gave her professional, friendly smile. She wondered if the woman ever relaxed; she sounded annoyed all the time. 'There's a beautiful room on the second floor with a very relaxing colour scheme,' she offered.

'Perfect,' said Olga.

Helen looked at the bags and cases scattered on the floor. 'Now then, can I help anyone take their luggage up to their room?'

'I need help with Marty's suitcase,' Marilyn said.

'Now, now, sweet cheeks. I'm not so decrepit that I can't manage my own luggage,' Marty replied. As if to prove his point, he heaved himself up and hoisted a golf bag over one shoulder, then picked up a suitcase with his free hand. Helen marvelled at his strength. For an older man, he looked fit and healthy, and he moved with ease despite the heavy luggage.

'So many golf clubs,' she said, glancing around as the rest of the group picked up their bags. 'Don't you just need one each for crazy golf?'

Alice Pickle dropped her bags to the floor. Marty and Marilyn froze. Freddy gave a snort of derisive laughter, while Olga sucked air through her lips.

'What?' Helen said, looking around. 'What have I said?'

Olga stepped forward. 'Many holes need many clubs. One club per hole. Sometimes two, even three, depending on the course.'

'That's right,' Marty said. 'We professionals need different clubs and different balls to play a crazy-golf course.'

'But—' Helen began.

Olga held up a hand to silence her, and Helen felt affronted. Then Marilyn turned her baby-blue eyes on her and smiled sweetly.

'We have a lot of equipment to help us play our best game. The balls we use have different weights, depending on whether the course runs fast or slow. Speaking of which, we can't waste any

21

more time. We've got to head out for a practice round, to see how the land lies and how the course seems.'

'Oh, I see,' Helen said, although she wasn't sure that she did. Her long-held belief that crazy golf was a fun game was being put to the test. She kept her thoughts to herself, however, and helped carry bags and cases up the stairs, dropping everyone off at their rooms. She showed Olga the location of the Seaview's quiet room for the team's meditation and pep talks, and the room for their yoga sessions.

'I'm happy,' said Olga approvingly.

Once the guests were all in their rooms, Helen picked up her new four-star plaque from where she'd hidden it earlier, then walked down the path to collect Suki.

'Good girl,' she said, stroking the dog's head.

She was about to head on to King's Parade and around the corner to the back of the Seaview when she was stopped in her tracks. The front door of the Vista del Mar was flung open, and there stood Miriam, resplendent in cream twinset and pearls.

'Helen, dear, would you be a sweetheart and help me out with a favour?'

A favour? She'd known Miriam for over twenty-five years, and in all that time, the woman had never once asked her for a favour.

'I've got a team of crazy golfers staying with me for the tournament,' Miriam continued. 'But I've made a mistake and overbooked. Their team captain . . .' She looked behind her to ensure no one was listening before she whispered, 'He's the most unpleasant man I've ever met. He turned up late and insists he must stay on King's Parade – something to do with his feng shui obsession. He's superstitious about which direction he faces, says it affects his golf performance. I've already told him there are no rooms left, but he won't have it. Helen, dear, the brute's threatening to sue me for breach of contract.'

Her cheeks turned red and she put a hand against the door frame to steady herself. 'I can't have my hotel's good name dragged through the courts. I'm desperate, Helen. I don't know what to do. I don't suppose you could put him up next door, could you? His name is Ricky Delmont.'

Ricky Delmont. The man Alice, Freddy and Olga had mentioned; the top crazy golfer they all wanted to beat. Intrigued, Helen leaned forward.

'Tell me more,' she said.

Chapter 4

'What more do you need to know?' Miriam said.

Helen had doubts about taking in someone Miriam had described as unpleasant. 'Could I come in and meet him?' she asked.

Miriam looked like she'd been slapped. 'I'm not inviting you in with your brute of a dog. You know I don't allow pets in Vista del Mar.'

'Suki's not a brute, she's the softest dog you'll ever meet,' Helen said defensively.

Miriam tutted out loud. 'Look, dear. Can you take this chap or not? A simple yes or no will suffice.'

Helen looked at the Seaview, where the Vacancy sign hung in her window. Yes, she could take him. She had two rooms spare. But there was clearly animosity between her guests and Ricky Delmont, and she didn't know whether it was such a good idea. She might be putting the cat amongst the pigeons.

Miriam tapped her watch impatiently. 'Come on, make your mind up. He's waiting in my lounge. He's given me an hour to find him somewhere to stay before he gets on the phone to start legal proceedings. Please, Helen, help a fellow landlady out.'

Helen wavered. The last thing she wanted was to bring Miriam's guest into the Seaview if it meant causing problems for the guests she'd already checked in. However, her bank manager would be grateful for the income to help pay off her business loan.

'I might be able to help, but there's something I need to do first,' she said.

Miriam tapped her watch with more force. 'Hurry, dear.'

Helen raced to the back of the Seaview and let Suki in through the door.

'Coffee, Helen?' Jean called. 'I've saved you a job, as I've just called Sally's mum, Brenda. She's coming in to talk about the cleaning.'

'Can't stop, Jean, I've got to see Alice Pickle on urgent business. Depending on what she says, we may have another guest moving in.'

Helen sprinted up the stairs and knocked on Alice's door. When it opened, she noticed that Alice had changed from her denim shirt and jeans into a navy tracksuit and trainers. Her long red plaits were now tied up and pinned in a neat circle on top of her head.

'Hi, Helen, everything all right?' Alice asked. 'We didn't leave anything downstairs, did we?'

'No, everything's fine,' Helen said. She girded herself before she continued. 'Look, Alice, there's no easy way to say this, so I'm just going to come out with it. You and your teammates mentioned a chap called Ricky Delmont earlier, when you were checking in.'

Alice backed away and her face visibly blanched. She narrowed her eyes. 'What about him?'

'I'm almost embarrassed to continue, because it seemed to me that there was no love lost between Ricky and your team.'

Alice steadied herself with a hand against the door. 'Not only is Ricky Delmont the captain of our rivals, he's also one of the most unpleasant men I've ever met in my life.'

Helen recalled that those were the exact words Miriam had used. She realised she might be making a terrible mistake if she took Ricky in, and so took her time before she continued.

'Ah, I see. Well, what I'm going to say next mightn't be what you want to hear, but I'm asking as a favour for a friend. Although she's not a friend really. I mean, we've got nothing in common apart from living next door and both trying to make a decent living. It's not easy, you know, running a seaside hotel.' She was aware she was rambling and decided to get to the point. 'Look, how would you feel if Ricky Delmont stayed here during the crazy-golf tournament?'

Alice's mouth dropped open. 'Ricky Delmont? In here? With our team?'

'That's the long and short of it. He's threatening to sue the landlady next door if she doesn't find somewhere else for him to stay within the hour.'

'Sounds like typical Ricky,' Alice muttered darkly.

'Would it be too much of a problem?' Helen asked. 'Because if it would, say the word and I'll tell the woman next door there's no deal.'

Alice beckoned Helen into the room. 'Close the door,' she whispered.

As Helen stepped inside, Alice plonked herself down on the bed and crossed her legs. Her right foot jiggled, and her left hand tapped the duvet. Helen could see that she was giving her request serious thought. In her experience, the body language of her guests rarely lied. She watched as Alice bit her lip, thinking things through.

'I'm sure I can square it with Marty, Marilyn and Freddy, although heaven only knows what Olga will say. But it might work . . . yes, it could work. It might be for the best. You know what they say about keeping your enemies close and all that.' Alice stood up and began to pace the floor. 'We'll be able to keep an eye on him at breakfast, see what he's up to, find out what he eats, what superfoods he's fuelling his body with. We might even over-hear him speaking on the phone to his teammates, working out their tactics and techniques.'

Helen held up her hands. 'Now stop right there,' she said sharply. 'I will not allow spying on any of my guests. If Mr Del-mont stays here, you'll treat him with respect and allow him his privacy.'

A mischievous smile made its way to Alice's lips. 'All right, it's a deal. Let him stay.'

'And you promise to leave him alone?'

She shot her hand out. 'I promise.'

Helen looked at the hand for a few seconds, trying to decide whether Alice was telling the truth.

'Oh, come on, Helen,' Alice teased. 'I'll speak to my teammates and warn them against bothering Ricky. I swear to you we'll leave him alone.'

Helen tentatively shook the woman's hand. 'Thanks, Alice. I'll go and give my neighbour the news.'

However, as she was about to head out to talk to Miriam, she was stopped in her tracks. She stood stock still in the hall, listening to the sound of raised voices coming from the other side of the wall, from the Vista del Mar. She quickly looked behind her to ensure no one was watching, then gently leaned to one side and laid her ear against the wall. She could hear a man's angry voice.

'I need a room to stay in!' he yelled.

'But Mr Delmont,' Miriam pleaded, 'I've rung my fellow hoteliers and no one has space for you. The crazy-golf tournament is big news for the town and every room has been booked up for months. I'm offering you the chance to stay at the Seaview next door. The only reason it's got rooms spare is because the place isn't up to scratch, but it's better than nothing, surely?'

Helen clenched her jaw. The cheek of the woman, how dare she? Then she heard the man's voice again, still angry, but with less power now.

'I'm not happy about this, and I'll be talking to my solicitor about taking further action.'

She headed to the Vista del Mar and knocked on the door. When Miriam answered, she looked flustered. 'Oh, it's you,' she said glumly.

'You could look a bit happier, Miriam, considering I've come to save your reputation.'

Miriam's face lit up and she clapped her hands in glee. 'Thank you, dear,' she said with relief. She walked to the end of the hall and called into the lounge. 'Mr Delmont? There's someone here I'd like you to meet.'

Helen waited on the doorstep. Despite agreeing to put up Miriam's troublesome guest, she still hadn't been invited inside. She wasn't surprised. If she'd learned one thing about her neighbour over the years, it was that she was a complete and utter snob.

A man walked towards her. He was tall and lean, with muscled arms. He wore a red sports cap, jeans and a T-shirt. Casual but smart was the phrase that came to Helen's mind. He had a neat brown beard and moustache. He also wore an intense scowl. She pegged him in his thirties.

'Mr Delmont, this is Mrs Dexter, landlady of the Seaview Hotel next door. She has a room available and has agreed to take you in.'

Helen held out her hand, but Ricky didn't shake it. He just glared at her.

'Is the room at the front? I must have a sea view.'

'Yes, it's a sea-view room on the top floor,' Helen replied.

'And will all my dietary requests be met? I have a long list of power foods I need.'

Helen thought of Jean struggling with the strange requests they'd already received from Alice Pickle's team. 'My cook will cope perfectly,' she said. She crossed her fingers against the little white lie. Then she uncrossed them, relieved to be telling the truth again. 'She's won awards for her breakfasts.'

Miriam muttered, just loud enough for Helen to hear, 'Keep talking to her the way you did this morning, and she won't be cooking for you much longer.'

Helen turned to her. 'What's that supposed to mean?'

Miriam waved her hand dismissively and smiled sweetly at the man at her side. 'Now then, Mr Delmont, I'm sure Mrs Dexter will be only too happy to help take your luggage into the Seaview. Now she's got her four stars, it's all part of the service she offers.' She turned to Helen and the smile dropped from her lips. 'Isn't it, dear?'

Helen gritted her teeth, then looked at Ricky Delmont's luggage. 'I'd be happy to help carry those,' she said.

'No need. I'll manage on my own,' he said. 'I never let anyone touch my golfing equipment, it only ever brings bad luck.'

Helen led Ricky into the Seaview. Before he paid the deposit on his card, she decided it was only fair to tell him the truth about who he'd be sharing the hotel with.

'I should let you know, Mr Delmont, that there's another team staying here, a team competing in the tournament.'

'Really? Who's their captain?'

'Alice Pickle.'

He didn't move. He fixed his gaze to a spot on the wall, and a wicked smile slowly made its way to his face. Helen didn't like the look of it.

'I understand you know her?' she dared herself to say.

'Oh, I know her all right. She's a nasty piece of work.'

Helen was shocked to hear this. Alice had seemed perfectly nice to her. 'If that's the case, are you sure you want to stay here?' she asked.

Ricky stood firm, still staring at the wall, avoiding eye contact. 'Oh, I'll stay. Seeing that woman every day will spur me on even more to beat that miserable team of amateurs again. I'm not called Ricky "hole-in-one" Delmont for nothing, Mrs Dexter. I've trained too hard and sacrificed too much to lose. No one beats me.'

Helen had met some cocky people in her time as landlady of the Seaview, but Ricky Delmont took the biscuit. There was something about him that she disliked already. 'Alice seems pretty confident that she and her team are in with a good chance of winning,' she said, realising she was already taking sides.

For the first time since entering the Seaview, Ricky turned his steely gaze on her. 'Let me tell you one thing, Mrs Dexter. The only way that Alice Pickle and her team will win this tournament is over my dead body.'

Chapter 5

'This way, please,' Helen said, ushering Ricky into the lounge. 'If you'd like to wait a moment, I'll check you in and hand over your keys.'

As she busied herself at the reception desk in the hall, she heard a noise on the stairs and looked up to see Olga, dressed like Alice in a navy tracksuit and trainers. The older woman peered around the living room door, then walked over to Helen.

'So it's true. Hole-in-one Ricky is here,' she said.

'Yes, it's true. And Alice has sworn that your team will allow him his privacy.'

'We'll leave him alone, I assure you. Alice won't have anything to do with him now.'

Helen was filling in a guest form with Ricky's details. Now she paused with her pen in mid-air. There was something dark in Olga's tone. 'What do you mean?'

Olga's beady eyes scanned her face. 'You mean you don't know? Alice never told you?'

'Told me what?'

'She and Ricky, they were married. Not long, three years. It was a bad marriage and he was a terrible husband.'

Helen dropped her pen. Well, Alice was turning out to be quite the dark horse. She wondered what other secrets her guests were hiding. Not that it was her business to know about their private lives. Still, she was shocked that Alice hadn't mentioned this when she'd asked about letting Ricky stay. Despite the bombshell, she remained professional and carried on filling in Ricky's guest form, though her hand was shaking with shock.

'We're going out now,' Olga said. 'To practise on the course. I'll wait here for the team to descend.' She snapped her heels together and stood up straight.

Helen heard more noise from upstairs, doors opening and closing, then footsteps on the stairs as the rest of the team came down. Each of them was dressed in a navy tracksuit and pristine white trainers, with a golf bag slung over their shoulder, while in their free hand they clutched a small, round black bag.

'Balls!' Olga barked.

Alice swung her bag towards her. 'Check! Got mine.'

'Got mine too,' Marilyn said. 'And Marty's got his.'

'Freddy?'

'You know I always got my equipment,' Freddy drawled.

Olga shuffled to stand in front of the young man. She just about reached his chest. She tilted her head back to take a good look up at him. 'Be polite, always.'

Helen watched as Freddy blushed red. 'Sorry, Olga,' he said.

Olga clapped her hands together. The team, and Helen, focused their attention on her. 'Everyone out. Left, right, left, right.'

Helen watched as they began marching down the hall. There was someone else watching too. Ricky walked out of the lounge, leaned against the door frame and gave a slow, sarcastic hand-clap. Everyone turned to look. Helen saw a smile flicker across Marilyn's lips at the sight of him, then Marty laid his arm protectively around his wife's shoulders. Freddy backed away and dropped his gaze to the carpet, while Olga remained impassive, giving nothing away. It was Alice who stepped forward, standing close to Ricky, just inches from his face.

'You can clap all you want,' she sneered, 'but you won't put our team off our game. I never thought I'd end up living under the same roof as you again, but it looks like we're lumped with each other in here until the tournament ends.'

Helen raised her eyebrows. 'Excuse me? Lumped with each other? Don't forget that you agreed to him staying here, Miss Pickle.'

'It's *Ms* Pickle,' Alice said, still glaring at Ricky. 'I'm no longer Mrs Delmont. I should never have married you. My mother always said you couldn't be trusted.'

'You should have listened to her and saved us both three years of misery,' Ricky snarled.

Helen watched as the pair bristled at each other. Alice was seething with anger. Her fists were clenched and her body rocked from side to side like a boxer ready to throw a punch. Ricky looked more relaxed, leaning against the door frame with a smirk on his face.

'Alice. We're going now,' Olga ordered.

'Too right we are,' Alice said, still staring at Ricky.

He shooed her away with his hand. 'Go and practise. You need it. You never were very good. I taught you everything, Ms Pickle, and don't you forget it. You'd be nothing without me.'

Alice spun on her heel and marched out behind her teammates.

Helen swallowed hard, trying to compose herself. 'Well, now that they've gone,' she said, 'let me take you up to your room.'

Ricky delved into his sports bag and pulled out a large white envelope. 'First I need you to sign this,' he ordered.

Helen peered at the pages he slid from the envelope. She'd never been asked by a guest to sign anything before.

'It's an NDA,' he said. He handed her a black biro. She looked from the biro to the paper.

'A what?'

'A non-disclosure agreement. A legally binding contract that establishes a confidential relationship between you as landlady of the Seaview and me as your paying guest. By signing it, you agree that any sensitive information you may discover about me while I stay here will not be made available to anyone else.'

'What sort of sensitive information?' Helen asked, concerned.

'The sort of information that my rivals, if they got their hands on it, would use against me to nobble my performance on the course.'

Helen was none the wiser.

'Mrs Dexter, I'm talking about my strict dietary requirements, which build muscle mass for my crazy-golf game. You need to sign this NDA because I don't want details of my diet to be made known to my ex-wife and that team of misfits. No one knows what goes into my power breakfasts and I'd like to keep it that way.'

She tried to keep a straight face. 'Oh, I see,' she said. 'Well, as long as that's all it involves, then I can sign it, I suppose.'

'You'll also find a list of the foods I require, along with details of my allergy, which you need to observe.'

Helen flipped to the second page and scanned it. There was only one item he was allergic to, and she breathed a sigh of relief. 'You have nothing to worry about, Mr Delmont. I don't allow peanuts at the Seaview. There was an incident during the first year my husband and I owned the hotel. A young boy was rushed to hospital when he choked on a peanut his parents had given him. We haven't had peanuts here since.'

'I'm glad to hear it,' Ricky replied. 'But you must not, under any circumstances, share my allergy information with anyone else. There's something else you need to know too.'

What now? she wondered.

'You are to turn a blind eye to anything untoward you may find in my room while I stay here. This is also covered in the NDA.'

Helen gave him a hard stare. 'Now hold on a minute. I don't know what sort of establishment you think this is, but if I find something that shouldn't be in your room, you can rest assured I'll have strong words with you about it. Just what kind of things are we talking about?'

'You'll find out, Mrs Dexter.'

'I want nothing illegal or immoral going on under my roof,' she said sternly.

'I promise you that it will be neither of those things, but what you may find could be construed as odd. Now, do you want my business or not?'

'This is most unusual,' Helen said. She hesitated a moment, then sank on to a seat and began to read the NDA. Although it was the first time she'd ever seen such a document, she'd had legal dealings before and was used to signing contracts and forms at Benson Brown & Co., her solicitor in town. To her eyes, the NDA looked amateurish, and she even spotted spelling errors. She wondered if it was worth the paper it was printed on. But, satisfied that it seemed straightforward, she signed both copies, then handed them to Ricky, who signed too before passing one back. As he did so, she noticed a mass of coloured plastic bangles on his wrists, all branded with the logos and names of crazy-golf courses: South Shields, Skegness, Worthing, Great Yarmouth.

'You folks take crazy golf seriously, don't you?' she said.

Ricky stowed his copy of the NDA safely inside his bag. 'Of course. Why wouldn't we? Whether a course has windmills or lighthouses, dinosaurs or pirates, it's always more than a game. It's a fight to the death.' He picked up his clubs and his sports bag, then beamed at her. 'Now, what time is breakfast in the morning?'

Helen thought for a moment. 'Well, it's usually any time between seven thirty and nine, but may I suggest, under the circumstances, that you choose a different time to Alice and her team, or even eat alone in your room? I could bring a tray up to you. I wouldn't normally ask such a thing of my guests, but after what I've just witnessed, it might be best to keep you and Alice apart. Plus, if we do it that way, her team won't find out what you fuel your, er, sportsman's body with.'

She made it sound as if she was doing him a favour when what she really wanted was to avoid any fighting between the warring ex-spouses. Their argument had shaken her up.

A smile made its way to his lips. 'Good idea. I like your thinking, Mrs Dexter. Now, lead the way to my room.'

Later, downstairs in Helen's apartment, Jean brewed a cafetière of coffee and slid a plate containing a slice of freshly baked lemon drizzle cake across the table.

'Brenda's due any time now,' she said as she poured the coffee.

'You called her? When? How did you find her number?'

Jean set the cafetière on the table. 'See! I knew you weren't listening to me when I told you earlier that I'd called her. I don't know where your head's at half the time these days.'

Helen gritted her teeth. 'I've got a lot on my mind.'

Jean crossed her arms. 'I rang her while you were busy with your guests. I looked in the staff book, and Brenda's details were there as Sally's next of kin. But I'll say it again, I'm really not happy about you bringing an outsider in. We're a close-knit team here. I've already told you I'll do the cleaning.'

Helen didn't think it fair to expect Jean to clean rooms at the Seaview after spending hours cooking breakfast. She wasn't a young woman, and her energy quickly flagged. Lugging a heavy vacuum cleaner up and down stairs was hard physical work that took its toll on Helen, never mind someone Jean's age.

'You've got too much on, what with doing all the cooking and looking after your mum in the care home. How's her legs, by the way?'

'Never mind my mum's legs. Stop trying to change the subject. If you're set on having Brenda come in, so be it. But don't say I didn't offer when it all goes wrong.'

'Why should it go wrong?'

'We don't know the woman.'

'She's Sally's mum, she'll be fine,' Helen said, dismissing Jean's concerns. She sipped her coffee and broke off a chunk of cake. She was about to pop it into her mouth when she remembered Ricky's NDA. 'We've got another crazy golfer staying. I've put him on the top floor. He's given me a list of food he wants served up for breakfast.'

Jean tutted out loud. 'I tell you, Helen, people these days are just faddy.'

Helen swallowed her mouthful of cake. 'Smashing lemon drizzle, Jean.' She took another sip of coffee and cradled the mug with both hands.

'What are the guests like?' Jean asked.

'They're a bit odd. I mean, for normal people, people like us, crazy golf is fun. It's sticks and coloured balls and playing with family and friends. But these people train for their games. They're all in tracksuits and trainers, and they've even got a team coach. They seem to have a whole set of clubs each. And they've got bags of balls.'

'That's because they need courage to play in such a big tournament,' Jean chipped in.

Helen laughed out loud. 'No, I mean they've brought lots of different balls in special bags. They're serious competitors with professional equipment. What with their power food requests, their petty squabbles and NDAs, my head's spinning right now.'

'NDAs?'

Helen tapped the sheet of paper on the table in front of her. 'Non-disclosure agreement. The new guest I've just checked in made me sign it. He says it means I have to keep quiet about his food requests and anything else I find out about him while he stays here. I read it through and there's nothing I was concerned with.'

'You should have had it checked over by your solicitors.'

She shook her head. 'If I ever find the time to visit them, I will. Anyway, it looked harmless, as if he'd typed it himself. But he's asked us not to tell anyone about his food requests or his allergy, understand?'

Jean took the sheets, glanced at them briefly, then laid them face down on the table. 'Nothing on there I can't handle,' she said. 'At least he's not asking for stuff I can't pronounce like the first lot did. I'll put this with the other food requests in the blue folder.'

Helen looked around the apartment. 'Where's the dog, Jean?'

'How am I supposed to know?'

'Suki!' she called. She walked to her bedroom, thinking the greyhound must be in there, but was surprised to see that she wasn't. 'Suki?' she called again, puzzled. She walked back to the living room, out on to the patio, and even looked in the bathroom, but Suki was nowhere to be seen. Her heart began to thump as anxiety set in. She marched to the back door and flung it wide, but Suki wasn't in the yard or out in the back lane.

She scratched her head in confusion. She knew the dog had been with her earlier that morning after she'd been to see Miriam about checking in Ricky Delmont . . . Suddenly it dawned on her where she must be. Feeling both relieved and hopeful that she was right, she ran up the stairs, grasping the handrail, and pushed open the door to the hallway. Sure enough, there was Suki, pacing the floor. Helen was just about to call out to her when Ricky Delmont's angry voice stopped her in her tracks.

'Bloody stupid dog. Get out of my way!'

She watched in horror as Ricky lunged at Suki, who backed away nervously. She'd never seen the greyhound look so cowed before. She had an unbroken rule about never losing her temper with a guest, but Ricky had gone too far.

'What the hell do you think you're doing?' she cried.

He started at the sound of her voice and turned to look at her, pushing a hand through his hair. 'Are you talking to me?' he said, looking around the hallway as if he expected to find someone else there.

Helen's heart began thumping again, but this time with anger at Ricky. She walked towards Suki and stroked her head as Suki nuzzled against her leg.

'You were threatening my dog!' she cried.

Ricky laughed out loud, which made Helen more determined to stand her ground.

'Don't patronise me,' she said. 'Suki's scared, I can tell.'

He shrugged. 'She was in my way. I was trying to get past her to go up to my room. You should keep her on a lead, she's vicious.'

Helen pulled Suki as far from Ricky as she could. She didn't like the tone of the man's voice, or the way he kept eyeing the greyhound. She knew that dogs scared some people, and that was why she always ensured that Suki stayed downstairs. She realised she must've closed the door on her earlier in error, while she had other things on her mind, and the dog had been locked out of the apartment.

'Suki's not vicious, she wouldn't hurt a fly,' she replied firmly. 'I'll take her downstairs, then you'll be free to move about as you need.'

Something didn't feel right to Helen. Ricky was acting too arrogantly by half, but she had no proof that he'd been about to hurt Suki before she entered the hallway. She had to give him the benefit of the doubt this time, so she adopted a professional stance, remembering the standard she needed to maintain in order to keep her four stars.

'I'm sorry if you were put to any inconvenience, and I promise it won't happen again.' As the words left her lips, she glared at

Ricky, holding his gaze. He nodded curtly, then turned and marched briskly up the stairs.

Helen breathed a sigh of relief as she returned to her apartment, making sure Suki followed this time. But as she reached the kitchen, the doorbell rang. She glanced at the CCTV screen on the wall and saw a woman's face crowned by tightly permed hair.

'Brenda's here,' she said. 'I'll go and let her in.'

Chapter 6

Helen was taken aback by Brenda's dishevelled appearance. She wore an unflattering green cardigan that had seen better days and a pair of black trousers that hung loose and trailed on the floor. She shuffled into the Seaview gripping her handbag under her arm.

'Thanks for coming, Brenda,' Helen said, as cheerfully as she could. 'It's good to see you. Have you heard from Sally on her honeymoon? It was a beautiful wedding, wasn't it? She's got herself a good man in Gav.'

'Aye,' Brenda said in a monotone, giving nothing away, no comment or praise about her new son-in-law. She didn't even say hello.

'I've known Gav for a few months,' Helen continued, trying to lift the mood. 'He's done a lot of work for me at the Seaview, handyman jobs, that kind of thing. He's been very helpful. It's been difficult running the place on my own since my husband passed away. Having Gav around has been great. Anyway, come downstairs and meet Jean. We'll have a coffee and a chat and I'll tell you about the job.'

She led the way downstairs, and when she entered the kitchen, Suki padded towards her.

'I can't be doing with dogs,' Brenda moaned.

Helen grabbed hold of Suki's collar, led her to the patio doors and put her outside. Suki lay on the ground, staring in through the window. 'She's very friendly,' Helen said, 'but I know not everyone likes dogs. However, she lives here, and if you come to work with us this week while Sally's away, you'll be crossing paths with her.'

Brenda pulled out a chair and sat down at the table. Helen sat opposite her, next to Jean.

'Coffee, Brenda? Slice of lemon drizzle? It's fresh out of the oven this morning. Jean's just made it,' she offered.

'Aye,' Brenda replied.

Jean sprang into action, pouring coffee and slicing cake. She cut herself another slice and topped up Helen's coffee. Helen opened her mouth to start telling Brenda about the work, but was cut short when Brenda spoke first.

'How much will I be paid?'

Jean beamed a big smile at her. 'My word, lass, you're a woman after my own heart, coming straight to the point like that. I always say there's no need to beat around the bush. Don't I, Helen? I always say—'

'How much?' Brenda repeated.

Helen's mouth opened and closed. 'The same hourly rate I pay Sally.'

'And is there much work?'

'A few hours each morning. You'd be helping me clean the guest rooms and en suites, the lounge and the dining room. Then there's the hall and making sure the outside is presentable, the steps are swept, that sort of thing.'

'I'll do it,' Brenda said.

Helen glanced at Jean, who gave a subtle wink.

'Thank you, Brenda. I appreciate your help. Sally's a great worker and I know you will be too.'

Brenda didn't acknowledge the flattery. Instead, she said, 'I need paying in cash. Every day.'

'Now, Brenda,' Jean said sternly. 'It's one thing being forward and another being rude. You're overstepping the mark.'

Helen looked at Brenda's bloodshot eyes, her sallow skin, her downturned mouth and the frizz of her badly permed hair. There were holes around the neck of her T-shirt where stitching was coming away, and her green cardigan was worn and thin.

'It's all right, Jean. I think I can manage to pay Brenda each day. I'm sure it'll be fine.'

'I need the money in advance,' Brenda said, without missing a beat.

Now it was Helen's turn to look askance. She took a moment before she replied. 'Let's see how it goes, Brenda. Come at seven tomorrow morning and you can have breakfast with me and Jean. The dog will be here, but I promise she won't harm you. You have my word on that.'

'Breakfast?' Brenda's eyes lit up. 'You mean the Seaview's award-winning full English comes as part of my job, for free?'

Helen had been thinking of cereal and toast. 'If that's what you'd like, then I suppose we could stretch to it,' she replied, thinking quickly. She could hardly refuse Sally's mum a meal.

Jean leaned across the table and narrowed her eyes at Brenda. 'You're not one of them vegetarians, are you?'

'Definitely not. I'm a sausage and bacon girl.'

She sank back into her chair with relief.

Brenda looked from Jean to Helen. 'Is that it, then? Can I go?' Without waiting for a reply, she scraped her chair back and stood up. She picked up her slice of untouched cake and popped it in her handbag. Jean's face was a picture.

'We'll see you tomorrow, Brenda, seven o'clock sharp,' Helen said. 'I'll show you out.'

'Bye, Brenda,' Jean called, but Brenda was already marching to the door that led upstairs and ignored her completely.

Helen followed her up to the hall. She was about to pull the front door open to let her out, then hesitated.

'You must be missing Sally and little Gracie,' she said. She didn't want to pry, but it seemed that something lay heavy on Brenda's mind. Why else had she looked so miserable at her own daughter's wedding, and at the Seaview that morning? 'Look, Brenda, if there's anything you want to talk about . . . I mean, with me, this week, while you're working here, I'm always free for coffee once the cleaning's been done.'

'Aye,' Brenda said. 'I'll be off, then.'

Helen pulled the door open, and Brenda shuffled out.

'Bye, Brenda, see you tomorrow,' Helen called, but the woman didn't respond.

Helen didn't have time to give her another thought, however, as just then, an open-top red sports car zoomed to the kerb. In the driving seat was her best friend, Marie.

'Helen!' Marie yelled. 'I can't stop, but I've got something to tell you.'

Helen ran down the steps to the car. She leaned over and kissed Marie on the cheek. 'Oh, you smell lovely. What's that perfume?'

Marie winked. 'It's the sweet smell of success. I'm expanding Tom's Teas, opening another branch in Filey. I think Tom would approve, don't you?'

'That's fantastic news, and yes, he'd have been very proud. Thank you, my friend, for keeping his memory alive. Ooh, is that a new trouser suit you're wearing?'

Marie flicked her long, silky brown hair over one shoulder, then ran a hand along her ruby-red trouser leg. 'Yes, it's new. I treated myself. Divorcing Daran Clark, that lowlife, gangster husband of mine, was the best thing I ever did.'

'Well, you look gorgeous as usual,' Helen said.

Marie ran her gaze over Helen, all the way from her brown boots to her old jeans and her tabard with the Seaview logo embroidered in blue. 'And you look very Helen,' she said. 'Look, love, why don't you let me take you clothes shopping in York or Harrogate? We could make a day of it, go to Betty's tearooms, eat cake. You could do with smartening up. Isn't Jimmy coming back soon? Surely you want to wear something nice when you see him. We've got so much to catch up on. We haven't spent time together in ages.'

'And yet you've got time to spend with Sandra DeVine,' Helen said. She realised how petulant she sounded at the mention of their old school friend, but she couldn't help it. 'Jean spotted the two of you in the Angel Inn. You know she always peers in through the window when she's walking past.'

'Are you jealous?' Marie laughed.

'I'm just missing spending time with my best pal, that's all. What've you been up to with Sandra?'

'Helping her arrange a school reunion. It's this week.'

'This week? That's short notice, isn't it?'

'I'm finding that Sandra's a short notice sort of girl. She's impetuous, impulsive. Plus, she's been connected online for years to everyone we went to school with. She posted an invite in her group, and half the school's turning up. It's on Thursday night, in the function room at the Royal Hotel. Want to come?'

Helen shook her head. 'You know I'm not a party person.'

Marie tapped her manicured nails against the steering wheel. 'You need taking out of yourself. You're holed up at the Seaview when you should be having fun.' She lowered her gaze before delivering her killer line. 'Tom wouldn't want you to be missing out on life.'

'Oh, don't play the Tom card,' Helen said, feeling a rush of anger.

'Then what card do I need to play to get you out and about? You're in danger of losing yourself to the hotel, becoming part of the wallpaper. You're still a young woman, you deserve to have a life. Speaking of which, it's your fiftieth soon. We should go out and celebrate.'

Helen sighed heavily. 'Don't you start. I've already got Jean on my case about having a party. I keep telling her I'm not up for it, but she won't listen.'

Marie's hands-free phone beeped on the dashboard. 'I've got to go, Helen, I've got an appointment to sign the lease on the new place in Filey. About the school reunion . . .'

'I'm not going,' Helen said.

'. . . I'll come for you on Thursday,' Marie said, putting the car into gear, checking her mirrors.

'I'm not going,' Helen repeated.

'I'll pick you up at seven,' Marie said, and before Helen could reply, she drove off.

Helen walked back up the steps to the Seaview, noticing the holes she'd drilled in the wall to hang the new plaque. She'd have to do something about it. It couldn't languish indoors after all the hard work she'd put in to earn the four stars. Just then, her phone beeped with a message. She pulled it out of her pocket and saw Jimmy's name.

Hi Helen, I've got 2 surprises for you! Hope you enjoy them both, bit nervous about your reaction tbh, but can't wait to see you. Not sure when I'll be back but I'll let you know asap. I've tried ringing but you don't answer, guess you're busy with guests. Speak soon, Jimmy x

She paused at the door, looking out at the sea, letting the message sink in. Jimmy had been nothing but kind, patient and courteous with her by text, phone and email while he'd been working as an Elvis impersonator in Spain. It had been easy to push him to the back of her mind and not deal with what his return would mean. But now he was coming back and she knew she had to make a decision. Did she want to share her future with him or not? Oh, if only she could get rid of the fear and the guilt about what it might mean to move on. If she decided to make a go of things with Jimmy, it meant closing the door on her life with Tom. And each time she thought of that, a lump came to her throat and tears welled in her eyes.

She swallowed hard, then looked ahead, taking in the sweeping beach vista she adored. An ice-cream van trundled noisily along King's Parade, the strains of 'Greensleeves' trailing in its wake. The tune pulled her from her thoughts about Jimmy. Seagulls flew overhead, tourists walked along the prom. Down on the beach, surfers headed into the waves, determined to make the most of the swell. Dogs ran on the sand. In the distance, a colourful line of brightly painted beach huts shimmered in the sun. She was about to head back indoors when she spotted one of her guests walking along King's Parade. It was Freddy, the crazy-golf wunderkind, and he was speaking into his phone. He looked angry, she thought, but it wasn't her business to pry.

She walked inside and through the door that led to her apartment just as Freddy entered the hall. Then she heard another voice and her heart dropped. It was Ricky Delmont; he must have been sitting in the lounge.

'It's people like you who bring this sport into disrepute,' he sneered.

'Say what now?' Freddy replied.

Helen stood rigid on the other side of the door as the two men argued in the hall.

'Just look at the state of you. You're a walking billboard, not a crazy golfer,' Ricky continued. His bitter tone made Helen wonder what Freddy had done to incur such wrath.

'If you mean my sneakers, they're branded, yes, but—'

'But nothing,' Ricky snapped. 'You take money to put company logos on your cap or adverts on your sports bag. You should be ashamed of yourself.'

'Why?' Freddy replied. 'If companies want to pay me for advertising, then sure, I'll take their cash. I need the money to help support me through crazy-golf training. What's so wrong about having a sponsor who pays me to show off their goods?'

Helen was pleased to hear the young man sounding so confident.

For one awful moment, she'd been worried she might have to go into the hall to rescue him in the same way she'd rescued Suki earlier.

'You're a joke, boy,' Ricky said. 'You know that the crazy-golf community nickname you Fake Jake because of your stupid American accent? You should hear the things they say about you when they know they're playing against your bunch of losers. You should have joined my team when I offered you the chance in Brighton last year.'

'I wouldn't join your team if it was the last one on earth, I told you that before. And why would I care what people say about me? It's not a popularity contest. I'm in this to win with my golf skills.'

'You haven't got the fight in you to win. Sure, you wear all the right gear, but where it counts, on the course, you haven't got a chance.'

'You're just jealous because you lost out on the sponsorship deal.'

'Me? Jealous?' Ricky sneered.

'We all know why the sponsors dropped you, Ricky. They found out about you threatening one of the players in the Brighton tournament.'

There was silence. Helen leaned forward so that her ear was against the door. She heard footsteps above her; someone was climbing the stairs, but there was no way of telling if it was Ricky or Freddy.

She dug her boots into the carpet. Her heart was beating wildly beneath her tabard. After a moment, she heard Freddy's voice on the other side of the door, and what he was saying made her heart beat even harder. He was no longer speaking with the cod-American accent he'd affected so far.

'Yes, Mum. Sorry for what I said earlier. I'll be careful, I promise. Yes, Mum, I'll get him. I swear on my life that I'll get revenge on Ricky Delmont for what he did to us both.'

Chapter 7

When Helen woke the next morning, her heart lifted to see sunlight streaming in through the window. It looked set to be a perfect Scarborough day. From the kitchen she could hear Jean shoop-shooping along to a song on the radio. She got out of bed and wrapped her dressing gown around herself. As soon as she walked into the living room, Suki padded to her, and Helen greeted her with a stroke behind her ears. 'We'll go out soon,' she said.

Suki slunk outside through the open patio doors.

'Morning, Jean!' Helen called.

'Morning, love,' Jean called back.

Helen was about to ask Jean how her elderly mum was. She was in her late nineties and lived in a care home in the middle of town, and Jean was constantly worried about her. But before she could say a word, the doorbell rang. Puzzled, Helen glanced at the CCTV screen in the kitchen, then looked at the clock.

'It's Brenda. She's an hour early,' she said.

'Strange woman, if you ask me,' Jean said. 'I hope she doesn't think you're going to pay her overtime for turning up before she's due. You've never paid me overtime in all the years I've worked here.'

Helen ran her hand through her hair, then walked up the stairs.

When she pulled the door open, she was saddened to see Brenda in the same dishevelled state as the day before.

'Morning, Brenda. I wasn't expecting you this early. Jean's just turned up to start cooking. I won't need you for another hour yet.'

'Aye, well, I'd like to come in, if it's all the same to you,' Brenda said. She lifted her gaze and looked directly at Helen. 'You did promise me Jean's award-winning full English before I start work.'

Helen was about to reply that she hadn't promised anything, but to keep the peace, she kept her thoughts to herself.

Brenda stepped into the hall and shuffled towards the door that led to Helen's apartment. 'I'll go down. I hope you've got your dog tied up. I can't be doing with dogs,' she said. She didn't wait for a reply.

Helen was flabbergasted. 'Er . . . excuse me, love,' she called out, but Brenda was already on her way downstairs.

She wondered how someone like Sally, who was personable and cheerful, polite and kind, could have such a sullen mother. And yet there was something about Brenda that stopped Helen from complaining. The woman looked down at heel, and even at Sally's wedding she hadn't seemed at ease. Besides, she was only working at the Seaview for a few days until Sally returned from honeymoon. How hard could it be to feed her and keep her sweet until then?

When Helen returned to the kitchen, she was surprised to see Brenda sitting at the table, delving into her handbag.

'I've brought my own knife and fork,' she said, laying the utensils on the table.

Jean spun around and tutted loudly, then returned to her task of placing hash browns on a metal tray. But Brenda wasn't finished. Next, she took out a large piece of cloth, which she spread on her knees.

'I've brought my own napkin.'

'Good grief,' Jean muttered.

Helen looked at Brenda. 'That's, er . . .' She struggled to find the right words. 'That's very organised of you,' she said at last.

'Aye,' Brenda replied.

Suki walked from the patio to the kitchen table. Helen caught her before she reached Brenda. 'Outside, now,' she told the dog, and Suki returned to lie on the flagstones warmed by the morning sun.

'Cup of tea, please,' Brenda said.

Jean looked at her with a face full of thunder.

'With two sugars and a splash of milk. And for my breakfast, I'll have two sausages, bacon, black pudding, hash browns, a poached egg and plenty of beans. I'd like my beans on a slice of white toast, buttered.' Brenda looked around the apartment. 'Have you got something I can read while I'm waiting?'

Helen's mouth opened and closed. She was lost for words. Jean, meanwhile, was turning red in the face, gripping a wooden spoon tightly. Helen walked towards her.

'You all right, love?' she murmured. 'Don't let her get to you.'

'I'll be all right in a few days, when Sally's back,' Jean said through gritted teeth. She cast a dark look at Brenda. 'Would madam like her tea served in a silver cup?'

Helen laid a hand on her arm. 'There's no need to be sarcastic.'

Jean shook her head and turned back to her work. Helen looked around, searching for something to keep Brenda occupied. An old copy of *The Scarborough Times* lay on the sofa. She picked it up. 'This all right for you, Brenda?'

'Aye,' Brenda said.

Helen was about to hand it over when Jean called out, 'Do you want me to iron it for you, Brenda?'

'Jean!' Helen snapped.

Brenda took the paper without a word of thanks. Jean turned the radio up.

'I'm going to get dressed,' Helen said. 'You two, don't fight while I'm gone.'

Helen quickly showered and dressed. Her usual routine was to take Suki for a walk on the beach while Jean was cooking breakfast. She knew Jean's habits off by heart after their years working together. The older woman didn't like anyone to fuss around while she cooked. But that morning, something told Helen she might not appreciate being left alone with Brenda. And she could hardly invite Brenda for a walk with her and Suki when Brenda didn't like dogs. She was unsure of what to do, but when she walked into the kitchen, her decision was made for her, as Brenda was already tucking into her breakfast.

'That was quick, Jean,' she said.

'I thought I'd cook hers first, because if she's using her mouth to eat then she can't use it to give me orders.'

'Give the woman a break,' Helen sighed. 'Look, will you be all right here if I take Suki out? You know she needs to go out first thing each morning. She hates changes to her routine.'

Jean raised her eyebrows. 'Don't we all,' she said pointedly. She looked at Helen. 'Yes, I'll be all right, but don't expect me to become firm friends with the woman. I'll tolerate her, for Sally's sake and yours. But that's it.'

Helen gave a wry smile. 'Try your best, Jean, for the Seaview's sake. I won't be long.' She clipped Suki's lead to her collar, then walked to the back door and out into the warm day.

When she returned, she found Brenda on the sofa, reading the newspaper, feet up on a pouffe. Jean was working her socks off in the kitchen, scrambling eggs, heating beans, turning sausages under the grill. Normally such a scene would have cheered Helen no end, but today there was something troubling her.

'What about the superfoods the guests have asked for?' she asked Jean, looking around, exasperated. 'Where are the chia seeds and manuka honey and all the other stuff they requested? Olga asked for an egg-white omelette, but I don't see the omelette pan ready.'

Jean pushed her glasses up to the bridge of her nose and gave her a hard stare. 'I've no idea what to do with half the stuff on the list. Who eats an egg-white omelette, for heaven's sake? How would I know when it's cooked? They'll have to fend for themselves. I'm just an old-fashioned cook doing old-fashioned breakfasts. It's what I do. It's who I am, and I deserve some respect for it.'

Helen let Suki off her lead and shooed the dog to the patio. She stood close to Jean and positioned herself so that Brenda couldn't hear what she said. Having the woman around was already proving harder than she'd expected. She wondered if Jean's warnings about taking an outsider on had been right. Jean was rarely wrong, and Helen began to realise she should have listened to her.

'Jean, please. I'll help you. We worked hard to get upgraded to four stars and I don't want anything to put that in jeopardy. Speaking of which, I should have another go at fixing our new plaque to the wall.'

'Pfft,' Jean said.

Helen sighed. 'Come on, it isn't like you to be petty. What's upset you so much? Did Brenda say something to you while I was out?'

'It's not Brenda.'

'Then is it the golfers' food requests?'

'It's not the food.'

'So what is it?'

'You really want to know?'

'Yes, I do.'

Jean banged the slatted spoon on the kitchen top and Helen jumped in shock. Behind them, pans of water bubbled. Sausages, bacon and black pudding sizzled under the grill, beans swam in sauce, hash browns turned golden. Jean's face flushed red. 'It's you.'

Helen was startled. 'Me? What have *I* done?'

'It's what you've *not* done,' Jean said, her voice rising. 'You've not once said flaming thank you for all the help I gave you while the hotel inspector was here earlier this year. I cooked pancakes specially and you know I didn't want to. I felt like you forced my hand.'

'Jean, I—' Helen began, but Jean raised her hand to silence her.

'And now you won't let me help with the cleaning when I offered. Instead, you bring an outsider in.'

'Keep your voice down,' Helen whispered, glancing at Brenda.

'No need, I've heard every word,' Brenda called from the sofa.

Helen was exasperated. 'Jean, love—'

'Oh, don't you *Jean, love* me! You've taken me for granted long enough. Forcing me to cook porridge and kippers and goodness knows what, all for the sake of getting an extra star. The Seaview doesn't need star ratings, Helen. It needs love, warmth and friendship, things that've been missing for some time.'

Helen felt lead pouring into her heart as Jean continued.

'This hotel is just as much a part of my life as it is yours. In fact, I've been here longer than you.'

'Jean, I know that, but look . . .' Helen was pleading, desperate.

Jean stood firm. 'The Seaview's changed, Helen. *You've* changed. You've got a hard side to you that you never used to have. And now you're flashing that extra star around like a magnet to faddy eaters. You should know me well enough to know that I don't do faddy. I do what I'm good at, and, may I remind you, I win awards for it.' She began untying the knot in her apron strings.

'Jean!' Helen cried. 'What are you doing?'

'I've had enough. I'm worried sick about my mum. I've got you taking me for granted. And now her ladyship over there waltzes in and starts treating me like muck. It's too much. I'm off.' Jean pulled the apron over her head and threw it on the kitchen floor. Then she stormed to the sofa and picked up her handbag and coat.

'You can't leave!' Helen cried.

'Just watch me,' Jean replied. She raked in her handbag, pulled out a bunch of keys and threw them on to a side table before disappearing through the back door.

Helen felt tears spring to her eyes. This couldn't be happening. Jean couldn't leave the Seaview. She ran after her. 'Jean, please, don't go. I need you.'

'You don't need me. You've got Brenda now,' Jean shouted.

'Jean!' Helen cried, but Jean walked on and didn't look back.

Stunned, Helen returned to the kitchen. Her heart felt like it had been smashed into pieces. She couldn't run the place on her own. She had no cook. The staffing agency weren't returning her calls. And on top of everything else, she had Brenda to deal with. What on earth was she going to do?

Chapter 8

The smoke alarm beeped and smoke filled the kitchen.

'The bloody beans are burning!' Helen cried.

'Aye, I thought they would,' Brenda said from the sofa. Suki was sitting on the patio, staring into the living room through the glass doors.

'Didn't you think to turn them off?' Helen said angrily.

She took the pan off the gas and wafted a tea towel under the alarm. When it fell silent, she put her hands on her hips, closed her eyes and counted to ten. She couldn't believe Jean had gone. Running the Seaview without her was unthinkable. Apart from when she had taken holidays, not a single day had gone by when she hadn't cooked breakfast at the hotel.

'Brenda! I need a hand,' Helen called, and when the woman didn't move, she yelled, 'Now!'

Brenda swung her feet to the floor and ambled into the kitchen. 'Aye. Jean's gone,' she said when she reached Helen.

Helen narrowed her eyes, ready to explode. Then she thought of Sally and little Gracie and bit her tongue. The last thing she wanted was for Brenda to tell her daughter that Helen had lost her temper with her. If that happened, she might not just lose the best cleaner she'd ever had, she'd lose Sally as a friend too.

'Yes, Jean's gone . . . for now, and I need your help with breakfast. Now listen, I'll do my best to cook, then you serve, right? I'll go upstairs to the dining room and pacify the guests. Tell them we've got an emergency situation and the special food they've requested isn't available.'

'Aye,' Brenda said. 'But you'll have to pay me more.'

'You can have more,' Helen said quickly, turning to the grill, where the sausages were starting to darken.

'How much more?'

Helen stared at the woman. She really was unbelievable. 'Brenda, I'm in the middle of a crisis. We'll talk money later. Now come and help. Open more beans and get rid of the burnt ones.' She handed Brenda a tabard with the Seaview logo embroidered in blue. 'Here, wear this. You're one of the team now, at least until Sally comes back.'

Helen worked quickly, issuing commands to Brenda to chivvy her along. She tried cajoling her, encouraging her; then, when that didn't work, she resorted to yelling. The guests complained, of course, that their power breakfasts had been replaced by bacon sandwiches and burnt sausages. When Ricky Delmont learned what had happened, he declared that he'd be eating out and would expect a refund on his bill.

Brenda relayed all the complaints to Helen once breakfast had ended. By then, Helen was too exhausted to care. 'I don't know how Jean copes,' she said.

'Coped. She's gone,' Brenda said.

Helen waved her hand dismissively. 'She'll be back, you'll see.'

Brenda shrugged. 'I wouldn't be so sure. If you spoke to me the way you spoke to her, I wouldn't want to work here either.'

Helen sat at the kitchen table and buried her head in her hands, then looked up at Brenda, who was standing at her side. 'Am I really that bad?'

'Aye.'

She gazed out to the patio, where Suki was lying Sphinx-like with her caramel limbs tucked beneath her. 'I'll visit Jean at home to apologise. I'll take flowers.'

'You'll need more than a bouquet,' Brenda said. 'You've been tetchy with her for months.'

Helen frowned. 'How do you know?' Then it dawned on her, and she felt sick. 'Sally told you, didn't she? Oh crikey. I had no idea I was getting so short-tempered.'

'Not just with Jean. Sally too. She told me all about it. Said you'd not been right since Jean mentioned throwing a party for your fiftieth birthday. It's a tricky age for a woman. You need to be careful. You might end up losing your temper with my Sally and end up with no staff at all.' Brenda looked around the living room. 'Mind you, now I've had a crack at waitressing, I think I've got a knack for it. I could work here, you know. Course, we'd have to talk about the hourly rate. It'd have to improve.'

'I'm sure Jean will be back,' Helen said, more confidently than she felt. 'And you working here is just a temporary measure, don't forget.'

'Aye, well, we'll see,' Brenda replied. 'So, do we have our coffee and cake now? Sally says it's her favourite part of working here, having coffee and a chat with you and Jean.'

Helen stood and walked to the cupboard under the stairs, where she kept the cleaning equipment. 'No. We have coffee after we've cleaned. Here, take these.' She handed Brenda a mop, bucket and blue rubber gloves. 'We start upstairs and work down. Every surface you see you must dust, polish, vacuum, wipe, swipe, shine and clean. Bleach is for bathrooms and toilets. We clean the bedrooms, en suites and stairs. Then we do the dining room, lounge and hall. You'll soon get the hang of it. Oh, and under no circumstances must you interfere with guests' belongings. You should only move their stuff to dust or vacuum underneath. You replace items on the tea tray, but that's it. If in doubt, don't do it and ask me for advice.'

'Aye.'

Helen and Brenda headed to the top floor, each of them lugging a heavy vacuum cleaner along with their buckets and mops. This was the floor where Ricky Delmont was staying. In all the commotion of the morning's crisis, Helen had completely forgotten about his odd request for her to turn a blind eye to what she might find in his room. She knocked at the door.

'I know this guest has already gone out for breakfast, and I saw the others heading off wearing matching tracksuits. I think they're training on the course. However, we always knock, just in case guests are in their rooms,' she told Brenda. She knocked again for good measure, and when there was no reply, she slid the master key into the lock and held the door to one side for Brenda to enter. 'Right, you do this room and I'll clean the landing before I go down to the next floor and start on the rooms there.'

As she was about to plug the vacuum cleaner in, she was stopped in her tracks by a blood-curdling scream. It came from Ricky's room. Brenda staggered on to the landing with her hands fluttering at her heart.

'What is it?' Helen gasped.

Brenda could hardly speak. The shock of what she'd seen was clearly too much.

'In there . . .' she whispered. 'In there . . . There's a dead body in the bed.'

Chapter 9

Helen felt faint. She put a hand on the wall to steady herself and swallowed hard. Many unusual things had happened at the Seaview Hotel, but no one had ever died there. Brenda slid down the wall and sat on the carpet, weeping. Helen took a deep breath. She knew she had to see for herself.

She approached the door to Ricky's room, expecting the worst, hesitating on the threshold. Closing her eyes, she braced herself, then stepped inside. Her heart was beating too fast. Behind her, Brenda wailed. Once she felt prepared, she slowly opened her eyes. There was no blood, gore or mess. The room looked normal apart from a body-shaped lump under the duvet. She walked briskly towards it – no point in lingering now, better to rip the plaster off and be done with it – and pulled the duvet back, ready for the horror. But it wasn't a body at all. It was Ricky's golf bag, with his clubs inside.

Relief rushed through her, so fast and strong that she thought she was going to faint. Her legs wobbled and she fell into a chair by the window.

'Brenda,' she tried to call, but her voice didn't work. 'Brenda,' she said again, louder this time. 'It's all right. It's not a body. You can come in.'

There was movement on the landing, sniffling, then Brenda

peeked around the door. Her eyes opened wide. 'Golf clubs?' she said, puzzled.

'Indeed,' Helen said. 'But I can understand why you thought it was a body. It fooled me too for a second. Oh, my poor heart. It's just as well Jean's not here, because if she'd found this, I think the shock would have done her in.'

'I'll need compensation,' Brenda said, her voice shaking.

'You can have a brandy downstairs. I could do with one too.'

She crossed her arms. 'I don't need a brandy. I want paying more for dealing with this. You never told me there'd be odd things going on.'

Helen looked at the golf bag. She couldn't argue that it wasn't unusual, and she wondered if Ricky always slept with his clubs. Was this what he'd meant when he'd said she might find strange things in his room? 'You can't tell anyone about this, Brenda,' she said sternly, remembering the NDA she'd signed. 'What we find in guests' rooms is strictly confidential.'

Brenda looked around the room. 'Well, I'm not cleaning in here after the shock I've just had. I'll do the landing instead.'

Helen kept glancing at Brenda as they worked that morning, checking that she was all right.

'You OK?' she asked.

'Aye,' Brenda replied, her status returned to normal.

Helen unlocked Olga's room after she'd cleaned Ricky's. When she stepped inside, she stood still by the door trying to take in what she saw. The smart navy suit and crisp white shirt that Olga had worn on arrival at the Seaview was replicated all over the room. Identical suits and shirts hung on the wardrobe door, on the hook behind the main door, on the mirror and even from the wall-mounted TV. Tentatively she walked to the wardrobe. Its door was ajar, as there were three suits and shirts hanging there keeping it from closing. She pulled it open an inch, surprised to see more navy suits inside. She counted a total of twelve suits and shirts. Three identical pairs of flat black shoes were lined up at the bottom of the wardrobe. Seven more pairs lined the walls.

Helen cleaned the room quickly, taking care not to disturb the clothes. Brenda cleaned Marilyn and Marty's room and Helen took a quick look after she had finished to ensure her cleaning was up to par. She was relieved to see it was. When all the rooms were done, the dining room and lounge cleaned and the hall vacuumed, the two of them headed downstairs.

'Coffee, Brenda?' Helen asked.

'Aye. And cake. Sally says there's always cake.'

'There usually is, when Jean's here.' She shook her head. 'Look, I'm going to have to leave as soon as we've had our coffee. I need to apologise to Jean.'

'Do you want me back tomorrow?' Brenda asked.

'Yes, please. Thanks for all you've done today. It's been a baptism of fire, and I apologise. What should have been a straightforward cleaning job has turned into something more, but I need all the help I can get. You can see how I'm fixed. I'll have to apologise again to the guests about their breakfasts. They've requested super-foods and power meals, seeds and protein and heaven knows what else. Instead, they've had bacon sandwiches and beans on toast. None of them were happy.'

'Aye,' Brenda said.

Helen brewed coffee and opened a pack of ginger snaps. She

was missing Jean already. She wanted to tell her about Brenda finding what she'd thought was a dead body, about the golf clubs in Ricky's bed and about Olga's suits. She wanted to reminisce with her about Tom and discuss the future of the Seaview. She longed to give her the good news about Marie opening a new tearoom in Filey. She wanted to mention her doubts about going to the school reunion. Most of all, she desperately needed some no-nonsense advice about her wavering romance with Jimmy. Instead, she looked across the table at Brenda's sad eyes, tired face and badly permed hair.

'So,' she said as cheerfully as she could manage. 'What are you doing for the rest of the day?'

Brenda dunked her ginger snap into her coffee and sucked noisily on it. 'Not much I can do.'

Helen raised an eyebrow. 'Oh?'

Brenda didn't reply. She took an unusual interest in her mug instead, running her finger around the base.

'Sorry, I didn't mean to pry,' Helen said.

Brenda shrugged. 'Doing things costs money, that's all, and I don't have a lot. I've got debts to pay.'

So that was why she'd asked for payment each day, Helen thought. She also wondered if this was the reason Brenda looked like she carried the weight of the world on her shoulders.

'Then I'll pay you now for the work you've done this morning.'

'Aye,' Brenda said immediately. 'Cash.'

Helen walked to the cupboard under the stairs where she kept her cash float. 'I'm sorry you got such a shock earlier,' she said, handing over the money.

Brenda didn't count it; she just stuffed it into her cardigan pocket. Then she threw the rest of her coffee down her throat, gathered her handbag and stuck it firmly under her arm.

'Oh, you're off then?' Helen said, surprised.

'Aye,' Brenda said.

'Same time tomorrow?' Helen asked.

'Aye.' And with that, Brenda walked towards the door that led upstairs.

'There's a back door, Brenda, just for our use down here. Let me show you.' As Helen stood, she spotted Jean's keys lying on the small table by the door. 'Here, you might as well take these. You can let yourself in when you arrive in the morning. I might be out walking Suki, but I trust my staff to let themselves in and out of my apartment. It's how things have always worked here.'

As soon as Brenda had left, Helen went to the patio doors and let Suki in. 'Fancy a walk to Jean's house?' she asked the dog.

Suki cocked her head in reply.

Before Helen left the house, she quickly ran upstairs to see if any post had been delivered. She pushed open the door at the top of her stairs and walked into the hallway. Two raised voices, arguing in the lounge, filled her with dread. She paused a moment and soon realised it was Ricky. Again. This time he was arguing with Olga.

'Leave Freddy alone,' Olga said. 'If you're going to be nasty to people, pick on someone your own size. Freddy's a great lad, I'm lucky to have him on my team.'

'Lucky? Pah!' Ricky scoffed. 'He's a long, tall streak of nothing, a clothes horse for loaded American companies.'

'You would have taken the money to do the same if the sponsor hadn't dropped you like a stone when they found out about your threatening behaviour. He's more than a clothes horse and you know it; he's as good as you as a player. That's why you tried to poach him to join you after the tournament in Brighton.'

'Why would I want to poach a useless lump like him?' Ricky yelled, angrier than Helen had heard him before.

She knew Olga was ex-military and probably able to take care of herself if push came to shove. But she was concerned that pushing and shoving might lead to fighting between them. She swallowed hard. She'd heard enough. It seemed that ever since Ricky Delmont had turned up, arguments had unfolded each time he was in the Seaview. Well, she wasn't prepared to listen to him any more. She coughed loudly to announce her presence, then walked into the lounge. Both Olga and Ricky looked at her, startled.

'I heard raised voices,' Helen said calmly, looking Ricky straight in the eye. 'And I'd rather not hear any more. The Seaview's a friendly place, a family hotel, and I don't take kindly to arguments under my roof.'

Ricky stormed from the room, leaving Helen alone with Olga.

'Are you all right?' she asked.

Olga nodded. 'He doesn't scare me, Helen. Mind you, I'd give anything to see someone take him down a peg or two.' And with that she marched from the room.

Helen took a second to watch her go. She wondered what might have happened if she hadn't turned up when she had.

Later that day, armed with a bouquet of white freesias from Louise, the florist on Huntriss Row, Helen set off for Jean's house, a neat semi-detached on Dean Road, near the cemetery. On the way, she tried to settle her mind. She was confused about what she'd

71

overheard Freddy the wunderkind golfer say on the phone to his mum about taking revenge on Ricky Delmont. What exactly was going on? Then there was odd Olga and her identical power suits. And as for Ricky's ex-wife, Alice, oh, there was no love lost between those two.

That wasn't all she had to contend with. Jimmy had texted again asking her why she wasn't returning his messages. The truth was, she still hadn't thought of the right words to say. Was she looking forward to seeing him? Without doubt, she was. He was a hand-some man, a talented singer and entertainer who was fun to be with, and he treated her well. He was polite and charming in an old-fashioned way that Helen admired. But she also knew that as soon as she saw him, she'd need to decide whether she was ready to put the life that she'd shared with Tom behind her and start anew. Then there was Marie, who was asking what she was planning to wear for the school reunion, saying she needed to know so that they didn't clash. This had made Helen laugh. As if she would ever wear anything as glamorous as the tight-fitting trouser suits and designer dresses that Marie favoured. And she'd never be able to walk in strappy stiletto sandals. She was much happier in her old jeans and boots.

When she reached Jean's house, she knocked at the door. She waited, but there was no answer. She rattled the letter box, opened it and called out for Jean, but still no one came. At the house next door, an old man with a round, cheery face popped his head out.

'I heard you calling for Jean. You've just missed her. Said she was going into town to visit a hotel landlady on Windsor Terrace.'

Helen's heart lifted. That could only mean one thing: Jean was returning to the Seaview. Oh, this was good news. She'd keep the freesias and give them to her later over coffee; maybe she'd even bake a cake to welcome her back.

'Thanks a lot,' she replied happily. 'Come on, Suki, let's take the scenic route home.'

Relief flooded through her as she walked to the South Bay beach. Jean was coming back and all was good with the world. The dream team would soon be back in action. The A team. The top team. The Seaview team. The Jean team. She smiled as she walked, holding Suki's lead in one hand and the freesias in the other. When she reached Sandside, she spotted an ice-cream van parked on the prom. It was offering *2 4 1 Ice Creams*, and it took her frazzled brain a second to work out that that meant two ice creams for the price of one. Well, it was certainly more succinct than saying *Buy One, Get One Free*.

She decided to stop for coffee on the prom, somewhere Suki might be given a bowl of water and a sausage. Before she could reach one of the pretty cafés opposite the harbour, however, she noticed colourful bunting and large flags fluttering next to the funfair at Norman's Nine crazy golf. She glanced at the course and spotted Alice's red plaits, Freddy's gangly frame, Marilyn's bleached hair whipped up in a beehive. She saw Olga and Marty too, all of them dressed in their navy tracksuits and white trainers. Intrigued, she crossed the road to take a closer look.

The nine-hole course was lovingly designed, with each hole modelled on a Scarborough landmark. There was the castle; the iconic Grand Hotel, once the largest hotel in Europe; the Victorian Spa; the *Hispaniola* pirate ship that took tourists on pleasure rides around the South Bay; the ornate art deco Stephen Joseph Theatre; the market hall; a huge tuna fish, in a nod to Scarborough's fishing past; and the clock tower from the historic South Cliff Gardens. The final hole was a windmill. If you scored a hole-in-one there, your winning shot would set chimes off playing the folk song 'Scarborough Fair'. Even better, you'd win a free game.

Helen stood by the railings and watched her guests practise. None of them spotted her; they were too intent on their game. Freddy was preparing to take a shot. Olga stood at his side, giving him instructions, while the others clustered around. He lifted his putter, hit the ball and it went sailing through a green and pink arch of the Stephen Joseph Theatre. A perfect hole-in-one. He jumped up and down on the spot, three times, in celebration. Helen smiled. How good it was to see her guests enjoying themselves.

As the group moved on to play the next hole, she spotted Ricky Delmont push past a small boy. 'Excuse me, I think you'll find I was here first,' he said rudely.

The boy's mum protested and the child began to cry, but Ricky didn't apologise. How cruel he was, Helen thought. She watched as he delved into a small canvas bag and pulled out three balls: red, green and yellow. He rolled each one in his hand, feeling the weight of it. He decided on the red one and put the others back. Then he did a most unusual thing. Instead of placing the ball on the ground to hit it, like any normal crazy golfer would have done, he brought it to his lips and kissed it.

'That's weird,' Helen said out loud.

Just like Freddy had done, Ricky positioned himself carefully at the tee-off spot and put his ball down. He lifted his putter and hit the ball, which sailed easily through the arch and into the hole. And then he did another odd thing. He jumped up and down on the spot, three times. Just like Freddy.

Helen's gaze flicked between the two men. Both had short brown hair. Ricky's face was half hidden by his beard, whereas Freddy was clean-shaven. As she watched them, she noticed the way they both swung their arms, the way they held themselves . . . Yes, there was definitely something similar in the way they looked and moved. She turned away; she knew she shouldn't be prying.

She walked on a few steps and noticed three middle-aged men huddled together, all of them talking into their phones. Well, there was no law against that, but the way they kept ogling Olga and blowing kisses to Marilyn, Helen found seedy. She saw Olga and Marilyn exchange looks of irritation; neither was happy about the intrusion. As she walked past, she was hit by a sharp whiff of aftershave that caught in her throat and made her gag. She could hear one of the men clearly as he spoke into his phone.

'You want to bet a grand on Alice Pickle's team to win, yeah? OK. I can give you good odds.'

Helen's eyes opened wide. Well, this was a surprise. It sounded like serious money was being placed in bets on the game. There was a lot more going on with this tournament than she had realised.

'Nah, keep your money, mate,' one of the men said. 'Ricky Delmont won't win this year, trust me. Let's just say I've got inside information. Some people think crazy golf is a matter of life and death, but I can assure you it's more serious than that, and I'm telling you now, put your money on Alice Pickle and her team. Delmont's dead in the water.'

Helen didn't like what she was hearing, so she walked to the end of the course, where a small hut painted in red and white stripes stood. This was where putters – long for adults, short for children – cheerfully coloured balls, score cards and pencils were dispensed.

In the doorway was an old man wearing a flat cap and an oversized black duffel coat.

'Morning, Norman, how are you?' she asked.

'Morning, lass,' Norman replied.

When he spotted Suki, he put his hand out to stroke her. The greyhound obliged and let him scratch her behind her ears. Then she tried to peer into the hut, but he abruptly moved to block her way.

'There's nowt for you in there, get out,' he said defensively, and firmly closed the door.

'The course is busy today,' Helen said, making polite conversation.

Norman's smile dropped from his face. 'It's all the crazy-golf teams coming into town for the tournament. They're mostly decent people, but some of them can be a flaming nuisance, especially him there.' He pointed at Ricky.

This piqued Helen's curiosity. 'Really?' she said.

'I was given an honour from the mayor for the maintenance of this course, you know,' Norman said proudly. 'I was even featured on the local news. I made every single model with my own two hands.' He gestured behind him to the red and white hut. 'Crafted them all in there. It takes me months to build a new one. But that fella there, every time he misses out on a hole-in-one, he smashes his putter against them. I've had to have words with him. He's a nasty piece of work, rude and offensive. He swore at me and told me to mind my own business. He made my blood boil. I tell you what, though, if he does it again, I'll have him. If he damages another of my models, I'll kill him.'

Chapter 10

Norman shifted so that he was standing in front of the hut door and held his arms out wide. 'Stay where you are, you're not going in my hut,' he said sternly.

Helen was flabbergasted. 'I had no intention of going in,' she said.

Just then, a young couple walked up to the hut. The man pulled a card from his wallet. 'Two adults, please.'

'I'll be off then,' Helen said, pulling Suki away. Norman was dealing with his customers and didn't acknowledge her. She walked off wondering why he was so protective of his hut. Was he hiding something he didn't want her to see? She thought about how rude Ricky had been to the little boy, who was still bawling his eyes out.

When she returned to King's Parade and was almost at the Seaview, she saw Jean walking towards her along the pavement. Her heart lifted and her shoulders relaxed.

'Look, Suki, it's Jean. She's back,' she said. The dog whined with pleasure.

Helen stood straight, beaming a smile as she waited for Jean to reach her. How happy she felt. And how dreadful too, for having sent her off in a huff in the first place. She'd make sure she never did it again. She held the freesias out.

'Oh Jean, I'm so pleased to see you. These are for you. I'm sorry and . . .'

Jean walked past without a word.

'Jean?'

She watched in horror as she realised where the older woman was heading. 'Jean? No, Jean, please. Tell me you're not going where I think you're going!'

Jean turned sharp left and walked up the path to the Vista del Mar.

'I've got myself a new job,' she barked over her shoulder.

'Jean! No!' Helen cried.

The door of the Vista del Mar opened and Miriam appeared with a triumphant smirk on her face. Helen thought her legs were about to give way. She felt dizzy and sick. Surely Jean wouldn't go to work for snobby Miriam next door? But when Miriam ushered Jean inside and the door closed, she knew there could be no other explanation.

'I've lost her,' she told Suki. 'I've lost everything. Jean's gone.'

She was so distraught that instead of taking Suki into the Seaview through the back door as usual, she walked to the front instead. Her heart felt heavy, her legs were weak and nothing made sense. Jean working next door was unthinkable. She slid her key into the lock and opened the door, then unlocked the door that led down to her apartment and shooed Suki downstairs out of the way in case any of her guests were in the hotel. They wouldn't be happy to see a dog on the premises when the Seaview advertised itself as pet-free. She was picking up her mail when she heard voices coming from next door. She recognised Jean's voice immediately. She had to know what was going on and laid her ear against the wall.

'I'm here for my interview,' Jean said.

'Oh, there's no need for formalities, Jean, dear,' Miriam cooed. 'The job's yours, as I told you when we spoke on the phone. I can't believe my luck that I ran into you just as you stormed out of the Seaview after arguing with Helen.'

'We can't talk here; she listens to everything through that wall,' Jean said.

Helen gasped and jumped back, then headed downstairs with tears in her eyes. She threw the freesias on the kitchen worktop and sank down on to the sofa, laying her head on a cushion and closing her eyes. In all the years Jean had worked at the Seaview, Helen had never known her venture inside Miriam's hotel. In fact, Jean had been Miriam's worst critic, always calling her out for thinking she was a cut above. But now this . . . She had crossed to the dark side and her defection cut Helen in two. It was the ultimate betrayal. Helen would have to make do with Brenda and struggle on until Sally returned.

The thought of having to work with taciturn Brenda instead of Jean brought her to her senses. 'The Seaview's what's important here. Whatever happens, you've got to look after it,' she told herself sternly. She pulled her phone from her pocket and dialled the number for the staffing agency. She hoped they might have a decent chef on their books. Someone who knew what to do with chia seeds, or even had an idea what they were. However, the agency told her they had no one available at such short notice.

She dropped her phone on the sofa and it rang immediately. Jimmy's name was displayed on the screen.

'Not now, Jimmy,' she whispered, and let his message go to voicemail.

*   *   *

The next day was a struggle the likes of which Helen had never known. It was horrible, unthinkable, that Jean was preparing breakfast for Miriam's guests next door. She imagined Miriam's gloating face.

'I bet she can't wait to lord it over me that she's got Jean working for her,' Helen told Brenda.

'Aye, you've already told me that this morning,' Brenda said.

'She's always had her eye on Jean, always wanted her after her breakfasts won an award for best on the Yorkshire coast.'

Brenda rolled her eyes. 'So you've said. Twice.'

'I can't cook to Jean's standard or manage this kitchen in the way she does . . . I mean, did. A basic breakfast will have to suffice. If the guests don't want it, they don't have to eat it.'

'You're starting to sound like Jean,' Brenda said.

And so it continued, with Helen complaining bitterly and Brenda pretending to listen. Helen sent breakfast up in the dumb-waiter for Brenda to serve. She went through the familiar motions, but her heart wasn't in it and her thoughts were far away. Well, not too far, just next door in the Vista del Mar.

'Jean won't bake croissants for Miriam, I can tell you that now,' she said out loud in the kitchen, but when she looked around, she only had Suki for company, as Brenda had headed upstairs.

'You need to stay outside, Suki. Brenda's working here and she doesn't like dogs.'

Suki obediently trotted outside and lay down on the patio.

The door swung open and Brenda came in carrying dirty plates on a tray. Helen tutted out loud.

'I've already told you not to walk downstairs carrying heavy things. Put them in the dumbwaiter. If you tripped on the stairs, you'd hurt yourself and things could get smashed.'

'You'll have insurance. I'll be covered,' Brenda replied.

'This is a business, Brenda. You must stick to health and safety rules. We ran through them, remember? Use the dumbwaiter, don't carry stuff yourself.'

'Aye,' Brenda replied. 'Oh, by the way, him upstairs wants a word.'

'Who?'

'The weird one who sleeps with his golf clubs. I said you'd be straight up. He's waiting in the lounge. And the little woman with the black hair wants to talk to you too. She's not happy about the food. And the girl with the red hair says the honey's not the kind they asked for. You might want to calm her down.'

'Oh crikey,' Helen moaned.

'And that's not all,' Brenda continued. 'The woman with the blonde hair and her dad—'

'He's her husband,' Helen chipped in.

'Aye, well. I heard them talking about moving out and trying to find another hotel. So if you want to keep them all sweet, I suggest you go up and talk to them now.'

Helen made for the door, ready to pacify her guests.

'By the way, I spotted a bunch of freesias in your bin. Can I have them?' Brenda said.

Helen stopped with her hand on the door. 'Take them,' she said, then marched upstairs.

When she appeared in the hall, the guests all rushed at her at once.

'Mrs Dexter . . .' Olga called.

81

'Ah, Helen, I need a word, in confidence,' Ricky said. 'You do realise that your hotel's four-star status is in jeopardy because of this food fiasco. I could report you for this.'

Helen gritted her teeth. Of course she realised, and she didn't need to be reminded, especially from someone as arrogant as him.

'You've sure got yourself a whole lot of problems here, Miss Helen,' an American voice drawled. She looked up into Freddy's smooth, boyish face. She knew from years of experience with guests that each had their odd little quirks. However, Freddy's fake accent was definitely one of the most unusual. Still, he was young, and had time to grow out of it.

'Helen, we need to speak to you urgently. It's about having a heart-healthy breakfast for my husband,' Marilyn said, casting a worried look at Marty.

But it was Alice who stepped forward. She held up a hand to silence the group, including Ricky. 'I'll speak on behalf of us all,' she said. Everyone quietened down.

'Please, let's go into the lounge to talk,' Helen said, leading the way. 'Take a seat, everyone.'

Marilyn and Marty sat on the window seat, and Ricky pulled up a chair and sat beside Marilyn. Helen noticed a smile pass between them. Then Marty put his arm protectively around Marilyn's shoulders and she snuggled into his side. Olga sat straight in her seat in her navy suit, white shirt and sensible shoes. Freddy took a stool at the bar, letting his long legs dangle to the floor. Alice paced from the bar to the window, and each time she turned, her red plaits swung over her shoulders. However, before she could begin, Helen started to speak. Better to get in first with her excuses, she thought.

'I can't apologise enough,' she said. 'We've had problems with our cook, unexpected problems. You'll not be charged for your breakfast, of course, and I'll work out a room-only rate for your stay.'

This took the wind from Alice's sails, as Helen had expected. If she'd learned a thing or two about catering for guests, it was that they expected value for money.

'I've failed you all, and I'm very sorry indeed,' she continued. 'I can recommend a couple of places in town for breakfast instead.'

'Do these places cater for athletes? We need power food. We have a tournament coming up!' Marty snapped.

Marilyn patted his hand. 'There, there, darling. No need to upset yourself. Remember what the doctor said, you must avoid stress. It's not good for your heart.'

Helen nodded at Marty. 'Try the excellent Eat Me café inside the Stephen Joseph Theatre on Eastborough.'

'I'm happy with that,' Olga said.

'Everyone else OK?' Helen asked, looking from Marilyn and Marty to Freddy, Olga and Alice.

'If Olga's happy, we're all happy,' Alice said.

Ricky suddenly jumped up and stormed from the room.

'Ooh, get him!' Alice taunted.

'I heard that,' he shouted from halfway up the stairs.

'Don't tease the man, Alice, he's bad,' Olga warned.

The smile dropped from Alice's face. 'You don't need to remind me of that.'

Helen wondered just what had gone on between Alice and Ricky in the past.

Olga clapped her hands together. 'Come, everyone, we need to go and practise.'

Marilyn stood and smoothed her hair with her hand. 'I just hope those guys aren't hanging around again. They really gave me the creeps.'

Helen's ears pricked up, remembering the men in the suits and the strong aftershave. 'What guys?' she said innocently, wondering how much they might reveal.

'A group of gamblers who watch us play. They take bets on the game.'

'Oh, I saw them,' she admitted. 'And I heard them placing bets when I walked past them. They were acting kind of furtive. Do they bother you in any way?'

Marilyn cast an anxious look at Olga, who took up the story. 'Yes, they bother the women in our team especially. There's something seedy in the way they watch us. They take photographs of us then tap away at their phones. I've tried reasoning with them and have often asked them to leave us alone.'

'And I've tried threatening them,' Marty added. 'But they still hang around.'

'We have to do our best to ignore them. Don't give them the satisfaction of letting them know they've rattled us,' Olga instructed, then she clapped her hands again. 'Right, everyone, it's time to go to work.'

Chapter 11

On the morning of the school reunion, Helen woke with a heavy heart. She wished she'd stood up to Marie and told her she wasn't going. What did she have in common now with the people she'd been to school with? She hadn't seen most of them for decades and hadn't felt the need to keep in touch. Some of them, the ones who'd stayed in Scarborough, she saw around town. And a handful, Marie included, were still her close friends. But as for the rest of them, she had no desire to meet them again.

'It'll be fun!' Marie had told her in a phone call the previous night. 'You'll enjoy yourself once you're there.'

Helen wasn't convinced. The thought of the evening filled her with dread.

'Come and have one drink, that's all. Sue and Bev will be there. And the Royal Hotel is gorgeous, you've always liked it in there.'

Knowing that Sue and Bev were going was the main reason she'd eventually agreed to attend. She hadn't seen them in a while, ever since they'd declared themselves a couple and moved in together. And Marie was right, she did like the Royal Hotel. It had enough leftover glamour from a bygone age for anyone to see that it had once been something special. It was a white confection of a hotel on St Nicholas Street with commanding views over South Bay beach. From its front door it was a short step to the Central

Tramway cliff lift, one of Scarborough's two remaining funiculars that carried passengers up and down the steep hills. Inside the hotel was a stunning staircase, and the opulent ladies' powder room had a faded grandeur about it, a throwback to an age of sophistication.

'Oh, all right,' she'd sighed. 'But if any fellas with beer bellies and bad breath that I knew as spotty oiks from school start coming on to me, I'll run a mile.'

'You'll be fine, trust me,' Marie said, then, unusually for her, she fell silent.

'Marie? You OK, love?'

'Look, it's slightly awkward, but would you mind if Sandra came with us in my car? She's asked for a lift, but I won't say yes to her if you don't want me to. I know you're not that keen on her.'

'She's a bit full-on for my liking,' Helen agreed.

An image of Sandra DeVine flashed through her mind. She was tall and skinny, with oversized breasts and a nipped-in waist. She dressed in 1950s retro clothes, and her long hair was dyed as black as midnight and swept up into a candyfloss whip. Her eyes were perfectly made up with smoky eyeliner, and her lips painted blood red. The whole effect was compelling, if somewhat unsettling, especially when she was at work serving fish and chips on the seafront.

'I really don't know why she insists on calling herself Sandra DeVine when we all know she's Sandra Potts,' she tutted.

'Oh, you know Sandra. She's always liked a bit of drama.'

Helen sighed. 'Of course it's all right to offer her a lift.'

'Attagirl,' Marie said, and rang off.

Helen pulled herself out of bed and threw her dressing gown on. She missed Jean with all her heart. Normally she'd wake to the sound of the older woman singing along to the radio, slicing mush-rooms and opening and closing cupboard doors. As she cooked, she'd comment on the weather, her mum's legs, the lovely chops she'd bought from the butcher in the market. But that morning there was silence. Either Brenda hadn't arrived yet or she was being very quiet.

She opened her bedroom door and walked into the living room. Brenda was nowhere to be seen. Suki walked to her and nudged her leg, in need of some attention. Helen obliged with a stroke behind her ears, and Suki pressed her head against her knee. Then she remembered with a sickening thud why Brenda hadn't arrived. There was no cooking to be done that morning, as her guests had chosen to eat their power breakfasts elsewhere. The Seaview kitchen stood silent, unused. She slapped her hand against her forehead. How could she have forgotten? Brenda wasn't due until later to help her clean the rooms.

She sank into a chair, tears welling in her eyes. Without Jean, without breakfast, it felt like the Seaview's heart had stopped. There was just the sound of the clock ticking on the wall. But then she heard voices outside. Two men, arguing. She walked to the patio doors and unlocked them, and Suki padded outside. The patio was below street level, and whoever was arguing had no idea she was there. They didn't realise she could hear every word. She immediately recognised the voices. It was Ricky and Marty, going at each other hammer and tongs.

'I've warned you! Keep away from my wife. If I have to tell you again, you'll know about it.'

'What are you going to do, Grandad? Hit me with your walking stick?' Ricky sneered.

Helen grimaced. Oh, that was a low blow.

'She's too good for you, she always has been,' Ricky said. 'I don't know what she sees in a wrinkled old fella like you. Apart from the size of your wallet.'

There was a beat of silence. Helen held her breath. She took a step forward in her slippers to hear better.

'Stay away from Marilyn. She's with me now and she's happy, and I intend to keep things that way. I might be old, but I've still got power where it counts.'

'In the bedroom? Don't make me laugh!' Ricky said.

'No, lad, somewhere much more important. My power's in my muscles. I train every day at the gym. Every day I work hard to keep fit for my crazy-golf game. I might look past it to you, but all that exercise gives me the stamina of a twenty-year-old. I've got a putting power arm, Ricky Delmont, and I'm not afraid to use it.'

'What tosh!' Ricky laughed.

'Oh, you can laugh. I might look old to you, but I'm muscled and ready to fight. Leave Marilyn alone, and remember, if I see you so much as glance at her again while we're forced to share this hotel, I'll hit you so hard you won't know whether you're in Scarborough or Scunthorpe.'

'*You?* Hit *me*? With your power arm?' Ricky sneered.

Helen strained to hear and shuffled forward again.

'Let me tell you something, Ricky Delmont,' Marty said. 'If I catch you again with your filthy hands on my wife, you might just live to regret it. Understand me?'

There was another beat of silence.

'Yeah,' Ricky said eventually, resigned.

Helen heard footsteps walking away. She didn't know who was

88

leaving, as she couldn't see up to street level. She stood a while pondering on what she'd heard, then she heard Marilyn's voice.

'Hey, darling. There you are. I wondered where you'd gone. Are you all set to head out for breakfast? Olga and Alice have already gone. Freddy's going to walk with us.'

'I sure am,' a male voice said with an American twang.

'I've just been taking in the sea air. Such a beautiful view,' Marty said. 'So, if we're all set, let's head off for a proper breakfast. Such a shame the landlady of this place can't make it herself. I wonder what the problem is with her cook . . .'

Helen heard their discussion fade on the breeze. She walked into the living room and sank down on the sofa. Suki followed and laid her head in her lap. She stroked the dog's head and gazed into her glassy eyes.

'Well, Suki, there's a to-do. I wonder if Ricky's been carrying on with Marilyn.'

Suki stared back in silence.

'You're not Jean, are you?' she sighed. 'Jean would have loved this bit of gossip.'

Her phone pinged with an email notification. She scrolled through her messages, noting new reviews on the online rating website HypeThatHotel. She smiled when she saw that more guests had left 5-star reviews from recent stays. Out of curiosity, unable to resist looking, she read the recent reviews for the Vista del Mar.

Superb breakfast. Best I've ever had. They must have a different chef since the last time I stayed here. The improved breakfast will definitely make me want to return. Five stars, and I take my hat off to the new chef!

Good location, clean rooms, nice view of castle and beach. Fabulous breakfast. However, the landlady's a bit of a snob.

Helen sighed. Jean's breakfasts were already improving Miriam's online ratings.

She was about to put her phone away when the Vista del Mar's website opened on the screen. She must have touched the link after reading the reviews. There was a picture of the hotel taken on a sunny day, showing the place to its best advantage under a clear blue sky. Her heart missed a beat. Under the logo was a picture of Jean working in the kitchen, with the strapline *Award-winning breakfasts!* Her stomach turned over. How dare Miriam do this? Stealing the Seaview's thunder! As if it didn't hurt enough that Jean had upped and left her. The Vista del Mar didn't have award-winning breakfasts, Jean did. The Seaview did. The award had nothing to do with Miriam and her hotel. Oh, she was going to have words with the woman about this!

She enlarged the photo on her screen. Jean didn't look happy. In fact, she didn't look as if she knew her picture was being taken. She was working at a stove, stirring a spoon around a pan, not looking into the camera.

As Helen closed the website, her phone rang. It was a local number with the area code for Scarborough. She sat up straight in her seat.

'Seaview Hotel, good morning.'

'Helen, it's Jimmy.'

She took a moment to gather herself. She hadn't allowed herself to think about Jimmy. The decision she had to make about her future with him needed careful consideration. She'd foolishly thought that if she kept busy, things would somehow work themselves out. But now Jean had left, and for the first time in the Seaview's history she'd had to send guests out for breakfast. In addition, she had truculent Brenda to deal with. Then there were all the strange goings-on with her crazy-golf guests.

'Helen?' Jimmy said.

'Sorry, Jimmy. I was miles away. How are you? It's good to hear your voice.'

'It's good to hear yours too. This is my new number, by the way. It's my landline.'

'Your landline? But it's a Scarborough number.'

When he didn't reply, she let the realisation sink in. 'You've moved here?'

'Yeah. It's one of the two surprises I said I had for you. I've finally bought a house, on West Park, by Falsgrave Park. It's beautiful, Helen, I love it. There are two bedrooms and I'm hoping Jodie will stay now and then.'

Helen recalled Jimmy's daughter Jodie, who'd been living rough in Scarborough when they'd first met. She knew the street that Jimmy mentioned. The houses weren't cheap there. She was impressed.

'She's in a shared flat now she's moved out of the hostel and says she's happy there,' Jimmy continued. 'You should come and visit. I'll cook dinner one night. Or lunch. Your choice.'

Helen's head spun. 'That'd be great, Jimmy, thanks. I'm a bit shocked to hear that you live here now.'

'You don't sound so happy about it.'

'Oh, I am, really,' she said, her mind still whirling from the surprise. 'It's just that I had no idea you'd sold up in London. It's happened so quickly.'

'My divorce came through too. I'm a single man again. I'm yours, Helen, if you'll have me.'

Helen took her time to reply. 'I need to take things slowly.'

'I know, and I'll respect that, always.'

His words helped reassure her. 'So what's the second surprise?' she asked, more cheerfully. She hoped he would tell her something that might put a much-needed smile on her face. Something that would take her mind off Jean for a while. Something that didn't involve her warring guests and their desire to win the crazy-golf tournament. She'd had just about enough of crazy golf, and if she never heard the tournament mentioned again, it'd be a day too soon.

'Oh, that.' He laughed. 'Meet me at the official opening of the crazy-golf tournament on Saturday at two, then you'll find out. I rather think you're going to like it.'

Helen let out a long groan.

Chapter 12

That evening, Helen's phone beeped with a message from Marie.

I'm outside. Sandra's with me. X

She stroked Suki behind her ears, then locked the basement door and headed upstairs and out of the Seaview's front door. Marie's cherry-red sports car was parked by the kerb, Sandra DeVine in the front passenger seat. The cheek of the woman, she thought. That was *her* seat, next to Marie. She sashayed down the pavement, her swaying hips emphasising the swing of her floaty blue dress.

'You look lovely,' Marie said as she crawled into the back seat. 'You OK there?'

'Bit squashed, but I'm in,' Helen replied. 'Sandra, I don't suppose you could pull your seat forward a little, could you?'

Sandra obliged, and the seat moved forward, giving Helen much-needed leg room. She looked at the back of Sandra's black beehive, which obstructed her view through the windscreen.

'How are you, Sandra?' she asked, making polite conversation. 'I haven't seen you in ages. You still seeing that policeman fella you were going out with a while back?'

'He's a detective, not a policeman. DS Hutchinson. Yes, he's moved in. We're very happy together,' Sandra replied. 'What about you, are you seeing anyone?' Her beehive shook as soon as the words left her mouth. 'Sorry, Helen. I didn't mean . . . I know you and Tom were soulmates, and I wasn't thinking when I said that. I don't want you to think I was implying you were moving on to someone else. Oh heavens, me and my big gob. It always gets me into trouble.'

'You're all right, don't worry,' Helen said, but she kept quiet about Jimmy. He was nobody's business but hers.

'Helen's seeing Jimmy, the Elvis impersonator,' Marie said.

'I don't want to talk about it. It's complicated.'

'You like him and he likes you, it's not complicated. You just need to let yourself go. He's a good-looking man, Jimmy Brown. You need to be careful you don't keep him hanging on too long. You might lose him to someone else.'

Helen shifted her knees to get comfortable and pulled at the seat belt, which was digging into her neck.

'Bev and Sue aren't coming,' Marie said.

Helen felt disappointed. 'Oh no, why not?'

'Bev's got flu and Sue's looking after her.'

They drove in silence the short distance to the Royal Hotel. Marie parked on St Nicholas Cliff, then Helen unfolded herself from the back of the car.

'Is that a new outfit?' Helen said when she saw what Marie was wearing. Marie obliged with a twirl, showing off a spangly silver dress that shimmered with tiny sequins under a smart black jacket. Sandra was dressed in her trademark 1950s rock-and-roll style, looking every inch the retro prom queen in an electric-blue dress with matching shoes. Helen admired Marie's style and Sandra's confidence. She looked down at her own sensible shoes, which didn't quite match her dress.

'You look gorgeous,' Marie said.

She threaded her arm through Helen's on one side and Sandra's on the other, and together they made their way into the Royal Hotel.

'Oh, it's lovely in here. So glamorous,' Helen sighed as they entered.

A board in reception pointed the way to the reunion, which was being held in a large room at the back of the hotel where music was playing, a pulsing seventies track they all knew.

'We used to dance to this at school discos,' Helen said.

Marie gave her a cheeky wink. 'You might have been dancing, but I was snogging Kevin Maynard when this song was in the charts.'

Sandra shot daggers at Marie. '*I* was snogging Kevin Maynard when this song was in the charts. He told me I was his girlfriend.'

Helen held her hands up. 'Ladies, please. Kevin Maynard was clearly a two-timing love rat, and as it was decades ago, I say we move on.'

'I hope he's not here tonight,' Marie said.

The pounding beat of a Bowie track greeted the threesome as they walked into the room. It was a long, narrow space with a bar down one side. Round tables were decorated with starched white linen tablecloths and posies of cream-coloured roses. There was a buffet table at one end of the room laden with sausage rolls, vol-au-vents and quiches. Marie headed straight to the bar.

'What'll it be, ladies? Cocktails? I'm driving, so I'll have lime and soda. I've got to keep a clear head; I've got business with my solicitor in the morning about the contract on the new Tom's Teas.'

'That's fantastic, Marie. I'm proud of you and I know Tom

would have been too,' Helen said. 'Oh, and I'll have a Scarborough Sunrise.'

'Me too,' Sandra piped up.

Helen turned to look into the room. It seemed to be full of dumpy middle-aged women and overweight men. She scanned the faces, trying to recognise people she might have known at school.

'There he is, over there,' Marie whispered.

'Who?' Helen said.

'Kevin Maynard, the two-timing love rat. I'd recognise those teeth anywhere. They were always getting in the way when we snogged.'

Sandra took her cocktail. 'Ladies, I hope you'll excuse me. As one of the organisers, I've got a speech lined up, so I'd better go and take the mic.'

As she walked off, Helen and Marie headed towards the buffet.

'Hey, Helen Armstrong!' a man's voice called.

Helen turned, taken aback that someone was addressing her by her maiden name. She saw a man approaching. He was short, bald, fat, with ears that were too large for his face. His crooked nose looked like it'd been broken more than once. He wore a synthetic blouson jacket in turquoise and white, a style popular in the eighties. She racked her brains trying to recall who he was. But try as she might, she couldn't place him.

When he reached her and Marie, he shot his hand out. 'Remember me? Arthur Mason. My word, it's good to see you again, Helen, and you, Mary.'

'Marie,' Marie replied sweetly, offering Arthur her hand.

A woman in a black trouser suit marched up and dragged Marie away, leaving Helen alone with Arthur. There was something about him that rang a distant and not too unpleasant bell in her mind. It started coming back to her then. He had been a sporty type, and she rarely mixed with those at school.

'Arthur . . . you used to be on the rugby team, right?' she said, hoping she was correct.

'That's right. Played for the county after I left school.'

Ah, she thought, that explains the broken nose. 'And what are you doing now?' she asked. 'Do you still live in Scarborough?'

'I work in sales. I've just moved back here, to Cayton Bay, after years living on the Norfolk coast.' He took a sip from his pint. 'And you?'

Helen beamed with pride. 'I run a guest house on the North Bay, the Seaview. We've won awards for our breakfasts.' The words almost choked her when she said this, thinking of Jean at the Vista del Mar.

'Can't say I know it,' Arthur said. 'Do you enjoy it?'

'It's interesting, every day's different. I've got crazy golfers staying this week – they're in town for the tournament on Saturday. A whole team, and the captain of another, Ricky Delmont . . .'

Suddenly Arthur's jaw dropped and his gaze fixed on a spot beyond Helen's left shoulder. 'Kiss me, Helen,' he gasped.

'What?' Helen said, stunned.

'I said kiss me. Or at least pretend to. Now!'

He lunged for her, and her cocktail sloshed from her glass as he grabbed her in an embrace that was far too intimate for her liking. She managed to turn her face from his lips, but couldn't struggle free.

'Just pretend, Helen, please,' he whispered in her ear as he relaxed his grip on her. 'Remember Penny Smith from school?

She's been stalking me online. She's just walked into the room. I need her to think I've already got a girlfriend so she'll leave me alone.'

'Get off me!' Helen hissed, and pulled herself away.

Arthur scanned the room. 'Where's she gone? I need to leave. I can't stay if she's here. I should've known better than to come tonight. I'm sorry for putting you through that. I'm a gentleman really, honest to heaven I am.'

Helen was shaken, but before she could say anything, Arthur was striding to the exit. As she watched him leave, she was shocked to see Jimmy hovering by the door. She set her glass down on a table and walked towards him. She hadn't seen him in months, and he looked even more handsome than she'd remembered, with his brown eyes and his dark hair greying at the temples.

'Hey, it's good to see you. You're looking well. What are you doing here?' she said.

She noticed he didn't look happy, and his bottom lip quivered. He laid his hand against the door frame and seemed to be having trouble looking her in the eye.

'Are you doing an Elvis impersonation with that lip quiver or is something else going on?' she asked.

'I was having a drink in the bar with the manager,' he explained. 'He was talking about a hotel he knows that needs an Elvis imper- sonator. Anyway, I spotted you when you walked through with Marie, and I just came in here to say hello, but . . .' His bottom lip continued to shake. 'I saw you with that man, Helen. I saw you kissing him.' He hung his head and gazed at the floor. 'I guess that's why you haven't returned my calls. I thought it was because you were busy at the Seaview, but now I know the truth. I wish you'd been honest and told me there was someone else. I wish I hadn't found out this way.' He turned to walk away.

'Jimmy! You've got the wrong end of the stick!' Helen cried. She set off after him along the lushly carpeted hall, desperate to tell him the truth, but a man was beckoning to him from the bar area.

'Come on, Jim. I've got you another pint. I need to talk to you about Elvis. Do you want the job or not?'

The moment was lost. She'd have to ring him later to explain. Why did this have to happen now, just when she was beginning to feel brave enough to give serious thought to her future with him? If Jimmy thought she had another man, he'd probably never want to see her again. Had she lost him for ever? She was surprised how upset this thought made her feel.

Just then, Marie appeared at her side. 'What are you doing out here? Come back in, the party's getting started. Sandra's about to give her speech and Kevin Maynard's bought us all drinks.'

Chapter 13

'I'm not in the mood for drinking with Kevin Maynard,' Helen said.

Marie raised her perfectly manicured eyebrows. 'What's up?'

Helen nodded to the corridor. 'Jimmy was here.'

'Elvis Jimmy? *Your* Jimmy?'

'He is not my Jimmy!' Helen snapped.

Marie looked at her with concern. 'Whatever he is, you seem upset that he was here and now he's not. What happened?'

'He saw me snogging Arthur Mason and stormed off in a huff.'

Marie put a hand over her mouth to stifle a giggle. 'Arthur Mason who played on the school rugby team? Oh Helen. I never had him down as your type.'

'Come on, Marie, give me some credit. He's not my type at all.'

'No, your type is tall, dark and Elvis. So why were you kissing Arthur? It must have been quite a smooch if it caused Jimmy to storm out. And what was Jimmy doing here in the first place?'

Helen glanced beyond Marie into the function room, where people were sitting on the floor rowing a pretend boat, singing along at the top of their voices. She looked down the corridor again, hoping, she realised, to see Jimmy walking back, but there was no sign of him. 'It wasn't what it looked like. Arthur grabbed me in a clinch to make another woman think he had a girlfriend.

But what really happened was that Jimmy thought I had a boyfriend, and now he's gone and I'll probably never see him again, and oh, Marie, I'm fed up.' She looked into the room again, at her ex-school friends laughing and singing, enjoying themselves. She only remembered half a dozen of them, at a push, and wanted to be a million miles away from them all. It was no fun without Bev and Sue. 'I wish I hadn't let you talk me into coming tonight. You know I don't like parties.'

Marie gently laid her hand on Helen's arm. 'You used to enjoy them when Tom was alive. Every holiday weekend in the summer, the two of you ran your Elvis parties at the Seaview. Look, love, would you like me to take you home? To be honest, I need an early night, so it's no skin off my nose if we leave now. Wait for me while I say bye to Sandra and a couple of the others.'

Helen began walking along the corridor. 'I'll meet you by the entrance in ten minutes,' she said. 'I want to find Jimmy. If he's still in the bar, there's a chance he'll let me explain.'

She crossed the reception area at the foot of a sweeping staircase and walked into the bar, but Jimmy wasn't there. She waited for a few minutes in case he reappeared, but when there was still no sign of him, she gave up and went to stand by the main doors. A few moments later, Marie swanned up, the silver sparkles on her dress swaying in time to the song she was singing, a hit from their school days.

'Come on, let's go,' she said, pulling her car keys from her bag.

They left the Royal, walking past the funicular and the Grand Hotel to Marie's car on St Nicholas Cliff. Driving back to the Seaview, Helen blurted out her bad news.

'I've lost Jean, she's gone.'

101

Marie took her eyes off the road ahead and glanced across at her. Her face blanched. 'No!' she cried. 'But she wasn't ill, was she? She always looked as fit as a fiddle.'

Helen tutted loudly. 'I don't mean she's dead, for heaven's sake! I mean I lost her to Miriam. She walked out after we argued and went to work at the Vista del Mar.'

'Want to talk about it?'

She sighed. 'It's a long story. I'm sure you don't want to listen to my woes when you've got so much going on in your life.'

'Nonsense!' Marie said quickly. 'What are best friends for if not to listen, give advice, and be a bit judgemental?'

A smile made its way to Helen's lips. 'You sure?'

'Certain.' Marie tilted her left wrist and glanced at her silver watch. 'How about I come in for a nightcap before I drive home? You can make me one of Jean's famous hot chocolates and tell me what happened.'

Marie parked outside the Seaview. The light in the lounge was on, and through the windows, Helen could see Olga marching back and forth. She also saw the back of Alice's head, with her red hair tied in a ponytail.

'Do you need to go in to see to your guests?' Marie asked.

Helen shook her head. 'No, they've specifically asked me not to open the bar while they're staying here. They're teetotal as well as faddy eaters. It looks like they're having a meeting, probably discussing power tactics for Saturday's game. Let's leave them to it and go in through the back.'

When she opened the door to her apartment, Suki bounded straight to her. 'What's up, Suki? Something spooked you?' She got down on her knees and stroked the dog behind her ears, calming her and soothing her with soft words. 'She's not normally like this,' she told Marie, worried. 'Something's upset her. I'll see if she needs to go outside to stretch her legs.'

But when she went to pull the dog's lead from the peg, Suki backed away. Helen tried the magic word guaranteed to send her to the back door – 'Walk?' – but for once, Suki didn't move.

'That's odd. She usually enjoys a quick once around the block before bedtime.'

As Helen soothed the dog, Marie laid her handbag on the sofa and slipped her feet from her sandals.

'These cost a small fortune, but they don't half pinch,' she said. 'Anyway, let me make the hot chocolate while you sort the dog out. Where do you keep your milk pan?'

Helen felt pressure on the back of her knee, and when she looked down, Suki was right behind her. She stroked the dog's head. 'It's all right, girl.'

Suki stayed where she was. Normally she'd have wandered off to her favourite spot by the patio doors by now.

'I wonder if she's feeling all right. Perhaps she's eaten something she shouldn't have while I've been out,' Helen mused.

Marie looked up from the pan of milk she was warming and cast a nervous glance at the red sandals she'd slipped off. 'She hasn't still got a thing about eating shoes, has she?'

'Yes, she has. I always keep footwear out of her reach,' Helen replied.

Marie quickly walked to the sofa, picked up her sandals and put them on the table. Suki finally slunk away from Helen's side and lay on the floor, all the while keeping her eyes fully on her mistress.

When the milk boiled, Marie poured it into two chunky blue mugs. She opened another cupboard door. 'Where do you keep your marshmallows?' she said, peering inside.

'I don't have any, love. I'm not a marshmallow fan.'

She shrugged and carried the mugs into the living room. Suki came to lie on the carpet next to Helen and rested her chin on her feet. Her eyes kept flicking to Helen's face, which concerned her a lot; it wasn't the dog's normal behaviour.

Marie handed Helen a mug, then curled up on the sofa with her legs tucked under her. She gave Helen a hard stare.

'Come on then, tell me everything. I want to know all about Jean. And while we're having this catch-up, I want to know if I should bring anything to the party next week.'

Helen had been blowing on her hot chocolate to cool it. Now she stopped and looked at Marie.

'What party?'

Marie took a sip of her drink. 'Your fiftieth, of course. My invitation came in this morning's post. I was surprised to receive it after you'd told me you didn't want a party. And why did you post it? You knew you'd be seeing me tonight. You could have saved yourself the price of a stamp.'

Helen set her mug on a coaster on a table by the armchair. 'An invitation? But I haven't sent any,' she said, confused. 'I don't suppose you've got it with you, have you? I need to see it. I need to find out who's sent it. Was it a Scarborough postmark on the envelope? Who'd do such a thing?'

'Calm down, love,' Marie said. 'I'm sure there's a perfectly good explanation.'

Helen raised her eyebrows. 'Really?'

'There must be. Look, I haven't got it with me, and I can't remember what postmark it had. I just assumed it was from you, so I chucked the envelope away. It sounds like someone's organised a surprise party for you. Do you think it might have been Jean or Sally?'

Helen thought for a moment. 'Jean's the only person I've talked to about having a party. She kept going on about it, but the more she went on, the more I shut her down. She wouldn't have dared organise a surprise I didn't want. And Sally's got Gav and Gracie to think about as well as her college work. She hasn't got time to organise a party. Who on earth is behind it?'

'Maybe one of our school friends?' Marie suggested.

Helen shook her head. 'Bev and Sue wouldn't do it without my say-so, and I don't know anyone else well enough any more. Sandra DeVine's got too much on her plate with her job at the chippy and her detective boyfriend.'

'Maybe we should play detectives ourselves to get to the bottom of this mystery,' Marie said.

'What was it like, the invitation?' Helen asked.

'Small, square, tasteful. Exactly the sort of thing you would have sent.'

Her shoulders slumped. 'This is awful. It feels like my life's spiralling out of control. Someone's nicked my identity!'

'There's no need to overreact,' Marie chided. 'It's only a party.'

'But I don't want a party,' Helen said, her voice rising. 'I don't want to celebrate turning fifty. Who would? It's not a milestone, it's a dead weight around my shoulders.'

'Oh, someone's feeling tetchy about getting old,' Marie said.

'I'm not tetchy,' Helen said tetchily.

Marie looked at her over the top of her mug. 'I'm the same age as you, but I'm not dreading my birthday. I plan to celebrate every day for a month. I'm going on a yoga retreat in Santorini for ten days once the Filey tearoom's up and running and I know I can trust my staff. Anyway, enough about me. Is there anything I can do to help with your party?'

Helen shook her head. 'You don't get it, do you? There *is* no party. I've got absolutely no idea who sent the invitations.'

'Must've been Jean, if she's the only one you've talked to about it,' Marie said. 'And on that note, tell me what happened between you and her.'

An unexpected lump made its way to Helen's throat, and when she began to speak, tears pricked her eyes. She picked up her mug and took a long, sweet drink. 'She walked out after we argued. She said I was taking her for granted.'

Marie nodded in agreement.

'Don't look at me like that,' Helen said.

'The woman's got a point,' Marie said calmly. 'You've been acting strange with her whenever I've called in for breakfast. Jean never complains, always works hard, turns up and puts the hours in. Then there's everything else she's done for you. She was there for you when Tom died, she even moved in so you wouldn't have to cope on your own. And there was all the work she did when the hotel inspector came. If it wasn't for her, you wouldn't have got your four stars. Jean's a marvel, Helen, and perhaps you *have* been taking her for granted. When was the last time you gave her a pay rise? Or treated her to a night out? You know she loves to go and see new Alan Ayckbourn plays at the Stephen Joseph Theatre. Do you ever treat her to a night at the theatre or a bunch of flowers, or make the coffee for your morning chats, or just say thank you to her?'

Marie's words cut Helen's heart in two. She knew her friend was right. She looked across the room to where the plaque with four stars leaned against the wall. She stood and walked to it, picked it up and ran her fingers over it. 'I want to apologise to Jean, but she's working next door for Miriam now. It's the ultimate betrayal, a real slap in the face.'

'Oh my word,' Marie said slowly. 'I bet Miriam's gloating.'

Helen remembered the photograph on the Vista del Mar's website. 'Without Jean, I'm lost. That's why I don't think she's the one behind the party invitations. She was mithering me for a party while she was still here, but now we're not speaking, she'd hardly have sent out invitations behind my back. I don't know if I want to carry on running the Seaview without her. Look, this is the plaque they sent us, proof that this place has earned its four stars at last. I tried fixing it to the wall by the front door, but it wouldn't hang straight. I might ask Gav if he can do something with it when he and Sally are back from honeymoon.'

'Could I have a look at it?' Marie asked.

She shifted in her seat to take the plaque, but as Helen handed it to her, it slipped from Marie's hand to the floor. When Helen picked it up, she saw a scratch down the side where it had caught the table leg.

'Oh, this is all I need after everything I'm going through. Jean's left me. Miriam's gloating. Sally's mum, Brenda, is a cross I have to bear. My crazy-golfing guests are arguing with each other. Jimmy's got the wrong end of the stick about me going off with another man at the school reunion. I'm worried I might have lost him just when I was getting ready to start putting my past with Tom behind me. Even Suki's rattled about something. And this plaque won't stay where it's put. I think it's trying to tell me something.'

'What are you saying, Helen?'

She looked Marie square in the eye. 'What I'm saying is . . .' She paused, aware that her explanation would sound ridiculous, but she couldn't think of any other way to put it. 'What I'm saying is that it feels like getting these four stars has put a curse on the Seaview Hotel.'

Chapter 14

The following morning, Helen noticed that Suki was still out of sorts and wouldn't leave her side.

'Do I need to take you to the vet?' she said, looking into the dog's grey eyes. She ran her hands over Suki's thin face. 'You're eating all right, so it's not that. What's wrong, girl?'

Suki pressed her head into Helen's hands. Just then, Brenda walked in.

'Morning, Brenda. You all right?'

'Aye.'

Give me strength, Helen thought.

'I went to the bingo last night and won fifty quid. It'll help pay some bills.'

'Well done, that's great!' Helen beamed. 'Er . . . you didn't see Jean at the bingo, did you? She likes the odd game.'

Brenda shook her head. 'Didn't see anyone other than me and my mates. I keep myself to myself. Well, usually.'

Helen was curious. 'Usually?'

'Aye. I had a bit of bother with my handbag,' Brenda said. She took her coat off and laid it over a chair. 'Thought someone had pinched it. But it turns out I'd only left it on the café counter when I'd gone to buy a coffee. Mind you, there was something odd about it when I got it back.'

'Oh?'

'Aye. I couldn't find the keys you gave me.'

Helen stood stock still. 'The keys to the Seaview's back door and my apartment?'

'Aye.'

'Jean's keys, the ones I gave you after she walked out?'

'Aye.'

Helen didn't like the sound of this. She bit her lip as she ran Suki's ears through her fingers. She tried to count to ten to calm her racing heart but only managed to get to four before irritation got the better of her. 'When did you last see them?'

Brenda rested both hands on the back of a chair and looked at her. 'I know I had them when I left here yesterday, because I went out the back door and locked up. Then I put them in my handbag, see, in the inside pocket where I always keep keys. It's got a zip, so it's safe and—'

'Brenda,' Helen said, trying to keep a lid on the pressure cooker building inside her. 'Are you telling me you haven't got the keys any more?'

There was a pause before Brenda replied. 'Aye.'

Helen's head spun. She looked at Suki. She looked around the kitchen, at the milk pan in the sink from the night before, at the tin of hot chocolate Marie hadn't put away. Then she looked at Suki again.

'Brenda . . . think carefully. Is there any chance that someone could have taken the keys from your bag during the time you thought you'd lost it, when you'd left it on the café counter?' She tried to control her anger. After all, it was hardly Brenda's fault that the keys had disappeared.

110

'I don't know. But even if someone did take them, there's no way they'd know where they were for. There was no fob, nothing on them to say where they belonged.'

Helen took a quick decision to protect her hotel, her livelihood. 'To be on the safe side, I'll get the locks changed on the back door and the door to my apartment.'

Brenda was silent for a moment. 'Our Sally's home tomorrow,' she said quietly. 'I expect you'll be glad to see the back of me.'

It was on the tip of Helen's tongue to say *Aye*. Instead, she forced a smile. 'As I've said, I'll get new keys cut today.'

Helen and Brenda worked together cleaning rooms while their guests were out for breakfast. As always, Helen began on the top floor. She entered Ricky Delmont's room, no longer surprised to find his golf bag beneath the duvet. His bag of golf balls was neatly tucked under a pillow. How odd that man was, she thought. She polished and vacuumed, tied curtains back and opened windows to let in the June air. She cleaned showers and basins, replaced used towels, straightened bedding and cushions. She made sure tea trays were replenished with tea bags, coffee sachets, biscuits and milk pods. And when every room was cleaned, the landings vacuumed, the staircase done to her satisfaction, she went downstairs to vacuum the hall.

When she'd finished, she bent down to pull the plug from the socket. Straightening up, she was met by the sight of her guests walking up the path. She smiled at them through the glass panels in the front door, then moved the vacuum cleaner to one side and swung the door open to greet them.

'Morning, everyone. Did you enjoy a good breakfast?'

Olga stepped forward in her navy suit and white shirt. 'I had a power breakfast to maximise my efficiency.'

'Well, that's lovely. I'm glad it all worked out in the end,' Helen said as cheerfully as she could manage.

'I'd also like to arrange a discount from you in our final bill,' Olga said.

'Of course,' Helen agreed. She gave a wry smile at the thought of her profit margin being slashed. She knew her bank manager wouldn't be happy. Her guests were going out for breakfast, but what else could she do when they insisted on eating all kinds of strange foods and she had no professional cook?

Olga turned to Alice, Marty, Marilyn and Freddy, who were filing in behind her. 'Team meditation in ten minutes,' she barked. 'Afterwards, we'll go through the crazy-golf rulebook again. I need to make sure everyone completely understands section 3.3.4.'

Alice sighed theatrically. 'Not again, Olga. We've been over this before. It's the sudden-death play-off rule – we know it by heart.'

'We should know *all* the rules,' Olga replied firmly.

'If only there was a rule that prohibited weird guys from hanging around the course taking pictures of us,' Alice sighed.

Olga began walking up the stairs. 'Left, right. Left, right,' she commanded.

The team members followed her along the hall. Alice was directly behind her, but she hung back for a few seconds, marching on the spot, which made her red pigtails swing. She turned to Helen and whispered, 'Is he in?'

'Who?' Helen whispered back.

'Ricky, my good-for-nothing ex-husband.'

'No, I've just cleaned his room. He wasn't there.'

'Good. I can't bear to bump into him today. It's the tournament tomorrow and I need to focus. If he sees me, he'll start playing mind games to try to throw me off my stride.'

'Alice!' Olga shouted from the landing.

Alice raised her eyebrows. 'Got to go,' she said, marching in step to Olga's command.

Marty was next to pause beside Helen. 'Have you seen the goddam rat today?' he hissed.

'Who?'

'Ricky the rat Delmont, that's who!'

Helen shook her head and Marty marched by, swinging his muscular arms. Then it was Marilyn's turn. As she leaned towards Helen, Helen caught a waft of expensive perfume, the same one Marie often wore.

'Have you seen him this morning?' Marilyn asked in her breathy voice.

'Let me guess . . . Do you mean Ricky Delmont?' Helen replied. My word, he was in demand. 'No, I haven't seen him.'

Marilyn's scarlet-lipped smile dropped for a second before she hurried to catch up with her husband. Then Freddy ambled towards Helen, swinging his arms in time to Olga's command.

'Left, right. Left, right,' he mumbled under his breath.

'Don't you want to ask me where Ricky Delmont is this morning?' Helen asked as he passed. 'Everyone else seems to be interested in his whereabouts.'

Freddy stopped and turned to her. There was something desperately sad about the way he looked, she thought, something innocent and lost. He opened his mouth to speak, then seemed to think better of it and snapped it shut.

113

'Are you all right?' she asked.

Freddy simply nodded, then marched up the stairs to join his teammates.

As Helen headed to the door that led down to her apartment, she could just about make out Olga's voice issuing orders upstairs.

'Team meditation in eight minutes, thirty seconds.'

She lugged the vacuum cleaner down the stairs and pushed open the door into her apartment, heartened by the sight that greeted her. Brenda was seated at the table in front of a cafetière of coffee, two chunky blue mugs and a discount supermarket brand of chocolate digestives.

'Brenda, you didn't have to buy biscuits. Thank you so much,' Helen said.

'I bought them from my winnings on the bingo. It's the least I could do. You've given me work this week and I'm grateful,' Brenda replied.

She filled two mugs with coffee and milk, then slid one across the table to Helen. Suki padded over and lay down at Helen's feet.

'You seem less anxious about having the dog around,' Helen noted.

'Aye,' Brenda said.

Helen stroked Suki's head. 'I'm sorry about losing my temper with you before, Brenda. But I was upset about the way Suki was acting, and then you said you'd lost the keys. I seem to be losing my temper a lot lately.'

'You need a holiday,' Brenda said.

Helen laughed. 'I can't remember the last time I took time away. The Seaview is my life. I need to be here every day of the year.'

Brenda dunked a chocolate biscuit into her coffee, then raised it to her lips and sucked it. 'I could look after your guests if you took a holiday,' she offered. 'I reckon my customer care skills are up to scratch.'

'Thanks, Brenda, I'll, er . . . bear that in mind,' Helen said. She straightened in her seat. 'Anyway, I'm looking forward to having Sally back. Of course, that means I'll no longer need you here. I'll sort out your wages and pay you in cash before you leave.'

'Aye,' Brenda said as she dropped her gaze to the floor.

Chapter 15

The day of the tournament dawned with a clear blue sky.

'Jean used to call these perfect Scarborough days,' Helen told Suki as she stroked the dog's ears. She took a bite of toast smeared with butter and jam and glanced at her phone, hoping there might be a message or a missed call from Jean or Jimmy. But there was just a barrage of business emails. She'd called Jimmy the previous evening to try to explain what had happened on the night of the school reunion. However, she'd received his voicemail and left a message, and now she was on tenterhooks waiting – and hoping – for him to call back. She wished she'd been more assertive with him after he'd caught her in the unwanted clinch with Arthur. She was saddened that he hadn't called. Was he busy, or was he ignoring her?

She set to work on her emails with a heavy heart. Five new bookings had been received, one cancellation, a reminder for insurance renewal and a special offer from her laundry company. She was relieved at least that Suki seemed her usual self, not as clingy as she'd been. 'Whatever upset you seems to have gone now,' she said.

Suki cocked her head to one side.

'I've got good news for you,' Helen said, patting the dog's neck. 'Sally's coming back today.'

Helen had had new keys cut for herself and Sally, and another set for whoever would replace Jean as cook. Her heart sank each time she thought about Jean. It hurt her deeply that her old friend was no longer working at the Seaview. She knew that Jean was a grafter who needed to keep earning, but of all the hotels in Scarborough, why did she have to walk into the Vista del Mar and accept work from snobby Miriam? Well, Helen knew she only had herself to blame, and now she was paying the ultimate price for taking Jean for granted. She'd learned a few home truths from Marie and Brenda about the way her relationship with Jean had soured and she hadn't even noticed. She realised now just how much she'd assumed Jean would always work at the Seaview, no matter what happened, and now it was too late. Her stomach turned with anxiety at the thought. She'd rung her a few times at home, ready to apologise, ready to talk, but all her calls had gone unanswered.

A sound at the back door made Suki jump up and pad to the door. Helen knew there was only one person it could be. Her heart lifted a little and a smile made its way to her lips.

'Sally!' she cried when the young woman walked in. Sally was petite and slim, with long blonde hair and a fresh complexion. She looked much younger than her thirty-two years. 'Oh love, it's good to have you back.' Helen embraced her for a long time, then stood back and gazed at her. 'My word, you're looking well. Married life suits you. How are Gracie and Gav, and how was the honeymoon? I'll put the kettle on and you can tell me everything. Well, not everything, of course.'

Sally made a fuss of Suki, then sat at the table while Helen made a pot of tea.

'Gracie's well, Gav's great, all's good. The honeymoon was wonderful. Gav's going to be a fantastic stepdad to Gracie. And the caravan, Helen, you should have seen it. It had three bedrooms, two showers, and a conservatory on the side.' Sally pushed her hair behind her ears and shot Helen a look. 'But I'm concerned about you, and how things have been here. Mum told me about Jean walking out. She feels terrible about losing her keys, by the way.'

'I've had the locks changed down here,' Helen said. 'There's a new set of keys for you on the table.'

'How was Mum when she worked here?'

Helen paused, holding a carton of milk. 'She was . . . well . . . helpful cleaning the rooms,' she said, choosing her words carefully.

Sally picked up her new set of keys and popped them in her handbag. 'I'm grateful you asked her, Helen, she really needed the money. I don't know if she mentioned it, but she's got debts she's trying to clear, old bills she's let slide. Her vice is a trip to the bingo once a week, but she only spends a few quid. To be honest, I'm not sure she even feeds herself properly. She can't afford to buy much.'

Helen thought about this for a moment. 'If she's in such dire straits, she can always come here for breakfast. I expect she's already told you that our guests are going out for theirs. They're a strange lot, Sally. Crazy golfers, desperate to win the tournament today.'

'Oh that, yes. I'm taking Gracie to watch it. There's all sorts going on at the beach – face painting and balloons. Would you like to come with us? *The Scarborough Times* says a local celebrity is opening the event, but I've no idea who it is. I hope it's Sunshine Sam. I love his gig nights. He's got a lot of fans in Scarborough.'

'What time does it start?' Helen asked as she poured water into the teapot.

Sally took her phone from her handbag, swiped it into life and consulted her calendar. 'Two o'clock.'

Helen looked at her. 'Oh, it is good to have you back. I might take you up on your invitation and ask Marie if she wants to come too. Our friends Sue and Bev are going. They're huge crazy-golf fans and will be sitting right at the front, watching the action unfold. Well, as long as Bev's recovered from the flu.'

She made a mental note to speak to Bev and Sue about the party invitations. She needed to see the whites of their eyes when she raised the subject. It was the only way to know if they were telling the truth. She needed to get to the bottom of who was behind arranging a party she didn't want.

'What about asking Jean if she wants to come to the tournament too?' Sally asked.

Helen shook her head. 'I can't ask her, love. She's not answering my calls.'

'Things are that bad between you?'

'I'm afraid so. Did your mum tell you Jean's working for Miriam next door?'

'She did. You must be gutted.'

'I'm shocked and hurt. I'm lost, truth be told. I'm not sure which way to turn. Everything's gone wrong. Our new four-star plaque won't stay on the wall, and now it's scratched too. Suki's been spooked. Keys have gone missing. Jimmy . . .' She stopped, unsure about burdening Sally with the problems of her love life.

'What about Jimmy?' Sally said gently.

'He and I had a misunderstanding at the school reunion. Things have gone wrong between us and I don't know how to make them right.'

'Have you tried calling him?'

'Yes, but he hasn't called back. It's complicated.'

'You're thinking about Tom, aren't you, and what it'll mean if you and Jimmy get together properly?'

'I'm never not thinking of Tom, that's the problem,' Helen said. 'Anyway, let's put Jimmy to one side and talk business. I've got guests staying without having breakfast, and that's never happened before. Mind you, I've never had guests like these. They demanded all kinds of strange foods, most of which *I'd* never heard of, never mind Jean. I just expected her to cope when I should have helped her out. I guess it was the final straw.'

'She'll be back, I'm sure.'

'I wish I had your confidence,' she said, then quickly changed the subject. Talking about Jean was too upsetting. 'Come on, let's have a cuppa before we start cleaning.'

Later that day, Helen was sitting next to Marie in a blue and white striped deckchair on the beach. Beside them were Sally and Gav and Sally's little girl, Gracie, who was enjoying a chocolate ice cream. The deckchairs were arranged in rows around the course. Behind them, a small crowd was standing to watch. With the day warm and still, Helen wore a T-shirt, cut-off trousers and plimsolls. Marie, as usual, was dressed to the nines. She wore a sleeveless blue linen dress that perfectly matched her high-heeled strappy sandals.

Helen held out her hand. 'Let's have a look at it, then.'

Marie seemed confused. 'At what?'

'At the party invitation you said you'd bring to show me.'

She slapped her hand across her forehead. 'Oh dammit, I forgot. Sorry, love, I'll bring it next time.' She whipped her sunglasses from her handbag and snapped them on to her face.

Helen eyed her friend keenly, but before she could say more, Marie nodded at the ice-cream van.

'Fancy an ice cream? They're offering two for one.'

'No, thanks. But you have one if you like.'

'It's not as much fun if you don't have one too,' Marie sulked.

Helen looked again at the van, wondering if she could force down an ice cream for Marie's sake, but decided against it. However, her gaze was taken by a small group of men clustered at the van. She recognised them straight away as the gamblers she'd seen before. They were dressed in the same suits as last time and were tapping at their phones. They kept glancing at the golfers queuing up at Norman's hut, then muttering amongst themselves. She wondered if they were placing bets again.

She was pulled from her thoughts when Marie tapped her arm. 'Which ones are your guests?'

Helen pointed. 'See the short woman with cropped black hair in the navy tracksuit? That's Olga. She's ex-military. The woman next to her, the one with red hair in a bun, she's called Alice Pickle and she's the team captain. The tall guy next to her is Freddy Morgan. He's a nice lad, a bit shy, and he talks in an American accent.'

'Because he's American?' Marie smirked.

'No, he's just young and putting on an act. I overheard him on the phone saying something about one of the team's rivals. It's all a bit weird. You know I don't like listening in on guests' private conversations, but it's difficult when they're living under my roof.'

Marie sprayed suncream on her arms as Helen continued. 'Anyway, next to Freddy, that muscular chap is Marty.'

'Ooh, he's a dish, a real silver fox,' Marie cooed.

'He's also married to the woman who's standing beside him,' Helen added.

Marie lifted her sunglasses to get a better view of Marilyn. 'But she's young enough to be his daughter!' she cried.

'Shush, keep your voice down! Yes, they seem an odd match, but they're very protective of each other. It takes all sorts, I guess.'

A commotion by the hut made them both turn and stare. Helen saw Norman arguing with Ricky Delmont.

'He's another of my guests,' she told Marie.

'Which one, the old man or the young stud?'

'The young one, but he's no stud. He's one of the most unpleasant men I've ever had the misfortune to host. He's called Ricky Delmont and he's been very rude and aggressive to me, to the other guests and even to Suki.' Marie's mouth opened in shock as Helen continued. 'Now it looks like he's arguing with Norman. I was chatting to Norman the other day, and he said he'd had a run-in with Ricky after he caught him smashing models on the course with his putting iron. It looks like they're having another fight now.'

While Marie craned her neck to see what was going on, Helen glanced around and recognised faces in the crowd sitting opposite. She waved. 'Hey, look, there's Bev and Sue. I need to have a word with them about the party invitations to find out what they know.'

As she struggled to stand from her deckchair, she felt Marie's hand on her arm.

'The tournament's about to start, Helen, you can speak to them later.'

She flopped back into the low-slung chair. Despite herself, she found she was scanning the crowd to see if she could spot Jean. Then her thoughts were interrupted by a man's cheery voice over the loudspeakers. 'Ladies and gentlemen, I'd like to welcome you all to the Scarborough crazy-golf tournament!'

A cheer went up from the crowd.

'Please give a warm welcome to a local celebrity we've invited to open the event.'

'Sally's hoping it'll be Sunshine Sam,' Helen said.

Marie shook her head. 'No, it's not him. Look . . .' She pointed at Norman's hut.

Helen's jaw dropped.

'Ladies and gentlemen, I give you Jimmy Brown, otherwise known as the one and only Mr Elvis Presley!'

The crowd went wild, cheering and clapping, yelling and screaming. Helen couldn't believe her eyes.

'Jimmy?' she repeated.

'You didn't know?' Marie asked.

'He hasn't returned my last call. He said he had a surprise for me, but I had no idea this was it.'

Jimmy made his way to the centre of the course to stand by the model of Scarborough Spa. He held a microphone in his hand and was dressed in an Elvis white suit, showing off his snake hips and long legs.

'Ah, thank you very much,' he said, his voice oozing from the loudspeakers.

'He looks fantastic,' Marie said, clapping and cheering.

Helen was too stunned to speak. She listened as Jimmy gave a rousing welcome speech. After he announced the competition officially open, recorded music started playing. It was the Elvis hit 'Suspicious Minds'. He began clapping along, encouraging the crowd to join in. Soon everyone was singing, those sitting in the deckchairs swaying from side to side and the spectators at the back dancing. Jimmy's voice floated high in the air above the bunting and flags. When the song ended, the crowd shouted for more, and he happily obliged with the ballad 'Always on My Mind'. When he took a final bow, the voice over the loudspeakers announced: 'Ladies and gentlemen, Elvis has left the crazy golf.'

As Jimmy walked off the course, he turned and looked directly at Helen. Bringing the microphone close to his lips, he crooned the title of the song he'd just sung, and the notes rang clear and true, without music or backing tape: 'Always on my mind.'

'How romantic,' Marie sighed.

Helen was about to reply when a woman screamed. At first she thought it was an Elvis fan screaming for more, part of the crowd enjoying the show. But it soon became clear that something else was going on, something serious. The crowd began to shift and part. Faces that had been filled with joy just minutes before now turned to horror. Ricky Delmont staggered on to the course, clutching his throat, then dropped like a stone to the ground.

Chapter 16

Helen leapt to her feet as the crowd surged forward. Everyone was clamouring to know what had happened. Ricky Delmont lay at Jimmy's feet, with his head on Jimmy's blue suede shoes.

'Stand back, everyone!' Jimmy called, then he whipped his phone from his trouser pocket. 'Ambulance, please,' he said urgently.

Two first-aiders rushed to Ricky, whose chest, Helen noticed, wasn't moving. She gawped at the scene; the shock was too much. He couldn't be dead, could he? Beachfront officials wearing hi-vis tabards arrived, instructing everyone to move back. She had noticed them in the crowd earlier, community police officers brought in to manage the crazy-golf crowd. Reluctantly people began to disperse.

Jimmy switched his microphone back on. In an even voice – no trace of Elvis now, no cod-Memphis accent – he asked the onlookers politely but firmly to move away. 'An ambulance is on its way,' he announced. 'They'll need access to the beach. Please, with respect, could you all clear the course.'

He began to help the beach marshals as mothers gathered their children and husbands laid their arms around their wives' shoulders. Gracie started asking questions. 'What happened to that man, Mummy? When will the crazy golf start? Can I have another ice cream from the van?' Sally and Gav ushered her away.

Helen glanced at Marie. 'I can't believe what just happened.'

'Do you think he's . . .' Marie paused.

'Dead?' Helen whispered.

Marie nodded.

Helen looked at the first-aiders kneeling over Ricky's body. The expressions on their faces confirmed the tragic news. She watched as someone covered Ricky's head with a large floral beach towel. Another towel, decorated with a cartoon duck, was used to cover his legs.

'Oh my word,' she breathed.

A stocky marshal with a red face and a ginger beard approached. 'Come on, ladies, move on, we need to clear this area.'

Helen began to walk away. Marie followed, but her strappy sandals sank straight into the sand. Helen grabbed her by the arm and they set off together, holding on to each other for support. It was like a horrible dream, Helen thought. One minute they'd been sitting in deckchairs on the beach, the next Ricky was dead.

'My legs are shaking from the shock. I need a drink,' she said.

She led the way across the seafront to the nearest pub, the Golden Ball. At the bar, she ordered two large whiskies while Marie found a table by the window. She brought the drinks over, sat down and raised her glass.

'Here's to . . .' She stopped short. 'I feel I should make a toast; we've just seen a man die. But I don't know what to say.'

Marie didn't wait for her to find the right words, and downed her whisky in a single gulp.

The sound of a siren came through the pub's open window, and within minutes, an ambulance had reached the course. Helen and Marie watched as people milled around trying to see what was happening. The beach marshals had sealed the area off, using deckchairs to shield Ricky's body. Then two police cars arrived.

'I can see Jimmy talking to the cops,' Helen said. 'Poor man, he must've had such a shock.'

Marie peered out of the window. 'What about your other guests, are they still there?'

Helen scanned the scene. 'I can't see them. They must've moved on. At least the crowd are giving the medics some space, although there's nothing they can do for Ricky now.'

The noise of the siren had drawn other customers to the window.

'Look! Elvis has killed someone!' laughed a man, pointing at Jimmy.

'Elvis has killed no one,' Helen said firmly. 'Somebody fell ill over there, that's all.'

The customers slunk back to their tables. Marie leaned forward. 'What do you think happened?' she whispered.

'You saw as much as I did. We'll have to wait and see.'

'Will you speak to Jimmy to find out?'

Helen looked across the road. Norman the hut man was talking to a policeman. She saw Jimmy sitting on the wall that ran along the seafront. A uniformed policeman was beside him, speaking into his walkie-talkie. On the other side was a beach marshal, who offered him a bottle of water.

'I'll go over there in a minute and tell him we're here. He might want to join us for a drink.'

Marie picked up her empty glass. 'I need another. Would you like one?'

Helen drained her glass and passed it over.

When Marie returned from the bar with two more whiskies, Helen said she was going to speak to Jimmy. When she stood, she was surprised by how much her legs were shaking. She carefully made her way to the beach. Jimmy was alone now, swigging from his bottle of water. The paramedics were closing up the ambulance, with Ricky's body inside. The police were wrapping yellow and black warning tape around Norman's hut, stretching it around the crazy-golf course, tying it to each of the models.

'Jimmy? You all right?' Helen asked.

He swung around and attempted a smile. Helen thought he looked completely done in. His Elvis quiff had dropped and his blue suede shoes had gone. She looked at his fluffy black socks and he caught her staring.

'The police took my shoes for forensics. The guy landed on my feet.'

'Look, Jimmy, Marie and I are just across the road in the pub. We're having a drink to cope with the shock. It looks like you could do with one too. Come and join us. It's not too busy inside. That's if the police are finished with you here?'

A policeman wrapping tape around the model of the pirate ship looked up. 'You're good to go, Mr Brown,' he called. 'We'll be in touch about your shoes and will let you know when you can have them back.'

Jimmy pushed his hair from his eyes and looked at Helen but didn't move. 'You sure you want to share a drink with me?' he asked.

'Yes, I'm sure. I wouldn't have asked you otherwise,' she replied.

He nodded slowly, then looked at the sea. Helen scanned the horizon, wondering what he was concentrating on that she couldn't see. But when he turned his gaze to her, there was a hard, cold look in his eyes.

'You didn't want to talk to me or share a drink when I ran into you at the Royal Hotel. In fact you seemed to be enjoying yourself with another man.'

Helen's shoulders slumped. 'Look, Jimmy, you've got the wrong end of the stick. It was someone from school, that's all. I hadn't seen him in decades and he threw himself at me. He said he was being stalked by a woman he used to know and he wanted her to think he already had a girlfriend. What you saw wasn't what you think. It was a horrible mistake.' She reached for his hand. 'You've got to believe me.'

She waited with bated breath while he absorbed this information. She was surprised by how anxious she felt, and how important it was to her that he understood there was no one else in her life. In that moment, she knew she wanted nothing more than to move on with Jimmy Brown. She was relieved when his face softened and he curled his fingers around hers. They exchanged a smile, then Helen led him across the road to the Golden Ball.

'No shoes, no service!' the beefy barman barked when he saw Jimmy. 'Can't you read the bloody sign?'

Helen flashed him a warning look. 'This man's had a terrible shock and needs a stiff drink.'

The barman glanced out of the window at the ambulance slowly moving away, then looked carefully at Jimmy. 'Well, all right, you do look a bit shook up, pardon the pun. My old man was an Elvis fan. I'll get a whisky for you, on the house. If you want peace and quiet, you can sit in the room at the back. There's no one in there.'

Jimmy padded off in his socks while Helen collected Marie and the drinks. Once they were in the cosy back room, Helen closed the door. Jimmy lifted his glass. 'He died, Helen. Right at my feet,' he said, then took a sip. 'And I've got no idea who he was.'

Helen and Marie exchanged a look.

'I know who he was,' Helen said.

Jimmy took another sip as she explained.

'He was one of my guests. He shouldn't have been staying with me, he should've been next door at the Vista del Mar, but there was a mix-up with the booking and Miriam asked me to take him.' She stopped herself from saying any more about Miriam at the risk of getting upset again over Jean. Now wasn't the time for that. But oh, how she wished her old friend was with her now. Jean would know the proper thing to say. She'd put it bluntly, but she'd be right. 'Sorry, I'm babbling. Did the police say anything about how he died? What caused it? Was it a heart attack? And why was he holding his throat?'

Jimmy shook his head. 'They don't know anything yet. They asked me what happened and I told them everything from the moment I turned up until the moment he dropped at my feet. I was only supposed to sing two songs and walk off, that was it. I never expected this. I'm in bits.' He put his glass down, then leaned on the table with his head in his hands. 'The police want to talk to me again. They said they'd be in touch. I never want another day like this for as long as I live.' He lifted his glass again and Helen noticed that his hands were shaking.

'Look, Jimmy,' she began. 'Why don't you come back to the Seaview? You're in no fit state to be on your own at home. You can use my apartment until you pull yourself together. If you need to stay overnight, you can sleep on the sofa.' She felt Marie's eyes on her, but she didn't care.

'Did he have family?' Jimmy asked.

'If he did, they weren't with him in Scarborough. The other guests I've got staying with me all knew him, and . . . well, it's wrong to speak ill of the dead, but . . .' Helen lowered her voice, even though they were the only ones in the room, 'he wasn't well liked. In fact, he was rude and nasty.'

'That doesn't mean he deserved to die,' Marie said.

'Sorry, I didn't mean that. Of course he didn't; no one does.'

A loud knock at the door made Jimmy jump and Helen stare. Marie took a swig of her drink. The door swung open and the barman's stocky frame filled the doorway.

'Just thought you'd like to know summat's happened at the beach.'

'That's the shock my friend's recovering from,' Helen said politely.

'Nah, what I mean is, the police have taken someone away. I've just been over there to see what's going on. I know one of the beach marshals. He told me that Norman the hut man's been arrested for murdering a crazy golfer.'

He made to leave, then paused, and a wicked grin filled his fat face as he turned back.

'Maybe Norman the hut man should be called Norman the hit man.' He chortled at his own joke. 'Anyway, I thought you'd want to know.' And with that, he walked away.

Chapter 17

Helen was shocked. 'Norman? But he seemed so . . . ordinary,' she said.

Jimmy took a swig of whisky. 'He was arguing with the dead man while I was waiting to open the competition. Everyone around them must have seen and heard him. He was threatening him, Helen. It sounded like the dead guy . . .'

'Ricky Delmont,' she chipped in.

'. . . well, it sounded like Ricky had damaged some models on Norman's course.'

'Models that Norman built by hand,' Helen said. 'He told me all this when I spoke to him recently.' A chill went down her spine as she recalled Norman's words. 'Oh no,' she groaned.

Marie laid her hand on Helen's arm. 'What is it?'

'I've just remembered what Norman said. He told me that if he caught Ricky damaging any more models, he'd kill him. I thought it was just a figure of speech. Mind you, Norman was upset, red in the face, very angry when he said it. He was shooting daggers at Ricky all the time I was there. And there was something else that I thought a bit odd.'

Marie and Jimmy both leaned forward.

'He was really protective of his hut. It's where he keeps the golf clubs and coloured balls, his cash till and card machine. But I remember Suki made a move to the door, and Norman stood in front of it to stop her going further. Then later he held his arms out either side as though to stop me from peering in. I'd forgotten all about that, but now that we know he's been arrested, his behaviour strikes me as particularly odd. Maybe he was hiding something in the hut, something that he used to kill Ricky.'

'You should probably tell the police,' Jimmy said.

Helen thought for a moment, trying to make sense of what had happened. 'What exactly did you see before he stumbled towards you, Jimmy?'

Jimmy ran his hand through his thick dark hair. 'Norman was pushing Ricky in the chest, but Ricky had his hands full with a putter in one hand and a red ball in the other and he didn't fight back. Then he swung his club at Norman, but it was clumsy and he missed. The whole thing looked comical more than anything else. Anyway, I left them to it once I was called. I walked on to the course, sang my songs, adding in an extra line for an extra-special lady . . .' he looked at Helen and smiled, and a butterfly took flight in her stomach, 'and when I was walking off again, Ricky came staggering towards me clutching his throat. He'd dropped his putter and the ball was rolling through the model of Scarborough Castle. He fell down dead right at my feet. I didn't know he was dead then, of course, I thought he'd just collapsed, but I whipped my phone straight out, which is no mean feat when your trousers are as tight as these, and dialled 999.'

Helen dropped her gaze to Jimmy's white-trousered thighs before looking into his eyes again, his lovely deep brown eyes.

'I've never had anyone die on me before,' he said.

She reached across the table and gently took his hands. 'Let me take you back to the Seaview. You can rest there as long as you need. I'm not letting you go home in such a state.'

He swung his legs from under the table and wiggled his toes. 'I can't walk far without shoes.'

Marie took her phone from her handbag. 'I'll call us a Gav's Cab.'

'Thanks, Marie,' Helen said.

A bright orange Gav's Cab took them to the Seaview. Jimmy got out first and held the door open for Helen. Then he took her hand as she climbed from the cab. His polite, old-fashioned manner was one of the many things she admired about him.

'Are you sure you won't come in for coffee?' she asked Marie.

'No, I'll let you and Jimmy catch up. You must have a lot to talk about, although if you ask me, in the words of Elvis himself, a little less conversation and a little more action might be a good idea. He's a good man, Jimmy Brown. Worth hanging on to.'

Helen leaned into the car and kissed Marie on the cheek. 'I'll call you,' she said.

She watched the orange car speed off along Windsor Terrace, then caught up with Jimmy, who was waiting outside the Seaview. 'Let's go in the back way,' she said. 'I can't face meeting my guests. I need to gird myself first. They'll be shocked at what's happened to Ricky. One of them used to be married to him, and another . . .' She thought about Freddy, and what she'd overheard him say on the phone about taking revenge. She thought about Marilyn and Ricky exchanging secret smiles, and about Marty threatening him. 'Well, they all knew him well.'

Jimmy offered his arm, and they walked round the corner of Windsor Terrace. When they reached the back door, Helen pulled her set of newly cut keys from her bag. She slid the key into the lock and was just about to turn it when, to her horror, the door swung open. She gasped loudly.

'What's wrong?' Jimmy asked.

'Someone's inside,' she whispered. 'The door's open. Someone's in my apartment.'

Jimmy pushed past her, but she grabbed the back of his jump-suit and pulled him back.

'No . . . let me go first. Suki might be in there. If she sees you first, she'll be confused.'

'But there might be a burglar inside!' Jimmy cried.

'Shush, keep your voice down.'

Helen looked around the yard for something to hit someone with, just in case.

'Pass me that piece of wood next to the bin,' she said.

Jimmy did as she asked. 'You're mad, Helen. Please let me go first. If there's someone inside, you brandishing a bit of wood isn't going to scare them. You need a—'

She spun around. 'A man? I hope that's not what you were going to say. A woman with a stick trumps Elvis in his socks.'

She gripped the stick with both hands and pushed the door wide. Immediately she could see that the internal door was open too. She was scared, on the brink of being terrified. She'd never had a break-in before. Slowly, though, that terror began to change into something else. Knowing someone was in her home turned her fear into anger. And where was Suki? Normally the dog would come to her the minute she walked through the door. An awful thought passed through her mind. Had the burglar left and taken Suki with them?

Then she heard a noise. She paused, took a deep breath and stepped forward. Her heart was beating nineteen to the dozen. Jimmy was behind her, his breath hot on her neck.

'Hello?' she called out. 'Who's there? Show yourself! Now!'

She lifted the stick in the air, ninja-style, ready to bring it down on the burglar's head the moment she saw them. She took another step and peered around the door. The kitchen was empty, there was no sign of Suki. Cupboard doors and drawers were closed. Her iPad and laptop were on the table where she'd left them. Her heart caught in her throat.

'Look!' she whispered to Jimmy. The patio doors from the living room were wide open, and she caught a flash of something brown. The burglar was out there. She charged at the doors, holding the stick in the air, Jimmy still behind her. She was ready to crash it down and nobble the intruder. Adrenaline raced through her.

But when she saw who was there, the stick dropped from her hands and she almost collapsed in shock. A woman was sitting in a patio chair, with Suki asleep at her feet. Helen felt her heart melt. She had to steady herself with her hand against the wall. Despite her shock, she couldn't keep the smile off her face.

'Jean!'

Chapter 18

She was so excited to see her old friend that when she tried to speak, her words tripped over her tongue. 'What are you . . . How did you . . . I thought . . . What's going on?'

Jean stood and brushed her hands down the front of her apron. Helen was confused enough already, but when she saw that Jean was wearing her work apron with the Seaview logo embroidered in blue, her head began to spin. She had so many questions to ask and didn't know where to start.

'Can't sit and chat, Helen. I've got sandwiches to make. Your guests are upstairs and I've offered them something to eat.'

'You've done what? How? When? But . . . your keys shouldn't work!'

Jean nodded at Jimmy. 'Nice to see you again.'

'And you, Jean. It's been a long time.'

Jean bustled into the kitchen with Suki behind her. Helen looked at Jimmy. 'I think I need another drink.'

'What's wrong? It's just Jean, isn't it?'

'There's a lot more to it than that,' Helen whispered. 'It's a long story.'

'What are you two doing standing there whispering?' Jean called. 'Come and sit down and I'll put the kettle on. I dare say you could use a cuppa and something to eat after what you've been through. I heard all about the dead man on the golf course. When I learned he was one of your guests, I came here straight away to do what I could to help.'

Helen and Jimmy sat at the kitchen table as Jean filled the kettle, buttered bread and sliced tomatoes. Helen didn't know what to say, but she knew she had to say something. Jean was acting as if nothing had happened. She straightened in her chair and clasped her hands on the table in front of her. She needed an explanation. But just as she was about to ask Jean what she was playing at, Jean, as always, got in first.

'I was with you-know-who next door . . .'

'Who?' Jimmy mouthed to Helen.

'Miriam,' Helen mouthed back.

'. . . and some of her guests are on the dead man's crazy-golf team. They were with him when he died and were taken in for questioning by the police. Apparently this Ricky chap had enemies, he wasn't well liked, and the police needed to know what his teammates could tell them. When they came back to the Vista del Mar, they were upset, as you'd imagine. I served them a drink at the bar and sat with them a while. Poor loves.'

All the time Jean was talking, her hands worked non-stop. She lifted the kettle, poured water into a cafetière and the teapot, buttered bread, turned from the fridge to the cupboard to the sink, never stopping, always moving. Helen was still confused and in shock after having a front-row seat to Ricky's death on the seafront. Having Jean back, talking as if nothing had changed, making sandwiches, brewing tea, was too much to take in.

'Jean?' she said forcefully as soon as she could get a word in. Jean stopped what she was doing and held a butter knife in the air.

'Yes, love?'

Helen stood and walked towards her. 'I'm confused. Are you back for good or just passing through?'

Without missing a beat, Jean began buttering again. 'Yes, I'm back,' she said matter-of-factly. 'I figured it was better the devil I know. Now, if you'll excuse me, I've got work to do. As I said, you'll find your guests upstairs. I told them there'd be nothing fancy to eat. I don't do fancy. It's ham salad sandwiches on brown bread. I told them I can't be doing with their faddy foods and power proteins.'

'And they were all right with that?' Helen asked.

'They were too shocked to argue.'

She looked at her apartment door. 'How did you get in? I've had the locks changed since you left.'

Jean paused in her work and gave a cheeky wink. 'Think a changed lock can defeat me? You should know me better than that.'

'Come on, Jean, I need to know. Security's important.'

She opened a wholemeal loaf. 'I met Sally at Bonnet's café in town after she finished work this morning. I told her I was thinking of coming back. I wanted to test the water, see how things stood. She reckoned you'd welcome me, and so here I am. She loaned me her keys and I had a set cut for myself.'

Helen gently laid her hand on Jean's arm. 'You're really back? For good?'

Jean's whole body softened, and when she looked at Helen, there were tears in her eyes. Then she stiffened again and began slicing cucumber. 'I'm back. And I'll tell you summat else. If I'd known for one second . . .' she brought the knife down hard, 'what it would be like working for Miriam next door . . .' down came the knife again, harder, faster, 'I'd have never gone there in a million years. She's a stuck-up so-and-so, that one. And you should hear what her guests call her behind her back.' She tutted loudly. 'I'll tell you all about it sometime. First let me take the sandwiches upstairs with flasks of hot drinks. Here, there's a cup of coffee each for you and Jimmy.'

'Plenty of sugar for me, Jean, please,' Jimmy said.

Helen spun around at his voice. She'd been so wrapped up in the joy and confusion of having Jean back that she'd almost forgotten he was there.

'He needs sugar for the shock,' she explained. 'Ricky Delmont died at his feet.'

Jean closed her eyes for a few moments, letting this sink in.

'The police have arrested Norman the hut man from the crazy-golf course,' Helen said. 'He was arguing with Ricky in front of the crowd; there were lots of eyewitnesses who saw them pushing and shoving.'

Jean's eyes opened wide. 'Norman Lawson?' she said, confused. She looked from Helen to Jimmy. 'Norman wouldn't hurt a fly. I've known him all my life. No, the police must have it wrong. He's one of the sweetest men I know.'

'He wasn't so sweet when I had a word with him earlier this week. He was angry, threatening to kill Ricky for damaging his hand-made models. Of course, I thought it was a figure of speech. I didn't think for one minute he was serious.'

'Norman?' Jean said again. 'I can't believe it. Mind you, I did hear he's got a few personal problems and went downhill after his wife left.'

'Helen?' Jimmy got up. 'I'm just going to use your . . .'

'Right you are,' she replied.

When he'd disappeared, Jean raised an eyebrow. 'You two back together?'

'It's complicated. We're still working through it,' Helen said.

Jean sniffed. 'Shame. You make a good team.'

'Let me get there at my own pace, Jean,' Helen said seriously. She paused. 'It's really great to have you back, but there's a question I need to ask, and I need an honest answer.'

Jean looked at her suspiciously. 'When have I ever lied to you?'

'It's about my fiftieth birthday party,' Helen began.

Jean's eyes lit up. 'Oh! So you've decided to have a party after all? Good girl, I knew you would. Now, let me start planning the food. I'll cook and bake and—'

Helen held her hand up. 'Stop right there. There will be no party. You know my feelings on the subject. I didn't want a party before you went to work for Miriam and I still don't want one now. But someone's arranged one for me. Invitations have gone out and I haven't sent them. Marie swears blind she hasn't sent them either. The only other person who knows about my birthday is you. So my question is . . .'

Jean turned away, busying herself at the sink.

'Jean, look me in the eye and tell me the truth. Are you behind this party?'

Her shoulders dropped and she turned back to look at Helen. 'No.'

'Have you received an invitation?'

She nodded. 'Yes, I have.'

'Why didn't you mention it to me?'

'I didn't know if we would ever speak to each other again. But now that I'm back and we're friends again, we can put the past behind us.'

'But the invitations, Jean . . . I can't let people turn up to a party I don't want. I need to get to the bottom of this and stop it immediately.'

Jean pushed her glasses up to the bridge of her nose. 'I see your point, love, but don't you think you're getting worked up over nothing? Where's the harm in it really? You should feel flattered that someone wants to throw a surprise party for you.'

'Flattered?' Helen cried. 'It's anything but flattering. It's . . . it's scary, if you must know.'

'If it'll help, I'll bring my invitation for you to see. It's on the mantelpiece at home. It might go some way to solving the mystery of who's behind it.'

'Thanks, that'd be good. Did you keep the envelope too? Was it a Scarborough postmark?'

'I threw the envelope away,' Jean said quickly. 'But don't worry, the invitation's very tasteful, exactly the sort of thing you'd have sent. Anyway, I'll put these plates in the dumbwaiter, then I'll go up and serve the food.'

Helen was perturbed at the way she had quickly changed the subject. But too much had happened that day for it to linger any longer on her mind. Having Jean back at the Seaview was wonderful. She would worry about the invitations later. 'I'll come up with you,' she said. 'I want to offer my condolences to my guests. They all knew Ricky, even if none of them seemed to like him.' An image of blonde and brassy Marilyn popped into her head. 'Well, apart from one.'

142

'When are they due to leave?' Jean asked.

'Tomorrow,' Helen said. 'Then the Seaview's empty until next weekend.'

'No guests at all until then?' Jean said. 'That's odd. Miriam's empty until next weekend too. Do you know, I've been hearing a lot about smaller guest houses like ours lying empty during the week and only doing decent business on a weekend. I blame the cheap and cheerless box hotels moving in on the edge of town.' She lifted a platter of sandwiches and placed it in the dumbwaiter along with two large flasks.

'Jean?' Helen said softly.

'What, love?'

'It's good to have you back.' She reached her arms out and the two of them embraced, briefly, before Jean pulled away.

'That's that,' Jean said firmly.

The bathroom door swung open and Jimmy walked out. 'I should probably go home,' he said. 'My hands have stopped shaking and I'm feeling a lot calmer. I'll call Gav's Cabs.'

'Nonsense!' Jean called. 'You haven't had a cuppa yet, and there's a sandwich here for you too.'

'I'll take it with me, Jean. You've both got work to do, I won't hold you up. I'll call you later, Helen, OK?'

'You sure you're going to be all right?' Helen asked.

He nodded. 'Jodie's coming over tonight, so I won't be on my own.'

Jean handed him a plastic tub with sandwiches inside, along with a tumbler with a lid.

'The coffee's hot, be careful you don't spill it. You'd never get the stains out of that jumpsuit.'

Helen followed him to the back door and they waited for the taxi to arrive. It came far too soon for her liking. She reached up and kissed him on the cheek. 'We'll speak soon,' she said.

The cab driver leaned out of the window and waved. 'Hey, missus!'

Helen peered at the familiar face. 'Gav!' she cried. 'How's married life going for you?'

'Ah, it's grand. Sally's the best thing that's ever happened to me.'

Jimmy turned to Helen. 'I could say the same thing about you.'

Her heart fluttered. She kissed his cheek again and breathed in the scent of his lemon spice aftershave. Then she watched as he walked to the cab and curled his long legs into the front seat.

'See you at your fiftieth birthday party next week!' Gav yelled, then the cab turned and drove away.

Helen stormed back into the kitchen. 'Jean! I want another word with you about this party. Gav knows! He . . .' She looked around the room. 'Jean? Where are you? Jean!'

She stopped and took a breath, remembering what Marie and Brenda had told her about treating Jean with kindness. Losing her for just a few days had shaken her to the core. It had made her realise that without Jean, there was no Seaview Hotel. She was as much a part of the place as Helen herself. She was woven into its fabric, part of its history and future.

'I mustn't upset Jean or take her for granted,' Helen muttered like a mantra. 'I mustn't upset her or take her for granted.'

Her heart rate slowed and her rage subsided. She'd speak to Jean about Gav later, because now was not the time. She had a dead man's rivals to deal with.

When she reached the hall, Jean was unloading the dumbwaiter.

'Let me help,' Helen said. She took the flasks of tea and coffee and placed them in the dining room. She heard noises coming from upstairs, footsteps getting louder, and she knew her guests were coming down. She walked to the foot of the stairs.

Alice was first. Her face was blotchy and red and she was dabbing her eyes with a paper hanky.

'I'm sorry for your loss,' Helen said.

Alice sniffed back her tears. 'I know he was my ex, but we were happy once and he'll always be a part of my life,' she said.

Next was Olga, stiff-backed and ashen-faced. 'I'm in shock,' she said, then she turned to follow Alice to the lounge.

Marty and Marilyn came downstairs arm in arm. Helen noticed that Marilyn's usually immaculate make-up was skew-whiff, with one of her false eyelashes hanging at an angle. Marty patted his wife's hand. 'She's got one of her headaches,' he said.

Last down the stairs was Freddy. He was so tall he had to bend his neck when he reached the bottom stair, otherwise he'd have banged his head on the low ceiling. Helen noticed that he looked as if he'd been crying, his face puffy and his eyes raw.

'You all right, Freddy?' she asked.

'Sure, everything is just fine and dandy,' he replied in his fake American accent.

Helen turned and walked into the dining room, helping Jean with cups and saucers. Then she braced herself to face her guests.

Chapter 19

In the lounge, sunlight streamed through the windows. Normally Helen enjoyed being in this room, with its gorgeous view of the North Bay beach. But today it seemed stifling and claustrophobic. Marty sat with his arm around Marilyn's shoulders. She was sniffing back tears, her fake eyelash hanging perilously. Freddy was hunched over, head down, furiously tapping at his phone. Alice sat rigid in her chair. Her red hair, which had been so carefully wound into a bun at the top of her head earlier, now fell in plaits either side of her face. Olga paced between the bar and the window with her hands clasped behind her back.

Helen plastered a smile on her face. 'Now, who'd like tea? Coffee?'

'Can I have coffee?' Olga said. 'Strong.'

'Alice? Freddy?' Helen said when there was no response from anyone else.

Alice shook her head, but Freddy didn't look up.

'Marty, what about you?'

'My wife and I will have coffee, Helen, thank you.'

Helen walked to the dining room to find Jean pouring coffee into mugs. 'I'll take one myself, Jean. Think I'm going to need it.'

Jean obliged and poured an extra cup. Then she set the mugs on a tray. 'Would you like me to take these in?' she asked.

'I'll do it, Jean. And thanks again for making them something to eat. But mostly, thank you for coming back.'

Helen was about to tell Jean that having her back was more than she deserved, more than she'd dared dream. She was about to say that the Seaview wouldn't have been the same without her. She was even going to mention that without Jean, she didn't know if she wanted to keep the business going. But her words went unspoken when Jean waved dismissively.

'Ah, it's nothing, love.'

She laid her hands on Jean's shoulders. 'No, Jean,' she said, looking into her friend's eyes behind her large, round glasses. 'It's everything.'

Jean patted her hand, acknowledging the moment. Then it was over, and Helen knew they would never speak of it again.

'I'll bring the sandwiches in,' Jean said, stepping away. Helen swallowed a lump in her throat and picked up the tray with the coffee mugs.

In the lounge, she set mugs down in front of Marty and Marilyn and placed her own and Olga's on the bar.

'Jean's made sandwiches for you all,' she said.

Alice glanced in her direction and gave a weak smile. Freddy stopped tapping his phone and slid it into his back pocket. He looked up and seemed surprised, as if realising for the first time that other people were there.

'Coffee, Freddy?' Helen asked, eyeing him carefully. There was something about the boy that troubled her. He looked vulnerable and young, lost and completely alone. She thought again about what she'd overheard him say on the phone, about taking revenge.

She hoped with all her heart that he hadn't been involved in Ricky's death.

She shook the thought from her mind. How could he have been? Ricky had died in front of witnesses. Norman had been arrested, and the police would bring the killer to justice. But still, an uneasy feeling settled in the pit of her stomach. It seemed that each of her guests had history with Ricky one way or the other, and from what she'd learned so far, none of it was good. She'd overheard Freddy swearing revenge on him, but for what she didn't know. Then there was the eerie likeness between the two of them. Surely she couldn't have been the only one to have noticed it. Were the others too used to the similarity to comment, or was she reading too much into it?

As for the rest of them, Alice couldn't utter Ricky's name without adding vitriol, while Helen could only guess at the problems the man had caused in Marty and Marilyn's marriage. From the little she had learned, it seemed that he had tried to woo Marilyn away. Marty, despite his age, was fighting fit and not prepared to let her go without a fight. But what, she wondered, did Marilyn want for herself? Then there was Olga, the enigma in the blue suit and white shirt. The only time *she* mentioned Ricky's name was to damn him as wicked or bad. Was it purely a professional relationship they had shared? Had Ricky been nothing more to her than a rival crazy golfer?

All these questions whirled in her mind as Jean entered the lounge carrying a tray piled with sandwiches.

'Thanks, love.' Helen smiled.

'I'll go downstairs to tidy the kitchen.' Jean laid the tray on the bar, then bustled away.

Helen perched on a stool at the bar and steadied herself with her arm on the counter top. A tiny figurine behind the bar caught her eye. It was a plastic model of Elvis Presley, no more than three inches high. She'd been given it by Jimmy's troupe of twelve Elvis impersonators, Twelvis, and the thought of them made her smile. They'd called it her good-luck charm. Above it, in a silver frame on the wall, was a photograph of her late husband, Tom. He was dressed in his white Elvis suit, the photo taken at one of the Elvis parties they'd held at the Seaview each summer. There'd been few parties since he'd died. Helen looked at his face, his eyes creased in a smile. How she wished he was there by her side. Familiar, painful grief sliced through her heart and she forced her gaze away.

She glanced around the lounge again. Olga was now sitting next to Alice. The only noise in the room was the scrape of coffee mugs against coasters.

'I . . . er . . . I heard some news from the scene of the . . . you know . . . what happened earlier,' Helen began, awkwardly.

All eyes turned towards her.

'You have news?' Alice said.

'Tell me,' Olga demanded.

Helen looked at their faces, from Freddy to Marty and Marilyn, from Alice to Olga.

'Apparently Ricky was involved in a fight before he . . . you know,' Helen said.

'He died, yes,' Olga said, and this time Helen noticed a catch in her voice. A chink in her armour. The woman was capable of emotion after all. 'I saw the fight.'

'Y'all saw the fight,' Freddy chipped in. 'The guy who runs the crazy golf was prodding Ricky in the chest. They were arguing in front of everyone.'

Marty removed his arm from Marilyn's shoulders and leaned forward. 'We saw Ricky swing his club at the guy who looks after the course.'

Helen nodded. 'I heard about that. And what I've heard since is that Norman the hit . . . hut man has been arrested.'

'I tried to stop Ricky fighting with him,' Marty said.

'But I pulled him back,' Marilyn added. She blew her nose on a lace-edged handkerchief, then turned to her husband. 'I didn't want you to get hurt, honey.'

Olga banged the table with her fist. 'Ricky Delmont was a terrible man!'

At Olga's side, Alice shifted uncomfortably. 'He always had a wicked temper, it's one of the reasons we divorced,' she said. 'Well, that and him sleeping with his putters and balls. It wasn't conducive to a happy marriage. Anyway, we all saw him argue with Norman. We were waiting to tee off, getting ready to start the game as soon as Elvis finished singing. Ricky's team was playing first – we'd flipped a coin to choose order of play. Ricky was furious, as he considered it unlucky to go first.'

'Was he still fighting with Norman when the coin was tossed?' Helen asked.

Alice shook her head and her plaits swung left to right. 'No, he pushed Norman away so that he could see which way the coin landed. When he knew his team were playing first, he stood in position at the start of hole one.'

'And where was Norman when Ricky stepped forward?'

'He was ranting and raving outside his hut. Ricky was trying to focus, but he lost his patience with Norman and started swinging his club to scare him away. In the chaos that followed, he managed to get away from Norman and laid his ball on the tee. He had a ritual he always carried out before he teed off; he liked to kiss his golf ball for luck. So he kissed the ball and put it on the ground, then Norman came at him again. The ball rolled away through the model of Scarborough Castle.'

Using the little that Jimmy had told her, along with this new information, pieces of a deadly puzzle began to form in Helen's mind.

'Was that when Ricky staggered on to the course clutching his throat?'

'Right,' Marilyn said, sniffing back tears. 'Then he collapsed and . . . well, we all know what happened.'

Helen was about to carry on asking about Ricky's demise, but Marilyn began to sob. Marty was shushing her, wiping away the tears that streaked her make-up, mascara running down her cheeks. Helen looked at the bar, where Jean had left the ham salad sandwiches.

'Let's not talk any more about what happened, it's too upsetting. Please, help yourselves to something to eat.'

Marilyn choked back her tears, then held up her hand. 'I can't stomach anything,' she said, sniffing loudly into her hanky.

'You need to keep your strength up, my dear,' Marty said. 'Let me get you some food.'

He walked to the bar and picked up a plate. Freddy followed and took a sandwich, then Alice and Olga.

'It's important to keep our energy levels high,' Olga said approvingly as each team member helped themselves. 'We're all in shock.

Tomorrow we'll be leaving, though, because the tournament will surely be cancelled after what happened to Ricky.'

Freddy's phone beeped with a message as he was about to bite into his sandwich. He pulled it from his pocket and looked at the screen, and his eyes grew wide. He stood and walked towards Olga and showed it to her. She nodded curtly.

'Well, that's a surprise,' she said.

'I guess we're staying in Scarborough a little longer than expected,' Freddy drawled.

Helen was confused. 'But you've just said the tournament will be cancelled and you're all planning to leave. What's going on?'

'The crazy-golf match is still going ahead. Ricky's teammates are staying next door to play against us, and it'll be a charity match. We'll all wear black armbands as a mark of respect for Ricky's passing.'

'That's more than he deserves,' Alice muttered darkly. She had stuffed half her sandwich into her mouth and was chewing furiously.

'We need to find another hotel,' Olga said.

Helen slid off her stool. 'You can stay on here if you wish. My next guests aren't due in until the weekend.'

'I vote to stay,' Marilyn said.

'If my wife's happy, then I'm happy,' Marty said.

'I'm happy,' Olga said.

'Me too,' Alice said. 'Freddy, are you happy to stay?'

'Sure am,' Freddy said with a smile.

'Then that's fixed,' Helen said. 'Oh, but there's just one thing.'

Olga arched an eyebrow.

'It's about the food. My cook, Jean, is back at work after, er . . . a little break. She's what you'd call the more traditional kind of cook.'

'You mean there'll be no power foods and super protein?' Marty said.

'I'm afraid not. You see, we're not that kind of hotel. We're traditional, old-fashioned, just like Jean. So if you'd like to take breakfast here, it won't be chia seeds and tofu, it'll be sausage and beans.' She braced herself for the flak she felt sure was coming. She saw Olga and Alice exchange a look. She felt her shoulders tense. Freddy shrugged. Marty whispered something in Marilyn's ear.

'If the team's happy, I'm happy,' Olga said, looking around at the others.

'Happy to have a traditional breakfast?' Helen said, unsure what was going on.

'I'm happy having the full English,' Freddy said, glancing at Olga.

Marty shrugged. 'Me too, and I speak for my wife on this also.'

'Thank you, honey,' Marilyn said, patting his hand.

'As we're playing the game as a charity event, we can relax in all kinds of ways, not least by having an award-winning full English breakfast,' Marty said approvingly.

'Then that's sorted,' Helen said. 'I'll tell Jean so she can prepare for tomorrow.'

She felt relieved to be leaving the lounge. There was a tension in the air she didn't like. While she was grateful that she was going to have guests, and income, for longer than expected, a part of her was anxious about the golfers staying on. She'd much rather welcome in families, couples enjoying a cheeky weekend, tourists coming to see a play at the Stephen Joseph Theatre, a gig at the

Open Air Theatre or a concert at the Spa. The last thing she needed was Ricky Delmont's death hanging over the hotel like a cloud. She guessed the police would come and take Ricky's belongings away. Well, she'd deal with that when the time came.

She forced her spine straight. 'Come on, Dexter, you can get through this,' she said.

Then she went downstairs to tell Jean.

Chapter 20

The following morning when Helen woke, Ricky's death came rushing at her. She thought of him kissing his golf ball, staggering to the course, falling dead at Elvis's feet – Jimmy's feet. The thought of Jimmy made her reach for her phone on her bedside table. She was ready to text him to ask how he was, but was pleased to see he'd already sent her a message.

Come for dinner soon. Let's talk x

She quickly replied, *Sounds great.*

Her finger hovered briefly over the bottom line of text, and then she returned his kiss.

A sound caught her unawares, something she hadn't heard for days. It was the sound of the radio playing in the kitchen, with Jean singing along. She lay still, savouring the moment. Jean was back at work and all was well with the world. She felt able to cope with almost anything now. However, something continued to niggle at her about the party invitations. The more she tried to work out who'd sent them without her knowledge or permission, the more her mind whirled.

She slid out of bed and into her dressing gown, pulled it around her and fastened it tight.

'Morning, Jean,' she said as she padded to the kitchen in bare feet.

She sat at the table, and Suki came obediently to her side.

'Morning, Suki my love,' Helen said, scratching the dog's neck, making her groan with pleasure.

Jean didn't look her way. She pushed her glasses up to the bridge of her nose and carried on placing sausages under the grill.

'Are you going to sit there all day or get on with some work?' she said.

Helen gave a salute. 'Aye, aye, Captain. It's good to have you back.'

She was about to head to the shower when she stopped and turned back.

'Jean?'

'What, love?'

'Did you bring your party invitation for me to look at?'

Jean hesitated a moment, then returned to her work. 'Sorry, love. I was all set to put it in my handbag last night when my sister-in-law rang from Bridgend. Well, she can't half talk, and by the time we'd finished chatting, it was bedtime and I forgot all about it. Not to worry, I'll remember tomorrow.'

Helen walked into the bathroom feeling unsettled. Was she being paranoid, or were Jean and Marie, the two people she trusted most in the world, lying to her?

The morning went by in a blur of activity as normality returned to the Seaview. Well, as normal as it could be considering her guests were in shock over Ricky's death. When Sally arrived for work, Helen hugged her.

'Please be respectful to our guests, under the circumstances,' Helen said.

Sally shot her a look. 'Aren't I always?'

Helen laid her hand on Sally's arm. 'Course you are. Sorry, I'm just a little on edge.' She coughed to clear her throat. 'Sally, love, can I ask you a question?'

'Go on. I bet it's about Jimmy, isn't it? Do you need some love-life advice? Because what I would do if I were you is—'

She held up her hand. 'It's not about Jimmy. I need to ask you a question and I want an honest answer.'

Sally looked at her. 'OK,' she said.

Helen sat up straight in her seat. 'Are you the one who's arranging my surprise birthday party?'

There, she'd said it. But one look at Sally's crestfallen face and she knew the younger woman wasn't involved.

'It's not me, Helen, honest.' Sally bit her lip, then stood and walked to the cupboard under the stairs, pulling out her tabard. 'Come on, we need to serve breakfast,' she called.

Helen watched as she disappeared out of the door. She already had a feeling that Marie and Jean were holding something back, and now Sally was acting strange. Something wasn't ringing true.

Helen and Sally served breakfast, walking from the dumbwaiter in the hall to the dining room with plates of sausages and beans, bacon and hash browns, black pudding and scrambled egg. Marty ate his with gusto, slathering brown sauce all over. However, Marilyn barely picked at her beans on toast. Olga had a small bowl of low-fat, low-calorie, gluten-free cereal with a cup of black tea. Freddy and Alice enjoyed the full works and ate every morsel.

'More tea? Coffee?' Helen asked when all was done. 'Toast with marmalade, jam or honey?'

'I'm finished,' said Olga.

Marty patted his taut stomach. 'That was wonderful, my regards to your cook.'

'What are your plans for today?' Helen asked.

Alice cast a nervous look at Olga before she replied. 'We're going to the golf course. We need to know what's happening before we play the charity game.'

Olga stood up. 'Let me check the rulebook regarding the interruption of a tournament.'

Freddy rolled his eyes. 'You're quoting the 3.4.1. rule at a time like this?'

'No!' Olga snapped. 'You're wrong. It's rule 3.4.3. Players must be ready to continue the tournament at any time.'

'Come on, Freddy, leave her to it. You know she's a stickler for the rules,' Alice said softly.

Helen's phone rang in her tabard pocket. 'Excuse me,' she said, moving away from her guests.

Alice followed Olga up the stairs, the others filing behind her. Left, right. Left, right. Helen watched them go as she spoke into her phone. 'Seaview Hotel, good morning.'

'Mrs Dexter, it's DS Hutchinson from Scarborough police.'

Helen's heart sank. Best to get this over and done with, she thought. She'd been expecting the call, as Ricky's things were still in his room. She walked to the lounge, closing the door behind her, and sank on to the window seat, gazing at the sun shining like diamonds on the waves of the North Bay. 'DS Hutchinson, how are you?'

'Busy,' he replied tersely. 'I'm sure you don't need me to tell you why I'm calling. We understand that Ricky Delmont was staying at the Seaview. Is that correct?' Without waiting for her to confirm, he barged on. 'I'm sending forensics this morning to go over his room and take his belongings away. I must insist that no one enters the room until my people get there. I should warn you, Mrs Dexter, there's likely to be press interest in the Seaview and in the hotel next door where the dead man's teammates were staying.'

'Oh no,' Helen groaned. She hadn't had time to give a thought to the press.

'DC Hall and I will visit you this morning. We need to speak to your guests. Are they all there?'

'Yes, they're here. They've just had breakfast. They said they were planning on going out.'

'Don't let them leave, whatever you do. Keep them inside the hotel,' DS Hutchinson said darkly. 'We need to question them all.'

'All of them? Why?'

'Mrs Dexter, we've got a dead man on our hands.'

'But he died in front of witnesses. Everyone saw him fighting with Norman, and I heard you'd arrested him. Why do you need to speak to my guests?'

There was a pause before he spoke again. 'Because, Mrs Dexter, the fight with the attendant at the crazy golf course isn't what killed Mr Delmont. Prepare your guests to be interviewed. From what we've learned about the victim, it seems he was a most unpleasant man who rubbed people up the wrong way. In my experience, men like that often make enemies, and initial enquiries reveal that a lot of people have a reason for wanting him dead.'

Helen's head began to throb painfully. 'Are you saying you're treating his death as suspicious?' she asked.

'That's exactly what I'm saying.'

'So it wasn't Norman who killed him? It wasn't the fight?'

'No, it wasn't the course attendant's shove in the chest that killed Ricky Delmont. That much has become clear, and we've released Mr Lawson this morning.'

Helen was surprised to hear this. 'But if Norman didn't kill him, who did?' She glanced at the lounge door, aware that any of her guests might be hovering in the hall.

'Mrs Dexter, I've told you enough so that you understand the seriousness of the situation we're dealing with. Now you know why I'm asking you not to let your guests leave. I need them all there when I arrive with my colleague. I need to speak to them to find out if they can shed light on what Mr Delmont ate that day, relating to his allergy.'

Helen gulped. 'His allergy?'

'His peanut allergy, Mrs Dexter. Ricky Delmont died from anaphylactic shock caused by a deadly reaction to peanuts.'

Chapter 21

DS Hutchinson cleared his throat. 'The toxicology report confirmed the cause of death in the early hours of this morning. It normally takes a few days for test results to come back, but the chief pulled a favour. Mr Delmont's death could prove damaging for business in Scarborough, and we don't want to scare tourists away. The sooner we have this nasty business solved, the better.'

Helen was stunned. She was trying to get her head around the news when DS Hutchinson said something else that rocked her back in her seat.

'Surely Mr Delmont mentioned his allergy to you when he checked in at the Seaview? He knew how serious it was. He knew it could kill him.'

'Yes . . .' she stuttered. 'He, um, gave me a sheet of paper with a list of foods on it that he could and couldn't eat.'

'You read it, I presume. Were peanuts on that list?'

Helen screwed her eyes shut. Of course she'd read it; it was attached to the NDA he'd made her sign. Once she knew he was allergic to peanuts, she hadn't given it another thought, though, because peanuts weren't allowed at the Seaview and there was nothing to be concerned about. In addition, Ricky had eaten

161

breakfast in town each day, somewhere different to Alice and her teammates. Besides, her mind had been elsewhere, feeling sorry for herself over losing Jean, thinking about Jimmy and keeping Brenda on her toes.

'Yes, peanuts were on the list and he told me about his allergy. But I never keep peanuts at the Seaview, or any products containing them. It's a rule I adhere to strictly after an incident years ago.'

'No peanuts at the Seaview,' DS Hutchinson said. It sounded to Helen as if he was writing it down.

'We need to collect this list from you,' he said sternly. 'We're gathering all evidence that might be crucial to the investigation.'

She thought for a moment. 'Didn't Ricky carry an EpiPen to counter the effects of anaphylactic shock? Or wear a bracelet to let people know he was allergic?'

'He wore many bracelets on both wrists, Mrs Dexter. Mainly plastic bangles bearing the names of seaside towns where he'd played crazy golf. In amongst those on his left wrist, we found a medical alert bracelet stating his allergy. However, it's highly unlikely anyone would have found it unless they knew what they were looking for. As for an EpiPen, his GP would have advised him to carry one, but one wasn't found on his body.'

'Oh, the poor man,' Helen said, trying to take it all in.

'Mrs Dexter, my colleague has just walked into my office. We'll be on our way soon.' He rang off.

Helen walked from the lounge, her heart beating wildly. She glanced up the stairs, then at the door that led to her apartment. She wasn't sure what to do first. She needed to speak to her guests to advise them they shouldn't leave, but she didn't want to scare them by announcing that the police were coming. More than anything, she needed to speak to Jean. She laid her hand against the wall and gave herself a stern talking-to.

Sally walked out of the dining room carrying a tablecloth splattered with brown sauce. 'You all right, Helen? Thought I heard you talking to someone.'

'I'm fine, Sally,' Helen said, forcing a smile, thinking fast. 'Look, could you . . . I mean, would you mind staying here a few moments?'

'Here?' Sally looked around. 'In the hall?'

'Right here, don't move. I'll be five minutes. Ten tops. I've got to speak to Jean about something. It's important.'

Sally made a move towards the door that led down to the apartment. 'Then let me help if it's so important.'

Helen jumped towards the door, blocking Sally's way. 'No!' she cried. 'Stay here. If any of the guests try to leave, don't let them. You mustn't. You hear me? You've got to keep them inside. It's necessary, trust me. If they come downstairs, tell them I'll explain everything as soon as I've spoken to Jean.'

She left a flabbergasted Sally and ran down the stairs, flying into the kitchen where Jean was washing up. She needed to find Ricky's NDA and his list of food to hand to DS Hutchinson when he arrived. 'Where's the blue folder with the guests' dietary requirements?'

Jean lifted her hands from the soapy water and dried them on a small towel. 'Not that again,' she moaned. 'I've already told you that I'm not cooking stuff I don't understand. I've had it up to here with you pushing me out of my comfort zone. And don't get me started on what I had to cook for madam next door. She buys frozen croissants, Helen. Frozen.' She shook her head in despair.

Helen rifled through the kitchen drawers. 'Jean, I need the blue folder for the police, the one with the guests' food lists. Where is it?'

'It's in here, where I always put it,' Jean said, calmly pulling open a drawer. Helen was about to breathe a sigh of relief when Jean's face clouded over. 'That's funny. It's not here.'

Helen stood next to Jean while she lifted everything out of the drawer. There were old parking permits, tourist leaflets, invitations to the opening of a new café in town. The invitations were so old that the café had closed and was now a vaping shop.

'It must be there. Find it!' she urged. She began rifling through more drawers and cupboards.

Jean stood back and put her hands on her hips. 'Why the rush?'

Helen pulled a ball of string from a drawer, an instruction manual for a microwave that she no longer owned, and the guarantee on her fridge freezer.

'What's going on?' Jean demanded.

'I need to find the list of food Ricky Delmont gave me with his NDA. It's important. The police have just called. They're on their way, and they say . . .' Helen paused and swallowed hard, 'they say he died from an allergic reaction to peanuts. I have to find that list. The police have asked to see it. Where the devil is it?'

The two women emptied drawers and pulled cupboards open,

without any luck. When they were satisfied the folder wasn't there, they sat at the kitchen table.

'Think, Jean, think. What did you do with the folder after I gave you Ricky's paperwork?'

'I put it in the middle drawer, where it always lives.'

'Are you sure?'

Jean narrowed her eyes. 'Are you doubting my word?'

'No,' Helen said. 'But I'm panicked. The police are on their way. Is there anywhere else it might be?'

Jean thought for a moment, then banged the table with her fist. 'Sally's mum could have moved it when she was working here while I was next door.'

'Brenda! Of course!'

Helen leapt to her feet and pulled her phone from her tabard pocket. Suki walked towards her and nudged her head against Helen's leg. 'Not now, Suki, we'll go out later,' Helen said. The dog slunk away to lie outside. Helen held her breath as she pressed Brenda's name on her phone.

Brenda picked up after three rings. 'Aye?'

'Brenda, it's Helen Dexter at the Seaview. Listen, I need to ask you something important. When you worked here, did you take anything from one of the kitchen drawers, a blue folder with sheets of paper inside? Think carefully before you reply.'

There was silence on the other end of the phone.

'Brenda? You still there?'

'Aye. I'm thinking carefully, like you said.'

Helen glanced nervously at Jean, who held up crossed fingers on both hands. 'Brenda?'

'No.'

165

'What do you mean, no?'

'I mean, I took a lot of things out of a lot of drawers when I worked there. But I can't remember a folder.'

'You're certain of that?'

'Aye.'

'If you do remember anything, call me straight back,' Helen said. She rang off, then looked at Jean. 'Brenda didn't take it. I think she's telling the truth.'

'What about Sally? She might have it,' Jean said, then shook her head. 'No, she wouldn't have, would she? Sally never has anything to do with the kitchen. It's my domain and I always keep her out. Oh Helen, it's my fault. If only we hadn't argued; if only I hadn't gone off to work for Miriam, the folder would still be there now. I'm certain it was there when I left that day. Someone must have taken it. But if it wasn't you, me or Brenda, then who else has been in here?'

Helen slapped her hand against her head. 'Poor Sally! She's upstairs holding the fort, trying to stop the guests from leaving. I forgot all about her. Oh Jean. What a nightmare.'

Jean stepped towards Helen and laid her hand gently on her arm. 'Listen to me. You didn't kill Ricky Delmont, and neither did I. He had an allergy. He died on the golf course, in front of witnesses. People saw him, Helen. He was fine one minute, arguing with Norman, then he fell flat on his face and died. Something happened to cause that allergic reaction, something that can't possibly have anything to do with the Seaview.'

Helen's head was reeling. She looked round the kitchen, where the contents of the drawers were strewn messily. 'Something's not right, Jean. I feel it.'

The door to the apartment swung open and Sally burst in, red in the face, still holding the dirty tablecloth. 'Helen, I know you told me to stay upstairs, but I had to come down. It's all right, the guests are in their rooms, I told them not to leave. But you've got two visitors.'

'Visitors?' Jean said, looking at Helen.

A worried look crossed Sally's face. 'It's the police.'

Chapter 22

DS Hutchinson was a tall, good-looking man with broad shoulders and short-clipped silver hair. Helen guessed he was in his late fifties. It was easy to see what Sandra DeVine saw in him. When she came into the hall, he was hovering by the front door reading a leaflet about the Scarborough Fair Collection and Vintage Transport Museum at the Flower of May holiday park.

'Good choice, it's a wonderful place,' she said. She tried to keep her voice as calm as possible, although she was shaking inside.

He stuffed the leaflet in his pocket, extended his hand and gave a wry smile. 'I'd say it's good to see you again, but I wish we could stop meeting like this.'

Helen shook his hand. 'Believe me, the last thing I want is another death connected to the Seaview. You'd better come into the lounge; we'll have privacy there.'

DS Hutchinson pointed through the glass panels of the front door. 'My colleague, DC Hall, is next door at the Vista del Mar. He'll be joining us soon.'

As Helen led him into the lounge, she glanced nervously upstairs. All was quiet.

'My guests are in their rooms,' she said.

'You can call them down after we've had a little chat. I've got some news to share.'

'Oh?' she said. She sat on the window seat. DS Hutchinson took a chair opposite. She looked into his steel-grey eyes. 'Is Sandra well?' she asked.

A smile made its way to his face. 'She's well and we're happy,' he quickly replied.

'She's an old school friend of mine.'

'Yes, she told me she saw you at the reunion last week. Now then, Mrs Dexter, if we could concentrate on the matter at hand. I'm not here to talk about Sandra.'

Helen shifted in her seat. 'Yes, of course. Anything to bring this nasty business to a close. You said you had news?'

DS Hutchinson nodded. 'The press are sniffing around. News of the death of a man on the seafront in a crazy-golf game could ruin the summer season. The tourists will be scared to come here. They'll go to Filey or Bridlington instead. We can't afford to let this drag on. That's why the chief pulled another favour after the toxicology report showed Ricky's cause of death. We did some tests and discovered traces of peanut on the golf course.'

Helen's eyes grew wide.

'It looks like someone deliberately planted it there, Mrs Dexter. Someone who knew about Mr Delmont's allergy.'

'But why would anyone do such a thing?'

'As I mentioned on the phone, the man had enemies, and plenty of them. We're treating his death as possible murder.'

'No!' Helen cried.

'I'm afraid so. You see, peanut was also found on the golf ball he used. While he was arguing with Norman Lawson, he picked the ball up, ready to place it on the first hole to tee off. But before he did that, he . . .'

169

'Kissed it,' Helen said.

DS Hutchinson narrowed his eyes. 'How do you know about that?'

She swallowed hard. 'It's a ritual he carried out before each game. I saw him do it when I was watching him practise last week. Oh my word, that's awful. So he kissed the ball without realising it had peanut on it, and that's what killed him?'

'Exactly,' DS Hutchinson said. 'What I need to ascertain from your guests this morning, and what DC Hall is checking next door, is who knew about the allergy and who didn't. And of those who knew, I need to find out if anyone had a motive for his murder.'

Tears sprang to Helen's eyes. 'This is dreadful, just terrible.'

'On the phone to me earlier, Mrs Dexter, you said that Mr Delmont told you about his allergy when he checked into the Seaview. Is that correct?'

Helen's right leg began to bob up and down. She pressed her hand against her knee to try to stop it. 'He, er . . . he gave me a list of foods that he'd requested while he was staying with me, and his allergy was mentioned on there.'

'Could I have that list, please?'

She bit her lip. There was no way out of this without telling the truth. 'I don't have it.'

'But he gave it to you?'

'Yes. And I gave it to Jean, my cook. She looks after the guests' food; she's done so for decades.'

'Is Jean here? Can I speak to her?'

'She's downstairs, but it's not her fault the list has gone missing. It's mine.'

She felt DS Hutchinson staring at her for a very long time. 'Jean and I have looked for Ricky's list, but we can't find it,' she said. 'I don't usually lose things. Jean left for a few days, she went to work somewhere else, and the folder we kept the list in has vanished. We've turned the kitchen upside down, but it's not there.'

'Could anyone else with access to the property have taken it?'

'Just Brenda, that's my cleaner Sally's mum. She came in to help out while Jean was working elsewhere and Sally was on honeymoon,' Helen explained. 'I called her this morning, but she swears she didn't take the folder, and I believe her. No one else has been downstairs. It's my personal apartment, my home, no one else has keys.' As the words left her lips, her mouth dropped open. 'The keys . . . oh no,' she gasped.

'Mrs Dexter? Are you all right?'

She stood and began pacing the room. Then she stopped pacing and turned to DS Hutchinson.

'Brenda's keys were taken from her handbag while she was at bingo. I had to get the locks changed.'

'So it's possible that someone stole the keys and used them to let themselves in to your apartment?'

Helen gasped again as the horrible realisation of what might have happened sank in. 'That night, when I returned home, my dog, Suki, wasn't her usual self. She was spooked in a way I've never seen before. It was as if . . .' She paused, hardly daring to say the next words. 'It was as if something or someone had frightened her. She was acting weird. There was no sign of a break-in, nothing had been touched, but her eyes were darting around the room as if she was looking for something, and she stayed close to my side. It wasn't like her at all.'

'Mrs Dexter, I think you need to face the possibility that

someone entered your apartment and might have taken the folder with Ricky's list inside.'

'Oh no,' Helen groaned. 'Then they might have discovered his peanut allergy and used the information to kill him.' She sank into a chair. 'I can't go to prison, I'm too young.'

'You won't be going anywhere. None of this is your fault. But we do need to check your CCTV. You have got CCTV, I assume?'

The blood pounded in Helen's ears as she tried to make sense of what he was saying. 'Sorry, what?'

'Mrs Dexter, are you all right? You've gone very pale.'

'I need a minute to pull myself together. This is the worst thing that's ever happened to the Seaview. We're responsible for a man being killed.'

'Mrs Dexter, I will need to speak to this . . .' DS Hutchinson checked his notepad, 'this Brenda you mention, and I'll speak to security at the bingo hall too.'

Helen turned to the picture of Tom. 'Forgive me, my love,' she breathed. She couldn't comprehend the enormity of what had happened. Was it really possible that someone had been in her apartment? She crossed her fingers and hoped not. And yet Suki had acted oddly. There was only one thing for it, she'd have to check her CCTV as DS Hutchinson had suggested.

The doorbell rang, startling her out of her thoughts.

'That'll either be forensics or my colleague DC Hall,' DS Hutchinson said. 'If it's forensics, I'd be grateful if you could show them up to the dead man's room. Once they've finished up there and taken all his belongings, you can treat the room as normal.'

'Normal?' Helen gasped. 'I don't think anything will be normal again.'

She pulled herself up to standing using a table for support, then walked slowly to the lounge door and out into the hall. She was in shock and had to force her legs forward. Two forensics officers introduced themselves, then a plump, jolly-faced man with short brown hair walked into the Seaview.

'Morning, Helen. Remember me?'

'DC Hall, of course,' she replied. 'Your colleague's in the lounge.'

'Any chance of a coffee?' he beamed. 'The miserable woman next door wouldn't put the kettle on.'

She closed the door and ushered DC Hall into the lounge. Then she took the master key from her tabard pocket and indicated to the forensics team. 'Please, follow me.'

Upstairs, she left the officers to get on with their work and headed back down. As she passed Olga's room, the door opened.

'Olga!' she cried, alarmed.

'Yes?' Olga said.

'Are you heading out now?' Helen cast a nervous glance down the stairs.

'I demand to know why we are under house arrest!'

'We have a small problem . . . I mean, there's someone who needs to speak to you before you leave.'

'Who? Why?'

'It's the police, Olga. They need to speak to all of you, about Ricky.'

'Oh.'

'I'm afraid so.'

Olga marched upstairs and Helen heard her rap hard at Alice's door. 'Alice. Come.' Then she returned to the first floor and did the same at Freddy's door.

173

Alice and Freddy both arrived on the landing at the same time as Marty and Marilyn came out of their room together.

'Everyone. Come,' Olga said.

Helen watched as she began marching down the stairs and the team members followed.

'Left, right. Left, right,' Olga commanded as they walked. Helen was at the back, and found herself marching and swinging her arms in time to the older woman's call.

'Halt!' Olga said once they reached the hall. The group lined up and looked at Helen. She pushed open the door to the lounge, where DS Hutchinson and DC Hall were seated.

'Please come in, everyone,' DS Hutchinson said, waving his hand at the empty seats.

As the crazy golfers filed into the room, Helen offered to send up some coffee. DC Hall sidled up to her and whispered in her ear. 'About this coffee . . .'

'Yes?'

'Might there be a slice of Jean's cake too?'

Chapter 23

Helen ran downstairs as fast as her shaking legs would carry her. When she reached the kitchen, Jean was drizzling citrus icing over a lemon cake, and Sally was stroking Suki's ears. All three of them looked up when she walked in.

'What's going on?' Jean asked.

Helen sank into a chair, then ran her hands through her hair. 'The police think someone let themselves in here with Brenda's missing keys.' She slowly raised her eyes. 'They also asked me if anyone apart from us three has access to the kitchen.'

'Just my mum when she worked here while I was on honeymoon,' Sally said.

'I've rung your mum; she swears she didn't touch the folder or take Ricky's list.'

'Jimmy?' Jean asked.

Helen shook her head. 'No, it's someone else. Someone who stole Brenda's keys from her handbag while she was playing bingo. Someone who knew that Brenda was working for me and that Ricky Delmont was staying here.'

'Sounds a bit far-fetched, if you ask me.' Jean turned away to put the kettle on. Helen reached her hand out to Suki and the dog walked towards her to sit at her side.

'What did you see that night, love?' she said.

Jean spun around. 'Who, me?'

'I'm talking to the dog, Jean.'

'I wouldn't hold your breath for a reply.'

Helen stared into Suki's glassy eyes and stroked her under her chin. 'Who was it, girl? Was someone in here? Did you see them? Is that why you were acting so strange?'

'Wouldn't she have gone for anyone who'd broken in?' Sally asked.

'No. If someone had been threatening me, raising their voice, she might have growled or bared her teeth. She might have been curious if someone had let themselves in without any fuss or aggression towards her, but otherwise she wouldn't have batted an eyelid. You know how placid she is; she wouldn't hurt a fly. A stranger coming in without forcing the door, letting themselves in with a key, she'd accept that, although it would confuse her. Anyway, a forensics team are in Ricky's room now. DS Hutchinson and DC Hall have arrived to question the guests. I've offered to send coffee up.' She looked at Jean's cake cooling on the kitchen top. 'I don't suppose I could take a few slices of that too?'

Jean opened a drawer and pulled out a knife, then gathered a pile of plates and began to slice the warm cake. A wonderful zesty lemon aroma filled the air. She gave a wry smile.

'Anything to keep the police sweet.'

Helen leaned back in her chair and sighed deeply. 'Oh Jean, why is this happening again? Another guest murdered, the police here . . . It's too much to cope with. Just when we've got our four stars, this goes and happens. It'll ruin us, I know.'

'Don't be daft, lass,' Jean replied without looking up. 'Let the police do their job. Things will soon get back to normal, you'll see.'

'I wish I could believe you. But this is the third time one of our guests has died in mysterious circumstances. My head's swimming. One minute I think we did everything right by Ricky and his allergy and we can't possibly be to blame. But the next, I doubt myself and blame myself for all of it.'

Jean pushed her glasses up to the bridge of her nose.

'Now listen to me. The Seaview's always been peanut-free, ever since that incident with the little boy that summer you and Tom bought the place. Nothing that Ricky ate or touched in here killed him. Nothing.'

Helen dropped her gaze for a second, then leapt out of her chair. 'I should check the CCTV from the night I was out.'

'Surprised you haven't done it before,' Jean said.

'I didn't think I needed to.'

Jean and Sally huddled around her as she moved to the small monitor on the kitchen wall. She picked up her phone and opened the app that controlled the system. Within seconds, the screen was displaying the night she had been out at the reunion.

'There's someone there, look!' She pointed.

'Probably a lost tourist walking along the back lane,' Jean said.

'No, Jean, that's not a tourist ambling about. That's someone heading straight to our back door.'

They watched as a figure in a thick black anorak with its hood up, obscuring the person's face, walked directly to the back of the Seaview and raised an arm. Immediately the display went black.

'They covered the camera up with something!' Helen cried.

'Crikey, Helen. So it looks like there was someone in here after all,' Sally said. 'Why didn't you switch the burglar alarm on?'

Helen looked at Suki. 'Same reason as ever: the dog would set it

177

off. I've always given her the run of the place. It's not right to keep her outside on the patio when it gets cold at night.' Her hands began to shake. She stepped back from the monitor and looked around the kitchen. 'I should tell the police about this, but I can't bear it. My beloved Seaview the scene of a crime. There must be fingerprints all over the kitchen.'

'I doubt there'll be any at all,' Jean said sagely. 'If the person who stole Brenda's keys is the same person we've just seen on the monitor, they came equipped to cover the camera. They knew you had CCTV; they might have staked the place out.'

A shiver ran down Helen's spine. 'Oh no,' she moaned as Jean carried on.

'And if they'd planned in advance to bring a cloth to hide the camera, they'd have made sure to wear gloves so they'd leave no trace.'

'What am I going to do?' Helen said, looking from Sally to Jean.

Jean turned away and poured water from the kettle into a large flask to make coffee. Then she arranged cups and saucers on a tray, along with slices of drizzle cake. 'Where were your guests on the night you went to your school reunion?'

Helen thought for a moment, then shrugged. 'They were all upstairs in the lounge when Marie drove me home. I suppose they must have gone out for dinner somewhere, but I've no idea where.'

'Helen, you've got to tell the police what we've just seen on the monitor,' Sally urged.

Jean pushed at her glasses again. 'Sally's right. Do the decent thing and come clean about everything. It's the only way we'll get through this. There are two detectives upstairs. Let them earn their wage and do their job. I'll stay here for as long as you need me today. I don't need to visit Mum in the care home. They've got her on new tablets for her legs and they knock her out, so she sleeps most of the time. I'll send the coffee and cake up in the dumbwaiter.'

Helen and Sally left the kitchen and walked up the stairs. At the dumbwaiter in the hall, Helen lifted the first tray and handed it to Sally. Then she took the second tray and walked into the lounge. As the two of them poured coffee and handed out slices of cake, the Seaview's doorbell rang.

'Excuse me, I'll be right back,' Helen said.

She walked along the hall, curious about who might be there. There were no guests expected, and the *No Vacancy* sign was hanging in the window, so no one would be enquiring on the off chance. She pulled the door open and was met by a bookish-looking man wearing tortoiseshell glasses. Her first impression was that he looked like an owl. He had a high forehead with swept-back auburn hair, and was well dressed in a blue jacket and dark jeans.

She smiled. 'Hello there, can I help?'

The man was standing halfway up the steps, but when Helen greeted him, he took two steps forward. He wasn't exactly invading her space, but he was close enough to make her uncomfortable. She gripped the door handle and stood her ground.

'Jack Malone,' he announced as he thrust a card into her hand. Automatically she glanced down at it. It was black, with silver lettering. He was talking non-stop, and she tried to make sense of what he was saying. Catching the words 'Ricky Delmont . . . suspicious death . . . staying here . . .' she glared at him. DS Hutchinson had warned her that the press would be on to the story, but she hadn't expected them so soon.

'You vultures don't waste much time, do you?' she said, trying to shut the door against him. But he was too quick, too well practised, too full of himself. He stuck his big boot into the doorway to stop it from closing.

'I'm a busy man, Mrs Dexter. Or can I call you Helen?'

She rattled the door against his foot, but it wouldn't budge. 'You can't call me anything. Now get lost, go on.'

'I just need a few words!' he called.

'No chance,' she said, squashing the door hard against his boot.

Eventually he pulled his foot away, and Helen shut the door and locked it. Then she drew the heavy green curtain that she used only in winter to keep out the cold sea air. She waited a moment, her heart beating wildly. She needed to calm down before she returned to the lounge. The curtain twitched.

'Helen. I need to speak to you.'

It was Jack Malone again, poking his fingers through the letter box. Helen bent down.

'I've got nothing to say to you. And I don't appreciate being doorstepped.'

'I'll be back. I don't give up easily, and I know that you don't either.'

'What's that supposed to mean?' she said, perturbed.

'I know all about you, Helen Dexter,' he said darkly. 'And I know about the Seaview's history. I know Ricky Delmont is the third person to have stayed here who's died. That's a rather unfortunate number of dead guests for a small hotel. If you know what's good for you, you'll talk to me first, before you speak to *The Scarborough Times*.'

'Get lost,' Helen said, more assertively than she felt.

As she stood up, she felt her knees shake. She leaned against the wall, straightened her tabard, then walked back into the lounge to face the detectives and her guests. But as she did so, through the bay window she spotted Jack Malone on the pavement outside. He was deep in conversation with her best friend, Marie.

'What the . . .?' she muttered. Nothing made sense. What was the journalist doing with Marie? More to the point, what was Marie doing with him?

'Helen? Is everything all right?' DC Hall asked. 'This is smashing cake, by the way.'

Helen wanted to run back to the hall, to yank the door open and yell to Marie not to say anything to Jack. But her legs wouldn't move. Her mind refused to believe what her eyes were telling her. And yet there it was, unfolding in front of her. She watched in astonishment as the two of them walked to Marie's red sports car. Jack slid into the passenger seat, Marie took her place behind the wheel, then the car roared off down Windsor Terrace.

Chapter 24

'Mrs Dexter, have a seat,' DS Hutchinson said.

Helen was reeling from what she'd just seen. What on earth was Marie doing with the journalist, and why had he got in her car? She racked her brains to try and remember whether her friend had ever mentioned Jack before. 'Sorry, what?' she said.

DS Hutchinson indicated the chair next to Sally. Helen sat down, and patted Sally's hand when she saw the worried expression on her face. Then she turned her gaze to the detectives. DS Hutchinson was leaning forward in his seat. DC Hall was wiping crumbs from his lips with one of the Seaview's linen napkins. She glanced around the room at her guests. They all looked as nervous and tense as she felt. She saw Freddy and Olga exchange a look, before Freddy whipped his gaze away and stared at the carpet instead. She saw Marty drape his arm around Marilyn's shoulders, holding her close. There was a distant look in Alice's eyes.

Her worried thoughts turned to the intruder in her apartment. Her gaze lingered on each of her guests. Was it possible it had been one of them? They all had a reason for hating Ricky, but did they hate him enough to want to do him in? The thought of someone in her apartment made her feel angry, violated and sick to the stomach. The idea of someone rummaging around in her private rooms was unthinkable. And yet there had been no break-in, no rummaging, and nothing of value had been taken. She hadn't noticed anything out of the ordinary, apart from Suki acting oddly. But whoever had been there had taken the folder with details of Ricky's allergy inside. Was it possible that that person had used the information they'd found there to kill him?

She looked at Freddy again, at his long legs sprawled across the carpet. The figure in the anorak caught on CCTV couldn't have been Freddy, as he was too tall; his gangly frame would have been obvious. Likewise, it couldn't have been Olga, for she was too short. She looked at Marty, Marilyn and Alice. Yes, it could have been any one of them. But Alice had been married to Ricky and would have known about his allergy; there was no need for her to steal a list of food. That only left Marty and Marilyn, and there was a lot to unpick about that peculiar couple and Ricky's efforts to split them up.

She suddenly became aware of DS Hutchinson's voice. To her embarrassment, she noticed him staring straight at her.

'Well, Mrs Dexter, is that something you could do for us?' he asked.

She shifted uncomfortably in her seat. What was he asking? What had she missed?

At her side, Sally turned to her. 'I'm sure we can allow the police to use the dining room to question the guests one by one, isn't that right, Helen?'

'What? Yes. Yes, of course,' Helen replied quickly, breathing a sigh of relief. She smiled at Sally. 'Thanks,' she whispered.

DS Hutchinson stood. 'I think we'll start with more questions for you, Mrs Dexter,' he said. 'Please, lead the way to the dining room.'

Helen walked from the lounge with DS Hutchinson in tow. As

they crossed the hall, two forensics experts walked down the stairs carrying Ricky's belongings in bags.

'Speak to DC Hall before you leave,' DS Hutchinson ordered them.

He entered the dining room and sat at a table. Helen closed the door and sat down opposite him. 'What can I help you with?' she asked.

'Everything, Mrs Dexter. I want to know all about your guests. How they behaved around Ricky Delmont and how he was with them. Tell me everything you know.' He pulled a notepad and pen from an inside pocket of his jacket.

'Everything? I'm not sure I know where to start.'

'I always find the beginning's a good place,' he said.

She looked at his rugged face, where silver hairs sprouted in a neat moustache. 'Well, I should probably start by telling you something I've just found out.'

'Oh? And what's that?'

'After you mentioned my CCTV, I took a look at it, and it does show an intruder on the night I was out.'

DS Hutchinson's eyebrows shot up as Helen told him about the hooded figure captured on camera.

'We'll need to watch the footage, of course,' he said. 'Did you recognise the intruder?'

'I couldn't see them, never mind recognise them. They put something over the camera.'

'I see. Well, tell me about your guests. I understand the young woman with the red hair was once married to the deceased. What was their relationship like while they were both staying with you?'

Helen unloaded everything she knew, and what a relief it was.

As words flew from her lips, DS Hutchinson had trouble writing his notes fast enough. She told him about Alice and Olga bad-mouthing Ricky at every opportunity. She told him about the phone conversation when she'd overheard Freddy saying he was out for revenge. This made the detective's forehead crease.

'Go on, please,' he urged. And so Helen continued, telling him about Marty threatening Ricky and telling him to leave Marilyn alone. 'No one ever thinks I'm watching them,' she said. 'But a hotel landlady notices everything. There's not much gets past me.'

'Is there anything else you can remember?'

She bit her lip. Her stomach churned with anxiety about the missing blue folder. 'Look, I'm feeling dreadful about it all because I have the most horrible feeling that the Seaview is responsible for his death. I keep blaming myself. See, I had a falling-out with my cook, Jean, and she went to work for the woman who runs the Vista del Mar, next door. If only we hadn't argued. If only Jean hadn't left. If only I hadn't been so wrapped up in my own problems, maybe I would have noticed that someone had been in my apartment and taken the folder. It's going around in my head all the time.'

'We'll get to the bottom of it, Mrs Dexter, you'll see. Please, try not to worry. In the meantime, I need to ask you to keep a close eye on your guests. Anything suspicious, call me at once. Is there anything you can tell us about Ricky Delmont? What was he like when he stayed here?'

'Unpleasant,' Helen said, without thinking. Then she put her hand across her mouth. 'I'm sorry, I shouldn't speak ill of the dead.'

'Go ahead. I'd appreciate your honesty.'

She decided not to hold back. 'OK, then. He was rude and nasty, not just to me but to the others staying here. He even threatened my dog! And he did something unusual when he checked in. He asked me to sign a non-disclosure agreement.'

DS Hutchinson stopped writing and laid his pen on the table. 'Do you have a copy?'

'No, it was in the folder that's disappeared. It was an odd document, amateurish. I'm not sure how legally binding it was. It looked like he'd typed it himself. I did think about having it looked at by my solicitor in town, but I never got around to it. He kept a copy for himself. It might be with his belongings.'

'What did it say precisely?'

'That I mustn't reveal what was on his list of foods, or his allergy, or divulge anything unusual that I found in his room.'

DS Hutchinson leaned forward. 'And did you find anything unusual?'

'Yes, he slept with his golf clubs and balls. Or at least, they were under the duvet when I cleaned his room. It gave my cleaner, Brenda, a shock the first time she saw it. She screamed the place down. She thought she'd found a dead body.'

DS Hutchinson leaned back in his seat. 'Sleeping with his putters and balls? That's highly unusual.'

'Very,' Helen said. 'Not something I've seen before. But his ex-wife, Alice, said it was one of the reasons she divorced him.'

'Can't be easy sharing the marital bed with crazy-golf equipment,' DS Hutchinson mused. 'Right, before I bring your guests in here to speak to each of them separately about the deceased, I'll accompany you downstairs to watch the CCTV. We'll need to take a copy. I'll ask DC Hall to stay up here to ensure nobody leaves the lounge. Thank you for everything you've told me, Mrs Dexter. Is there anything else at all that you remember?'

Helen thought for a moment. 'Oh my word, yes.'

'Go on,' he said.

'Last week I took the dog for a walk along the seafront, and I was talking to Norman at the crazy-golf course – the man you arrested for Ricky's murder.'

'He's been released now,' DS Hutchinson said.

'There were three men there, and they were acting . . .'

'Suspiciously?'

She shook her head. 'Not exactly. But they were taking bets on the game, talking into their phones. Real wide boys, they were, I don't know how else to explain them. They didn't have Scarborough accents – in fact they didn't sound like they were from Yorkshire at all, but that's par for the course around here, we get tourists from all over the country. I think these men sounded cockney. Anyway, they were unusually dressed for a day at the beach. Definitely not tourists. They wore expensive sharp suits, big gaudy watches, highly polished shoes with pointed toes. Lots of aftershave, I remember. They didn't half pong.'

'And they were taking bets on the game?' DS Hutchinson probed.

'Yes, serious money. One bet was a thousand pounds. I heard one of them on their phone when I walked past. He said something about it not being worth putting money on Ricky Delmont to win this year's tournament. He said he had inside information that Ricky's team wouldn't win . . . Oh no.' She paused as the words she'd overheard came rushing back.

'Mrs Dexter?' DS Hutchinson prompted.

She snapped her gaze to the detective. 'He said, "Delmont's dead in the water this year."'

Chapter 25

After Helen had been questioned by DS Hutchinson, she returned downstairs to Jean and found her sitting with her feet up on the sofa. The radio was tuned to a documentary about duffel coats, the presenter's voice calming and soft. Suki lay on the carpet. When Helen walked in, Jean swung her feet off the sofa.

'Don't get up, Jean, enjoy your rest. Where are your shoes? I hope you've put them somewhere safe; you know Suki likes to chew them.'

'I've worked here long enough to know that. Don't worry, they're shut away in the cupboard.'

Helen slumped into the armchair. 'Well, I told the detectives everything I know. They'll come down to take a copy of the CCTV, and they're calling forensics back to dust the kitchen and back door for fingerprints.'

'It's like *CSI: Scarbados* in here.'

'It's not funny, Jean. Once news gets out, we'll be ruined. I'll have to close the Seaview and sell up.'

Jean wagged a finger. 'I'll hear no more about you moving on and selling up. You're letting your imagination run away with you again. Now, let's get through the rest of today before you start getting daft ideas about spending your future elsewhere. Is Sally still upstairs with the guests?'

'Yes, but she's due to leave soon; she's stayed on longer than she was supposed to already. She says she doesn't mind, but I'll pay her overtime to compensate. Speaking of Sally, I've decided to visit her mum.'

'Brenda,' Jean sighed.

Helen couldn't fail to notice her tone of disapproval. The two of them hadn't hit it off.

'When you see her, give her some pointers on politeness,' Jean said.

Helen ignored the cutting comment, even if Jean was right. 'I want to ask her about the night at the bingo when her keys were stolen. I need to speak to her before the detectives do, because she'll be scared when they turn up. She'll be more relaxed talking to me. She might remember something that could help sort this mess out.'

'And stop you from doing something you'll regret, like selling the Seaview,' Jean added. 'When will you go and see her?'

'Tomorrow morning. I'll walk there and take Suki with me. I need the fresh air. It feels claustrophobic in here after everything that's happened.'

'How many times do I have to say it? The man died on a crazy-golf course on the seafront with no connection to the Seaview,' Jean said firmly.

'But I still can't help feeling to blame. I've got guests upstairs who are struggling with what's happened, and there are all kinds of bad vibes. I've heard things I shouldn't have, and you'll never guess what I saw while I was up there just now: only my so-called best friend talking to a journalist who was trying to doorstep me, asking for information on the dead man. He sounded threatening; said he knew about the other guests who'd stayed here who'd died.'

189

Jean looked over the top of her glasses. 'They died elsewhere in Scarborough. Nobody died here,' she said.

'Then there's Jimmy to think about . . .'

'Give him a ring, go and see him. He's good for you.'

Helen didn't stop to acknowledge Jean's words.

'. . . and on top of all of that, there's the mystery of the invitations to my fiftieth birthday. I can't be doing with the fuss of a party, Jean, you know I'm not up to it, even if I wanted to celebrate, which I don't. Are you sure you're not behind it?'

Jean held her hands up in surrender. 'Believe me, if I was arranging a party, I'd have asked you for suggestions to make a list for the cash and carry to buy all the food.'

Helen felt Jean was telling the truth. If she had been behind it, she would have been more preoccupied.

'It's unsettling, Jean. In fact, it's downright scary knowing someone's organising this without my consent. The last thing I need, with a dead guest on my hands, is to worry about a party.'

'Then think, love. Who knows you're coming up to fifty?'

'Marie. You. Sally. My friends Bev and Sue. I haven't seen either of them since the day Ricky died, but I've since spoken to them both on the phone. They wouldn't organise a party without involving me, and neither would Marie. Yet someone's gone to the expense of having invitations printed and sent to my family and friends. Tom's sister in Shetland rang the other day to say she'd received one. I had to tell her there's no party. How did the hoaxer even get her address? It's awful, Jean. It feels like someone's having a cruel laugh.' She thought for a moment. 'It wouldn't be Miriam next door, would it?'

'Pfft! Don't speak to me about her!'

Helen leaned forward. 'What exactly happened between you two when you worked at the Vista del Mar? What was she like? You know she put your picture on her website, offering *our* award-winning breakfasts to her guests. The cheek of the woman.'

Jean tutted. 'Miriam's as patronising as you'd expect. Everything we've ever assumed about her is true. She thinks she's slumming it in Scarborough, you know. Oh yes, she's always going on about how much better Bridlington is, how it attracts a better class of guest. I said to her one day, I said, "Miriam, love, if Bridlington's more your cup of tea, why don't you sell up and move there instead?" and do you know what she said in reply?'

Helen shook her head.

'She said . . .' Jean sat up straight, pushed her glasses up to the bridge of her nose and affected an accent that made Helen laugh. She sounded exactly like Miriam. 'She said, "Jean, dear, I couldn't possibly leave Scarborough. It needs me and the Vista del Mar. You see, my hotel offers a quality break for the more discerning guest. If I left, where would those guests stay?" Well, you can imagine the look I gave her. All the time I worked there, she kept calling me "Jean, dear", which really got on my nerves. And you should hear the way she treats her cleaners.'

'Cleaners? She can afford more than one?'

'No, she only has one at a time, but she doesn't half get through them. She had two in the short time I was there. They don't stay long once they've suffered her biting remarks. She's lucky if they last more than one day. In fact, she's looking for a new cleaner right now. She's got agency staff working until she finds someone permanent.'

Helen sank back in her chair.

'You look tired, love,' Jean said.

'I'm worn out. My head's scrambled after everything that's happened. Once the detectives have taken the CCTV, and forensics have finished dusting the kitchen for fingerprints or whatever they need, I'll take Suki for a long *w-a-l-k* on the *b-e-a-c-h*.' She spelled out the words so the dog wouldn't leap to her feet and stand by the door before Helen was ready. 'I've got to clear my head.' She ran her hand through her hair. 'Jimmy wants me to go to his new place for dinner. I've been blowing hot and cold with him. The least I can do is accept his offer and sit down with him to lay my feelings on the line.'

'His *new* place? He's living in Scarborough now?' Jean said, surprised.

'He's bought a house on West Park, by Falsgrave Park.'

'Nice.' She nodded approvingly. 'Look, love, I can handle the detectives and forensics in here. I can show them the CCTV, I know how it works. There's cake left and I'll make more coffee. I'll lock up when I leave. You go out with Suki for your walk on the beach.'

Suki stood to attention and padded to the door. Helen grimaced. 'I was trying not to get her worked up for that yet. That's why I spelled the words out.'

Jean shrugged. 'It looks like she knows what's best for you.'

'Well, I do need to get out. I might even treat myself to a bite to eat at the Hideout café by Peasholm Park. They've got seats outside and I can take Suki there.'

Jean stood up and smoothed down her skirt. 'Go,' she ordered. 'I'll see you tomorrow.'

Helen walked to the cupboard under the stairs and fetched

Suki's lead. She clipped it to the dog's collar, then picked up her fleece jacket and tied the sleeves around her waist.

'Thanks again, Jean,' she said as she went to the door.

Outside, she glanced up at the camera by the back door. She wondered again who had been in her home. Who had taken the folder? There'd been no sign on the CCTV of the intruder leaving the apartment, so the cloth they'd used to cover up the lens must still have been there on their exit. She had to assume that it had blown away in the wind.

She rounded the corner on to Windsor Terrace with Suki at her side. The beautiful wide sands of the North Bay beach spread out in front of her, and the sun glistened on the sea. On Marine Drive, she saw an open-top bus filled with tourists. An ice-cream van, three motorbikes and two caravans were following it. To her right stood the impressive ruins of the castle, overlooking both bays.

As she headed towards King's Parade, planning to walk down the hill to the beach, she spotted Alice sitting on a bench. Her first instinct was to keep walking. But as she drew closer, she saw that Alice was crying, and her heart went out to the young woman. Despite his many faults, Ricky had been her ex-husband, and she must have loved him once. Helen knew only too well what it was like to lose a loved one. She carried her grief over Tom close to her heart, like a pebble tucked safely away.

'This way, girl,' she told Suki as she headed towards the bench.

Chapter 26

'Alice?' Helen said gently.

Alice looked up, pulled a paper tissue from her pocket and wiped it across her eyes. Then she shifted along the bench and Helen took her cue to sit down. Suki lay at her feet on the ground.

'I don't mean to intrude. I'll go if you want to be alone. But I was concerned when I saw you. I was passing with the dog, taking her for a walk.'

Alice swallowed hard and screwed the tissue in her hands. 'It's all right, you can stay. I've just finished with the police. Or rather, they've finished with me. They put me through the wringer in there.'

Helen was saddened to hear this. 'They should be more sensitive. I'll have a word with DS Hutchinson if you like. I know him.'

Alice shook her head. 'No, please don't say anything. I'm just glad it's over. They knew I was married to Ricky, of course. I mean, something like that isn't going to stay quiet and there's no reason why it should. But the way they spoke to me in there, it felt as if they were accusing me of his death . . . of his murder. I'd never do anything like that. Sure, the guy had his faults, and yes, he had enemies. As a couple, we'd fallen out of love years ago, but I'd never hurt him, Helen. I wouldn't hurt anyone. I'm not like that.'

She began crying again and pulled another tissue from her pocket. Helen looked at the sea and waited for her sobs to subside.

Her mind whirled with questions, and although she knew now was not the right time to ask them, when Alice was so upset, she also knew that she might not get another chance to speak to her alone. It was the first time she'd seen her away from Olga's watchful eye.

'I guess Olga's being interviewed now,' she said, watching Alice's reaction.

'Yes, but there's not much she can tell them.' Alice sniffed. 'She never had a lot of time for Ricky, even when we were married. She avoided him like the plague, said there was bad energy about him. I should have listened to her. She was right all along.'

Helen kept her gaze fixed ahead at the sea.

'Did you know about his allergy?' she asked.

From the corner of her eye, she saw Alice nod her head. 'He was always strict about what he ate, always careful about letting people know about his allergy when he ate out. I'm sure he must have given you his list of foods when he checked in. He always handed it over wherever he was staying in a hotel. Although the only things he wouldn't eat were peanuts and porridge.'

'Porridge?' Helen said. Her voice came out in a squeak. She couldn't remember porridge being mentioned on Ricky's list.

Alice was blowing her nose and wiping her eyes and didn't seem to notice. 'Oh, he couldn't stand the stuff. He wasn't allergic to it, but just the look of it used to set his nerves on edge. It was only peanuts he was allergic to.'

'Did your teammates know about the allergy?' Helen asked.

'No, there was no reason for them to know,' Alice replied. 'Olga's the only one who knew Ricky outside of the crazy-golf world, and that's only because she and I were once good friends.'

'Does that mean you're not good friends now?' Helen probed.

Alice shrugged. 'Not so much. People change, you know how it is.'

She turned her head away, and Helen let the subject drop. They sat in silence for a few moments before she dared ask another question.

'Does this mean Marty and Marilyn didn't know Ricky outside the world of crazy golf?'

'No, none of them knew him on a personal level. They only ever met him at crazy-golf matches.'

Helen was intrigued. This wasn't what she'd gathered when she'd overheard Marty ordering Ricky to leave his wife alone.

'Ricky's reputation went before him and he wasn't well liked,' Alice went on. 'There was no reason why any of the team would socialise with him away from the circuit. I don't even think his own teammates liked him that much. They tolerated him because he was such a good player.'

Helen looked down the hill at the waves frilling on the shore. Dogs ran on the sand, chased balls and bounded into the sea.

'*You* must have liked him once upon a time.' She looked at Alice, ready to gauge her reaction. She was worried she'd gone too far and Alice would think she was sticking her nose into her business. Which of course she was. But she needed to find out more about her guests to help uncover Ricky's killer. The sooner this was over, the better for the Seaview and her own peace of mind.

Alice dabbed the tissue at her eyes. 'Oh, I loved him, Helen, once. I thought the sun shone out of him. He was kind, loving, sweet. He was the one who got me involved in crazy golf. I hadn't played it before I met him, not seriously. Of course I'd played while on holiday, but that was all it was then, a game. Ricky was obsessed by it, and I was in love, obsessed with him. I'd have done anything to please him, and so I started playing seriously and we became the dream team. We played tournaments as a couple, then Olga spotted us on a course in Tynemouth. It was a gorgeous course by the beach, with dinosaur models that sprayed water when you scored a hole-in-one.' She stifled a laugh. 'Sorry, it feels wrong to bring up happy memories after what happened.'

'It's not wrong,' Helen said gently. 'You loved him once and no one can take the good memories away. Believe me, I know.'

Alice gave her a look, but Helen stayed silent. She didn't feel the need to share her memories of Tom; she preferred to keep them securely inside.

'What about . . .' She paused. Glancing at Alice, she saw the girl sitting up straight on the bench. She looked brighter, more alert than she'd done when Helen had first found her. If there'd been any doubt in her mind that Alice was going to start crying again, she wouldn't have persisted with her questions. The last thing she wanted was to upset her in the same way the police had done, quizzing her about Ricky. But she needed answers, so she decided to press on. 'What about Freddy, did he know Ricky away from crazy golf?'

There, she'd said it. Maybe now she'd find out about the revenge she'd overheard Freddy say he was planning to take. But she was stunned when Alice shook her head.

'No, I don't think they ever met apart from when we played.'

'Oh,' Helen said, baffled. 'And when they did meet, were they, um, friendly?' She knew she had to be careful. She didn't want to make Alice suspicious about why she was asking. It might make her clam up.

'Not particularly,' Alice said. 'Ricky didn't open up to people, he wasn't a friendly sort of guy. Kept himself to himself. He was private. He hated anyone to know things about him.'

'Like his allergy?' Helen said.

Alice nodded. 'That's why he didn't carry an EpiPen, although his doctor insisted he should. He didn't want anyone to think he had a weakness, in case they exploited it. And now someone has, and he's dead.' She leaned forward, balled her hands in her eyes and began sobbing again.

Helen laid her arm gently across the young woman's shoulders. 'That's it, let it out,' she said soothingly.

Once Alice's tears began to subside, Helen asked if she'd like to go back to the Seaview.

'No, I want to sit here for a while. I find the sea very calming. Olga's going to join me when she's finished with the police.'

Right on cue, the older woman arrived, striding towards the bench and looking menacingly at Helen.

'I'm here. You can go now.'

'Well, yes . . . I, um . . . I'll leave you to talk,' Helen said. Olga's command struck her as rude. Nonetheless, she stood up, Suki too. Olga slid on to the bench in the spot she had vacated.

'Thanks, Helen,' Alice said.

Helen left the two women sitting together.

'Make it all go away, Suki,' she said to the dog as they walked down the hill to the beach.

Helen reached the main road that ran along the seafront at the bottom of the hill and waited for a gap in the traffic. Another open-top bus came towards her, filled with tourists waving and smiling. She waved back, and a cheer went up. The bus was followed by two cars and a motorbike. She stared in shock. One of the cars was a cherry-red sports car. Marie's car. Marie was driving, and in the passenger seat was Jack Malone.

'What the . . .?' Helen muttered under her breath. This was the second time she'd seen Marie and Jack together.

As the sports car sailed by, Helen waved, but Marie didn't notice.

When it was safe to cross, Helen walked on to the golden sands. Suki stretched her legs, although she didn't venture far. When Helen and Tom had first collected her from the rehoming centre, they weren't able to let her off the lead, as her instinct to chase was too strong. She'd be off like a shot, chasing balls, other dogs, a feather on the breeze, and they'd have trouble getting her back. Greyhounds were sighthounds, their chase instinct triggered by light and speed. But now Suki was older, calmer, and she usually, though not always, stayed close to Helen's side.

Helen's boots sank into the sand, and she breathed in the sea air and turned her face to the sun. She took a few moments to steady and ground her thoughts. She heard the whisper of the waves as they broke on the shore, seagulls cawing overhead, children laughing, dogs barking. She felt her shoulders sink. It felt good to be on the beach. It felt even better to be out of the Seaview, and that was something she felt guilty admitting. She thought of Jean dealing with forensics and detectives, wonderful Jean doing all of that for her. She made another vow never to take her old friend for granted. As for Marie, that was another matter. She needed to find out what was going on.

She pulled her phone from her pocket. Marie's voicemail kicked in and she left a message.

'It's me. We need to talk.'

Chapter 27

That evening, no matter how many times Helen checked her phone, Marie didn't call back. When her phone did ring, it was DC Hall calling to say that if he and DS Hutchinson had any more questions, they'd be back in touch.

'In the meantime . . .' he began.

From the tone of his voice, Helen knew what was coming. She'd been through this before, when two of her previous guests at the Seaview had been killed. One of them, an Elvis impersonator in town for a fan convention, had been found dead in Peasholm Park with his blue suede shoes stolen. The other, the leading lady in a theatrical troupe, had been found dead on the South Bay beach. Did other Scarborough landladies have as many problems as she had at the Seaview?

'In the meantime, you want me to keep an eye on my guests, is that right?' she sighed.

'I'm afraid so, Helen. It seems you know the drill by now. Any behaviour that strikes you as suspicious, anything you think we should know, call us right away.'

After DC Hall rang off, Helen sat on the sofa with Suki at her feet, watching TV. Jimmy texted to confirm his dinner invitation at his new house the following night. She smiled. Finally, something to look forward to and take her mind off the death of Ricky

Delmont. She sent a reply to say she'd be there. Then she opened her laptop to deal with emails, relieved to see that more bookings had arrived for the summer. But then she saw five cancellations. Five. That could only mean one thing. Word must surely be out about Ricky Delmont's death, and the Seaview would have likely been mentioned online. A quick search confirmed her worst fears. The hotel was named at the end of many news articles about Ricky's death as the place where he'd stayed in the town. She sighed. Her heart felt heavy.

She closed the lid of her laptop, then walked around the apartment turning off lights. Before she headed to her bedroom, she glanced nervously around. She went to the back door to double-check that she'd locked it, even though she was certain she had. She also double-checked the windows and patio doors. Knowing there'd been an intruder inside her home had really shaken her. The plaque with its four stars looked accusingly at her from its spot in the kitchen. A stab of guilt went through her for not finding the time to hang it by the front door. Reminding herself that she had more pressing problems to worry about, she turned away from the plaque and went to bed, where she fell into a fitful sleep.

When she woke the next morning, the first thing she did was check her phone, but there was nothing from Marie, no missed calls or texts. However, she was cheered to read a message from Jimmy saying he was looking forward to seeing her later. She couldn't recall the last time anyone had cooked dinner for her.

From the kitchen came the rattle of pans, cupboards and drawers, and Jean chirpy-chirpy-cheeping along to a song on the radio. Helen pulled herself out of bed and padded into the living room in her dressing gown. Suki immediately walked to her, and she sat in a chair, fussing over the dog, stroking her and reassuring her. How she wished she had someone to do the same thing to her. To run their hands through her hair, to tell her everything would be all right. It was still early days between her and Jimmy. Too early for that sort of thing. The thought of Jimmy made her smile, and she realised how much she was looking forward to seeing him that evening for dinner in his new home.

'Morning, Jean,' she said.

'Morning, love. You all right today?'

'Could be better. DC Hall rang last night. He confirmed his team are all done in here. Unless we can tell them anything about the guests, anything odd that we notice.'

Jean rolled her eyes. 'Odd? That lot upstairs couldn't *be* more odd. The dead man was sleeping with his putters and balls. The little woman with the black hair and the harsh face goose-steps like she's in a military parade. The young lad, the tall one, talks in an American accent for no good reason. And don't get me started on the old man and his fancy piece, the blonde bombshell.'

'She's his wife, Jean,' Helen said sternly. 'And whatever we think about our guests, we keep it to ourselves down here.'

Jean tutted loudly. 'Come on, you know me better than that. You can trust me. I'm not like Miriam next door. She gossips about her guests the minute their backs are turned.'

'She really does that?' Helen said, surprised.

Jean nodded. 'Oh yes. It's no wonder she doesn't get repeat visitors.'

Helen stood and pulled her dressing gown tight. 'I'll go and get dressed, then I'll take Suki for one of those things I have to spell out, so don't say the word otherwise she'll go straight to the door.'

'All right,' Jean said. 'Leave me to fix breakfast. What are your plans for today once we've finished in here?'

'I'm going to visit Sally's mum before DS Hutchinson can get to her. I'll set off as soon as I've served breakfast and cleaned the rooms with Sally. I've got to speak to Brenda to find out exactly what happened with her handbag at the bingo.'

'I warned you not to bring an outsider in,' Jean sniffed.

'You could come with me if you like. Meet her on her home turf. It might be a chance to lay the animosity between you to rest. Would you like to do that?'

Helen looked at Jean, waiting for a response, but Jean was doing her best to pretend she hadn't heard. She carried on opening a catering-size tin of baked beans, avoiding eye contact, giving Helen her answer.

'Fair enough,' Helen said. She returned to her bedroom to shower and dress.

Half an hour later, she left through the Seaview's back door to take Suki for her morning walk. She kept checking her phone, and was disappointed and upset that Marie still hadn't called. As she rounded the corner of Windsor Terrace, she spied Miriam outside the Vista del Mar. She was standing at the bottom of the steps that led to her front door, a plastic bucket at her feet. She wore her cleaning tabard over a smart black trouser suit, and yellow rubber gloves, and was sloshing soapy water on the steps, then scrubbing them with a small, hard brush. Helen slowed her pace when she spied her, trying to work out what to say. It was the first time they'd crossed paths since Jean had left the Seaview. She could have walked past, because Miriam had no clue she was there. However, she decided to clear the air.

'Morning, Miriam.'

Miriam froze. Then, slowly, she turned around, and the scrubbing brush dropped from her hand. Despite the early hour, she was already wearing full make-up, and her long grey hair was twirled in a stylish knot. It looked to Helen as if it was held up by gravity, for she could see no grips or pins. How did the woman manage to look so glamorous first thing in the morning? When did she find time to do such extravagant hair and make-up while running a hotel? Helen never seemed to have time for anything other than walking Suki. Suddenly aware of how drab she must look in comparison, in her green fleece jacket, jeans and boots, she pushed a lock of brown hair behind her ear.

'You stole from me, Miriam,' she said, keeping her voice as even as possible, despite the rage of temper she felt.

'Stole? Me?' Miriam cooed.

Helen felt her stomach turn over. 'You know what I mean. Taking my cook and passing her award-winning breakfast off as your own on your website. I could do you for fraud.' As the words left her lips, she realised how ridiculous she sounded. She had no idea what her rights were, or even if she had any.

Miriam peeled off her rubber gloves and draped them over the side of the bucket. 'If you mean Jean, I never stole her. How dare you accuse me of theft. She came to me of her own accord after her disagreement with you. And while she was in my employ, it was only right and fair to let my guests know about her award-winning breakfasts. I use my website for publicity just like every other hotelier in Scarborough. What I put on there and who I employ is no business of yours.'

Helen felt her neck and shoulders tense. How good it would feel, she thought, to let rip and lose her temper to get rid of her anger and frustration over Ricky's death. Instead, she held her ground. She had too much pride to engage in a slanging match in the street. Besides, it wouldn't be good for business if anyone saw her.

'Anyway, I can't stop and chat on the doorstep like a common herring girl,' Miriam sniffed. 'I've got my guests' breakfasts to see to. And heaven help me, I've got calls to make to find a new cleaner.'

She turned her back on Helen, picked up her bucket and began to climb the steps.

'Miriam!' Helen said firmly.

The other woman stopped in her tracks, but didn't turn around.

'If you ever do anything like that again . . . if you take the Seaview's award and pass it off as your own, I'll come for you. You hear me? You can't lord it over me any more now I've got my four stars. We're equal now.'

Miriam slowly turned, and Helen noticed her face drop. Her words had clearly rattled her. But she wasn't about to go down without a fight.

'You and I may both have four stars, dear, but some hotels are more equal than others,' she said smugly. 'At least I've never had a dead body to deal with. It's unfortunate the way your guests keep getting murdered. You've had the police in and out of your front door more times than I can count. However, this time, the trouble the Seaview has attracted impacts on me too, because I've got the dead man's teammates staying here. I'm having to act as agony aunt and grief counsellor to those poor men. Not to mention how annoying it is to have the police turn up on a whim to ask them more questions. If this affects my future bookings, you can be sure I'll have stern words to say.' She waved her hand as if to shoo away a fly. 'I've got to go. I've croissants to warm in the oven. You see, dear, it's little touches like French pastries that put the Vista del Mar ahead of the competition. Jean told me you never offer croissants at the Seaview.'

'And she told *me* your croissants are frozen!' Helen yelled.

Miriam stood stock still, then laid a hand against the wall to steady herself against the truth of Helen's words. Helen was ready to fling more insults, but when Miriam turned around, her bottom lip was quivering. She suddenly looked vulnerable and old.

'All right. You win this round, Helen. May I ask you to keep what you know to yourself?'

'About your croissants?' Helen asked.

Miriam nodded.

Helen pulled Suki's lead. 'Come on, girl, let's go.'

'Helen, dear?' Miriam said, all sweetness now, chastened.

Helen stopped. 'What?'

'Let's put this nasty business behind us.'

'If you insist.' At heart, she was relieved at Miriam's words, for she'd never had such cross words with her neighbour.

'Actually, I've got a favour to ask,' Miriam went on.

Ah, so that's why you've suddenly changed your tune, Helen thought. 'Go on.'

'Do you know anyone who's looking for work? I've got a cleaner's job going, but I can't find anyone suitable, and I really need some help.'

'Well, maybe. I can't promise anything, but if I have time, I could ask around,' Helen said, then she headed to the beach with the dog.

Back at the Seaview after her walk, Helen served breakfast with Sally. The guests were quiet in the dining room, sadness hanging over them. Even Olga seemed less officious than usual. After breakfast, Alice announced that the team were going to walk to the South Bay. They wanted to find out what was happening at the crazy-golf course before the charity game, which was now confirmed as taking place on Friday.

While Helen and Sally cleaned rooms, Helen kept checking her phone, hoping for a message from Marie. When they'd finished, they joined Jean for their morning coffee and cake. Jean poured from the cafetière and handed out slices of chocolate cake with thick, gooey icing on top.

'This looks gorgeous,' Sally said, taking her plate.

Suki came to the table, hoping for crumbs. Helen glanced briefly at Jean.

'Did you remember to bring the party invitation today, Jean? You promised you would, and I need it if I'm to get to the bottom of whoever is sending them out.'

Jean paused with her coffee mug in mid-air. Did Helen imagine it, or did she and Sally share a look before Sally quickly looked away?

'Sorry, love. What am I like? I'd forget my head if it was loose. I'll bring it tomorrow,' Jean said. Then she stuffed a large piece of cake in her mouth, preventing her from answering more questions.

Helen narrowed her eyes. 'Why do I get the feeling you two are up to something?'

'If you're having strange feelings, you're probably overtired,' Sally said.

Jean nodded in agreement and patted Helen's hand as she chewed her cake.

Helen thought for a moment. 'I'm going to make a list of all the people I know, all my relations, and I'm going to call them one by one, demanding to know who's behind this.'

Jean shrugged. 'If it'll make you feel better, love.'

'Oh, it will, Jean. It will,' Helen said, determined. 'I should have done this right at the start.'

Sally glanced at the clock on the kitchen wall. 'If you want to catch Mum at home, you'll need to leave soon.'

Helen sipped her coffee and took a bite of cake. They sat in silence for a moment and she thought about her run-in with Miriam. 'Gorgeous cake, Jean,' she said at last. 'Did you bake for Miriam while you were working at the Vista del Mar?'

Jean shook her head. 'No, love. I didn't do anything for Miriam that I wasn't paid for.'

'I'm still not sure how things lie between her and me, you know,' Helen said. 'We had a bit of a ding-dong this morning. I had a go at her about passing your award-winning breakfasts off as her own, then she threw croissants at me.'

Jean dropped her fork. 'She did what?'

'Oh, not literally. I mean she tried to lord it over me by saying the Vista del Mar was better than the Seaview because she offered croissants at breakfast.'

'She doesn't tell her guests they're frozen, you know. She passes them off as home-baked,' Jean said.

'She says she's making phone calls today to find a new cleaner,' Helen said.

Jean rolled her eyes. 'The only type of person who could stay the course with Miriam needs to have a rod of iron running through them and skin as thick as a rhino's. Someone who can turn a deaf ear to her condescending remarks and take insults with a pinch of salt. Someone who'll let criticism slide off them like water off a duck's back. Someone who's able to give as good as they get. In short, she needs someone who's as tough as old boots.'

Helen looked at Sally. 'Is your mum still looking for work?'

Chapter 28

Brenda lived in a terraced house on Vine Street, a narrow road in the centre of town. It was a cul-de-sac, and at the end was Scarborough's auction house and sale rooms. Helen remembered that Tom had been there once to bid on two garish paintings of Elvis he'd wanted to hang at the Seaview. She'd secretly been grateful when he'd returned home empty-handed, outbid by an Elvis fan with deeper pockets. She looked at the outside of Brenda's house. Two baskets filled with pink and white petunias hung each side of a white PVC door. Under the downstairs window was a horizontal planter filled with the same flowers.

'It looks pretty,' she said.

'Mum's got green fingers,' Sally replied. 'Gav buys the plants for her. She loves making hanging baskets.' She stepped forward, moving a green wheelie bin to one side. 'Come in, she's expecting us, I texted her. You can bring Suki in, she won't mind. She's getting used to your dog now.' She pushed the door open. 'Mum, it's just me. I've got Helen,' she called.

Helen stepped inside. The house smelled fresh, of something familiar, zesty and citrus. Brenda walked into the hall carrying a cloth in one hand and a bottle of lemon cleaner in the other. It was the same lemon cleaner they used at the Seaview Hotel. When she caught Helen's eye, she whipped the bottle out of sight behind her back and looked guiltily at her feet. She was dressed in the same shapeless cardigan and loose trousers she'd worn at the Seaview. Her tightly permed hair hadn't lost any of its harsh curl.

'It's nice to see you, Brenda. Are you keeping well?' Helen asked.

'Aye.'

She followed Sally and Brenda into the living room. It was sparsely furnished, just two armchairs and a three-seater sofa that had seen better days. The sofa sagged in the middle and the armrests were worn. The grey carpet was thin and worn too. A gas fire in a mock-brick surround dominated the room, next to a widescreen TV. Helen sat in an armchair and Suki lay at her feet.

'Would you like a cup of tea, Helen?' Sally asked.

'Don't go to any trouble.'

'It's no trouble. I'll go and put the kettle on.'

When Sally had left the room, Brenda looked at Helen. 'Well. Go on, ask me what you came to ask me.'

'It's about the man who died at the crazy-golf course,' Helen said.

'Aye. We've already spoke on the phone about him. I told you I never saw a folder or any notes about food he wasn't supposed to eat. I'm an honest woman, Helen. I'd never tell a lie, especially when it involves someone, heaven rest his soul, who's passed on.'

'It's not the folder I want to speak to you about. It's about the night you went to the bingo and had your keys stolen. I'm working on a hunch that whoever took the keys used them to enter the Seaview and stole something from my apartment.'

'No!' Brenda said.

'I'm afraid so. Anything you can remember about that night, anything at all, tell me, please. I want to bring this to an end. It's a nightmare. I'm not sleeping well, and I've lost bookings because

211

the story's in the news and the Seaview's been mentioned. I've even got a journalist hounding me. It could ruin my business. I need to do all I can to find out what happened, then I can rest easy again. Have the police been in touch with you yet?'

'Not exactly.'

Helen bit her tongue. She'd forgotten how infuriating Brenda could be. 'What do you mean? Either they have or they haven't.'

'They haven't. But they have been to bingo. Janet, the manager, told me they looked through the CCTV to see if they could spot anyone rifling through handbags.'

'Did they find anything?'

Brenda shook her head. 'Not a sausage.'

The sound of a whistling kettle came from the kitchen, and Sally popped her head around the door into the living room.

'Tea? Coffee?'

'Whatever's easiest,' Helen replied, then returned her attention to Brenda.

'Think, Brenda. Is there anything else you remember from that night? Anything that'll help?'

Brenda shrugged. 'Such as?'

'Well . . . did any of your friends see anything strange?'

Sally walked into the room carrying three mugs on a tray. She handed Helen one bearing the motto *I'VE BEEN TO BARBADOS*. Helen wondered if it was a holiday souvenir.

'Who were you with that night at bingo, Mum?' Sally asked.

Brenda took her mug and placed it on the thin carpet. 'Just the usual gang: Peggy, Dinah and Pat. Janet calls us the Four Musketeers.'

'And were your friends' handbags rifled that night?'

'No, but there's been a bit of trouble with young lads coming in, trying to take things. They think we're a load of old biddies. Dinah gave one of them a black eye when she caught him trying to steal her bag the week before.'

Sally laughed out loud. 'He should've known better than to mess with Dinah.'

'Was anything else taken from your bag, or was it just the Seaview's keys?' Helen asked.

'Just the keys,' Brenda replied. 'I didn't have much else. My house keys were in there, but they weren't touched. My purse was there too, but there was just a couple of pound coins in there. Oh, and there was an old phone that Sally gave me. It sends texts, that's all. It wasn't worth stealing.'

Helen mulled this over. 'And the friends you were with, did they know you were working at the Seaview?'

Brenda sat up straight in her seat and beamed. When she smiled like that, she looked a different woman, alert and engaged, almost attractive once her dour expression disappeared. 'Aye.'

'Mum was proud to be working for you, Helen. It's the first job she's had in a while. She was honoured to say she worked at the Seaview.'

'So, a lot of people knew you were working for me. Did you also tell them you had the keys?'

Brenda sank back in her seat, deflated. 'Aye. I might have mentioned it.'

'Who to?' Helen demanded. She drummed her fingers on the worn armrest.

'Just to Dinah, Peggy and Pat.'

'Oh Mum!' Sally cried. 'Helen trusted you with those keys. You should have known how important it was not to go shouting about them.'

'I wasn't shouting. I just mentioned them to my friends,' Brenda huffed.

Helen shifted in her seat. Sally leaned forward and looked at her.

'You don't think one of Mum's friends killed Ricky Delmont, do you?'

Helen shook her head. 'No, of course not. But if one of them knew Brenda had a set of keys, then who knows who else they might've told? Gossip spreads.' She sighed heavily. 'I'm grasping at straws, aren't I? Desperately trying to tie ends together.'

'It's the police's job to find the killer, not yours,' Brenda said sternly.

Helen looked into the older woman's worn face; at her sad eyes and pale, doughy skin. 'I know it's not my place to stick my nose in, but the Seaview is implicated in Ricky's death, and if I lose my hotel, I lose everything. That's why I want . . . no, why I *need* to uncover what happened. Someone came into my home, Brenda. They took something that ended up killing a man, and the police are treating it as murder. It doesn't get more serious.'

Brenda nodded slowly. 'Aye.'

Helen drained her cup, trying and failing to picture Brenda in Barbados. She stood, and Suki got to her feet too. 'I'll go. I appreciate all you've said, and I hope my questions haven't upset you.'

'Takes a lot more than that to upset me,' Brenda said.

Helen looked at her again. 'Speaking of which, are you still looking for work?'

'Aye. But I'm not coming back to the Seaview after what happened to that poor man.'

'I'd be grateful if you didn't mention that to any of your friends who might be gossiping at the bingo. Anyway, it's not me who's looking for staff. It's Miriam next door at the Vista del Mar.'

'That stuck-up cow? Oh, the things Sally's told me about her.'

'Mum!' Sally chided.

Helen laughed out loud. 'It's true she can be tricky. She needs a cleaner, though, someone who's tough enough to stand up to her when she gets high-handed. I thought about you. I could put a word in if you like.'

Brenda looked from Sally to Helen. 'Aye.'

'What Mum means is that she'd love to come and talk to Miriam about the job.'

'Pfft,' Brenda said.

'Well, Brenda? Should I speak to Miriam and put your name forward or not?'

'Aye,' Brenda replied. Then her face broke into a smile and her eyes lit up. 'Thanks.'

Helen left Sally and Brenda and walked out with Suki. Thoughts ricocheted in her mind like balls in a pinball machine. They pinged from bingo to handbags, from party invitations to Jean and Sally's shared furtive looks, from keys to peanuts, from models of windmills to golf balls. She was concentrating so hard on unpicking what Brenda had said that it took her a while to realise her phone was buzzing. She brought Suki to a halt and pulled her phone from her pocket, relieved to see Marie's name.

'Marie?'

'Hi, Helen. Are you at the Seaview?'

'No, I'm on Vine Street, near the auction house.'

'Why?'

'It's a long story. Anyway, thanks for ringing me back, and I'll get straight to the point. I saw you with that man, the journalist. He tried to doorstep me for a story about Ricky Delmont, then I saw him get into your car. Care to tell me what's going on?'

There was a pause.

'Marie? You still there?'

'I'm here,' Marie said at last. 'Meet me in Bonnet's coffee shop in half an hour, and I'll explain it all.'

Chapter 29

Helen glanced at her watch. She didn't have enough time to take Suki back to the Seaview and head out again to meet Marie. Instead, she decided to go straight to Bonnet's. She crossed her fingers that there would be empty seats in the café's courtyard, as she knew dogs weren't allowed inside. Bonnet's was Helen's favourite café in Scarborough. Nestled away on the narrow lane of historic Huntriss Row, it had an old-fashioned charm. It served traditional food made from local ingredients and had an on-site bakery, and the delicious aroma of home-made chocolates welcomed all who stepped inside.

As she walked from Brenda's house, questions crowded her head, and at the centre was Ricky Delmont. Spinning around him were Alice and Olga, long-legged Freddy with his strange accent, mismatched Marty and Marilyn, and the strangers on the seafront taking bets on the crazy golf. She gave her head a shake. She really should take Jean's advice, and now the same suggestion from Brenda, to let the police do their job. But with the Seaview implicated in Ricky's death, she felt there was too much at stake to sit back and do nothing.

'I've got to do something, Suki, but what?' she muttered as she walked. Unsurprisingly, the greyhound didn't respond; she just kept trotting at Helen's side.

When Helen reached Bonnet's, there was a phone message from Marie to say she'd been delayed for half an hour.

'Come on, Suki, that gives us time to walk on the beach,' she said.

At the end of Huntriss Row was the Central Tramway funicular, which ran down the steep hill to the beach. It was one of the oldest cliff railways in the country, and its pretty facade was painted a fetching red and cream.

'Ah, what the heck, Suki. Let's travel down in style.'

She bought a single ticket, then walked into the waiting car. A small boy was standing on one of the wooden benches that ran along each side.

'When will it move, Mum? Dad? Make it move,' he cried excitedly.

Helen felt his excitement only too well. She'd been riding on the funiculars in Scarborough ever since she was a child, and the joy of it had never left her. Suki sat dead still.

'Good girl,' Helen said.

The little boy caught her eye. 'What's your dog called?'

'She's called Suki.'

'She's skinny and big.'

'She used to be a racing dog,' Helen explained. 'But once she stopped winning races, she was given to a rehoming centre, and that's where I found her. I fell in love with her the minute I saw her.'

'I like her too,' he said.

The ticket master who managed the office came into the carriage. 'Hold tight, everyone.'

The door slammed shut and the car jerked forward on its descent. The little boy's dad lifted him up to look out of the window.

'Here we go, Barney,' he said, as excited as his son. 'Look out for the other car coming up the hill. We'll pass it in the middle.'

'There it is!' Barney yelled. 'There, Dad, I saw it. I saw it!'

All too soon the ride was over. At the bottom of the tramway, the door was pulled open by the ticket master. Helen was last out, with Suki. She crossed the road and walked along Foreshore Road, which bordered the South Bay beach. Scarborough's South Bay was bigger and busier than the North. Where the North Bay had restful Peasholm Park at its heart, along with the miniature railway and the Open Air Theatre, the South Bay was more commercial. It was the territory of candyfloss, ice cream and chips. Amusement arcades, souvenir shops and cafés lined the seafront. Helen was heartened to see the vintage Harbour Bar ice-cream parlour doing a roaring trade. Seagulls flew over fishing boats landing the day's catch. Pleasure boats took tourists along the spectacular Yorkshire coast.

She was about to head on to the sand to let Suki off the lead when she spotted one of her guests standing outside the crazy-golf course. Well, it wasn't hard to miss Alice's red hair, and once she'd spotted Alice, she noticed the others. Olga was chatting to Freddy. Marty was holding hands with Marilyn, who wore her brassy blonde hair in an elaborate curl pinned with a sparkly clip.

Alice spotted Helen and waved, then the others turned to look in her direction. Olga and Freddy stepped away and carried on their conversation, while Alice, Marty and Marilyn greeted Helen warmly.

'What's happening with the crazy-golf course?' Helen asked.

'It's reopening today,' Alice beamed. 'The police have finished, so it's full steam ahead for our charity game on Friday.'

'It's great news,' Marty said.

Helen noticed that Marilyn stayed silent. 'Are you pleased to be playing too?' she asked.

'Yes, I'm looking forward to it,' Marilyn replied.

However, her tone of voice made Helen think otherwise. She studied Marilyn's face. She looked tired, she thought, and a bit peaky, even under her heavy make-up.

Alice rocked back and forth on her heels and clapped her hands together. 'It'll be good to play on Friday, it'll give us closure after what happened. We'll dedicate the game to Ricky, raise funds for the allergy charity, then we'll go home and try our best to put this behind us.'

'I admire your spirit,' Helen said.

Olga and Freddy were still deep in conversation, but Olga was starting to look peeved, and her voice was rising with each word she flung at the young man.

'We need to follow the rules. Rules are important. Rule 3.1.7. is especially important. It states that no more than forty-five seconds is allowed for a player to complete a stroke.'

'But that's not long enough, Olga. Can't we bend the rules for a charity game?' Freddy pleaded.

But Olga wouldn't budge. 'No, it's the rule.'

Freddy spun away from her and his face showed surprise when he saw Helen. 'Oh, hi. I mean, er, howdy there,' he said.

'Howdy,' Helen replied with a smile.

Then Olga joined the others. 'I'm ready to leave,' she said.

The group lined up behind her. First Alice, then Freddy, who was followed by Marty. Marilyn brought up the rear.

'Now we go,' Olga ordered. 'Left, right, left, right.'

Helen watched in amazement as her guests marched away. Marilyn turned around and waved.

'Bye, Helen,' she said.

Helen nodded in acknowledgement.

The five crazy golfers marched along Foreshore Road, arms swinging, legs stepping in time to Olga's command. Tourists turned to stare. Cars slowed as motorists watched the strange sight. Some people took pictures on their phones. It was an unusual sight to see adults walking in unison; they were indeed striking to watch. Tiny Olga leading them with her clipped, barked instructions, cropped black hair and beady eyes. Alice with her red hair tied in plaits that swung from side to side. Freddy with his long legs and stooped shoulders. Muscled Marty with his broad chest and swathe of white hair. Then Marilyn, perhaps the most striking of all, with her white-blonde confection of a hairdo and scarlet lips.

'They're an odd bunch all right,' a voice said. Helen turned to see Norman the hut man. Where he'd come from she had no idea, as he hadn't been there when she'd been talking to her guests.

'They're staying with me at the Seaview,' she said.

'Oh, don't you mention your Seaview to me. It's where the dead man was staying, the one who died on my course,' Norman huffed. 'The police told me that when they took me in for questioning. They thought I'd done the fella in. Course, they had to let me go. They had no proof, see. Doesn't mean I wouldn't have belted him around the chops if I could have got my hands on him before he collapsed.'

Helen chose her words carefully, curious to know how much Norman might reveal. 'I heard you had a run-in with him, then he tried to hit you with his crazy-golf putter,' she said.

'I didn't kill him,' Norman said, his tone serious now. 'The police have told me what did for him, and it's nowt to do with me. I'm in the clear. He was a right bad 'un, though, smashing my course up. So yes, I went for him. He lost his temper with my course and I lost my temper with him. I don't normally attack my customers; I want to make that clear. But that Delmont fella was asking for it, he was a nasty piece of work.'

Just then, Norman noticed Suki. 'I'm going to have to ask you to leave,' he said.

'Leave? Why?'

'You can't bring the dog in here.'

'In where? I'm just standing on the road chatting to you. In fact, you were the one who started talking to me.'

Norman moved to stand in front of his hut. Helen noticed the door was closed.

'Go on, move along now. Get the dog away,' he said. His face was growing red and his voice began to shake.

Helen took a step towards him, holding Suki behind her. 'What are you hiding in there?' she asked.

Norman pulled nervously at his collar. 'Me? Hiding? Where?'

She took another step. 'What's inside your hut that you don't want me to see? You were cagey about it last time I walked by, before Ricky died. You were acting strangely then and you're acting strangely now.'

'I'm not,' he said, strangely.

'Are so,' Helen retorted.

'How dare you call me that!' Norman cried. 'Now leave my golf course immediately.'

Helen took another step closer to him. The toes of her boots were almost touching his shoes. Her nose was almost touching his. She was so close to him that she could smell something on his breath. As a hotelier running a bar, the smell was familiar. 'How many bottles do you keep in your hut?'

'Bottles? I don't know what you're talking about,' Norman blustered.

'Oh, I think you do. I think you keep bottles of spirits in there. Whisky is my guess. Take a few nips during the day to keep you going, do you?'

'No, it's just a—'

'Don't deny it, Norman, I know what whisky smells like.'

'It's not whisky, how dare you suggest it.'

His tone was turning nasty, and Helen knew she needed to keep her cool. 'I run a bar at the Seaview. I've had guests stay with me in the past who've had a drink problem. I've seen this secretive behaviour before.'

She took a step back. Norman's shoulders slumped and his face crumpled. He cast his gaze to the model windmill on the final hole.

'I want to stop, but I can't. I drink, then lose my temper; it sends me into a rage. I know that if I carry on, I'll end up losing all this . . .' He waved his hand at the golf course and the tremor returned to his voice. 'I can't lose it, it's all I've got. I've built it by hand. I want to give up the booze, of course I do. I know it does me no good.'

'There are people you can talk to. I'll bring you a phone number next time I walk by. Is there anyone at home you can confide in, someone who'll help?'

Norman shook his head. 'My wife left me when my drinking

got bad. She said she wouldn't play second fiddle to the other women in my life.'

'Oh Norman,' Helen said.

'It's not what you think. I started a love affair with Brandy, Margarita, Sherry. Well, you get the idea. And just when I thought things couldn't get any worse, Ricky Delmont dies on my course. My business might never recover.'

She laid her hand on his arm. 'You'll get through it, Norman, I promise. I'll put you in touch with someone who can help. The charity game on Friday could be a fresh start; it might be worth thinking about.'

He rubbed his stubbly chin. 'Friday, yes. Thanks,' he said.

'Norman?' Helen swallowed hard. 'Have you ever seen any gambling going on at games on your course?' She felt dreadful asking him when he was in such a state, but he'd been honest about his drinking; perhaps he'd be honest about what else he knew.

He gave a wry smile. 'The official line is that gambling on the game doesn't happen. But unofficially – and this is just between us – it does. I turn a blind eye to what goes on, because sometimes they cut me in if they have a big win. They've asked me to rig games in the past, but that's something I'd never do, although I've been offered big money.'

Helen let his words sink in. The fact that he was admitting this to her in the state he was in made her feel he was telling the truth.

'I've got to go, Norman, I'm meeting a friend. But I'll see you on Friday for the big game. In the meantime, promise me you'll think about what we've talked about. Your crazy-golf course on the seafront is too important for Scarborough to lose. It's been here all my life – I used to play here as a child. You can't let it go. You can't lose it, or yourself. Tell Stella and all those other women that you need some time on your own.'

Norman held his hand out to her. 'Thanks,' he said.

Helen shook his hand, then turned and walked away. She glanced back just once, and was horrified to see him raising a whisky bottle to his mouth.

'Oh no,' she moaned.

She was about to walk on when suddenly she saw him pause with the bottle inches from his lips. She watched as his arm dropped and he sank on to a bench. The bottle fell from his hand and rolled away, spilling its contents on the ground.

Chapter 30

As Helen hesitated, unsure, wondering how wise it would be to retrace her steps, she saw Norman stand, pick up the bottle and drop it into a waste bin. He looked up and caught her eye, then smiled weakly and raised a thumb in a gesture to let her know he was fine, at least for now. Helen nodded, then walked back to the Central Tramway.

'All aboard!' the ticket master cried once Helen and Suki were seated inside the funicular. Up the hill it went, passing the second car on its way down. Within a minute, Helen was back at the top and making her way from the station.

Rounding the corner to Huntriss Row, she walked into the court-yard at Bonnet's and was pleased to see Marie had already arrived. Her friend stood to greet her and threw her arms around her.

'I haven't seen you since the reunion,' she said.

Helen raised her eyebrows. 'Well, I've seen *you*, more than once . . . with Jack Malone,' she said archly.

Marie sank into her chair. 'I'll explain everything.'

Helen picked up the menu.

'No need to read it, I've already ordered,' Marie said.

Helen put the menu back down. 'How did you know what I wanted?'

'Because we've been coming here for decades and you always have the same thing.'

She gave a wry smile. Marie knew her too well. 'Fair enough, you've got me. I'm a creature of habit.' She eyed her friend's stylish black leather jacket, black jeans and high-heeled ankle boots. 'You're looking particularly lovely today. Off anywhere special?'

Marie shook her head, and her long, glossy hair bounced in curls around her shoulders.

'Not meeting anyone?' Helen pried.

Marie leaned forward, glanced from left to right, then beckoned Helen towards her. 'I know you're trying to ask me about my journalist friend. I told you I'd tell you everything, and I will.'

'All right. Let me start with the basics. Who is he? You know he doorstepped me yesterday?'

Marie's face clouded over. 'I didn't know that. I'll have a word with him next time I see him.'

'What on earth are you hanging out with him for?'

'He's my new publicity agent, one of the best. I've hired him to do the PR for the Filey tearoom. He's worked in London and now has an office in York. He's excellent at his job, a hard worker, tenacious like me. We've become friends.' She lowered her gaze, then looked Helen in the eye. 'Actually, we're more than friends.'

'You're seeing him?'

'It's early days, but yes, things have taken a romantic turn.'

The waitress came towards them carrying a tray. 'Two cappuccinos, two tuna mayo sandwiches on brown bread.'

'Thanks, love,' Marie said as the waitress set plates and cups down. Once she'd gone, Helen picked up the conversation.

'I don't understand. If this Jack Malone is a PR man, what was he doing knocking at my door threatening to run a story on the Seaview?'

Marie picked up a spoon and knocked the froth off her coffee. 'As I said, he's tenacious. He was a journalist before he set up his PR agency. One of his old contacts told him that Ricky had stayed at the Seaview. It piqued Jack's interest. He remembered Ricky's name in connection with an old story he'd run as a journalist on a paper in Gorleston-on-Sea. It's a little resort outside Great Yarmouth. There'd been a fight on a crazy-golf course in Yarmouth, and Ricky was involved. I swear I didn't tell Jack to question you at the Seaview. I'll make sure he doesn't bother you again.'

Helen picked up her cup and took a sip of frothy milk. 'Did he uncover anything about Ricky's death?'

'No. He hasn't made any connection between the fight in Yarmouth years ago and what happened here. The only thing that connects the two events is that they took place on crazy-golf courses.' Marie sipped her own coffee. 'What was Ricky Delmont like?'

'I told you all about him at the tournament before he died. He was awful, Marie. He was rude to me and my guests, one of whom was his ex-wife. He even slept with his . . .' Helen paused, mindful of the non-disclosure agreement she'd signed. Even if it was probably not worth the paper it was written on, and had been amateurishly drawn up by Ricky himself, a copy of it had been stolen from her apartment. 'Well, let's just say he took his crazy golf seriously.' She looked at her tuna mayo sandwich. But even though it was her favourite, her stomach turned with anxiety and she pushed the plate away.

'I can't eat this, Marie. I'm sorry. My mind's all over the place.

I'm worried sick about the party invitations . . .' She gave Marie a hard stare. 'The invitations that both you and Jean said you'd bring for me to see but neither of you has. I've also got Ricky's death to contend with, and as for the rest of my guests, it seems they're keeping secrets. Olga, their team coach, is a strange little woman who barks orders, and the rest of them fall into line like sheep. Do you know what it reminds me of?'

'No, but I have a feeling you're going to tell me,' Marie smiled.

'That scene in *The Sound of Music* when Captain von Trapp blows his whistle to command the children to line up. That's what Olga's like, but without the whistle. There's Freddy, who's just a boy really, still growing into his long limbs. He's awkward and shy and speaks with an American accent. But I overheard him talking on his phone without a trace of an accent. He mentioned Ricky, and swore revenge on the man.'

'Do you think he might have killed him?'

'I hope not,' Helen said quickly. 'Freddy's a lovely lad and I'd hate to think he was involved. Do you remember when I pointed out my guests to you on the day Ricky died, when they were lined up to play on the course?'

Marie nodded.

'Remember the older man you called a silver fox, and his much younger wife? To be honest, I think Ricky might have been having an affair with her, from what I've overheard. There's not much I miss at the Seaview. The problem is, I wish I didn't know any of this. It's doing my head in.'

'Have you told the police?'

'I've told them everything. They've asked me to keep an eye on the guests in case I overhear or see anything suspicious.'

'You're really going through the wringer, aren't you?' Marie said.

Helen nodded. 'The only ray of sunshine is that Jean's back, but I'll tell you something, I'll never take her for granted again. It didn't half give me a jolt losing her. I even thought about selling up and moving on, and I haven't thought that way since Tom died. While Jean was away, Sally's mum, Brenda, came in to help out. Anyway, some paperwork went missing that Ricky had given me about foods he required and those he wasn't allowed to eat. Turns out he was allergic to—'

'Peanuts?' Marie chipped in. 'Sorry, Helen. I read about his allergy on the front of *The Scarborough Times*.'

Helen groaned out loud on hearing the story had made front-page news. This didn't bode well for business. 'Well, before Ricky died, Brenda had her keys stolen from her handbag at the bingo. I'm starting to think that whoever took them let themselves into the Seaview, stole Ricky's food sheet, discovered he was allergic to peanuts and . . . well, you know what happened next.'

Marie bit into her sandwich, then swallowed hard. 'Oh Helen, that's awful. I had no idea you were going through this.' She stretched her hand across the table and took hold of Helen's. 'How can I help?'

Helen thought for a moment. 'There is one thing you can do.'

'Name it,' Marie said.

Helen looked her hard in the eye. 'Keep your journalist boyfriend away from my hotel.'

Chapter 31

Back at the Seaview after meeting Marie, Helen let herself in to her empty apartment. She experienced a frisson of fear that was beginning to feel horribly familiar. It had started after she'd seen the intruder on the CCTV. She hated feeling vulnerable in her own home, and it now made her feel angry. She made a mental note to ask Gav to fit a new alarm. Surely there must be something that Suki wouldn't set off? Did pet-friendly alarms exist? If anyone knew, Gav would. She let Suki off her lead and the dog went straight to her favourite spot in front of the patio doors.

Helen walked into the kitchen and turned the kettle on to make a pot of tea. Her phone beeped with a message, and she smiled when she saw it was from Jimmy.

Cooking chicken chasseur for our dinner. Do you like mushrooms? X

She texted back with a mushroom emoji, a thumbs-up and a smiley face. She glanced at the clock on the wall. She had enough time to spend a couple of hours doing admin on her laptop before getting changed for the walk to Jimmy's house. A note on the kitchen bench caught her eye. Jean's neat, small handwriting told her there was a freshly baked cake in the tin. 'Bless you, Jean,' she said.

She pulled the lid off the tin to reveal a ginger cake. She cut a slice off the end and took it with her tea to the table. Opening her laptop, she scrolled through emails, deleted spam and read a couple of new solid five-star reviews left by guests on HypeThatHotel. She opened the folder on her system where all her incoming bookings were automatically routed, but her heart dropped like a stone when she saw a stream of cancellations. She'd been dreading receiving more now that news of Ricky's death was out, and she girded herself to see how widely the story was being reported online.

She ran a search on the hotel. It was mentioned online on various news sites and in clickbait headlines in connection to Ricky's murder. She felt sick. Her head spun. Then she forced herself to remember what Jean kept saying: that this would blow over, and more importantly, that Ricky hadn't died at the Seaview. He'd died on the crazy-golf course and his death had nothing to do with the hotel.

She forced her mind back to her work, concentrating on adding the new bookings to the Seaview's calendar on her laptop. Then she braced herself and picked up her phone again. She rang Tom's family in Shetland first, then her friends, to ask if they'd received party invitations. They all replied that they had, and were both confused and upset when she told them there was no party and it had all been a mistake. She felt relieved that she'd made the calls, despite hearing everyone's concerned voices when she told them the invitations had been sent without her knowledge or consent.

All done, she then took a moment to take stock of business in the weeks ahead. She only had five more nights of the crazy golfers. Their plan was to play the charity game on Friday, then leave on Saturday morning. Once they'd gone, she and Sally would turn the rooms around for more guests coming in. She didn't recognise the names of any of the guests booked in on Saturday and Sunday. They were all new business rather than repeats. She racked her brains trying to recall if there was a big show on in town at the Spa or the Open Air Theatre, something that would bring tourists in for the weekend. She opened another web browser, but there were no blockbuster shows or gigs as far as she could see. Still, it filled her heart with pride to know that the Seaview would be full with families and tourists. It was exactly what she needed, and what the hotel deserved, after the tragic events of Ricky's death.

Later that day, Helen stood in front of her bedroom mirror holding two dresses against her body, one after the other. Suki peered around the door. 'Which one, Suki? Red or blue?'

The greyhound didn't offer an opinion. Helen decided on the red dress and slipped it on over her head. She did her make-up, styled her hair, then slipped her feet into a pair of heeled shoes.

'Crikey, I haven't worn these in ages,' she muttered. Then she thought about the long walk to Jimmy's house and slipped the shoes off. She was half minded to put her jeans back on, and her old boots to walk in. But she liked the way the dress felt on her shoulders and the way it floated around her knees, so she put the shoes back on. She'd call one of Gav's Cabs to take her to Jimmy's.

Her heart flipped. Would she need one to bring her back? She'd never spent the night with him before. She'd never felt ready. But now, wearing her new, flattering dress, looking forward to seeing him and spending time with him . . . who knew where the night might end? Tom had been the only man she'd ever shared a bed with, but she was ready to move on, and felt sure in her heart that Jimmy would be patient and kind. He already knew she needed to take things slowly, and that Tom had been her only love.

She glanced again in the mirror and admired her reflection. A confident woman in a pretty dress smiled back. She hadn't had a chance to dress up in ages; she didn't count the school reunion as a proper night out. She'd never wanted to go in the first place. What if Jimmy hadn't given her a second chance after he'd caught her being grabbed by the ex-rugby player? She realised in that moment that he meant more to her than she'd been able to admit so far.

She walked into the living room and called Gav's Cabs.

'It's Helen Dexter at the—'

'Seaview Hotel, course it is, missus!' a cheery voice boomed.

'Gav! How're you doing?'

'Loving life as a married man. Now, where can one of my chariots take you?'

Helen gave Jimmy's address, and Gav promised that a taxi would arrive straight away.

'Gav, while I've got you on the phone, is it possible to install a burglar alarm in my apartment that Suki won't set off?'

'Course it is, missus. There are plenty of pet-friendly alarms on the market. I'll pull some prices together for you, and once you decide, I'll send one of my lads to install it. I'll even charge you mates' rates, not the full whack.' And with that, he hung up.

Helen patted Suki, left water for her, and locked up the apartment. She tried the handle twice, to be sure, then walked upstairs. She was surprised to hear voices coming from the lounge. Pausing, she put a smile on her face and popped her head around the door. Olga and Freddy were sitting side by side on the window seat. When they saw her, they jumped apart.

'Hi, Helen, we were just . . . I mean, Olga and I were . . .'

'Tactics,' Olga said firmly. 'We were talking tactics.'

Freddy nodded too enthusiastically. Helen wondered what was really going on, because his face had coloured and Olga's had gone white. She frowned. Surely they weren't another odd couple like Marty and Marilyn? 'Yes, that's it,' he said. 'We were talking about tactics for the charity game on Friday.'

'Would you like a soft drink from the bar before I go out?' Helen asked.

'No, thank you,' Freddy said.

Helen noticed no trace of American accent this time. She wondered if he kept the accent for when he was part of the bigger group. Well, he was the youngest, and maybe he needed a way to assert himself with them.

'You look nice,' he said. 'Off somewhere special?'

'For dinner with a friend,' Helen replied.

The toot of a car horn outside saved her from revealing more.

'I'll see you at breakfast tomorrow,' she said, then turned and walked out of the door.

Sliding into the cab, she greeted the driver, who she recognised, then turned to look at the Seaview's lounge, the beautiful bay window with its views out to the sea. Olga and Freddy were sitting with their backs to the window. She saw Olga stroke Freddy's hair, then push a lock of it behind his ear. It was a touching moment, intimate.

'There's nothing so queer as the folk who stay at the Seaview,' she muttered under her breath.

When the cab reached Jimmy's house, Helen paid, then stepped out on to the road. She took a moment to appraise the neat two-storey terraced home. It looked well kept and smart. There was a small garden at the front and a black door with a polished knocker. She lifted the knocker and rapped twice.

Jimmy opened the door immediately, then pulled it wide and beamed. 'Helen, come in.'

She stepped inside. The aroma of something delicious cooking drifted to her along the hall. 'Something smells good,' she said.

'Chicken chasseur's my speciality. It'll be ready in ten minutes. To be honest, it's the only thing I can cook,' he admitted. 'I've done meringue nests for dessert.'

'I'm impressed,' Helen said.

'Well, when I say I've done meringue nests, what I mean is I bought them. But I put the raspberries in them myself. Here, let me take your coat.'

She slid her arms from her jacket and Jimmy stepped forward. They were standing close; so close that Helen could smell his lemon spice aftershave. He smelled good. It felt good to be there. She stood with her jacket in her hand, gazing into his eyes. Time seemed to stand still. Then he took her free hand, brought it to his lips and gently kissed it. She shifted her weight so that she was leaning towards him, ready to receive the kiss on the mouth that she felt sure was coming.

Jimmy closed his eyes and leaned forward. Helen held her breath, ready to offer herself to him, to meet him in a warm embrace. Who knew where it might lead? She still hadn't booked her return Gav's Cab. His lips brushed hers, gently, not forcing her, always polite, never rushing or asking for more than she was prepared to give. And oh, she wanted to give everything right there, right then. But just as she was about to lose herself in the kiss that she'd been longing for, she felt a tickle at the back of her nose. A sneeze building up. She pulled away, fast.

'Helen?' Jimmy said, alarmed.

She rummaged in her bag for a tissue. Her eyes began to stream, her nose began to water, and then came sneeze after sneeze. There was only one thing in the world that could make her allergy come on so quick and strong. She looked wildly around and saw the cause of the attack. A small brown kitten was staring up from the carpet, where it sat between Jimmy's feet.

He bent down and picked it up. 'Helen, I'd like you to meet Priscilla.'

Chapter 32

'Jimmy called his cat Priscilla? Why can't people give their pets normal names, like Tabby or Ginger?'

'Because his cat is neither tabby nor ginger, Jean. It's a scrawny brown kitten. You know I'm not keen on cats – they bring on my allergy.'

Jean wiped her hands on her apron, then looked across at Helen. 'Well? Come on then, tell me what happened next. You can't leave me hanging on a wink and a sneeze. I want to know the full story. What happened after your allergy started at Jimmy's house last night?'

'He put my dinner in a dish and I brought it home in a Gav's Cab,' Helen sighed.

'Oh dear me, no,' Jean tutted. 'That'll never do.'

'What else could I have done?'

'Haven't you heard of antihistamines?'

Helen picked up the note of sarcasm in Jean's voice but chose to ignore it. 'My eyes were streaming, my nose was running, I couldn't stop sneezing. As soon as Jimmy realised I was allergic to his cat, he locked it in the kitchen. But it wasn't enough. There were cat hairs on the sofa, on the carpet, on his shirt. I did my best, but I couldn't last more than ten minutes before I had to call it a night and ring for a cab.'

'You'll be seeing him again, though,' Jean said. It was a statement, not a question, and Jean's less-than-subtle tone wasn't lost on Helen.

'I'd love to, Jean. I was almost ready to . . .' She stopped herself. Jean didn't need to know the ins and outs of her love life. 'To get closer to him. But I can't stay at his place now I know he's got a cat.'

'Then there's only one thing for it. He'll have to stay here when you want to be together,' Jean said firmly.

'Jean!' Helen cried.

'Oh, don't spare my blushes and I'll not spare yours,' Jean said. 'I've seen it all before, love. I'm more experienced than you think. You don't get to my age without having your head turned once or twice by a handsome man.' A faraway look came into her eyes. 'There was a man once, you know, before I married Archie. Malcolm, he was called. His aunt lived in Hull, next door to Mum's friend Noreen, and I bumped into him each time I visited. He was a looker, was Malcolm. Anyway, what I'm saying is, life's too short not to try again with Jimmy. Invite him here, cook a meal, have him stay overnight, and I'll stay out of your way the next morning.'

'I'll think about it.'

'You've said that before, but you've never done anything about it.'

'This time's different, Jean. I think I'm finally ready to face my future with Jimmy. I'll always love Tom, always, but it's time for me to move on. Ricky's death has shaken me up and made me realise that you never know what's going to happen.'

'Too right. You could be hit by a bus tomorrow,' Jean chipped in.

'Or I could give myself to Jimmy and . . .' She stopped again. It really didn't feel right talking about sex with Jean. Cakes and pies, yes. Sausages and bacon, happily. But desire and lust? They were tricky subjects to chat about with her.

'You're ready for Jimmy, that's all that matters. And I couldn't be happier for you,' Jean replied, putting an end to their conversation.

Helen felt her face growing hot with embarrassment. 'I've already spoken to Tom's sister, to ask if she'd received a party invitation,' she said, changing the subject.

'Had she?' Jean replied.

'Yes, and I told her there was no party. I also rang Bev and Sue and had another long chat with them. I can't believe everyone has received invitations. Anyway, they all know the truth now. There's no party and that's that.'

'Who else did you call?' Jean asked.

'A couple of aunts in Bridlington, but they hadn't received anything. Mind you, I haven't seen them since I was a kid.'

Jean picked up a tea towel and flung it over her shoulder. 'What are your plans for today?' she asked.

Helen picked up her mug of tea. 'The usual. I'll take Suki out, then after breakfast I'll clean the rooms with Sally.'

'I don't mean work stuff,' Jean said. 'I mean, are you going to meet Jimmy to apologise for what happened last night?'

'Apologise? It wasn't my fault,' Helen huffed. 'I didn't know he had a cat.'

'I suggest you call him if you want to keep him.'

'Jean, that's my business. I'll sort things in my own time.'

Jean raised her hands in surrender. 'I'm just saying, that's all.'

Helen put her jacket on, and Suki walked towards her to have the lead snapped to her collar.

'I'll be back in half an hour to serve breakfast. And when I come back, I'd rather not talk about allergies and cats. Think you can manage that?'

Jean zipped her mouth shut and threw the key away.

When Helen reached the beach, she let Suki off the lead. The tide was coming in and there was a narrow strip of sand. Paddleboarders glided on the silky blue sea. Dogs chased sticks, and a little boy ran to the waves in bare feet, screaming with joy when cold water tickled his toes. She breathed in the fresh air, going over in her mind what Jean had advised her to do. She knew she'd ring Jimmy again – she wanted to see him – but there was the tricky problem of his cat to be solved.

As she walked, she saw a couple ahead of her holding hands. Her heart caught in her chest. It couldn't be them, surely? And yet it was. Olga, in her navy-blue suit and smart shoes, and Freddy. They were just metres away. Helen didn't know what to do.

'Oh crikey,' she muttered. The scene in the Seaview's lounge the night before came to mind. She thought she'd spotted a tenderness between them then, and now here they were, holding hands. She decided the best thing for it was to turn around and walk away before they realised they'd been spotted. But when she looked for Suki, the dog was nowhere to be seen. She spun around, desperate.

'Suki!' she called. She shaded her eyes from the sun and saw the greyhound walking at Olga's side. 'Oh no,' she sighed. There was only one thing for it.

She picked up her pace, marching towards Olga and Freddy, determined to get her dog back. Whatever happened next would be up to the courting couple and how they reacted. If they were going public with their romance – and it looked like they were being open – then she might as well congratulate them. In for a penny, she thought.

When she reached Olga's side, she greeted her guests warmly, as if it was the most normal thing in the word for Olga to be courting a young boy like Freddy. She had experienced many unusual things in her decades as landlady of the Seaview Hotel. She was prepared to chalk this down as another of them.

Olga dropped Freddy's hand and stiffened. 'I must go now,' she said.

She spun on her heel and left the beach. Freddy opened his mouth to say something, but seemed to think better of it and closed it again. Helen snapped the lead to Suki's collar.

'Sorry, I didn't mean to interrupt your walk. I just needed to get my dog back.'

Freddy watched Olga go, and Helen saw tears in his eyes.

'Freddy? Is everything all right?' she asked.

He didn't answer. Instead, he walked after Olga, following her from the sand to the prom. Helen trailed after them sheepishly.

Halfway up the hill was a children's play area, with swings, slide and a roundabout. Olga was sitting on a wooden bench, gazing out to sea. Helen watched as Freddy walked towards the older woman and sat down beside her. There was nowhere else for her to go. She had to walk past them or head back to the beach. She decided to front it out. Ordinarily she would have left her guests to it and turned a blind eye. But these weren't ordinary times. This time there was a murder to solve. There was something strange going on and she needed to find out what. And so she marched confidently on.

'Come, Suki,' she said.

Olga and Freddy both turned to look as she neared their bench. Without moving her gaze from Helen's face, Olga took hold of

Freddy's hand. The woman had nerves of steel, Helen had to give her that.

'Let me tell you something,' Olga said. 'Sit.' She patted the seat at her side with her free hand.

Helen did as instructed, and Suki lay at her feet.

'I love Freddy,' Olga said.

Helen was about to comment that she could've worked that out for herself, but decided to keep quiet.

'He is my life,' Olga continued. Helen noticed that an unusual softness had entered her voice.

'You don't need to explain,' she said, feeling awkward. 'I'm sorry I bumped into you on the beach. As I just told Freddy, I was collecting my dog to take her home.' She got up, and Suki stood too. 'I'm sorry, I should go. This is none of my business.'

'Sit!' Olga barked.

They both sat down again.

'Mum, please . . .' Freddy said.

Helen froze. Mum? Her mind tried to do a jigsaw, working out how to slot pieces together that wouldn't fit, no matter how hard she tried. It was a jigsaw with long legs, a short body, black hair, brown hair, long arms, a fake American accent. Freddy. Olga. Mum?

'Mum?' she squeaked.

'Freddy's my son,' Olga said, patting his hand.

Helen's mind spun. If Olga was Freddy's mother, that could only mean one thing. She'd already spotted the resemblance between Freddy and Ricky. She'd seen the way Freddy had jumped up and down three times on the golf course when he'd scored a hole-in-one, the same way Ricky had. 'Then you and Ricky . . .' she began, hardly daring to finish her thought.

243

'I'd rather not talk about Ricky,' Olga said.

'But he's Freddy's dad, right?' Helen heard herself say. What had she to lose now? She was already in for her penny, she might as well go for the pound.

'Right,' Olga said, nodding curtly.

'Don't tell Alice and the others, please,' Freddy pleaded, wiping his eyes. 'No one knows but Mum and me.'

Helen thought this unlikely. How could Alice, Marty and Marilyn not have noticed the resemblance between Freddy and Ricky?

'Dad . . . I mean Ricky, had an affair with Mum while he was married to Alice. It was one of his many affairs. And then I was born.'

'Freddy's the best thing to happen to me,' Olga added.

'I promise I won't say anything, unless this has something to do with Ricky's death,' Helen said.

'I'm not a killer.' Olga spoke firmly, narrowing her eyes.

'Mum's right, Helen. She wouldn't harm a fly, and neither would I. Besides, both of us know the best way we could have hurt Ricky. We'd planned to end his run as champion crazy golfer. I'd been training all year to beat him.'

'Yes, I'll admit it, I wanted revenge on him. He never paid child support when Freddy was younger. And he never answered letters from my solicitor,' Olga said.

Helen remembered Freddy's phone call, the one he'd made when he'd thought he was alone at the Seaview. His phone call to *Mum*.

'You wanted to beat Ricky on the crazy-golf course and get your revenge that way?' she said.

'We wanted to annihilate his game and publicly humiliate him,' Freddy replied with anger.

Helen now had the corner pieces of the jigsaw, and the straight edges began to line up. Norman the hut man had been ruled out as a suspect. Could she also rule out Olga and Freddy, or might they be lying, in cahoots to protect each other? They were convincing in what they'd said, she thought, but she only had their word.

Freddy took Olga's small hands and kissed her on her cheek. In that tender moment between mother and son, Helen hoped with all her heart that they were as innocent as they claimed.

Chapter 33

As soon as Helen walked through the door of the Seaview, Jean looked up from her task of whisking eggs in a bowl. Helen didn't even bother taking off her jacket as she flopped into a chair at the table.

'What's up?' Jean asked.

Helen sat still, staring at the wall.

'Helen?'

Questions whirled in her mind. How could Olga, tiny little Olga, have produced a tall, strapping lad like Freddy? Ricky Delmont hadn't been overly tall. Was Freddy's height a throwback to genes in Olga or Ricky's past? Did Alice know about Ricky's affair with Olga while she'd been married to him? She closed her eyes. When she opened them, Jean was standing in front of her with a tea towel over her shoulder. In one hand she held a white porcelain bowl and in the other a fork. It was the noise of the fork clacking against the side of the bowl that had pulled Helen from her thoughts.

'You're miles away, Helen. What's happened?' Jean placed the bowl on the counter top and put her hands on her hips. Helen noticed her left foot impatiently tapping the floor.

'I've just learned something about two of my guests,' she said.

'Which two? The old man and his young bit of stuff? It's not right, if you ask me.'

246

'Jean, please. I know we're from different generations, but I never had you down as narrow-minded. Marty and Marilyn seem happy enough. They're married, let's leave it at that. Anyway, it wasn't them I've been speaking to. It was two of the others, Olga and Freddy.'

Jean sat opposite Helen. 'What have you learned that's upset you so much?'

Helen leaned back in her seat. She unclipped the lead from Suki's collar and the dog slunk away to the patio doors to watch a sparrow in the birdbath. 'Olga's his mum, Jean.'

'Whose? Ricky Delmont's? The dead man?'

'No, Freddy. She's Freddy's mum.'

Jean laughed out loud, but when she saw Helen was serious, the laughter died away. 'But she's . . .' She lowered her hand to her knees. 'And he's . . .' She raised her hand above her head. 'Are you sure?'

'I'm sure. They told me themselves. And I've caught them together being tender and caring. I've noticed little things passing between them ever since they arrived, and they make sense now. Gentle touches, caresses, smiles. It's because they love each other. And that's not all. Brace yourself, Jean. Freddy's dad is . . . I mean he was . . . Ricky Delmont.'

'You mean Olga and Ricky were married?'

'No. Ricky had an affair with her while he was married to Alice.'

'Did Ricky know the lad was his son?'

'Oh, he knew all right. And by all accounts he wanted nothing to do with him. Wouldn't even pay Olga the child support she needed.'

'Oh, that's bad.'

'That's what Olga keeps saying. Each time she mentions Ricky, she calls him a bad man.'

Jean leaned towards her. 'Do you need to tell the police what you've found out?'

Helen thought for a moment. 'No,' she decided. 'This is personal to them. I can't see them being involved in Ricky's death, not now I know the truth about the revenge they were planning.'

Jean's eyebrows shot up in surprise. 'Revenge?'

Helen waved her hand dismissively. 'It's a long story involving a phone call I overheard. My hunch is that Freddy and Olga are in the clear. As is your friend Norman.'

'I heard the police let him go,' Jean said.

'Did you know about his drink problem?'

Jean nodded. 'Everyone knows. It's a sad state of affairs. His wife left him, you know.'

'He told me about it. That reminds me, I'll take the phone number of a support group next time I'm over his way. I'm sure some cards were pushed through the letter box the other day.'

'Poor Norman,' Jean said.

Helen thought for a moment. 'Do you know, I had a quiet word with Alice when I found her sitting outside after she'd been quizzed by the police. She didn't mention anything about Olga and Freddy, but I can't believe she doesn't know about her husband's affair with Olga. I mean, Freddy's the spitting image of Ricky. How can she not know?'

Jean stood and picked up the bowl, giving the eggs an extra whisk before setting them to one side. 'It's amazing what people, especially women, will turn a blind eye to if it stops them confronting something they don't want to face. Maybe Alice does know but doesn't mention it for fear of upsetting the team. You know how focused they are on winning. Maybe Marty the muscle man and the gold-digger know about it too.'

'Jean, you mustn't call her a gold-digger. Have some respect. Without our guests, whatever they're like, we wouldn't be in work. I'd have to sell up and move out.'

Jean shrugged and turned away. 'Doesn't seem right to me, a young girl like her being with a much older man. I don't like it.'

'You're not paid to like it, you're paid to cook,' Helen said tersely, then regretted her words immediately.

'I was better paid next door at the Vista del Mar,' Jean sniffed.

'How much was Miriam paying you?' Helen asked, shocked.

The door to the apartment burst open and Sally breezed in. 'Morning!' she called.

'Morning,' Helen muttered under her breath, shooting daggers at Jean as she did so. Sally stood stock still and looked from Helen to Jean.

'What's going on with you two?'

'She started it,' Jean said, without turning around.

'And she's being narrow-minded and mean,' Helen replied.

'Oh, for heaven's sake!' Sally exclaimed. 'I won't let you two fall out again. Remember what happened last time?'

Helen cast her gaze to the floor, then looked shyly at Jean. Jean's face flushed red. Helen walked towards her and gently laid her hand on her arm. 'I'm sorry, Jean. Ricky's death has turned my life, and the Seaview, upside down. I've lost bookings. The hotel's on the front page of the local paper, implicated in his murder. I'm upset and I'm taking everything out on you when I shouldn't.'

'Look, love—' Jean began, but Helen held up her hand.

'I'm not finished. I'm also upset about Jimmy having a stupid cat that triggered my allergy. And I'm rattled about the fiftieth birthday party that someone's organising behind my back. You still haven't brought the invitation in. It feels like you're hiding something. Marie said she'd bring hers too, and I've not seen that either. I feel like I'm going mad, Jean, or paranoid.'

Jean patted her hand. 'I'm sorry for what you're going through, love. It sounds to me as if you're not sleeping too well. You're getting all het up about something that'll blow over soon. Now, let's say no more about it. Least said, soonest mended. Let me get on, and the breakfast will be ready in no time.'

Helen's shoulders slumped. Maybe Jean was right. Maybe she needed to have an early night and catch up on her sleep. She hated arguing with Jean and was grateful that Sally had arrived when she had. If she hadn't, she hated to think how heated her words with Jean might have become. She might have lost her again.

She turned to Sally and mouthed, 'Thank you,' then changed the subject to something more cheerful. 'I spoke to your Gav last night. He was working the switchboard when I rang for a cab to take me to Jimmy's house. He said he was loving married life.'

Sally slipped her tabard over her head and snapped the fasteners shut at her waist. 'He's a great stepdad to Gracie, best thing to happen to both of us. We're taking Gracie to Cayton Bay at the weekend. There's a new ice-cream parlour opening. It's owned by Dinah's son.'

'Who's Dinah?' Jean asked.

'One of Mum's friends. It's got over fifty flavours of ice cream. Fifty! Can you imagine? I never knew there were that many. But don't worry, we'll be back in time for your party. Six o'clock start it says on the invitation.'

Sally gasped, then put her hand over her mouth and glanced at Jean. Jean pursed her lips. Helen knew that look on Jean's face; it was a warning to Sally not to say any more. She felt her shoulders tense. 'You know I don't want a party!' she said, aware that her voice was rising and anger was building. 'How many times do I have to tell you both? There is no flaming party!'

She noticed Sally and Jean share another look.

'What?' she said, turning from one to the other. 'What do you two know that I don't? Do you know who's organised it? Tell me now if you do, because this is driving me mad.'

She flung herself on to the sofa and sat with her head in her hands, eyes closed, trying to make the whole thing go away – the party and the mysterious invitations, Ricky's murder, Jimmy's cat, Olga being Freddy's mum. None of it made sense. Tears pricked the back of her eyes and a lump was forming in her throat. Then she felt movement on each side of her, and when she opened her eyes, Jean was sitting on her right and Sally on her left. Sally was holding her hand. Jean was sitting upright, looking into her eyes.

'We weren't supposed to tell you, love.'

'It was a secret,' Sally added.

'What was? What's going on?' Helen cried. Tears were rolling down her cheeks.

'This party,' Jean said.

'Your fiftieth birthday,' Sally chipped in.

'It's you two, isn't it?' Helen yelled, furious. 'The two people I trust most in the world, and you've gone behind my back and lied to me! I'm disappointed in you both.'

'No, love, it's not us,' Jean said gently.

'Then it must have been Marie,' Helen said. 'Or was it Sandra DeVine? Oh, I bet it was her. It's exactly the stupid sort of thing she would do to try to get in with me and Marie. Just wait till I get my hands on the conniving cow.'

'No, it wasn't Marie, Sandra, or Bev and Sue,' Jean said.

'We've got to tell her,' Sally said, looking at Jean.

'Tell me what? What on earth's going on? I feel as if I'm going mad. Will someone tell me once and for all who's arranged this blasted party?'

'You really want to know?' Jean asked.

'Of course I want to know. Tell me now, before I throttle you.'

A look of concern passed over Jean's face, and when she spoke, her words came out in a whisper.

'It was Tom, love. He arranged it before he died.'

Chapter 34

Helen sank back in her seat and closed her eyes, trying to make sense of what she'd just heard. 'Tom?' she whispered.

'Sally, run upstairs and fetch the brandy from the bar,' Jean ordered. She patted Helen's hand. 'It's all right, love. I know it's a shock. It shocked me too when I found out.'

'What? When did you know? How? What happened?'

'Let's wait for Sally to come back with the brandy. You'll need something to help you cope. I have to admit, I wouldn't mind a nip myself. I never wanted you to find out this way. It's not what Tom wanted.'

'What he wanted? What are you saying?'

Sally burst through the door carrying a bottle. She immediately went to the kitchen cupboard and took down two mugs. Pouring a splash of brandy into each of them, she handed them to Helen and Jean.

'Not having one yourself?' Jean asked.

Sally bit her lip, then shook her head and looked away. Helen took her mug in both hands and lifted it to her lips.

'That's right, love. It'll help you focus on what you're about to hear,' Jean said.

She sipped from her own mug, then placed it on the table, straightened in her seat and turned to face Helen.

'A few weeks ago, a letter came from Benson Brown & Co., addressed to me at my home.'

'A letter from my solicitor? You never mentioned it,' Helen said, confused.

'I was under strict instructions not to say a word. It was part of the contract I signed.'

'Jean, it feels like you're talking in a foreign language. My head's swimming. I don't understand what Tom's got to do with this. A contract? Solicitors? Is this some kind of joke?'

'I'd never do anything so cruel,' Jean said, shaking her head. 'Now listen to me.'

Helen took a sip of brandy and looked Jean in the eye as she continued.

'When Tom knew he was dying, when he was in the hospice, he called Benson Brown. He wanted you taken care of after he'd gone. He wanted to ensure that his will was up to date, all the insurance policies on the Seaview were in place, that kind of thing.'

'And he did take care of me, you know that,' Helen said. Tears brimmed in her eyes; the brandy tasted thick in her throat. It felt as if she was watching herself on the sofa, as if this was happening to someone else. She forced herself to concentrate on what Jean was saying.

'One of the things he wanted more than anything was for you to have a party at the Seaview on your fiftieth birthday. It was a party he knew he wouldn't be around to attend. He gave Benson Brown a list of people to invite, including his sister and her family in Shetland. She's driving down, staying overnight in a couple of places, before arriving in Scarborough on Saturday. There's a whole load of people coming to the party and staying at the hotel for two nights.'

'But . . . I had a look at this weekend's bookings and didn't recognise any names,' Helen said, trying to process what Jean was saying.

'It was part of the surprise. They were all booked in under false names. Tom even left money with Benson Brown to pay for them all.'

'Oh Jean, what have I done? I called everyone I knew to tell them there was no party. I've undone all Tom's work.'

Sally leaned forward. 'Don't worry. Each time you rang someone to tell them the party was off, Jean rang them to say it was on. Everyone's still coming.'

Jean wagged a finger at Helen. 'Now, there's something I want to say to you. It might sound as if I'm being cruel to be kind, but that's just the way I am. You know I don't mince my words. Since Tom died, you've not been yourself and that's understandable. However . . .' and here she cast a nervous glance at Sally before returning her focus to Helen, 'the Seaview hasn't been the same either. If you ask me, it's about time you stopped feeling sorry for yourself.'

Helen's mouth opened in shock as Jean continued.

'No amount of moping will bring Tom back. Arranging your birthday party was something he did because you were the love of his life. He knew how much you enjoyed a good party. We used to hold them here every weekend.'

'The Elvis parties,' Helen muttered.

'Yes, the Elvis parties, with rock and roll, guests dressed up in black wigs and white suits, diamanté belts and rhinestone capes.

Oh Helen, remember the fun? Everyone dancing and singing to the jukebox filled with your and Tom's Elvis records. When was the last time that jukebox was played?'

Helen tried to remember, but couldn't. 'Tom really did all that for me? Arranged invitations to go out and everything?' she asked.

Jean squeezed her hand. 'He was thinking of you and the Seaview.'

Helen drained her mug. She wanted to cry, she wanted to laugh. More than anything, she wanted Tom there so that she could hug him and kiss him and tell him she missed him. 'It'll take time for this to sink in,' she said.

'It will, love,' Jean agreed. 'When I got the letter from Benson Brown, it fair knocked me for six. Tom arranged with the solicitor to have the invitations printed, and they kept them in their office and sent them to me with his instructions. I had to ensure that people were still living at the same addresses before I sent the invitations on. He even left money to cover postage.'

'He always thought of everything,' Helen said softly. 'Oh Jean, I feel such a fool.'

'There's no need to, love. Look, I shouldn't have told you, but I couldn't bear to see you suffering after what happened with Ricky Delmont. I know the party's lying heavy on your mind, and I hated that it was making you feel terrible.'

'Tom might have thought of everything, but there's no way he could have known my fiftieth would coincide with a guest being killed.'

Jean bristled in her seat. 'Precisely. And he wouldn't have wanted Ricky's death to spoil your party. You've got to remember that.'

'Can I see it, Jean? This contract of Tom's that you signed with Benson Brown? Can I take a look at what he wrote? It's his legacy to me.'

'Course you can. I'll bring it tomorrow when I come in to work. Mind you, not a word to Tom's sister. I don't want anyone to know I've gone against the contract. But I had to tell someone, it was too big for me to keep to myself, and so I confided in Sally.'

'You must understand why we had to tell you, Helen,' Sally said. 'We've seen how you've struggled since Ricky's death.'

'I don't know what to say. I'm glad you told me, though. I thought a party was the last thing I wanted, but knowing that Tom's behind it changes everything. It'll give me a focus, something positive to concentrate on instead of my thoughts being mired in murder.'

Helen handed Jean her mug, then got up from the sofa. It felt like there was too much going on in her mind; her head was heavy and fuzzy. 'But how . . . I mean . . .' she began, questions spiralling. 'These invitations, I need to see one. I'd love to know what Tom wrote and see the cards he chose.'

'I'll bring it tomorrow, promise. We can talk about it as much as you want. Just don't mention it to Benson Brown, and remember to look surprised and set your face to stunned when we jump out on Saturday night in the bar with balloons, banners and cake.'

'Cake? Who's making cake?'

Sally pointed at Jean.

'Guilty as charged,' Jean said. 'And Marie's doing the catering with her staff from Tom's Teas. I had to bring her in on our secret, but I had a feeling Tom wouldn't mind.'

'Gav's decorating the outside of the Seaview with pink and white petunia hanging baskets. Mum's making them for you,' Sally said.

Helen thought her heart would burst with love for her friends. 'Who else is coming?' she asked.

Jean began counting on her fingers. 'Me, Sally, Gav and Gracie. Marie's bringing a plus one, some fella called Jack Malone. Your friends Bev and Sue are coming, so is Sandra DeVine. Sandra's asked if she can bring her fella, the detective.'

'DS Hutchinson? Tell her she can.'

'Tom's sister and her husband and their two sons are coming for two nights,' she continued. 'One of your nephews is bringing his boyfriend. Everyone's booked in upstairs and we'll have a celebratory breakfast on Sunday morning after the party. My sausage butties are a wonderful hangover cure. There's only one thing left to arrange.'

'What's that?'

'Well, Tom's clear instructions to Benson Brown were that your fiftieth should be a night to remember, a night to do the Seaview proud. He's asked for it to be an Elvis party. Which means, I guess, it might benefit from an Elvis impersonator.' Jean rubbed her chin and rolled her eyes, like a cartoon villain. 'Hmm, if only we knew where we could find one of those.'

'All right, I get the message. Subtlety was never your strong point. I'll speak to Jimmy. You don't think Tom would mind, do you?'

'Mind? I think he'd be delighted about you dating an Elvis impersonator. You know how much of an Elvis fan he was.'

'Dating? How old-fashioned that word sounds. But it suits

Jimmy; it suits us and the way we feel about each other. Am I making sense?'

'Dating, courting, whatever you want to call it, it puts a smile on your face each time you mention his name, and that's great to see. I'm looking forward to the party.'

'Ask your mum if she wants to come, Sally.'

Jean crossed her arms defensively under her ample bosom. 'You really want that woman back here?' she huffed.

'Jean, that's my mum you're talking about,' Sally snapped. 'I know she's not everyone's cup of tea, but she's all right once you get to know her.'

'Invite Miriam too,' Helen said. 'Might as well get her on our side, otherwise she'll only complain about the noise from the jukebox.'

'Well, if you're sure,' Jean said. 'Me and Sally will keep on co-ordinating the party as if nothing has changed. But please, not a word to Benson Brown. If they find out I've blown Tom's secret, they might do me for fraud.'

'You'll get banged up in Holloway for six months, Jean,' Sally teased.

'Oh, you two. What would I do without you both?' Helen said.

Jean waved her hands at her, shooing her out of the door. 'Breakfast's almost ready to serve to our guests, so get yourself upstairs. Square your shoulders and put on some lipstick to face the world. Work will take your mind off what I've just told you, for a little while anyway. I know it's a lot to take in. Once you're done upstairs, I'll have the cafetière ready, and one of my spiced apple cakes, warm from the oven. The three of us can have a good chat.' Jean turned to the stove, where sausages were grilling and bacon was sizzling.

'Sorry, I can't stop for coffee today,' Sally said. 'I've got an appointment in town.' She dropped her gaze to the carpet, and Helen took it as a sign that she didn't want to talk more about it.

'Come on, Sally, let's get to work,' she said. As she headed for the door, the brandy bottle caught her eye. She picked it up. 'I'll put this back in the bar. Thanks for bringing it down. Jean was right, it helped with the shock, but I hope I don't reek of booze.'

'You don't reek of anything other than the zingy citrus tang of our cleaning solution,' Sally joked. 'By the way, I'm sure a bottle of that has gone missing.'

Helen remembered Brenda hiding a bottle behind her back on the day she'd visited her. She'd obviously felt guilty about taking it, or she wouldn't have acted so furtively. She decided to keep quiet about it, and followed Sally up the stairs.

When they reached the hall, Sally stood by the dining room door, waiting for the guests to come down. Helen walked into the lounge to put the brandy bottle back. She slid it on to a glass shelf, then turned to look at the framed photo of Tom. It was a picture taken at one of the Seaview's Elvis parties. Tom was suntanned and smiling. He wore his white Elvis suit, collar up, shades on, dark hair slicked back. He was grinning, one hand on his hip and the other pointing at the camera, at Helen as she'd taken the snap. Carefully she lifted the photo from its hook and ran her fingers over Tom's face.

'Thank you, my love,' she whispered. She raised the picture to her lips and kissed it. 'Thank you,' she said again, then she hung it back on the wall.

As she turned to leave the bar, she noticed something that shouldn't have been there. She knew she hadn't left it there because she absolutely forbade such things at the Seaview. A shiver ran down her spine. She didn't like what she saw. Nestled between two glasses on the shelf was an open packet of peanuts.

Chapter 35

Helen froze. When she'd pulled herself together, she called out, 'Sally, did you leave this here?' She held up the packet of nuts in her hand as Sally walked into the lounge.

Sally peered at it. 'Of course not.'

'Well, someone did. It was with the glasses. Didn't you see it when you took the brandy?'

'I dashed in, picked the bottle up and ran out as fast as I could. You were in such a state downstairs that I wanted to get to you quickly. I didn't stop to look around. I didn't see anything.'

'No one was in the hall? None of the guests?'

'Not a soul,' Sally replied.

Helen looked at the packet of nuts. It was a high-quality brand. 'Why would anyone leave this here? It's as if someone has tried to hide it amongst the glasses.'

Sally's face clouded over. 'It was peanuts that killed Ricky Delmont.'

'It's worrying,' Helen said. 'I know it wasn't here last night, because I did a stock-take. Someone's placed it here since then.'

'I think you should tell the police,' Sally said.

Helen gave this some thought. However, she knew that if she rang DS Hutchinson, he'd send forensics back to dust for finger-prints in the bar. He might ask more questions of her guests and scare them into silence. No, she wouldn't call him. Someone was using her business, her home and her livelihood to hide incriminating evidence! She was determined to take matters into her own hands.

As she walked back into the hall, she heard Olga and Freddy's voices.

'I'm hungry,' Olga said, marching towards the dining room.

Freddy hung back and gave Helen a wan smile. 'I'm sorry about earlier, when you met us on the beach,' he said. She noticed that his accent carried no American twang this time. 'I was feeling confused over what had happened to Dad. See, he abandoned Mum when I was a baby. He didn't even acknowledge me while he was staying here, although he knew I was his son. Mum says he was a bad man, and maybe he was, but he didn't deserve to die. The shock of it has knocked me for six. That's why I was upset.'

Helen patted his arm. 'It's all right. I promise I won't say a word.'

He smiled more warmly. 'Thank you, Helen. This really is a special hotel. I felt at home the minute I stepped through the door. It's cosy and comfortable.'

'Comfortable enough to lose your American accent?' she pushed.

'Oh, that,' Freddy said, blushing. 'Mum brought me up on the army base, and I just loved the way the American kids spoke. They got me hooked on American TV and films and I started speaking like they did, just to fit in. It became a habit I couldn't shake – my way of putting a front on, of being someone I wasn't. Now that Dad's gone, somehow it doesn't seem to matter any more. I feel I can be myself now, to look after Mum.'

Helen felt a warm glow inside. 'She's lucky to have you.'

Freddy walked into the lounge and sat opposite Olga. A noise on the landing suggested someone else coming down. Helen stayed in her position at the foot of the stairs, peanuts on her mind, ready to start inspecting her guests, looking for any clues as to who had left the packet behind the bar. Alice appeared, her red hair loose, falling around her shoulders in curls.

'Morning, Alice. How are you? Did you sleep well?'

'No, not well at all, but it's no reflection on the bed or the room. I've got too much on my mind. I keep thinking about Ricky and the awful way he died.' She walked straight past and into the dining room.

Marty and Marilyn were next down, holding hands.

'Morning to you both,' Helen said.

'Morning,' Marty replied. 'Any chance of some iced water for my wife?'

'Of course. Coming right up.'

Helen glanced at Marilyn's face. She looked peaky again. Her brassy blonde hair was scraped back, tied with a scrunchie at the back of her head. She wore no make-up at all, and Helen noticed that her skin was blotchy and pale, and she had dark circles under her eyes. Well, it wasn't her place to ask, of course, because she never liked to interfere in her guests' lives, but that didn't mean she wasn't curious. Was Marilyn mourning Ricky, grieving for her lover? She'd seen the smiles pass between the pair before his untimely death.

She went downstairs to ask Jean for iced water, then walked into the dining room and set the jug in front of Marilyn.

'Is everything all right this morning?' she asked, glancing from Marty to Marilyn. She tried to keep her tone light, not too inquisitive, just the right side of caring. It was a gift she'd perfected over decades.

'My wife's feeling a little under the weather,' Marty replied.

Helen hoped Marilyn might add to her husband's words, but she simply reached for the jug. Helen left them to it and began to help Sally serve.

After cereal and juice, Jean sent up plates of cooked full English breakfasts. Sausages (pork or vegetarian), toast (white or brown), bacon, hash browns, black pudding, beans, eggs (fried, scrambled or poached) were sent up in the dumbwaiter. Helen and Sally walked back and forth from the dumbwaiter to the dining room, bringing brown sauce, red sauce, mustard, more toast, pats of butter (vegan spread on request), pots of milk (semi-skimmed or soya), marmalade (orange or lime) and jam (strawberry or plum). All of it washed down by tea (Yorkshire; the only kind that Jean served). Freddy devoured his breakfast with everything on it, then got stuck in to lashings of toast. Marty did the same, and all the while, Helen noticed that he cast anxious looks across the table at his wife. She kept her eye on Marilyn as the woman picked her way through a slice of dry toast.

'Nothing else for you this morning?' she asked.

Marilyn shook her head, then delicately popped a piece of toast into her mouth and washed it down with iced water.

Across the room, Alice ate scrambled eggs on toast, making appreciative noises. Olga, however, stuck to her usual bowl of low-fat cereal with skimmed milk, and a cup of black tea.

'I need to keep fit for training,' she said.

'You should eat more,' Alice remarked.

Olga shot daggers at her. 'I'm finished,' she said, then pushed her chair back from the table and stormed out of the room.

Helen pretended she wasn't paying attention as she gathered

Olga's bowl to send down to Jean. She noticed Freddy turn to Alice.

'Why do you have to upset her?'

Alice shrugged. Helen wondered what was going on. Did Alice know the truth about Freddy being Olga's son? She looked at them all and wondered who knew what. How strange it all was, she thought. She glanced again at Marilyn, who had pulled the crust from her toast and left it on the side of her plate.

She filled the dumbwaiter and sent it down to Jean, her mind working overtime, thinking about the peanuts. Had the murderer left them in the lounge on purpose, wanting her to find them? Or had they been left by mistake? Perhaps the killer had intended to implicate another guest in Ricky's murder, or even to compromise Helen and the Seaview. Her blood ran cold at the thought. A madcap idea began to form in her mind, a plan to trap whoever had left them. She needed to be discreet. It wasn't going to be easy, but she was determined to save the Seaview's reputation and its four stars.

Chapter 36

In the early hours of Wednesday morning, when the world outside was dark and sunrise still hours away, Helen lay under a table on the dining room floor. All the lights were switched off and the Seaview was silent. She had her phone with her to use as watch and torch and to call the police if things turned ugly. She crossed her fingers and hoped they wouldn't. Then she crossed them again and hoped she was doing the right thing.

She hadn't dared tell Jean or Sally what she was up to, as they'd have tried to talk her out of her madcap idea. And it was mad, of that there was no doubt. But whoever had left the peanuts behind the bar had left them there for a reason, and her plan was to nab whoever it was. Her jumbled thinking, as far as she'd got with it, was that if the person who'd left them in the small hours of the previous morning had done so by accident, they might come back to retrieve them at the same time this morning. But if they'd been left to implicate another guest, or to involve Helen and the Seaview, her eccentric plan might be in vain.

She'd waited until she was sure all her guests were in their rooms. She'd listened to their doors open and close, heard water running in their en suite bathrooms. It was almost 1 a.m. when she felt certain they were all in bed. Only then did she creep into the dining room with her phone in her back pocket and a sense of dread in her heart. She carried a packet of raisins in case she got peckish and a small bottle of water in case she built up a thirst. Well, she'd never been on a stakeout before and had no idea how long she might need to wait. She'd never felt so gung-ho, and also so foolhardy. She knew she had to be careful, and she also carried a hammer, just in case. Not that she'd use it, of course, but it'd be something to brandish. Something to frighten the living daylights out of whoever came for the nuts. And if no one came, if her stakeout proved pointless, then she'd ring the police and tell them what she'd found. They could send forensics, question her guests, do what the heck they liked, because frankly, she'd had enough.

Her neck was beginning to ache, so she changed position from lying on her stomach to lying on her side. She took her phone from her pocket, desperate to know how long she'd been waiting there for something to happen and someone to appear. It must have been two or three hours, at least.

Only twenty minutes? She moaned silently when she saw the time. This was going to be a long night. She slid her phone back and pulled out the packet of raisins, ripping it open and slipping half a dozen into her mouth. She chewed slowly and carefully, listening for noises from upstairs. At every creak, her heart skipped. But the creaks were just the old building settling down for the night, the Seaview yawning and stretching before bed.

She pulled her phone out again. Three minutes had passed since she'd last looked. She began to wonder if she'd made the right decision about spending the night on the floor. She hadn't even brought a sleeping bag or a pillow. What if she fell asleep and her guests found her there the next morning? She scraped her chin along the carpet, anything to ease the boredom. Another thirty seconds went by. She yawned, but kept her gaze firmly on the door to the lounge. If anyone came down to go in there, there was no way they'd see her unless they entered the dining room, and why would they do that? Suddenly a million reasons jumped into her mind why they might. She really hadn't thought this through. She scratched her head and checked her phone. Two more minutes had passed.

This is silly, she thought. I haven't a clue what I'm doing.

She pressed her hands on the carpet to push herself up, ready to call it a night, give in and go to bed. And that was when she heard it. She recognised it instinctively, her experienced landlady's ear attuned to each sound the Seaview made. Every door, every stair, every landing, she knew the noise of each one. It was faint, hardly there, but she heard it. She crouched low, out of sight of anyone coming down, swallowing the raisins she was chewing, gulping them down out of fright. Then she picked up the hammer. Another noise, this time louder. A creaking stair, and Helen knew exactly which one. She gripped the hammer and held her breath, listening. Another step, another creak. Someone was on their way down. She could hardly breathe. She had to keep silent and still. Had she turned her phone off? She didn't dare check in case the light alerted whoever was out there. She prayed she'd remembered to turn off the ringer, but who would be calling her at this time of night?

She tuned her ear back to the sounds. Her line of vision through the crack in the dining room door led straight to the bottom of the stairs, across the hall and into the lounge. All she could see was the carpet, and table and chair legs. She'd soon see the killer's legs too, and that made her determined to keep her cool. Nab them, grab them, threaten them with the hammer. She repeated the mantra in her head.

There it was, the first step into the hall. Whoever was out there was light on their feet. Was it Olga? She was small enough not to make a sound; tiny, like a doll. Marty would be heavier, louder. Alice might be quiet, Helen thought. She discounted Freddy because he moved clumsily, and she didn't think he'd make it downstairs without a lot of noise. She gasped. She saw a bare foot. Scarlet toenails. A woman, tiptoeing from the hall to the lounge.

As she eased open the dining room door, she heard the tinkle of glass from the lounge. Slowly and carefully she pulled herself up to standing then stepped out into the hall in her socked feet, hammer raised in one hand, packet of raisins in the other.

'Gotcha!' she yelled. She flicked the light on in the lounge. There was no one to be seen. 'I know you're hiding behind the bar. Come out now with your hands up and you won't get hurt.'

There was no movement, nothing. Helen had been afraid before, but now she was angry. She was tired and needed to sleep. 'I said come out. Show yourself.'

Slowly something rose behind the bar. It looked like a candy-floss caught in a net, and it took her a few seconds to realise what it was. Marilyn pulled herself to standing. Her blonde beehive was wrapped in a hairnet, her bottom lip was quivering, and her eyes were streaming with tears. She wore a pink satin nightgown with a frill around the neck and was holding both hands high in the air. 'Don't shoot!'

Helen's packet of raisins shot out of her hand and sprayed all over the floor. She was so nervous she could hardly hold the hammer. She put it down on a table.

'Marilyn?'

'I'm sorry,' Marilyn wailed.

'What are you doing?'

'I was just getting something from the bar. A drink, that's it. You said we could help ourselves if you weren't around.'

Helen narrowed her eyes. 'Just a drink?' she said accusingly.

Marilyn shook her head. 'No, something else. But please don't tell Marty.'

'I might have to tell the police if you're after what I think you are.'

Marilyn's breath came out of her in short, sharp bursts, and Helen saw that she was shaking. 'Can I put my hands down now?'

'Of course. Come out from behind there.'

Helen kept her eye on the hammer, ready to brandish it if Marilyn turned on her. But from the nervous look of the woman, she doubted she would. She sat on the window seat and gestured for Marilyn to sit next to her.

'What's going on?' she asked.

'I was after the . . . um . . . It wasn't a drink.'

'I guessed that much already.'

'It was the peanuts. I didn't know where to put them, so I left them behind the bar, out of sight. You don't seem to use the bar much, so I didn't think anyone would find them. I could hardly keep them in our room and eat them in front of Marty. I'm craving them. He doesn't know about this, and he can't know. It'd ruin us if he found out I'm . . .'

'Pregnant?' Helen offered.

Marilyn nodded, and her beehive wobbled.

'Is the baby Ricky's?' Helen dared to ask.

Marilyn waited a few seconds before she gave her reply. Her beehive shook from side to side. Helen took a moment before she asked her next question.

'It's Marty's?'

The caged beehive bounced up and down.

Chapter 37

'I don't understand. Why would Marty be unhappy that you're going to have his baby?' Helen asked.

'Because he insists he's too old to be a father,' Marilyn said softly. 'When we've talked about having children, I've always told him he'd make a good dad, no matter how old he is.' She gripped her hands together and brought them to her frilly pink heart. 'It's what's in here that counts.'

Helen rose and walked to the bar to pick up the peanuts. She put them in front of Marilyn. 'Would you like to eat them now?'

Marilyn shook her head. 'The craving's left me. I think the shock of bumping into you scared it away. What were you doing down here anyway? And why are there raisins all over the floor?' A look of alarm passed over her face. 'Is that a hammer? Were you going to hit me?'

'No, I wouldn't hit anyone. I brought it as self-defence in case any funny business went on. When I found the peanuts, I assumed it had something to do with Ricky's death.'

'Well, in a way it does,' Marilyn said sweetly.

Helen's blood ran cold. Her gaze fell on the hammer; it was a little too far away for her liking.

'After we learned how Rickster died . . .'

Rickster?

'. . . I haven't been able to stop thinking about peanuts. I started craving them, but had to hide them so Marty didn't find them. His sister craved peanuts all through her pregnancy. I'm worried he'll make the connection if he sees me eating them too. I don't know how I'll break the news to him about the baby.'

Helen was relieved to hear that Marilyn had a motive for leaving the peanuts at the bar, but she was shocked nonetheless. 'Hang on, did you just call him Rickster?'

'It was my pet name for him. Marty didn't like me calling him that.'

'I can understand why. It's a little familiar. Listen, Marilyn, I don't mean to pry . . .'

'You want to know if Rick and I were having an affair, don't you?'

'Well, no, but . . .' Helen said, knowing full well she'd been rumbled. She was quickly learning that there was a sharp mind behind the pink frills and peroxide.

'It's all right. The police have already asked me about it. I don't mind admitting it. Yes, we had a fling that lasted almost a month. Marty found out and threatened to kill Rickster. Neither of us saw him again for two years. Until this week, when we turned up here and Rick couldn't book in next door. I told Marty not to get his blood pressure up. He's under doctor's orders not to get stressed; it does his heart no good and he needs to be careful. But he went for Rick when he saw him; it brought back all the feelings of jealousy from two years ago. He had him by the throat at one point and threw him up against that wall.'

'In here?' Helen cried, looking around. She didn't like the

thought of guests fighting in the Seaview. It wasn't that kind of place. 'Listen, Marilyn, it seems I've put two and two together about the peanuts and come up with the wrong answer about Ricky's death. When I saw the nuts hidden behind the bar, I assumed the worst. I hung around the lounge most of yesterday trying to nab whoever it was when they came in to take them back. But no one did, so I hid in the dining room after everyone had gone to bed, and now it turns out to be a blameless mistake. I can't apologise enough. But can I offer you some advice?'

Marilyn snapped her gaze from the nuts to Helen's face. 'You're going to advise me to tell Marty about the baby, aren't you?'

Helen smiled. 'You can't keep this secret, no matter how you try. He's going to find out at some point.'

Marilyn laid her hands gently on top of her frilly pink nightie and cradled her stomach. 'It could bring us closer, I guess. And it's not as if we couldn't afford a nanny or some help if Marty struggles with his energy when the child comes.'

'Then you'll tell him?' Helen asked.

Marilyn nodded, and her beehive bounced again. 'I'll need to pick my moment carefully. It'll have to be after the charity game on Friday, because he's fully committed to that. It's more than a game to Marty and me. You might have noticed we're all rather taken with the sport.'

Helen didn't deny it.

'Some people say it's not about winning or losing but about how you play. To us, winning is everything. Some people go fishing, some people go to church, some people Morris dance. We don't just play crazy golf; we dedicate our lives to it. We travel the country from Land's End to John O'Groats.'

'There's a crazy-golf course at Land's End?' Helen asked.

'There are at least four there that I've played with Marty. He's trained hard for this tournament, and now that Rickster's dead, he's in with a good chance of getting on the board.'

'The board of the committee that runs crazy golf?'

Marilyn smiled and shook her beehive. 'No, the chalkboard that's screwed to the side of the hut at Norman's Nine. The top five players with the highest scores get to chalk their names on the board. It's a rite of passage in the crazy-golf world, something that Marty's never achieved. He's come sixth many times, just missing out on a chalkboard celebration. With Rickster gone, who knows – now might be Marty's time to make the top five. It'd mean the world to him, I know.'

'You really love him, don't you?'

Marilyn looked surprised to be asked. 'He's my husband; of course I love him. Yes, we had a wobble when I had my fling with Rickster, but that's all it was. It was a distraction during a difficult patch we were going through. I love Marty with all my heart and always have, from the very first moment we met.' Tears filled her eyes, but Helen still had a question that needed answering.

'I saw you, you know,' she began carefully. 'You and Ricky, before he died, exchanging secret smiles when you thought no one was looking. Was there really nothing going on between you, or was there still a spark there, a hangover from your affair?'

Marilyn sniffed back her tears. 'Oh. You noticed that?'

Helen nodded.

'Well, it was kind of nice to see him, I suppose, and I like a bit of flirting as much as the next girl. But my heart belongs to Marty.

Now, if you'll excuse me, I should get back upstairs. I'm sorry about the peanuts, Helen. Would you like me to get rid of them?'

'If you want to take them upstairs to satisfy your craving, you'll have to come clean with Marty. But if you leave them with me, I'll throw them out. I don't allow peanut products at the Seaview. You saw what a serious allergic reaction did to Rickster . . . I mean Ricky.'

'Then throw them away, Helen, please,' Marilyn said. She shivered in her pink nightie and rubbed her bare arms to ward off the cold night air.

'I'll let you go up to bed, you must be tired.'

'And hungry, thirsty and needing the loo. My friends tell me this is what it'll be like all the way to the birth. Do you have children, Helen?'

Helen shook her head. It was a question she'd been asked more times than she cared to remember, and each time the words hit her hard. She and Tom had wanted children and had tried many times, but it wasn't to be.

'No,' she said. 'I've got the Seaview instead.'

'I expect it keeps you busy.'

'Too busy at times. I could do without my guests being poisoned by peanuts. It's not a happy place to be right now.'

'The police will get to the bottom of it, you'll see.'

'I hope you're right. Please, Marilyn, don't let me keep you. Go back up to Marty and get some sleep.'

But Marilyn didn't move. 'We all know, you know,' she said firmly.

Helen was confused. 'Know what?'

'All of us, me and Marty and Alice, we know that Freddy is Rick's son. We never mention it, though, for Alice's sake. We heard on the crazy-golf grapevine that Rickster had an affair while he was married to her, and that Freddy's the fruit of that union.'

'Ah, I see,' Helen said. She wondered how much Marilyn knew about Freddy's mother, and decided to press on. 'Do you know who he had the affair with?'

'Could have been any one of a dozen women, and they're just the ones Marty and I know about,' Marilyn replied.

Helen decided against mentioning her conversation with Olga and Freddy, remembering Freddy's plea not to tell anyone. It seemed clear to her that Marilyn didn't know who his mother was.

'We reckon whoever it is must have been really tall.' Marilyn smiled.

Helen bit her tongue. 'I guess so,' she said. 'Anyway, I'm done in. We should both get some sleep.'

Marilyn stood, and her pink nightie floated as she wafted to the door. 'I'll tell Marty about the baby. I will. I'll tell him on Saturday when we return home. I'll settle him in his chair with the mug of cocoa that he likes every night before bed, tuck a blanket over his legs – the tartan one we bought in Fort William – and ask Alexa to play Michael Bublé.'

'He's a fan of the Bublé?' Helen asked. Well, it took all sorts, she supposed.

'No, but I am. It'll help me relax. Thank you, Helen, for making me see sense.'

'Goodnight, Marilyn, sleep tight.'

Marilyn walked away and up the stairs. Helen waited until she heard the sound of her door open and close, then she got down on all fours and scrabbled around, picking up the raisins. She threw them in the bin, then retrieved the hammer and the packet of peanuts. Before she turned off the light, she glanced at the framed photo of her beloved late husband behind the bar.

'Night, Tom,' she said. She blew him a kiss. 'Thanks for organising my party; it turns out it's just what I need.'

Chapter 38

Helen was dancing with Michael Bublé in the ballroom at the Royal Hotel and he was holding her in his muscled arms. Then it wasn't Michael Bublé; it was her guest, Marty, who was whispering in her ear, telling her he was going to be a father, telling her how overjoyed he was that his wife was pregnant. She woke with a start, staring at the ceiling, relieved that the whole thing had been a dream. She glanced at the clock on the bedside unit. It was exactly 7 a.m.

Popping her head around the bedroom door, she called out good morning to Jean. Then she showered quickly, stuck her legs into jeans and her arms into a T-shirt, then pulled her fleece from the cupboard under the stairs. Suki knew the morning routine off by heart and was already waiting by the door.

'Enjoy the sunshine, it's glorious out there. A perfect Scarborough day,' Jean said as Helen left the Seaview.

Down on the beach, Helen set Suki free off the lead. If only she could set Michael Bublé free too. How was it that some dreams insisted on sticking around for hours, while others – the really good ones, the nice ones where Tom came to see her and told her he loved her – disappeared within minutes after she woke? As she walked on the golden sand, the sunrise turned the sky yellow and pink. She marvelled at the watercolour wash of the sky mingling with the grey sea and pulled her phone from her pocket to take a picture. If she didn't have proof to show Jean and Sally, they wouldn't believe how beautiful it had been.

Thoughts of Jean and Sally meandered their way to her birthday party on Saturday. Her crazy-golf guests would have left by then, and she could relax. Well, as much as she was able to while the police were still investigating Ricky's death. She wondered why DS Hutchinson hadn't called her asking for an update. Maybe he was busy at the station; she'd heard about the cutbacks there. She noticed voice messages on her phone, and as she walked along, her boots sinking into the sand, she put it to her ear and listened. The first message was from Jimmy.

'Let's try again, Helen. Please. We'll meet somewhere in town for dinner. You won't need to see Priscilla again. We'll talk. Ring me when you can. Oh, it's Jimmy here, by the way. OK. Thanks, Helen, bye now.'

The second was from Marie.

'Want to meet for lunch? Call me.'

On her walk back to the Seaview, the open-top bus, empty of its passengers, made its way along North Marine Drive. A run-down ice-cream van trundled behind it, backfiring as it went.

When she arrived home, she was surprised to find Sally in the kitchen. She wasn't due to start work for another forty minutes.

'You're early this morning,' she said.

'Gav gave me a ride in one of his cabs; he was passing this way, so he dropped me off. He's printed estimates for you about having an alarm fitted. Oh, and he said that when he comes to fit the hanging baskets to the front of the Seaview, he'll fit window boxes too, if you'd like them.'

Helen took the estimates from Sally. 'I'll look at these later. As for the window boxes, that'd be great. How much do I owe him?'

'Consider it your birthday present,' Sally replied.

'Want a cup of tea and a bacon sandwich, you two?' Jean called.

'Please, Jean,' Helen replied.

'Sally?' Jean asked.

'Just tea, please, I don't think I can stomach anything else.'

Helen regarded Sally with concern. 'Are you feeling all right?'

Sally sat at the kitchen table and looked at Helen and Jean. 'I went to the hospital yesterday for a scan. That's why I had to get away early.'

Jean stopped what she was doing and paused with the teapot in mid-air. 'A scan? Everything all right, I hope?'

A smile made its way to Sally's lips. 'Everything's fine. No, better than fine. I shouldn't really announce it yet, but Gav and me, we're pregnant.'

Jean beamed at her. 'Oh love, that's fantastic. Just wonderful. Now, are you feeling all right? Do you need anything? Shall I put sugar in your tea if you're not having a bacon butty? Or can I fix you some cereal or toast?'

'Thanks, Jean, but really I'm fine, there's no need to fuss.'

Helen sat next to Sally and took both of her hands. 'It's wonderful news and I'm over the moon for you and Gav. This means Gracie will be getting a little brother or sister.'

Sally couldn't keep the smile off her face. 'It might be one of each.'

'What?' Jean cried.

'Twins?' Helen said.

Sally nodded. 'My GP told me there was a chance of twins because Mum's a twin and they run through the maternal line.'

'Your mum's got a twin? There's another Brenda? Heaven help us, we're doomed,' Jean muttered.

'Jean!' Helen said sharply.

Sally ignored Jean's comment. 'And because of that, he sent me for an earlier scan than normal. The hospital confirmed it yesterday. It is twins.'

Helen hugged her.

'I'd like you to be godmother to both babies,' Sally said.

Helen felt tears prick her eyes and a lump formed in her throat. 'I'd be honoured,' she replied. She pulled a tissue from her pocket and dabbed at her eyes. Then a practical thought hit. 'We'll have to plan who we get in to cover for you while you're on maternity leave.'

'I know Mum would be happy to return,' Sally said.

A pan clattered to the floor.

'Sorry,' Jean said.

'Your mum might be working next door by then if Miriam takes her on. Anyway, it's months away yet, we'll deal with that when we come to it. Sorry, my thoughts were jumping ahead. The Seaview is always at the forefront of my mind.'

'And rightly so, Helen, this place means the world to us all. Me and Gav, well, we wondered if we could hold a party upstairs after the christening at St Mary's church? Now it's my thoughts that are jumping ahead. Not that it'd be a party as such, but you know, a few drinks and a buffet, that kind of thing.'

'I'll do the buffet,' Jean said.

'And I'll provide the drinks,' Helen added. 'Consider it done.'

Jean poured tea and served bacon butties, then they all sat at the table talking about the future, about Helen's fiftieth party on Saturday night, about Tom, about Jimmy and about the Seaview. Jean handed Helen a large white envelope from her shopping bag.

'This is the contract I signed with Benson Brown, and one of the invitations that Tom designed.'

For a few moments, Helen pushed all thoughts of Ricky Delmont, murder, Michael Bublé, peanuts, intruders and crazy golf to the back of her mind as she pulled a postcard-size invitation from the envelope.

'It's gorgeous.' She ran her finger around the edge, scalloped in blue. 'It's so old-fashioned, really precious. Tom designed these himself?'

Jean nodded. 'It's all detailed in the contract. Read it with a glass of wine when you're feeling relaxed tonight. Put some of Tom's favourite Elvis tunes on. Take your time; it's worth going over every detail. You'll see that he stipulated you weren't to know about the party, that it was to be a surprise, but that afterwards you were to be told everything. Remember, you can't tell anyone that Sally and I broke the secret.'

'We only told you because you were in such a state about the guest who died at the crazy golf,' Sally added.

'It's perfect,' Helen said, turning the invitation in her hands. 'Just perfect.' She raised her eyes to Jean. 'I think my sparkle's coming back.'

But then her phone rang, and when she saw the name on the screen, she felt her pulse quicken.

'I've got to take this, it's the police,' she said, excusing herself.

She walked to the patio and sat in a chair in the sunshine.

'Morning, DS Hutchinson, how are you? Are you any further forward in finding Ricky Delmont's killer?'

'Not exactly, Mrs Dexter. The CCTV image of the intruder at the Seaview hasn't led anywhere yet. My men are on the case – we've got a murder to solve, after all – but I was hoping you might have news for me. I understand the crazy-golf game's now taking place on Friday and your guests are playing in it.'

'That's right. I know you asked me to keep my eye on them. They're upset, of course, shocked by what's happened, and it's bound to affect the way they act, but other than that, they've been completely normal.'

Helen crossed her fingers against her little white lie. She'd already decided there was no point in mentioning what she'd learned about her guests. What use would it be for the police to know that Olga was Freddy's mum, or that Olga and Ricky had once had an affair, or that Marilyn was pregnant? The feeling in her gut was that none of them were killers, and she didn't want to be responsible for bringing their private lives under scrutiny. Neither did she feel the need to mention that she'd spent the small hours of that morning staking out her guests from the dining room floor. Still, she was glad she'd done it.

'Mrs Dexter?' DS Hutchinson said, rather tersely.

'Sorry, what?' Helen said.

'I said we've followed up on the gambling syndicate, the ones taking bets on the crazy golf. They're a known outfit who travel the country placing high-stake bets on low-risk games, mainly for overseas punters.'

'Do you think one of them killed Ricky Delmont?'

'We're ruling nothing out. Carry on being vigilant, Mrs Dexter.'

Helen saluted. 'Yes, sir,' she said.

'Now is not the time to be flippant,' he said, sternly.

After she'd rung off, she stared at her phone and sighed. The last thing she needed was a run-in with the police, but she really didn't like the way DS Hutchinson was using her as the eyes and ears of the force. However, she couldn't give it any more thought, as she had pressing things to do. Breakfast was about to be served.

Upstairs in the hall and dining room, she and Sally worked together, passing plates, sauce bottles, teapots and toast racks, gliding from the dumbwaiter to the dining room with practised ease. When Helen walked into the dining room offering more tea, she found Olga consulting a black ring binder as she addressed the group.

'I'm testing them on the rules,' she explained.

'Oh, not this again, Olga,' Marilyn moaned.

'We sure know those rules off by heart now,' Freddy said. Helen noticed his American accent was back.

Undeterred by the complaints, Olga carried on, pointing at a page in her file.

'Marty!' she barked. 'Explain rule 3.1.6.'

'Players must be stationary and quiet.' Marty sighed. 'Which is something I wish you would be.'

She shot him a dark look. 'Don't disrespect me, just answer the question.'

Marty bit into a slice of toast.

'Alice! Explain rule 3.4.2.,' Olga said.

'Thunderstorms will stop play immediately,' Alice replied. 'Come on, Olga, we know all of this. It's Crazy Golf 101; all serious players know these rules.'

'I like to keep the team on its toes,' Olga said.

Helen caught Sally's eye and they exchanged a smile. Her heart swelled with love for her friend. She'd look after her especially well now she knew she was expecting – and not just one baby, but two. She'd really miss her once she went on maternity leave. And while she was grateful for Sally's offer of her mum to work in her place, having Brenda back would upset Jean. That was something she vowed she'd never do again. No, she could never employ Brenda, but she knew someone who might.

Chapter 39

The Vista del Mar had a polished brass knocker on its panelled oak door. Helen rapped it hard. As she waited, she glanced around, trying to work out Miriam's doorstep appeal. What did the Vista del Mar have that the Seaview didn't? Both had clean and tidy pathways, painted gates, wrought-iron railings. There wasn't a lot of difference between them except that the Seaview occupied a corner plot. She wondered if that was why Miriam was always rude to her; did she have corner-plot envy? The wooden plaque by the Vista's front door was hard to miss. Four brass stars shone in the sunshine.

'I really must get my plaque put up,' Helen muttered. She looked at the spot where she'd tried to fit it. Two holes in the brickwork were all there was to show for her failed handiwork. From the angle she was viewing them, she could see they weren't level. No wonder the plaque wouldn't hang straight.

The door swung open and Miriam appeared, looking even more grumpy than usual. Helen smiled brightly.

'Morning, Miriam. May I say you're looking very well today. What a lovely blouse you're wearing; the ruffle at the neck really suits you. And have you done something with your hair?'

'Don't flatter me, Helen. What do you want? I'm a busy woman, looking after my four-star abode and tending to quality guests. Speaking of guests, any news on who murdered yours?'

Helen was determined not to let Miriam rattle her. She began to count to ten in her head. When she reached four, she shot out her hand. 'There's no need for that attitude. I come bearing gifts.'

Miriam looked at the tea-towel-wrapped parcel in her hand. 'What is it?'

'One of my award-winning cook's lemon drizzle cakes, for you.'

Miriam's eyes lit up, then she checked herself. 'Well, I suppose I could take it, if you insist.'

'I insist,' Helen said, handing it over. 'You can keep the tea towel, I don't want it back.'

Miriam ran her fingers over it. 'I don't want this in my hotel, it's not a hundred per cent linen.' Yet she kept hold of it all the same.

She began to close the door, but Helen stuck her foot in to stop it from shutting. Then she felt guilty, remembering how angry she'd been when Marie's journalist friend had done the same to her. She pulled her foot away and took a step back. 'Sorry, Miriam. I got carried away. Look, is there any chance you and I can bury the hatchet and start again? Consider the cake a peace offering, if you like.'

Miriam's shoulders relaxed. 'If you want to, so be it. Now, is there anything else you want, or have you just come to butter me up?'

'I know you're struggling in there with no permanent cleaner, and I happen to know someone who's looking for a job. She's a hard worker, diligent, and I highly recommend her. She's able to put up with a lot.' Helen reached into her pocket and pulled out a slip of paper, which she handed to Miriam. 'She's called Brenda, and this is her number. I hope it works out for you both.' She turned on her heel, then walked away down the path.

'Helen, dear!'

She spun around to find Miriam holding the cake in one hand and the phone number in her other.

'Thank you, for both of these,' she said.

Helen nodded her acknowledgement, then walked away.

When she entered the Seaview, she was surprised to find Marty alone in the lounge, as she'd never seen him on his own before. She paused, unsure whether to leave him and carry on to her apartment. But curiosity got the better of her, and she strode into the room, pretending to be checking stock at the bar. 'Morning, Marty. Don't mind me, I'm just counting bottles of tonic.'

'Morning, Helen. Lovely breakfast again. Please give my compliments to your cook.'

Helen picked up two small bottles, carrying on the pretence that she was working. 'I noticed Marilyn didn't eat much. I hope there was nothing wrong with her food?'

Marty crossed his thick, muscled arms across his chest and sat up straight in his seat. 'She's not feeling so good, that's all.'

'Oh dear. I hope she'll be well enough to play the charity game on Friday.'

'There's no way she'd miss it. It means too much to her. She loves her crazy golf.'

She tried to keep her tone light as she carried on. 'On her way downstairs, is she?' she asked. She hated being nosy, but she had to make the most of her time with Marty before anyone else arrived.

'She's doing her hair and make-up; it could take a while. You know what young women are like.'

Helen smiled as if she knew only too well. Her brain was working overtime trying to figure out how to turn the conversation to Ricky's death. She could hardly blurt out that she'd overheard Marty threaten to kill Ricky if he didn't leave Marilyn alone. So how on earth could she bring up the subject? She picked up a cloth and rubbed it over the bar top, doing her best to think of the most subtle words to use. When she glanced at Marty, she was shocked to see that he was staring right at her.

'Everything all right, Helen? You look a bit tense. I always have a sports massage at my gym when I'm tense. Unknots the muscles and does me the power of good.'

'Basements!' Helen blurted.

Marty stared at her. 'What?'

She continued to polish the counter, not daring to look Marty in the eye. 'Basements, eh? Funny things, aren't they? I mean, it's amazing what a person can hear in a basement if they're outdoors and there are voices coming from the street when they think they're not being overheard.'

'Are you all right, Helen?' Marty asked, frowning.

Helen wiped the cloth harder and faster. 'Me? Couldn't be better. But I heard something when I was on my patio in my basement.' She stopped, hurried to the door, glanced left and right to ensure no one was coming, then closed the door and walked across the lounge to sit opposite Marty. There was no easy way to get out of this, so she decided to finish what she'd stupidly started. 'I heard you tell Ricky you were going to hit him if he didn't leave Marilyn alone.'

The colour drained from Marty's face.

'So was it you? Did you hit him? Perhaps you hit him hard enough to kill him?'

His left leg began to bounce up and down. His face went pink, then red. A warning thought went through her mind. Marilyn had said that Marty had a bad heart and his GP had warned him not to get stressed. What if her words proved too much for him?

He looked at her. 'I should report you for harassment,' he said, but then a wry smile played around his lips and a shiver of relief fluttered in Helen's chest. He didn't look like a man about to have a heart attack.

'The police quizzed me about my history with Ricky after my wife admitted her affair to them when she was questioned. And yes, I admit it, I did want to kill him when I found out about their fling years ago. If I'd caught him with her again, who knows what might have happened. But Marilyn gave me her assurance she wouldn't stray, and I believed her. And do you know why I believed her?'

Helen shook her head.

'Because I love her and I know she loves me. Oh, I know what people say. They say I'm her sugar daddy and she's my blonde piece of fluff.'

Helen tutted loudly, thinking about Jean.

'But there's more to my Marilyn than meets the eye. She's a lot stronger than she looks. She earns her own money with her beauty business and refuses to take a penny from me.' His face clouded over. 'But she's been acting strange lately, and she's gone off her food.'

'I'd speak to her if I were you. Ask her what's going on. Talk to her. Women like that sort of thing. Be tender. Put some Michael

Bublé on in the background, pour her a nice glass of wine. On second thoughts, no, make that a cup of tea.'

Marty gave her a puzzled look.

'I'm sorry I blurted things out,' Helen said. 'I've got a lot on my mind. Listen, Marty, do you know anything about gamblers taking bets on crazy-golf games?'

He slowly nodded his head. 'There's a syndicate of gamblers who follow us around the country, taking bets from overseas on our games. A lot of money changes hands. One of them approached me at Barnard Castle. Smashing little course, that one, right by the castle. He asked me to nobble a game by losing on the last hole. I told him where to go. I'd never do anything like that. Winning is everything to me. Why do you ask?'

'I overheard one of these gamblers on his phone, trying to talk someone out of placing money on Ricky before he died. He said that Ricky was "dead in the water" this year. Do you think one of the gambling syndicates would be desperate enough to kill in order to win a bet or skewer the odds?'

Marty gave this serious thought. 'It's possible. I've heard of up to three million pounds changing hands on one game. There's a gambler in Taiwan with more money than he knows what to do with. He's got a fixation with British pastimes, and gambles on pigeon racing, crazy golf, marbles, sometimes even on who'll win an egg-and-spoon race at a school fair. So it's possible that some of those in the syndicates choose to make a killing one way or another.'

Something Marilyn had said came to her. 'With Ricky gone, that means you're in with a chance of getting your name on the board.'

'It's something I've dreamed of all my life, but if you're suggesting I killed Ricky just to get into the top five, you couldn't be more wrong. All's fair in love, war and crazy golf, Helen. I'm as straight as they come when I'm playing my game. I don't take bets or bribes. I play by the rules. It's only in matters of the heart that my emotions get the better of me. And with a wife as beautiful as Marilyn, I need to be on my mettle. She attracts a lot of attention. Now, if you'll excuse me, I'm going to head over to the bench on the clifftop to do my press-ups. It's the perfect height for my frame.' He flexed his biceps. 'Got to keep these guns in shape.' He stood and walked from the room, leaving Helen alone.

She watched from the window as he headed across the street and began to do press-ups against the bench. She heard footsteps outside the lounge, then the sound of the front door opening and closing. Marilyn, hair and make-up done to perfection, strolled across the road. Marty stopped what he was doing. He kissed his wife on the cheek, then lovingly stroked her face and gazed into her eyes.

Helen looked out at the sea with much on her mind.

'Penny for your thoughts.'

She spun around to see Jean at the door.

'Oh, I was just thinking about Tom,' she said. 'He used to look at me the way Marty looks at Marilyn. Then it started me off thinking about Jimmy.'

Jean walked to the window and glanced out. Marty and Marilyn were now sitting on the bench, Marty's strong arm laid protectively across his wife's shoulders.

'What would you do, Jean?'

'About what?'

'I'll never forget Tom, nor would I want to. But I'm still holding back with Jimmy. I've used his cat and my allergy as an excuse not to ring him. And it's not the cat's fault. It's because I'm scared to let Tom go.'

Jean sat down next to her and looked her straight in the eye. 'You really want to know what I'd do?'

Helen nodded, and Jean patted her hand. 'I'd buy a box of anti-histamines and give him a call right now.'

Chapter 40

Jean left the room, and Helen continued to gaze through the window. She watched Marilyn and Marty walk off hand in hand.

'How romantic,' she sighed.

She pulled her phone from her pocket. Jean was right, she was always right. She turned to the framed picture of Tom on the wall.

'I'm going to ring him,' she said to the picture. 'Jean says I should. I'm going to invite him to the party on Saturday night. Oh, don't look at me like that, Tom. You'd like him if you knew him; he's an Elvis fan, just like you.'

She pressed Jimmy's name on her phone. He answered within three rings.

'Hey, how are you, Helen?' He sounded cheery, upbeat.

'I feel better now I've heard your voice,' she replied. 'Thanks for inviting me to dinner in town. We should definitely do it one night next week.'

'Why not this week?'

Because I've got a murdered crazy golfer on my mind and the Seaview is implicated. Because there's been an intruder in my apartment and it's given me a scare even though I've changed the locks. Because my head's spinning with secrets I've learned about my guests. Because, because, because.

'Are you free on Saturday night?' she blurted out before she could talk herself out of it.

'Sure am. Where would you like to go? What about the Italian restaurant on Queen Street?'

'Lanterna?' Helen cried. 'It's the best restaurant in Scarborough. We wouldn't be able to get booked in at short notice. We'll go there another time, because there's something happening here on Saturday night and I'd like you to come. There's a party for my fiftieth birthday.'

'You kept that quiet.'

'I didn't know about it.'

'You didn't know you were turning fifty?'

Helen laughed out loud. 'I didn't know about the party. I'm still not supposed to know. It's all a secret, a big surprise. And you can't tell anyone. Well, you can invite Jodie, it'd be good to see her again. But you've got to swear her to secrecy too. Neither of you can let anyone at the party know that I knew about it in advance.' She looked at Tom's photo. 'It's a long story, one I'll explain when I can.'

'Will it be one of your Elvis parties, like you told me you used to hold at the Seaview? I could dress as Elvis if you'd like, put my suit on and sing a few songs.'

Helen looked again at the photo of Tom in his white Elvis suit. 'No, don't come as Elvis, it'd feel as if you're working. Come as Jimmy.'

'So it's not an Elvis party?'

'Sort of,' Helen said. 'You can sing if you'd like to, but no dressing up.'

'Got it. What time do you want me there?'

'Arrive about six. It's family and close friends only. Tom's sister and her lot are coming from Shetland. I've told them about you and they're looking forward to meeting you. Should be a good night.'

'I look forward to meeting them too. Let me bring you a birthday present,' Jimmy said.

'No, you don't have to do that. Just bring yourself . . . and a pair of pyjamas, if you have them.'

'Pyjamas? I never wear the things,' Jimmy laughed.

There was a beat of silence between them.

'Oh. Are you asking me what I think you're asking me?' he said.

'Yes, I'm inviting you to stay over. I really would have liked to stay at yours when I came to your house for dinner, but Priscilla had other plans.'

'Are you sure, Helen?' Jimmy asked, concerned.

'I'm sure. I'd love nothing more. See you Saturday, about six?'

'Saturday at six works for me. I'll bring my toothbrush,' he teased.

'I can't wait,' Helen replied.

She rang off, then immediately texted Marie.

Yes to lunch. Meet you at Lookout on the Pier café at 1 x

Marie texted straight back with a thumbs-up and two smiling faces.

At quarter to one, Helen walked along Sandside towards Scarborough's West Pier with Suki at her side. Before she turned on to the pier, she looked along the seafront towards the crazy golf. She saw Norman by his hut, chatting to a young couple, handing out putters and balls. An ice-cream van was parked on the road, with its serving hatch facing the course. She recognised it as the one she'd seen driving past the Seaview and along Marine Drive. It looked like it had seen better days. The paintwork was peeling and faded, and she remembered hearing it backfire as it trundled past. It was the van with the sign offering two ice creams for the price of one. She remembered the wonky 'Greensleeves' tune it'd played, with some of the notes missing. It sounded like a gramophone that hadn't been wound up to full speed.

She turned right and headed on to the pier, walking past lobster pots and fishing tackle. Halfway along was a short set of iron steps, and she began to climb them, taking care that Suki's skinny legs could manage. At the top was the door to the Lookout on the Pier café. She pushed it open and entered the cosy room. It had large windows either side, giving views on one side to the harbour and on the other to South Bay beach.

'Table for one?' the waitress asked.

'Two, please. My friend's coming too.'

'Make that a table for three,' a voice behind Helen said. She spun around, happy to see Marie but surprised that there was someone else with her.

'Helen, this is Jack. I think you've already met.'

Jack Malone thrust his hand out. 'I'm pleased we get to meet again, as I want to apologise for the way I behaved last time.'

Helen looked at his outstretched hand, then at Marie. 'You didn't tell me we'd have company,' she said coolly.

'Come on, Helen, give him a chance.'

Helen looked at Jack's brown eyes through his tortoiseshell glasses. 'I felt threatened on my own doorstep.'

Jack withdrew his hand and ran it through his floppy brown hair.

Marie stepped forward. 'Oh, come on, you two, make friends, for my sake.'

Jack tried again with his hand. This time Helen reluctantly shook it, then she followed the waitress to a small table by the window overlooking the harbour. From her seat, she had a bird's-eye view of the crazy-golf course. She was pleasantly surprised to see the hut door wide open, and hoped Norman now had nothing to hide. Suki settled herself under her chair.

The waitress left three menus and a promise that she'd be back to take their order.

'Smashing place, this,' Marie said, looking around approvingly. 'It's a café by day and a bistro by night. It's got some of the best views in Scarborough.'

'I don't think anything beats the view from the top of Oliver's Mount,' Helen said, but Marie disagreed.

'I like being closer to the sea. Anyway, enough of the views, what are we going to eat?'

Marie inspected the menu while Helen inspected Jack. She wondered what her friend saw in him. He was bookish, a bit nerdy, not Marie's usual type, which was hunky, well groomed, tall, dark, rich and handsome.

'Marie tells me you're doing publicity for the new Tom's Teas at Filey, is that right?'

'Yes, that's right. I've got my own PR business, with a small team working for me.'

'And you used to be a journalist, yes?'

'For my sins,' Jack smiled. 'Sometimes my tabloid newspaper training kicks in. I'm sorry, Helen, for what I said to you at the

Seaview. I can't apologise enough. In fact, I insist on paying for lunch.'

'I won't argue with that,' Helen said. 'Marie also told me that you're digging into Ricky Delmont.'

He opened his mouth just as the waitress appeared to take their order. Once she'd gone, he began to speak.

'Years ago, Ricky was involved in a fight at a crazy-golf match near Great Yarmouth. He lost his temper with a rival player and started attacking him with his club.'

Helen and Marie winced at the same time.

'I asked an old contact of mine on one of the tabloids to investigate what happened,' Jack continued.

Helen looked at him. 'Why?'

'I asked him to,' Marie said.

Helen turned to her, eyebrows raised.

'You're my best friend and I know you've been going through the mill, blaming yourself for Ricky's death, wrongly believing that your beloved Seaview was implicated. I wanted to help and I thought Jack might uncover something about Ricky to bring this to an end.'

Helen pulled a jug of water towards her and filled a glass. She noticed that her hands were shaking. 'Go on then, what did you find out?' she asked Jack.

He had the decency to look sheepish. 'Nothing, I'm afraid. It appears no charges were ever brought against Ricky.'

She leaned back in her seat, crossed her arms. 'It's odd.'

'Very odd,' Marie agreed.

Helen turned to gaze from the window at the crazy-golf course.

She saw families playing, couples laughing, nine replica models of Scarborough landmarks made by Norman's own hand. Norman was chatting to an elderly couple, smiling, looking more relaxed than she'd ever seen him. And yet despite the happy scene, the innocent game had resulted in Ricky Delmont's death.

'There's more to this than meets the eye,' she muttered.

Chapter 41

Helen pulled her phone towards her. 'I need to let the police know,' she said.

Jack gently laid his hand on hers to stop her. 'If the police have done their job properly, they'll already know about Ricky's background,' he said.

Helen sat up straight in her seat and pushed her phone away. 'Can we talk about something else now? I've had it up to here with Ricky Delmont.' She eyed Marie carefully, wondering how much she should say about what Jean had revealed about the party. However, she didn't need to say a word, as Marie brought the subject up herself.

'Jean told me that you know about the you-know-what,' she said.

'Oh, she did, did she? Well, I'm glad you know I know. She told me to keep quiet; she's terrified of being hung, drawn and quartered if you-know-who finds out she's spilled the beans.'

'She's only told me; it'll go no further.'

'Thanks for offering to do the catering for it.'

'Oh, I'm not doing all of it. Jean insisted on making your cake.'

Jack twirled his spoon in his fingers. 'Is this a secret language between friends that I'm not allowed to decode?' he asked.

Glenda Young

Marie patted his hand. 'Don't be petulant, it doesn't suit you.' She turned to Helen. 'How's Jimmy, by the way?'

'He's fine, you'll see him on Saturday night at the you-know-what.'

Food and drinks arrived, putting an end to more party discussion. As they ate, Helen grilled Jack about his past and his work for Marie's new tearoom in Filey. After they'd finished, she eyed the cakes on the countertop. 'Fancy a dessert?' she asked.

'Can't stop, sorry. I've a meeting with the designer who's doing the artwork for the menus,' Marie said.

Jack stood and walked to the counter, where he paid for lunch on his card.

'That was good of him,' Helen noted.

'He's a very nice man, Helen. I find myself growing fond of him.'

'You make him sound like a pet dog,' Helen said.

Marie laughed, then stood and picked up her jacket and handbag. 'Are you going to be all right?' she asked, concerned.

'I'll be fine. Aren't I always? Besides, the guests I've got staying at the Seaview are leaving first thing on Saturday. I'll be glad to see the back of them, although it doesn't stop me feeling that the hotel is still implicated in what happened to Ricky.'

Marie hugged her and kissed her cheek. 'I'll see you Saturday, about six.'

Marie and Jack left the café together. Helen pulled Suki to her and followed them down the steps. While Marie and Jack turned left to walk along the seafront and up into town, Helen turned right. 'Do you know what, Suki? I fancy an ice cream.'

She headed to the crazy-golf course, to the ice-cream van with its *2 4 1* sign above the serving hatch. She looked at the pictures of the sweet treats on offer. Red and yellow striped lollies, orange juicy fruits, blue slush, ice cream in over fifty flavours.

'Fifty flavours, that's a lot,' she said.

A noise inside the van made her peer through the hatch.

'Sorry, love, I'll be right with you,' a voice said.

A short man heaved himself up from the driver's seat. It was his jacket she recognised first, a turquoise and white blouson. He was short, bald and fat, with ears that were too large for his face. His crooked nose looked like it'd been broken more than once. He beamed at Helen. The last time they'd met she hadn't recognised him, but there was no mistaking him this time.

'Arthur? What are you doing here?'

'Hey, it's Helen Armstrong!' he replied cheerily.

Suki looked up when she heard his voice. Then the sun caught the turquoise flash on his jacket, and she cocked her head to one side.

'It's Helen Dexter now, Arthur. I did tell you that when we met at the school reunion last week.' She looked at the tatty old van. 'Is this yours?' she said. 'When we met at the reunion, you said you were a salesman, and that you travelled a lot.'

He spread his hands wide. 'That's exactly what I do. I travel the Yorkshire coast selling ice creams. It's my own business. I call the van Dinah, after my mum.'

Helen wondered where she'd heard that name before. She tried to think, but Arthur was firing questions at her without taking a breath.

'Did you enjoy the reunion? It was good to see everyone, wasn't it? I left for a while to shake off Penny Smith. When I returned, I

305

was going to ask you to dance, but you'd already gone. Sandra DeVine said you'd left with a man. I assumed he was your husband.'

Helen shook her head. 'My husband died a while back,' she said. Oh, but it still hurt to say those words.

'I'm sorry to hear that. My condolences to you. Well, I'm not presuming anything, but if you should be free and single, would you like to go on a date?'

'Sorry?' she said. 'No, Arthur, no.'

She looked into his face, at his nose that was bent from too many years playing rugby. She saw a podgy stomach bulging under his jacket. Was that from eating too much ice cream? She didn't want to hurt his feelings, but the last thing she wanted was a date with Arthur Mason.

'What I mean is,' she began, thinking of Jimmy, 'I'm seeing someone.'

He tapped the side of his nose. 'I knew it. Pretty girl like you. What can I get for you? Name it and it's on the house.'

Helen surveyed the fading, peeling pictures stuck on the window. 'I'll take a vanilla ice cream with a Flake, please. It's very kind of you to offer.'

'It's the least I can do for an old school friend.' Arthur took a cone from a stand and pulled down a nozzle on a machine. Ice cream swirled into the cone. He stuck a Flake in it, wrapped the cone in a napkin and handed it to Helen.

'Thanks, Arthur,' she said. 'It's been nice seeing you again.'

'And you, Helen. You caught me before I moved along the prom. I find it best to keep moving. Stay in one spot too long and people don't see you no more.'

He returned to his driving seat and Helen walked along the seafront with Suki. To her left was the sparkling sea and golden sands of the South Bay beach. To her right were the amusement arcades, cafés, and shops selling rock dummies, lollies, candyfloss and chips. Plastic buckets for crabbing hung on hooks with fishing nets of orange and pink. Fridge magnets in the shape of seagulls and puffins competed for space with tea towels, flip-flops and gifts of all kinds, all branded with one word: *Scarborough.* An open-top bus passed her on the road. Out at sea, the *Regal Lady* was setting out with tourists for a trip around the bay.

She licked her ice cream, enjoying the cold sweetness, and thought about Arthur. He was a funny sort of guy, but he seemed harmless enough. Her mind turned again to her guests. She felt as sure as she could be that none of them had killed Ricky Delmont. If it had been Olga or Freddy, Alice, Marty or Marilyn, why would they have gone to the trouble of entering her apartment to steal a list of foods? That didn't make sense. Besides, now that she knew the truth about Freddy's mother, his words about taking revenge on Ricky made sense. She felt certain that Olga and Freddy were innocent. Odd, but innocent.

And then there was Alice, perky, pretty Alice, the team cheerleader. Ricky had broken her spirit with affair after affair while they were married, and Helen's heart went out to the girl. Alice was competitive, yes, and she'd admitted that she wanted to win the tournament using fair means or foul. But she wasn't foul enough to be a murderer, of that Helen felt sure.

She licked her ice cream again as her thoughts began to uncurl. She thought about Marty and Marilyn. Oh, Marty was in for a shock once he got home and Marilyn switched on the Michael

Bublé. He was strong and protective, staying fit in order to keep up with his much younger wife. And Marilyn loved him very much. An oddly matched couple, yes, but were they murderers?

'I don't think so, Suki,' she said.

Suki looked at her, her glassy grey eyes darting from Helen's face to the remainder of the ice cream.

'Oh, all right, then,' Helen said. She handed the dog the final bite of cone and ice cream, and Suki lapped it greedily from her hand.

They walked on, past families on the beach and children riding donkeys. Windbreaks fluttered in the breeze, a group of friends played cricket with a plastic bat and ball, another small group played rounders. As Helen stood and watched, the jingle-jangle of a familiar tune was carried to her on the breeze. It was 'Greensleeves'; unmistakable, mournful, and played out of key. She turned around and smiled when she saw Arthur's ice-cream van coming towards her. He lifted his hand from the steering wheel to wave as he drew parallel with her. But when the van passed her, she stood still and stared in horror. On the back, in lurid green letters, was the announcement: *NEW! Peanut ice cream!*

The vehicle trundled on a short distance, spluttering and coughing fumes, then stuttered to a halt. Traffic swerved around it. Car horns beeped in anger and frustration at the broken-down van bringing traffic to a standstill. As Helen walked closer, she couldn't keep her eyes off the sign at the back. Peanuts. Peanuts. Dinah the van. Arthur. Peanuts. Her mind whirled and her heart began to beat so fast she thought it might burst.

She thought of the night of the school reunion, when she'd met Arthur. They'd made small talk, and he'd mentioned that he'd lived on the Norfolk coast. Norfolk. That was where Great Yarmouth was, wasn't it? He'd told her he was a travelling salesman and he'd asked her what she did for a living. She'd told him about the Seaview. Oh no, she thought. They'd talked about crazy golf. She'd told him she had Ricky Delmont staying at the hotel. Arthur had known where Ricky was staying, and it was because of her. But where had she heard the name Dinah before? Was it Jean who'd mentioned it? No. Marie? No. Someone else, but who?

It came to her in a flash. It had been Brenda, when she'd been talking about her night at the bingo, the night her keys to the Seaview had been stolen. Dinah was one of Brenda's friends, along with Peggy and Pat. Helen felt sick. Was this the same Dinah, Arthur's mum? She glanced at the ice-cream van. She remembered Sally saying that a new ice cream parlour was opening on Saturday in Cayton Bay, owned by someone called Dinah's son. Sally was going there with Gracie and Gav, and there would be fifty flavours for sale. Suddenly her thoughts about Ricky's death began to take horrible, stomach-twisting, peanut-flavoured, ice-cream-coned shape.

Chapter 42

The ice-cream van sat idle on the road. Helen stood behind it, staring at the sign offering peanut ice cream. Her heart was pounding, her legs were shaking and the palms of her hands had turned moist with fear. She remembered how on the day of Ricky's death, the van had been at the crazy-golf course. She recalled that Gracie had been eating ice cream. Marie had offered to buy Helen one, but she'd declined. Her stomach twisted with anxiety. Was it just a coincidence that Arthur's van, with its peanut flavour ice cream, had been there that day? Or was there something more sinister going on? There was only one way to find out. 'Come on, Suki,' she said.

She knocked at the serving hatch window and peered inside. Arthur was sitting in the driver's seat, trying and failing to turn the engine over. It sounded to Helen as if he'd flooded it.

'Arthur! I need to speak to you,' she said.

He spun around in his seat. He was sweating and red in the face.

'Arthur, come out here, now!'

'What do you want?'

She wanted to be wrong about him, that was what she wanted. But all the signs pointed in one direction, and she didn't like it one bit. 'I need to ask a few questions about Ricky Delmont.'

Arthur froze. Helen saw horror etched all over his face. Her stomach dropped to the floor. She was right. 'Arthur, get out here, now!' she called, banging on the hatch.

He lunged across to the passenger door and flung it open. Traffic overtaking the stalled van screeched to a halt, and cars beeped their horns as he stepped out in front of them. Helen watched as he ran across the road. For a short, fat man he was surprisingly quick. Must be his years of rugby training, she thought. She started after him with Suki, but she had to manoeuvre carefully with the dog in tow, and by the time she'd crossed Foreshore Road, Arthur had disappeared into the Central Tramway funicular and it was already starting to move. She knew she had to catch him, but how? There was no way she could beat him to the top on foot.

As the second funicular car trundled down the hill, she realised that was her only option. She knew it was likely that Arthur would run as soon as he reached the top of the hill, but at least she could ask the staff which way he'd gone and follow him as best she could. He was hard to miss, in his striking turquoise and white jacket.

When the car arrived at the bottom, the passengers disembarked and she dashed straight in, standing right at the front with Suki. The car began to move up the hill, and at the same time, the first car started to descend. When they passed each other in the middle, Helen saw a flash of turquoise and white and couldn't believe her eyes. Arthur hadn't got out at the top; he was in the car going down! He must have watched her and Suki get in and decided to outfox her. She was livid.

'Stop that funicular!' she screamed at the top of her voice. The other passengers, and Suki, looked at her as if she'd gone mad. All she could do was move to stand by the door so she'd be first out of the car the moment it opened.

'Be careful, miss!' the ticket master warned as she leapt out at the station, but she barely heard him. Her heart was beating too fast, the blood rushing in her ears. She had to get Arthur. There was no point going back down in the funicular; he would only come up again, and they'd end up crossing each other all day. She looked down the hill. She saw him reach his van and jump into the passenger seat. She guessed he'd be trying the engine again, but if he was, the van didn't move. Then she gasped. He'd jumped out of the van and was running along the seafront in the direction of the Spa.

'Come, Suki,' she cried, pulling the dog with her as she set off parallel to him along the top of the hill. Did he know she was there and had him in her sights? She could see him clearly, but he didn't once look up. It seemed to her he didn't have a clue where she was.

'Run, Suki, run,' she urged, and the dog began to canter like the racing greyhound she'd once been, pulling on her lead, racing ahead. 'Slow down, Suki,' Helen called. 'You'll pull my arm out of its socket!'

Still Suki ran on, dragging Helen behind her. They ran past the Grand Hotel, past St Nicholas café and across the Spa bridge. Below, Arthur was still barrelling along the seafront, heading towards the Spa. Beyond the Spa were the South Cliff Gardens. Helen's problem now was how to get down the hill to stop Arthur before he disappeared into the gardens and out of sight.

She arrived at the Spa chalet puffing, panting, out of breath. 'Just a minute, Suki,' she gasped. But Suki didn't stop; she wanted to keep running and chasing now that her dander was up. Exhausted, Helen hung on to the blue railing of the Spa bridge while she got her breath back, continuing to keep her sights on

Arthur. Her grip on Suki's lead slackened, and in that moment, the dog took off with the lead trailing behind.

'Come back!' Helen yelled.

Passers-by stopped and looked at her, and then at Suki.

'You'll have your work cut out getting a greyhound back, love,' an old man told her. 'Once they've got the chase in them, they never lose it. If the dog's got its eye on something, it'll not stop until it's hunted it down.'

Helen had been watching Arthur intently, trying not to lose sight of him, but now she was focused on Suki. She saw the dog zip ahead along the narrow path that led into the gardens. She called after her, but Suki didn't stop; she just kept on running. Helen couldn't run any more. Her legs felt like lead. Her heart was beating too fast. Her head hurt and her feet burned. She wasn't used to such physical exertion. But she followed Suki as fast as she could. She had to get her dog back and she had to stop Arthur. Down and round the pathways she went, into the gardens. She prayed the dog wouldn't run up the hill and into traffic, as she had no road sense at all.

'Suki, come back!' she called.

When anyone walked towards her, she asked the same question: 'Have you seen a greyhound running loose?'

'That way.' A woman pointed further down the hill.

Helen hurried on through the gardens towards the sea. There was no sign of Arthur, and she was afraid that she'd lost him. Past the Victorian Spa was another funicular, the Scarborough Spa cliff lift.

'Ticket for one?' the station master asked when he saw her.

She shook her head. She could barely speak, she was so exhausted. 'Lost my dog. Greyhound.'

313

He nodded up the hill. 'With a lead trailing behind? It ran up there a minute ago.'

Helen looked at the many pathways winding up the steep hill through the gardens. She gasped her thanks and began to make her way up.

When she reached the short tunnel that ran under the funicular, she spotted Suki standing at the entrance. She ran to her and picked up her lead, and was stunned to see Arthur pinned up against the tunnel wall.

'Get that dog away, it's a monster,' he cried.

It took her a moment to understand what was going on. Arthur was in a tunnel; he could leave at any time through the other end, and yet it looked like he was glued to the wall. She saw he was trembling. She pulled Suki's lead and held the dog close. A monster? Suki wouldn't hurt a fly, but there was no need for Arthur to know that.

'Yes, she's a monster all right,' she said grimly. 'And I'll set her on you if I need to. All it takes is one word from me.'

Arthur began to cry. 'Please don't. I'm terrified of dogs.'

'Be quiet,' she ordered. 'And don't you dare move, or you know what will happen.'

Arthur whined in terror. Helen pulled her phone from her pocket and pressed the number for DS Hutchinson. 'I've found Ricky Delmont's killer,' she gasped when he answered. 'I'm at the tunnel in the South Cliff Gardens.'

'I'm on my way,' he said.

She put the phone back in her pocket. 'The game's up, Arthur. I know you murdered Ricky.'

Inside the tunnel, Arthur hung his head and started to weep. 'You don't know what he did to me,' he cried.

'I know he attacked you in Great Yarmouth,' she said.

He raised his eyes and looked at her. 'How on earth do you know that?'

'I have my sources.'

Suki strained on the lead and Arthur pressed himself further against the tunnel wall. 'Keep her away.'

'You'll have worse than my greyhound to deal with once the police arrive.'

He slunk down the wall to the ground.

'You stole the keys to my hotel from my cleaner's bag at the bingo hall, didn't you?' Helen said.

Arthur wailed out loud, then slowly nodded his head. 'Mum helped me get the keys when I told her that Ricky Delmont was staying at the Seaview.'

He made to stand up, but when Suki stepped forward, he slid down again, cowed.

'I thought the keys were for the hotel's front door. All I wanted to do was get inside, find his room and steal his putters and balls. But the keys didn't fit the front door. I tried the back door instead, and ended up in the kitchen. My mum warned me you had a dog because she knows I'm terrified of them. So she gave me some doggy treats which I threw onto your carpet once I entered your apartment. While the dog was distracted, I was still terrified and almost lost my nerve. But she seemed calm and friendly. She wasn't the growling monster she's turned into today. Anyway, I soon realised I couldn't get upstairs from your apartment, so I panicked and decided to take whatever I could find, anything to do with Ricky. I thought maybe you'd have his home address or his phone number in a file. I didn't know what

I was looking for, but then I found the blue folder with his allergy listed.'

'So you decided to poison him instead of smashing up his putters?'

'No!' Arthur cried. 'I didn't mean to kill him. I smeared peanut ice cream on the ball he was using at the tournament. No one noticed me, because Ricky was fighting with Norman and everyone was watching them. I knew Ricky always kissed his ball for good luck before he teed off. But the next thing I knew, he was dead. I just wanted him out of action. I wanted to put him in hospital, the same way he did to me all those years ago. I wanted revenge, that's all.'

Suki stepped forward, and Arthur recoiled.

'He broke my nose. After he attacked me, everything went wrong. My girlfriend left me, and I lost my job. I'd worked as a travelling salesman, but they said my nose was putting off customers. I ended up buying an ice-cream van and plying my trade along the Norfolk coast. Mum was the only one who cared. When I returned to Scarborough for the school reunion, it coincided with the crazy-golf tournament Ricky was playing in. Then you told me he was staying at the Seaview. I never meant for him to die.'

Helen heard sirens from the seafront. 'Save your words, Arthur; keep them for the police.'

Chapter 43

Uniformed officers bounded up the hill, followed by DS Hutchinson and DC Hall.

Helen nodded to the tunnel entrance. 'He's in there.'

Arthur was brought out in handcuffs, flanked by officers. Helen watched as he was taken away and bundled into a police car.

'Are you all right, Mrs Dexter?' DS Hutchinson asked.

Helen shook her head. 'My legs are wobbly.'

'I'm afraid you'll need to accompany me to the station to answer some questions.'

'Can I bring my dog? I can't leave her here.'

DS Hutchinson offered his arm. 'Yes, you can bring her. Let me help you down the hill.'

Helen took his arm, then, at the bottom of the hill, she accepted his help to lift Suki into a van. At the police station, DS Hutchinson whipped out his notepad and Helen told him everything, leaving no stone unturned. She unloaded all she knew about Arthur, about his past in Great Yarmouth, and about how he'd waited for years to take revenge on Ricky. She told him about his mum, Dinah, the peanut ice cream, and how her suspicions had led to her chasing him. DS Hutchinson wrote it all down.

'We discovered that Mr Delmont once attacked a crazy golfer in Great Yarmouth, but we hadn't made the connection to Arthur,' he said. 'My staff were working on it. It seems you helped solve the mystery for us, Mrs Dexter.'

Something popped into Helen's mind. 'Arthur was planning to open a new ice-cream parlour on Saturday.'

'With fifty flavours.' DS Hutchinson nodded. 'I never knew there were that many. Well, it won't be opening now.'

'I wonder where he got the money to invest in an ice-cream parlour when he couldn't even afford to keep his van in decent nick?'

'Oh, he didn't invest,' DS Hutchinson explained. 'The parlour was registered in his mother's name. She won a large sum at the bingo a few months ago. Everyone knew about it – she put herself forward to be featured in *The Scarborough Times*, and they ran a double-page spread. We'll be bringing her in for questioning after what you've told us.'

His phone rang and he excused himself. Helen watched him go, then sat for half an hour in the stuffy room, watching the hands on the clock slowly tick the minutes away. Her phone had no signal inside the station, so she couldn't call or text anyone. She hoped Suki was being looked after. A kindly policeman had taken her when they had arrived, and his eyes had lit up.

'I've always wanted a retired greyhound,' he'd said. 'Come on, girl. Come with me and I'll get you a drink of water.'

When DS Hutchinson finally returned, he apologised for taking so long. 'The ice-cream van has been towed from the seafront,' he explained. 'Arthur Mason has admitted everything. He's confessed to the murder of Ricky Delmont and confirmed that it was his mother who took the keys from your cleaner's handbag. I think we're done here, Mrs Dexter. You're free to go.'

'Please, call me Helen,' she said. 'You're going to be a guest at my birthday party with Sandra, after all. Jean's making hangover-cure sausage butties for Sunday morning. You're welcome to stay, if you're not at work, that is.'

'I'm looking forward to it, Mrs . . . Helen. Thank you.'

Helen stood, but didn't move. She needed assurance that her legs had stopped shaking after the shock of the day. When she was certain she wouldn't fall, she walked from the room.

'You can collect your dog from the front of the station; the sergeant's making a fuss of her there. Would you like one of my staff to drive you both to the Seaview?'

Helen shook her head. 'I need to clear my head with a walk, but I appreciate your offer.'

She walked home slowly. By now, it was late afternoon. Once she reached her apartment, she collapsed on to the sofa, trying to process what had happened. She felt exhausted. It had been a long day; she'd been up in the small hours staking out the dining room, and now here she was involved in the capture of a killer. She rang Marie to tell her the news.

'Do you need me? I'm free, I can be there in ten minutes.'

'No, I want to be on my own, just me and Suki,' Helen said firmly. 'I'm going to make myself something to eat, then have a very early night. I need to put today behind me. Saturday and the party can't come fast enough. I need my friends and family around like I've never needed you all before.'

'Are you sure I can't come over now?' Marie said.

'No, please don't,' Helen replied. 'Let me deal in my own way with what happened today. It's a lot to take in, but rest assured I'll call you if I need you. And if I don't see you before, I'll see you on

Saturday. There are only three more nights with the crazy golfers before the Seaview opens its doors to a party to remember. Oh, and I've got one more thing to tell you.'

'What's that?'

'After what I've been through today with Arthur, it's made me realise I'm more capable than I thought. Turning fifty doesn't seem so scary. I think I might be getting my sparkle back.'

Marie laughed out loud. 'Your what?'

'Oh, nothing. It was just something Jean said.'

'Call me if you need me.'

'I promise.'

After she'd hung up on Marie, Helen cooked dinner, fed Suki, then lay down on the sofa to watch TV. She closed her eyes and tried to let the day's events soften in her mind.

She woke the next morning to find Jean standing over her with a concerned expression on her face.

'You all right, love?'

Helen looked from left to right. What was she doing on the sofa? Why was the TV on? She tried to move, but her neck hurt, her legs hurt and she was aware she didn't smell good. Running around in the sunshine the previous day, chasing Arthur, chasing Suki, had done her body odour no favours. She sat up. 'I'm fine, Jean. I had a bit of a day yesterday. I'll tell you all about it after I've showered and changed.'

She was true to her word, and over poached eggs on buttered toast with a mug of tea, she revealed everything. Jean tutted and shook her head. She chipped in with questions at the right time and knew when to keep quiet.

'So you see, it was Brenda's friend Dinah who stole our keys. She gave them to her son, Arthur, to help him get revenge on the man who'd attacked him and broken his nose.'

'Oh love, it's awful,' Jean said, then she wiped her hands on her apron and pulled the fridge open. 'But it's all done with now. We can concentrate on happier things, like your party this weekend.' She shot Helen a look. 'I assume Jimmy's coming?'

Helen smiled. 'You assume right.'

Jean gave her a cheeky wink. 'I'll arrive an hour later than usual in the morning. We'll all enjoy an informal late breakfast. My sausage butties are the talk of the town.'

'Did you invite Miriam to the party?' Helen asked.

Jean pushed her glasses up to the bridge of her nose. 'I did, and she said . . .' She stuck her nose in the air and affected an accent exactly like Miriam's. 'She said, "Jean, dear, I'd love to come, and perhaps I will if I have nothing better to do."'

Helen laughed out loud. 'That sounds just like her.'

By the time Sally arrived that morning, Helen felt strong enough to start work. It was a necessary distraction from all that had happened, and she threw herself wholeheartedly into her routine. As she carried Jean's perfectly cooked breakfasts from the dumbwaiter into the dining room, all eyes turned towards her. Even Olga looked up from her folder of crazy-golf rules.

Alice stood. 'We heard from Ricky's teammates staying next door that there's been an arrest for his murder. Is it true?' she asked.

'Yes, it's true,' Helen said, looking around.

Olga and Freddy sank back in their seats. Alice sat down, then leaned on the table with her head in her hands. Marty and Marilyn held hands across the table.

'It was an old adversary of Ricky's, someone he attacked on a crazy-golf course years ago.'

Marty thumped the table with his fist. 'I knew it! I bet it was that man at the course in Southend!'

'Or the one in Paignton,' Alice said.

'I can guess which one,' Olga said. 'Great Yarmouth. I was there.'

'Yes, that was the one. His name was Arthur Mason,' Helen said.

'I even visited him in hospital. Took grapes,' Olga said.

'Arthur owns the ice-cream van that was at Norman's crazy-golf course on the day Ricky died. One of his new flavours was peanut,' Helen said.

Sally wafted past carrying plates. She set them down on the table in front of Marty and Marilyn. Helen was pleased to see Marilyn enjoying a boiled egg with buttered soldiers. 'Are you all right?' she mouthed. Marilyn nodded discreetly by way of reply.

As Helen left the dining room, she could hear her guests talking about Arthur, Ricky, Great Yarmouth and the Norfolk coast. She picked up a bottle of brown sauce and walked back into the room. The chatter and whispers immediately ceased.

'It's all right with me if you want to talk about Ricky's death. I do understand,' she said. 'Talking things through helps make sense of it. Please don't clam up on my behalf. The Seaview is a safe space, and confidential information will stay within its four walls.'

She glanced at Olga, who acknowledged her words with a sharp nod.

'I'd like to give a toast,' Olga said.

'I can't eat any more toast, I've had enough,' Freddy said.

Olga stood and raised her glass of freshly squeezed orange juice. 'To Ricky Delmont.'

More glasses were raised.

'To Ricky, whatever we thought of him,' Marilyn said.

Marty patted her hand. Alice pushed her chair back and held her glass of apple juice aloft.

'To Ricky. The worst husband ever. The man I thought was the love of my life but who became the bane of it instead. May he finally rest in peace.'

The rest of breakfast was eaten in silence. When all was done and the guests began to file from the dining room, Alice caught Helen's eye.

'I know it hasn't been easy having an unusual group like us staying here, especially with everything that's happened. I just wanted to say thank you, on behalf of our team, for putting up with us all.'

'It's nice of you to say that, thank you, Alice. Are you going to practise today at the course?'

'Oh yes, Olga's organised two long training sessions. Tomorrow's game might be a charity game rather than a tournament, but it's a game we all want to win. Well, at least it *was* a game we wanted to win, but there's been a change of plan now.'

Alice bounded up the stairs with her red pigtails flying. Helen wondered what she'd meant. Olga stepped forward and looked at her.

'I think it's ironic,' she said.

'Sorry?'

'The ice-cream van with its *2 4 1* sign.'

'What about it?' Helen said, confused. 'It means Arthur Mason was offering two ice creams for the price of one. I don't understand what's ironic about that.'

Olga opened her folder of crazy-golf rules and ran her finger down a page. She pointed at one of the paragraphs.

'Safety rule 2.4.1. Players must at all times exercise due care, responsibility and caution so as not to injure themselves or other persons.'

She snapped the folder shut and disappeared up the stairs, leaving Helen's head spinning. They really were an odd bunch.

Chapter 44

On the morning of the charity game, there was tension in the air. Helen felt it as soon as she walked into the dining room carrying a rack of brown toast. Instead of the usual chatter, her guests were silent. Olga, she noticed, was reading her folder of rules yet again. Freddy sat straight-backed in his seat. Alice's red hair was coiled in a twist at the top of her head. Marilyn was in full make-up, with her hair in a gravity-defying white beehive. Marty's face was clean-shaven and pink.

'Good luck today, everyone,' she said.

'We don't need luck, we're prepared,' Olga said.

'Thank you, Helen,' said Marty. 'Will you be coming to watch?'

'I wouldn't miss it for the world. It'll be a positive end to a difficult time, although I hear there won't be any ice-cream vans allowed.'

She left them to their breakfast. When they'd finished and were filing from the room, she and Sally cleared it quickly, then headed downstairs to the kitchen.

'How are things upstairs?' Jean asked.

'Tense. A bit serious,' Helen replied. 'Would you like to come and watch the game with me, Jean? Marie can't come, as she's working in Filey at her new tearoom, getting it ready for the grand opening next week.'

'I can't, love. I've got to pop to the care home to see how Mum's doing.'

'Sally? What about you?' Helen asked.

Sally shook her head. 'Me and Gav have arranged to go to Bridlington. There's a cab firm for sale and Gav wants to look at it. He's thinking of expanding Gav's Cabs.'

Helen looked at Suki. 'It's just you and me then, girl,' she said.

'You should ask Jimmy to go with you,' Jean said.

'He's working, Jean. I've already rung him. He's got a singing job in the bar at the Cumberland Hotel. They've been looking for an Elvis impersonator to take up a residency, and Jimmy jumped at the chance when they offered him the job. He's working lunchtimes and evenings until the end of September. It looks like I'll be watching the crazy golf on my own.'

Later that morning, after the rooms had been cleaned, Jean and Sally left for the day. Helen clipped Suki's lead to her collar and headed out of the back door. She rounded the corner of the Seaview on to King's Parade just in time to see her guests leaving through the front. They were dressed identically in navy tracksuits and white trainers, each of them carrying their sports bag and putters. Olga led the way, barking her commands.

'Left, right. Left, right.'

Helen waved at her guests as they marched down the path. 'I'll see you at the course,' she said.

The front door of the Vista del Mar swung open and five men walked out. They too carried bags of putters slung over their shoulders and small sports bags in their hands. Then Miriam appeared and locked the door behind her. She wore a smart grey trouser suit, and her sunglasses were perched on her head.

'Morning, Miriam, how are you?' Helen asked.

'Helen, dear. I can't stop to chat. I'm going to the crazy-golf game to watch my guests win. They're an elite team, you know. They brought in a new captain after the unfortunate death of Mr Delmont, your murdered guest.'

Helen sighed. 'I'm going to watch the game too. We could walk together, if you'd like?'

Miriam eyed Suki. 'As long as you keep your mutt away from my new slacks.'

The two women set off together, making small talk about the weather, art events at the Old Parcel Office and shows in town. When they reached the seafront, Helen was pleased to see that a sizeable crowd had turned up. She excused herself from Miriam and walked towards Norman, happy to see his hut door open.

'Morning, Norman, how are things?'

'Oh, you know. Busy,' he replied.

She nodded to the hut. 'Everything all right?'

'I have good days and bad days,' he said.

She slipped him a card with the number of a support group. He pocketed it and nodded his thanks.

'You'll get the best view of the game from the deckchairs on the beach,' he told her.

Helen took his suggestion and settled herself into a red and white striped chair in the shade of the hut. Suki lay in the shade too. When the crazy golf began, there was no big announcement like there had been last time. There was no Jimmy in his Elvis suit, no singing. There was no fuss or sparkle and, thankfully, no fighting. There was also no ice-cream van. Helen scanned the crowd and the prom. She was relieved not to see any of the gamblers, and hoped they'd had the decency to stay away.

Both teams lined up in front of the hut. Norman tossed a coin to decide which team went first.

'Heads or tails?' he asked Olga.

'Heads,' Olga said.

'Heads it is!' he called, holding up the coin for all to see.

Helen watched her guests and noticed the serious concentration on their faces as they putted their balls through the models of Scarborough landmarks. She clapped loudly when Olga scored a hole-in-one through Scarborough Castle. She cheered when Freddy sent a precise shot through the iconic Grand Hotel and watched as he jumped up and down three times to celebrate. And when Marty played a blinder on the model of the *Hispaniola* pirate ship, she took her phone out of her bag and snapped a picture. But her guests had stiff competition from their rival team staying at the Vista del Mar. They scored holes-in-one on the models of the art deco Stephen Joseph Theatre, the market hall, and the huge tuna fish marking Scarborough's tunny-fishing past. The game was tense. At the final hole, the windmill, the scores were level. The crowd waited with bated breath to see which team would win. Would any of them score a hole-in-one at the windmill to set the chimes playing 'Scarborough Fair'?

Helen couldn't bear the suspense. She wanted Olga and her team to win. It was what they deserved after the awful time they'd had. She looked across at Miriam, who was waving tea towels in the air, cheerleader style. She peered at the towels, certain one of them was hers.

Both teams lined up at the final hole. This was it. The team that won this hole won the game. Olga, Freddy, Marilyn, Marty and Alice huddled together, heads down. Helen wondered what instructions Olga was barking. Then they stepped back and played their shots in turn. They were good, oh, she'd give them that, but they weren't perfect, and Olga missed a hole-in-one by a hair's breadth. A polite round of applause went up from the crowd.

Now it was time for Miriam's guests to play. They too went into a huddle before they played the hole.

'Win it for Ricky Delmont!' someone shouted from the crowd. There was another round of applause.

The team stepped forward and the crowd fell silent. The players took their shots, and each of them scored a hole-in-one. Miriam's team had won and Helen's had lost. Helen glanced across at Olga and her team, but instead of looking as devastated as she felt, they were congratulating the rival team, shaking hands and sharing hugs.

Helen stood and walked towards them with Suki. 'Well played,' she said. 'Such a shame you didn't win.'

'I didn't need to win,' Olga said.

Helen looked at her, shocked. 'But you're all so competitive. You told me that winning is what it's all about.'

Marty shook his head. 'Not today, Helen. We drew lots last night to decide which one of us was going to play a deliberate bad shot. Olga drew the short straw. You see, today wasn't about winning. It was about letting Ricky's team win.'

Helen was beginning to understand.

'It was about letting Rickster rest in peace,' Marilyn said.

Marty took his wife's hand and they walked off the course. Alice and Freddy walked off together too, followed by Olga.

Miriam appeared at Helen's side. 'The best team won, dear,' she gloated. 'That's because they stayed at my Vista del Mar, you see. They were well rested, well fed. I gave them the breakfast of champions and it paid off.'

Helen gritted her teeth against Miriam's barbed comments. After years of living next door to the woman, she really should be used to her behaviour by now. And yet somehow Miriam always had the last word. A sharp retort hovered on the tip of Helen's tongue, but she was so exhausted, she simply turned and walked away.

The following morning, two orange Gav's Cabs waited at the Seaview to take her guests and their golfing equipment to the railway station. Olga paid the bill on behalf of the group.

'I'm sorry for any inconvenience,' she said as she handed Helen her credit card.

'She means about Ricky Delmont and everything that happened,' Freddy chipped in.

Helen returned the card. The hall was full of putting irons, sports bags and suitcases.

'Well, I'd like to say goodbye to you all and hope you have a pleasant onward journey,' she said, adopting her professional landlady manner. She shook hands with Olga and Freddy.

'Mum and I are heading to the States,' Freddy beamed. 'I can learn a lot there to improve my game.' He and Olga picked up their bags and headed outside.

Next was Alice, struggling with her suitcase and putters.

'The cab driver will help you with those,' Helen said.

Alice dropped everything to the carpet, then threw her arms around Helen, taking her by surprise. 'They think I don't know that Olga is Freddy's mum, but I do,' she whispered in Helen's ear.

Helen looked at her, astounded, but pretended not to understand. One thing she'd learned in her years running the Seaview was when to keep her mouth shut.

'Have a safe journey home,' she said.

Finally Marty and Marilyn stepped forward. Marty shouldered a heavy bag of putting irons, then lifted a suitcase in one hand and a sports bag in the other. The cab driver came towards him, offering to help, but he shook his head. 'I can manage. I might look old, but I'm more than capable.' He turned to Helen. 'Thank you, Helen, for all you've done. I know it's been difficult. Rest assured, I'll be leaving a five-star review on HypeThatHotel.' He walked off and began to load the luggage into the cab.

Marilyn leaned forward and kissed Helen on the cheek. 'I'm going to tell him about the baby tonight,' she said.

'I hope everything goes well for you both,' Helen said, and she meant every word.

Marilyn got into the back of the cab with Marty, and as one, the vehicles tooted their horns and revved their engines. Then they began to move, taking Helen's guests away.

She walked into the lounge, where she collapsed on to the window seat just as Jean and Sally walked in. Jean clapped her hands together.

'Come on. We can't sit around staring out of the window. You two have the rooms to clean before everyone arrives, and I've got a birthday cake to bake!'

Chapter 45

The party was in full swing by the time Jimmy arrived with his daughter, Jodie. He leaned towards Helen and planted a kiss on her cheek. Then from behind his back he whipped out a bunch of long-stemmed pink roses tied with a white satin bow.

'Happy birthday, Helen.'

'Jimmy, they're gorgeous, thank you,' she said.

'Sorry I'm late. I've been rehoming Priscilla; she's living at Jodie's house now.'

Jodie stepped forward and handed Helen a card and a small purple gift bag. 'My flatmate's looking after her and settling her in. Happy birthday, Helen. It's not much, but I wanted to bring something.'

'Thanks, Jodie,' Helen said, touched. She liked Jodie and hoped she would get to know her better now she was planning on getting closer to Jimmy. She ushered the two of them along the hall and into the lounge.

'Hello, Jimmy, it's good to see you again,' Jean said, offering him a plate. 'Fancy a sausage twizzle?'

Jimmy took a twizzle and a napkin. Helen laid the flowers on a table.

'Would you like me to put those in water?' Jean asked.

'Jean, you're a marvel. What would I do without you?'

Jean shot a look across the room to where Brenda was talking to Sally and Gav and swaying from side to side with a glassy look in her eye. 'Just keep me away from Brenda,' she muttered. 'She's had far too much to drink.' She picked up the bouquet. 'I'll top up Suki's water bowl for her while I'm downstairs,' she said as she bustled away.

'Jimmy, Jodie, these are my friends Bev and Sue. Jimmy, you met them when your troupe of twelve singing Elvises performed in Scarborough.'

'Twelvis!' Sue screamed. 'They were wonderful. It's nice to see you again, Jimmy.'

Jimmy hugged Sue and Bev before Marie swanned up and kissed him on both cheeks.

'It's good to see you, Marie,' Jimmy said.

'Likewise. It's even better to see the smile you put on my best friend's face,' Marie beamed. 'Now, has anyone seen my fella Jack? I'm sure I left him around here somewhere.' She walked off towards the dining room with a glass of champagne in her hand.

Helen took Jimmy to meet her sister-in-law and her nephews.

'They've travelled all the way from Shetland to be here,' she said. 'Now then, Jimmy, let me get you a drink, and you, Jodie.'

'A soft drink for me,' Jodie said. 'I've been off the booze and clean for six months.'

'I'll have a pint of whatever's going,' Jimmy said.

Helen headed to the bar, leaving Tom's sister and Jimmy chatting happily together. The jukebox on the wall played every kind of Elvis hit. Fast rock-and-roll numbers were followed by ballads and singalongs. Everyone was in the party spirit; even Miriam, who'd turned up carrying her own wine glass.

'Because, Helen, dear, you just never know if other hotels are going to be as clean as the Vista del Mar,' she sniffed when Helen challenged her.

Bev, now fully recovered from flu, was jiving with Sue in the lounge, their skirts flying. DS Hutchinson and Sandra DeVine were smooching cheek to cheek, even though the song that was playing was a lively one. Helen poured Jimmy a pint of Wold Top, the local brew. She raised her eyebrows at him.

'Did you, um, bring your toothbrush?' she said.

'Oh yes,' he replied with a cheeky smile.

Her heart fluttered. Tonight was the night. But first there was dancing to be done, eating and drinking and talking and catching up with all of her favourite people.

When the jukebox changed its tune to a song deserving a jive, Jimmy set his drink on the bar and turned to her.

'Are you dancing?'

Helen put her glass of champagne next to his pint. 'Are you asking?'

'I'm asking.'

'Then I'm dancing.'

She and Jimmy jived through the lounge and into the hall, and suddenly found themselves alone beside the Seaview's front door. Outside, the night air was warm, and she sat down on the top step. Jimmy sat next to her and they both gazed at the sea.

'It's calm tonight,' she said.

'It's beautiful.' Jimmy turned to her. 'Almost as beautiful as you. You've a lovely sparkle in your eyes tonight.'

She rested her head on his broad shoulder and breathed in the scent of his lemon spice aftershave. For the first time in weeks, she felt at peace. Just then, she felt something push against her shoulder.

'Sorry, missus.'

She turned around to see Gav. In one hand he held an electric drill and in the other the wooden plaque with the Seaview's four stars.

'Sally says you had trouble fitting this to the wall. I thought while I was here I might as well put it up.'

'Thanks, Gav, but there's no need to do it now. Go and enjoy yourself with Sally and Gracie.'

'To be honest, missus, I'm glad to get away from my mum-in-law for five minutes. She's had too much to drink.'

Helen stood so that Gav could step out of the Seaview. Jimmy got up too.

'Thanks, Gav. I appreciate this,' she said.

Gav got to work fixing the plaque to the wall. Jimmy laid his arm across Helen's shoulders, and she snuggled into his side as she watched Gav attach the four stars, finally, to the Seaview. He stood back to admire his handiwork, and she beamed with pride.

'It looks great, Gav,' she said.

'Superb,' Jimmy agreed.

Once Gav had made his way back inside, Helen turned her face to Jimmy's. This is it, she thought. Her heart fluttered, thinking of their night ahead. His lips brushed hers, gently and softly. She leaned further towards him. But before their lips could meet again, one of the guests came dancing and singing along the hall. Helen turned to see who was causing the commotion, and was stunned to see it was Brenda, a bottle of Prosecco in one hand and an overflowing glass in the other. The woman was so drunk she could barely stand.

335

'I'm shelebrating my new job at the Vishta del Mar,' she slurred.

And then she tripped and lost her footing. The glass flew from her hand and smashed against the wall, and the bottle thudded to the carpet. Jimmy leapt into action, ready to catch her, but he was too late. Brenda crashed into him, and Helen watched in horror as he staggered under her weight. She tried to stop him from falling, but it all happened so quickly that she didn't stand a chance. The pair of them tumbled down the steps and landed in a heap at the bottom, Brenda on top, belting out a drunken rendition of 'I Am What I Am'.

'Jimmy!' Helen called. She ran to him.

Brenda poked her in the arm. 'I love you. You're my besht friend.'

Helen ignored her; she was too focused on Jimmy.

Jimmy groaned. 'My leg. It's my leg, I can't move it.'

Gav appeared at her side, along with DS Hutchinson. 'He needs to go to hospital,' Gav said, 'but I can't take him, I've had too much to drink. Let me call one of my cabs.'

'No, I'll take him,' DS Hutchinson offered. 'I don't drink, I've only had lemonade.'

Jimmy stirred and his eyes opened wide. 'I'm all right,' he said, trying to sit up.

DS Hutchinson held three fingers in front of his face. 'How many fingers can you see?'

'Three. I didn't bang my head, I'm all right,' Jimmy said impatiently. 'But I can't feel my left leg. I think it might be broken.'

Jodie appeared. 'Dad? What's happened?'

'He fell down the stairs,' Helen explained. She looked at Brenda, who was now singing 'YMCA' and doing all the actions, moving her arms around on the ground.

'Let's get you up, fella,' DS Hutchinson said. 'Gav, you take his other arm and we'll get him into my car.'

Helen watched the men struggle to get Jimmy upright.

'Let me come with you,' she said.

Jimmy turned around. 'No, Helen. You've got to stay. It's your party, you can't leave. I'll ring you from the hospital as soon as I know what's happening.'

She watched with a heavy heart as he was carefully placed in the car. She was worried about his injury, saddened that he'd miss the rest of the party, and deflated after she'd spent all day looking forward to seeing him. Only moments ago, they'd been about to kiss, before Brenda had put an end to it all. Well, there'd be another time. She had everything to look forward to.

'By the look of your leg, you'll be kept in overnight,' DS Hutchinson warned.

Helen waited until Jimmy was safely in the car. Then she and Gav hoisted Brenda to her feet and walked her back inside. 'Jimmy's been carted off to hospital with a suspected broken leg and Brenda hasn't got a scratch on her,' Helen said.

Gav laughed out loud. 'The woman's indestructible, you should know that by now.'

Helen propped Brenda on a chair in the dining room, then dispatched Sally downstairs to ask Jean to brew coffee.

'I'll get you sobered up if it's the last thing I do,' she told Brenda.

'Shspoilshport,' Brenda slurred.

When Jean brought the coffee, she sat between Helen and Brenda. 'I warned you this woman was trouble.'

Just then the hotel landline rang in the hall. Helen made a move to answer it.

'You can't answer the phone tonight of all nights. It's your birthday. It's the middle of your party. Why not let it ring for once?' Jean said kindly.

'You know I'd never do that. The Seaview means everything to me. Keep your eye on Brenda.'

Helen walked into the hall and picked up the phone. 'Good evening, Seaview Hotel.'

It was a man on the other end; he sounded young and polite.

'Good evening. I was wondering if you might have rooms free for our ballroom-dancing formation team? We're performing at Scarborough Spa in the Big Ballroom Blitz. There are ten of us, you see, and we'd all like to stay in the same hotel.'

'Oh, that sounds exciting,' Helen said. She scrabbled under the reception desk and pulled out her tablet, then opened her bookings app. 'Now, what date would you like to come in?'

We hope you have enjoyed reading
Foul Play at the Seaview Hotel.

For more tales of murder and misadventure at Scarborough's
Seaview Hotel, don't miss Glenda Young's previous cosy crime
novels featuring amateur sleuth Helen Dexter and her trusty
greyhound Suki . . .

The first Helen Dexter cosy crime novel, *Murder at the Seaview Hotel*, is a hugely entertaining and intriguing mystery.

When twelve Elvis impersonators arrive at the Seaview Hotel in the charming Yorkshire seaside town of Scarborough, a murder is nothing to sing about . . .

Available in paperback and ebook now.

The second Helen Dexter mystery, *Curtain Call at the Seaview Hotel*, is sure to enthral crime fans everywhere.

Things take a dramatic turn in the charming Yorkshire seaside town of Scarborough when an acting troupe book into the Seaview Hotel and the stage is set for murder . . .

Available in paperback and ebook now.

Don't miss Glenda Young's unputdownable and heart-wrenching sagas!

Available in paperback and ebook now.

© Les Mann

Glenda Young credits her local library in the village of Ryhope, where she grew up, for giving her a love of books. She still lives close by in Sunderland and often gets her ideas for her stories on long bike rides along the coast. A life-long fan of *Coronation Street*, she runs two hugely popular fan websites.

For updates on what Glenda is working on, visit her website **glendayoungbooks.com** and to find out more find her on Facebook/**GlendaYoungAuthor,** Instagram **@flaming_nora** and X **@flaming_nora**.

THRILLINGLY GOOD BOOKS
FROM CRIMINALLY
GOOD WRITERS

CRIME FILES BRINGS YOU THE LATEST RELEASES FROM
TOP CRIME AND THRILLER AUTHORS.

SIGN UP ONLINE FOR OUR MONTHLY NEWSLETTER AND BE THE FIRST
TO KNOW ABOUT OUR COMPETITIONS, NEW BOOKS AND MORE.